CITY OF SECRETS

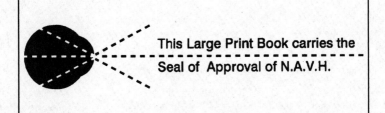

CITY OF SECRETS

KELLI STANLEY

THORNDIKE PRESS
A part of Gale, Cengage Learning

GALE
CENGAGE Learning®

Detroit • New York • San Francisco • New Haven, Conn • Waterville, Maine • London

Thorndike Press® Large Print Core.
The text of this Large Print edition is unabridged.
Other aspects of the book may vary from the original edition.
Set in 16 pt. Plantin.

LIBRARY OF CONGRESS CATALOGING-IN-PUBLICATION DATA

Stanley, Kelli.
    City of secrets / by Kelli Stanley. — Large print ed.
        p. cm. — (Thorndike Press large print core)
    ISBN-13: 978-1-4104-4521-6 (hardcover)
    ISBN-10: 1-4104-4521-6 (hardcover)
    1. Women private investigators—California—Fiction. 2. Serial murder—Investigation—California—Fiction. 3. Jewish women—Violence against—California. 4. Nineteen forties—Fiction. 5. San Francisco (Calif.)—History—20th century—Fiction. 6. Large type books. I. Title.
PS3619.T3657C587 2012
813'.6—dc23   2011043145

Published in 2012 by arrangement with St. Martin's Press, LLC.

Printed in the United States of America
1 2 3 4 5 6 7 16 15 14 13 12

For my mother,
Patricia Geniusz Stanley,
my best friend and the best person I
know. Thank you for your courage and
your Polish tenacity and your strength,
Mom, and most of all, for your love.

ACKNOWLEDGMENTS

The only constant in life is change — a fact that makes me all the more grateful to be writing thank-yous for my latest novel.

City of Secrets was a tough book to write emotionally, and without the unflinching and self-sacrificing support of family, and the cheer and friendship of extended family and colleagues in the crime fiction community, it would have been an even harder task.

My incomparable agent and dear friend Kimberley Cameron — my Rock of Gibraltar — helped keep me (relatively) sane as I chronicled Miranda's journey through 1940 San Francisco and a part of Napa Valley few tourists ever know about.

The brilliant and supportive Marcia Markland — whom I am so lucky to call my editor — helped buoy me through the rocky "second book" syndrome.

I am very proud to be published by

Thomas Dunne/Minotaur, and thank all the great people at Macmillan with whom it is such a pleasure to work: Peter Wolverton, Thomas Dunne, Andrew Martin, Sally Richardson, Matthew Shear, Talia Sherer, and Matthew Baldacci, as well as publicists extraordinaire Sarah Melnyk, Hector De-Jean, and Bridget Hartzler. Extra special thanks to the invaluable and indefatigable Kat Brzozowski, who is an utter joy.

City of Secrets is blessed with a great artistic team: Olga Grlic's stunning cover, Kathryn Parise on the sumptuous interior, Elizabeth Curione for peerless editorial production, and Sona Vogel for copy edits both sensitive and thorough.

Deep and heartfelt thanks are due to all the readers, reviewers, bookstores, librarians, Facebook friends, Tweeters, and friends who championed *City of Dragons* — your support has made *City of Secrets* and the Miranda Corbie series possible.

Thanks, too, to the Mystery Guild, the Book-of-the-Month Club, and Quality Paperback Book Club, Tantor Audio, Audible, and Thorndike Press for making *City of Dragons* available in multiple formats and through multiple venues. I'm enormously grateful, as always, to the bookstores that hosted me on tour, as well as Barnes and

Noble, for their outstanding support of *City of Dragons.*

Extra-special thanks to my home away from home, M is for Mystery, and my San Mateo family: Ed Kaufman, Pam Stirling, Jen Owen, Charlotte, Ann, and the rest of the stellar staff. Thanks to dear friends Fran Fuller and J.B. at the Seattle Mystery Bookstore, Whodunnit Books, Murder by the Book, Powell's, Barbara and Rob Peters and The Poisoned Pen Bookstore, Diane at the San Francisco Mystery Bookstore, Book Passage, Patrick at Mysterious Galaxy, Book 'Em, and the late, great Mystery Bookstore in Los Angeles — Bobby and Linda are family, and I, along with every other author in the crime fiction community, miss them and the store that brightened L.A.

More thanks are due to wonderful friends John and Ruth Jordan of *Crimespree Magazine,* the fabulous Kate Stine and Brian Skupin of *Mystery Scene,* the great George Easter of *Deadly Pleasures,* and the bloggers and groups and book club members who do so much to keep crime fiction news in the news.

A big thank-you to the real Bente Gallagher (fabulous author Jennie Bentley), who lent her name to Miranda's best friend, and mystery maven Lucinde Serber, who encouraged me to use hers.

Organizations are a big part of a writer's life — at least, this writer's life — and I'd like to add thanks to the Mystery Writers of America, the International Thriller Writers, and Sisters in Crime — and particularly to Margery Flax, who helps make every MWA member's life a little easier!

Extra-special thank-yous to all the readers who took time out of their busy lives to e-mail me. I truly appreciate hearing from you, and I'm grateful for your comments, memories, and corrections! Writing is a solitary act, and I never consider a book completed until it has been read. Thank you for reading!

Finally, some thanks to my high school English teacher Shirley Foster, for her personal support and for helping instill me with confidence at an age when we need it the most. This book would not have been written without her long-ago help.

I love writing and I love being an author, but my family is the most important thing in my life. Whenever I'm ready to give up and throw in the towel, they stand by me, keeping me going. Tana — thanks for keeping me on the right track, even through Miranda's darkest days. Mom and Dad —

thanks for always believing in me.
I love you all more than I can say.

AUTHOR'S NOTE

The plot of *City of Secrets* is fictional; the underlying tensions, motives, and many of the background details unfortunately are not.

German scientists were heavily influenced by the American eugenics movement. Anti-Semitism was relatively common in America, and Charles Coughlin, the Catholic priest-*cum*-radio broadcaster, remained popular throughout the country. Long before the term "right-wing militia" became a problem for Homeland Security — and before Timothy McVeigh became responsible for the second-deadliest act of terrorism in the United States — the "Christian Front boys" in New York were planning to blow up government buildings and fascistic groups physically harassed Jews on the streets of Manhattan.

I examined actual documents from the era — thanks to the American Jewish Committee online archives — and studied the many books of the period that were concerned with the potential for fifth columnists and American Fascism. The Musketeers were an actual group in San Francisco; lesser known than the Silver Shirts and the German-American Bund, they were representative of hundreds of hate organizations that sprouted up during the Depression, heartened and encouraged by Hitler's march to power. Anti-Semitism remained a threat to a cohesive, civilized society throughout World War II and afterward: Hollywood didn't specifically address the problem until *Gentleman's Agreement* and *Crossfire,* both released in 1947.

At the same time, there were many people who fought an unheralded struggle for human rights during this period. The Reverend L. M. Birkhead, who founded Friends of Democracy; Rex Stout, the creator of Nero Wolf, who served as the chairman of the organization, are but two examples.

Miranda fights the war in her own way, but she was walking side by side with other soldiers, struggling against oppression and for the right of all men and women to live in dignity, individuals and yet part of a collective, not subjugated to violence, malice, or hatred because of who they were. Such heroism is unusual in every age but, fortunately for us, not anachronistic. It is to these unheralded champions that we owe the progress we still strive for, and the peace we hope we shall find.

I hope you enjoy *City of Secrets,* and I thank you from the bottom of my heart for reading. You can find more about my books — including photos, historical documents, videos, and audio — at www.kellistanley .com, and I'm also on Facebook and Twitter. As always, I look forward to hearing from you!

■ ■ ■ ■

PART ONE:
THE FALL

■ ■ ■ ■

Must the entire world go to war for 600,000 Jews in Germany who are neither American, nor French, nor English citizens, but citizens of Germany?

— Charles Coughlin,
Detroit News, January 30, 1939

ONE

Pandora was still pretty. White skin, blond hair. Roots not faded back to black and brown. Stretched across the platform, breasts firm, nipples plump, pubic hair shaved. Head hung over the edge, upside down. Frozen, still, marble. Perfect artist's model, except for the blood dripping.

Drip-drop. Drip-drop.

Fred was standing in the stage shadows, hat in his hands. Tom skittered around Miranda, keeping up a monologue.

"I — I figure you know wh-what to do, Miss Corbie, bein' a detective an' all. You probably seen . . . She really is — dead?"

Fred choked, his large brown fedora crumpled with sweat from where he was squeezing it. He took a step toward Miranda.

"Ain't you better — ain't you better do somethin', Miss Corbie? Whoever did this to Pandora . . ."

She turned to face him. "Somebody threaten her? Try to get too close?"

He shook his head. "I can't say, Miss Corbie. Tom finds her like this — she ain't supposed to be here, she was always late, but you know, it don't take much time to take off your clothes, and she — she never had to wear much makeup. . . ."

He turned his back to her, faced the shadows again. A calliope started playing from the merry-go-round.

Miranda stood up from where she was crouched by the dead woman's face. "You touch anything?"

"I cain't — cain't remember, Miss Corbie. I saw her, might've shook her some." Tom's eyes came back to the dead girl, West Virginia accent thicker.

Miranda took the pack of Chesterfields out of her purse. Said carefully: "You know how this got here?" She pointed to Pandora's right breast, the one without a hole in it.

Under the swell, under the small, slow trickle crossing her chest and oozing from the stab wound. A word in blood.

Kike.

Bombs exploded from the Elephant Towers, rattling the wooden platform. Signal for opening time, second Golden Gate International Exposition, step right up, folks, and welcome to Treasure Island.

Miranda took a deep breath and lit a cigarette, staring at the dead girl.

May 25, 1940. Opening Day at the Fair to End All Fairs.

Closing day for Pandora Blake.

9:06 A.M. Miranda folded the newspaper over the B-western fence post outside Sally's and flicked the Chesterfield in the dirt, waiting for the bulls to make an appearance, waiting for someone official to show up and tell her to go away.

Another explosion shook the Gayway, drowning out the Hawaiian and Spanish music from the turnstiles. Some genius in the PR department figured bombs were news in Europe, why not drop them on San Francisco?

Girls in line at the hot dog stand tittered. Whiff of fresh scones from Threlkeld's, fog peeling off Ripley's Odditorium.

Tom stepped out of Artists and Models across the midway strip, his long body jerking itself in different directions. She waited, quick inhale, dropped the Chesterfield, crushing it in the sawdust. His hand shook when he grasped her arm. A little taller than her, about five eight. Patched and stained

21

dungarees, worn, covered in dirt, electrical wire hanging from his pocket. Blue eyes watery, wide, scared.

"They — they takin' her away, Miss Corbie. Don't know no family for her, but — God almighty, seems like she needs somebody."

Trembling all over. Rubbed his face into his blue work shirt, mouth contorted, tears on weathered skin.

Miranda said slowly: "You sure you didn't see anyone? They'll ask you. They'll try to break you. You know something, tell me."

Head shake, hair sandy and lifeless. "I don't see nothing. I'm settin' up the lights for the opening, she's the first act on the hour — we been practicin' for the last week. I see her stretched out already, figured she was playin' around." He plucked at his rough blue shirt, stained with oil and sweat, looking down, whispered voice. "I walk over, thinkin' maybe . . . maybe she . . . I don't know."

Miranda nodded, didn't say anything. He choked back a whimper. Wiped his face with his arm again. Met her eyes.

"So I get Fred, and he says to find you. Alls I did was — was touch her a little. I thought she was playin'. So help me Gawd, Miss Corbie — I thought she was playing."

The thin electrician held his face in his hands, shoulders convulsing with sobs.

9:27 A.M. Lost men in soiled pants sidling through early, looking for the sure bet, the certain thing, a grift at better odds than Tanforan. Couples, hand in hand, mouths open, blushing at buying a ticket for Sally Rand's, chubby brunette oohing over a cheap gold bracelet, boyfriend in glasses spending a buck for the engraving. "Nina," he says proudly, and she blushes.

Kids kick up the sawdust, dressed in faded pinafores and big brother's old knickers, clutching dimes for the roller coaster and the Roll-O-Plane and the lions in Captain Terrell Jacobs's African Jungle, buying cotton candy and popcorn, dropping peanuts down the Gayway.

Miranda waited and blew a smoke ring, missing Shorty and the rest of the Singer Midgets from last year.

Not the same Fair. Not the same world. Phony war over, a world war now, except we weren't a part of the world anymore.

We were Americans. Who needed the fucking world.

She shielded her eyes against the sun, checking attendance day numbers on the giant cash register. A shadow blocked her view. Grogan, smirk on his face.

"Time to talk, Corbie."

Herman sat and sweated, sad brown eyes following Grogan's cigar, crumpled derby on his lap. Looked back and forth between Grogan and Miranda.

He whined for the third or fourth time. "Lieutenant, it's Opening Day. Mr. Schwartz got a lot invested."

Grogan looked at the end of his cigar critically, stamped it out in the Firestone ashtray. "You think I like this any more than you do, Lukowski? We got fifty more men than usual today, whole goddamn city's been throwin' one hootenanny after another for the whole goddamn week. Fiesta Days, my ass. It's money, money for Schwartz, money for you. But there's a blond dame upstairs that got stabbed at your concession. And until the M.E. gets done with the crime scene, you can't get your girly peep show open again. So shut the fuck up."

Grogan glanced over at Miranda. "I'd apologize for my language if there was any ladies present."

Miranda blew the stream of smoke in his face. "How'd you manage to get promoted, Grogan? I figured you'd be headlining the Odditorium by now."

Grogan leaned back in his chair until it squeaked. "You're the freak, Corbie. First a whore, now a private dick. Get your picture in the fucking paper, and think you're Carole fucking Lombard."

She stabbed out the Chesterfield on his desk, rolling around the stub until the paper splintered and tobacco spilled out. "How long do I have to stay here? I can't wait long enough for you to find an idea. World doesn't have that much time left."

His lips stretched, eyes tight under the heavy bags. "Long enough to deal with Captain O'Meara."

Noise in the outer room. Sally's voice. O'Meara stuck his head in and scanned the room, not looking at anyone in particular.

Said: "My office, please." Grogan shoved his chair aside, gestured sarcastically for Miranda to go ahead of him. Herman sighed and shrank farther into the office wall.

Sally was already inside, draped in a brown fox stole and an air of irritation. Surrounded by men, and not the kind she liked. Too old, too fat, too lawyer.

Major Charles Kendrick, one of Dill's vice presidents, old man with a droopy white mustache and too much room in the seat of his pants. Francis Sandusky, director of

25

concessions, Threlkeld's crumbs still clinging to his potbelly. Randell Larson, stiff in
his young attorney starched Arrow shirt and
unobjectionable navy tie.

The fucking Firing Squad.

Sally smiled at Miranda, grabbed her hand
and squeezed it.

O'Meara struck a newspaper pose behind
his desk, gray black hair shiny with Wildroot
Cream-Oil, star on his chest as polished as
the black leather shoes. He cleared his
throat, spoke to the Certificate of Merit on
the wall.

"I'm sorry to bring you here under these
circumstances. As you know, there's been a
death on Opening Day. A young woman —"

"Was murdered, Captain. Or don't we use
that word during Fiesta Days?"

Larson shook his head, soft white hands
folded in his lap. O'Meara's blue eyes narrowed, crawling over her.

She wouldn't make it easy on the bastards.

"Miss Corbie, you've rendered service to
the Exposition company on several occa-
sions."

"She's the best protection my girls got on
the Gayway. I'm not here much — you
know me, I've got a finger in a lot of pies —
but everyone at Sally Rand Enterprises can
tell you Miranda Corbie is a valuable em-

ploy-ee." She enunciated carefully before blowing smoke out the corner of her mouth. "And a damn good broad. So what's the beef? I've got a show to set up and a plane to catch."

"Just a few questions, Miss Rand. Miss Corbie doesn't work solely for you, does she?"

"Ask me the goddamn questions, O'Meara. I know who I work for." Miranda leaned over his desk. "I work for myself. Worked for Leland Cutler, too, before he was cut loose. You might remember him. He was president of this circus before the moneymen replaced him with Dill."

O'Meara pulled open the mahogany desk tray, shut it. Trying to time it just right.

"As I said, Miss Corbie — you've been helpful. But the nature of this incident —"

"Who's the lawyer — you or Larson? Pandora Blake was stabbed and murdered. Somebody wrote 'kike' on her dead body, in her own blood. That sound like an 'incident' to you?"

The captain exhaled, color in his cheekbones. Larson shifted in the background, making a noise in his chest. Sandusky looked up from the floor, stomach quivering.

"Christ, you're not exactly known for

27

discretion. That Jap case a few months ago — you were asked not to investigate —"

"I was *told* not to investigate. A killing nobody gave a fuck about, except to hush it up." Voice derisive, eyes sure and hard. "I'll say it again. Pandora was murdered. Her body defaced. Because somebody doesn't like Jews."

Sandusky took a step backward. Gasp from Larson. Forbidden words. Fuck was fuck, but Jews were something more than profanity.

The major made a snorting sound, voice quavering. "She defiled herself. Appearing in a show like that."

Sally's voice slurred with the slight lisp she usually controlled. "Now wait a goddamn minute, sport. If you want to dress up in a powdered wig, maybe I'd better leave the room. My girls — all the girls — make money for this outfit. They're about the only ones who do." She dropped her cigarette to the floor and crushed it out.

The major retreated to San Juan Hill. Miranda set O'Meara's horse-head lighter back on the desk with a thump, quick inhale, second-to-last cigarette.

"You know damn well I'm a private detective, O'Meara. From now through September I work the Nude Ranch for Sally."

28

Never dodge, never run, no blindfold. Johnny taught her that.

"I'm sorry, but — not anymore, Miss Corbie."

Sally's chair scraped the tile floor. "I hire who I want to hire. Who the hell are you to can my employee in front of me? Jesus, what are you people — Gestapo?"

Grim smile from O'Meara, no teeth in it. Hair back to gleaming, hands steady. Audition for *Mr. District Attorney,* champion of the fucking people. Just make sure you're the right people, honey. No Jews or nudes allowed.

"Management considers Miss Corbie a security risk. We understand your position, Miss Rand, but keep in mind that private security personnel need approval by the Fair management. That's why we asked you to be present."

"And here I thought it was my figure." Sally shook her head, disgust making her face look its age. "Well, honey . . . that's that. I can always use you at the Music Box. Hell, I could train you in the act — you got everything it takes."

Miranda dropped ash on the floor, eyes locking on Grogan and his smirk.

"Thanks, Sally. I've still got my license."

O'Meara nodded at Larson. The lawyer

scurried forward with a typewritten document. O'Meara let it drop, the paper making a smooth, expensive sound against the dark brown wood.

"You will if you sign this. It says you promise to not give out any information about the homicide. Or contact the press. And that you won't initiate an investigation on your own or sign a contract with anyone who seeks to employ you in regards to it."

Sally made a guttural noise, left hand on her ample hip. "An hour ago I was carrying a midget and leading a parade of freaks down the Gayway. If you ask me, the only freaks in this whole goddamn fair are right here, right now, trying to find some balls to scratch and coming up empty." She motioned with her head to the door. "C'mon, honey. Let's drift."

"In a minute."

Sally rearranged her fur, flounced out. Miller's "Bugle Call Rag" and screams from the Roll-O-Plane filtered through the dusty window glass. Miranda rubbed out the stub on a corner of O'Meara's desk. Picked up the document, checked the signatures. Folded it, wedged it behind the *Chadwick's Street Guide* in her purse.

Sweat was beading up in O'Meara's hairline. Larson opened his mouth to say something, shut it again. Sandusky and the major faded against the wall, mute chorus, packed jury.

She placed her hands on O'Meara's desk, leaning forward. Felt his gaze draw downward, helpless. Spoke in soft tones, silky, like talking to an out-of-town Shriner at the Club Moderne.

"I know how many people depend on Treasure Island for their wages, Captain. Better than you do. But that's not what this is about."

She stepped back, staring down each man in turn. "You bastards want to look the other way, pretend it never happened." Her fingers closed into fists. They shook, and she held them at her side.

"Heil Hitler."

She was almost out the door when Grogan raised his voice.

"You gonna sign it, Corbie? Keep out of it?"

She threw it over her shoulder.

"There's a war on, Grogan. No more fucking peace in our time."

They were still standing in silence when the outside door to the station house slammed shut.

She stayed on the island for the rest of the

31

day, saying her good-byes. Electricians and stagehands and loud talk about a strike to get her back on the Gayway. Barkers with crumpled faces, voices hoarse, pat on the shoulder and free admission to anything she wanted to see. She talked to Sally's bunch, but the girls were mostly new, didn't know Pandora, didn't know Miranda, didn't know about how she started with the Fair or about Leland Cutler or Phil or the Incubator Babies case, except from hearsay.

She caught Sonny from the coroner's office at the dock, gave him a fin to let her ride back in the morgue boat. The sun was setting behind the skyscrapers as Miranda stood in the stern, smoking a new pack of Chesterfields.

Dead girl on the Bay, bier coming home. Blond and beautiful. *Willows whiten, aspens quiver.* Goddamn poetry, her fucking father the fucking professor and the fucking *Lady of Shalott. He said, "She has a lovely face . . ."*

Cigarette went out with a gust from the Bay Bridge, car lights crawling like ants on the top deck, Key System train shining, fast, modern, on the deck below. Took her Ronson Majorette three times to light the stick again.

Lovely face. Enough for big dreams. No family, not that anyone knew. Kept to herself, that one, always dreaming. Brushing her hair in the mirror. *"Tirra lirra," by the river.* Then the mirror cracked, no Jews allowed in Shalott. Restricted community, don't you know. Only Episcopalian knights allowed, and if you aren't one of those, lady, you don't sit at our table.

Sonny turned on a radio, Glenn Miller and Ray Eberle wishing on a star, goddamn Jiminy Cricket, and a little boy made of wood.

Geppetto's Italy, not Mussolini's.

The boat pulled up to Pier 5. The *Delta Queen* lay clean and quiet by Pier 1/1/2, overnight to Sacramento in style, but style was too old-fashioned for 1940. On September 29 the Fair would close for good, and so would the *Delta King* and *Queen,* faster world of train tracks and asphalt passing them by.

Red neon glowed on the Embarcadero, come to the Exposition, ferries every five minutes. Bored morgue attendants stood on the pier in white coats and threw a rope to Sonny. Two uniforms waited in a car. Last look back at Treasure Island.

The Gayway danced and drank and sparkled, salt spray exploding in green and blue. White Star Tuna sign the only star to guide by.

When you wish upon a star
She stepped off the boat, stood by when they took the body out.
Your dream comes true . . .

Two

Strauss, Sutro, Haas, Fleishhacker. Golden city and orange bridge built by Jews, mostly German, who took their place on hills, Nob and otherwise, and gave and gave and gave. Zoos, museums, schools. Jewish philanthropy and Chinese labor, founding fathers of San Francisco.

The early Jews tried to belong, heritage stretched as far as their pocketbooks: Christmas trees in windows, seders after the Easter parade. And they made her a city, more than a town, a grande dame sparkling with phony gemstones, showgirl flashing petticoats at the Palace Hotel.

Old San Francisco was gawdy and bawdy, but she had class enough to know it, posing for painters on the peninsula, strutting with ships through the Golden Gate. By 1915, she'd risen from the fire as the Athens of the Pacific, Paris of the West, her claim to cultural superiority owed to people she'd

35

kick out of the Bohemian Club a few years later.

Because the waves washed up on shore. Flotsam and jetsam.

Eastern Europeans, bad Jews, dirty Jews, Jews who didn't live in Cloud City, staring through the windows of Queen Anne mansions at the fog and the businesses they built over decades.

And then the private clubs and apartment houses found reason to object. No Jews, no Reds, because really, they're all the same. You can tell them, you can smell them, and they give the good ones a bad name.

Forget Hitler. We've got our own Jewish problem.

The phone jarred Miranda awake. Still wasn't used to the sound, and only four people knew the number. Her hand reached for the heavy black receiver.

"Hello? . . . Hello? Who is it?"

No answer.

She swore, squinted at the clock. Quarter to nine.

Miranda stretched, floor cold against her feet, and padded across the shiny waxed surface to the window, yellow silk of the nightgown caressing her skin. Reached for a pack of Chesterfields on the end table, lighting up with a Moderne matchbook. Leaned against the sill.

The City was open for business, the Fair back in town, and it was all colored lights and Hum-A-Tunes and progress in America! Cavalcade of a Nation, and Let's See the West in '40, Mary. You say there's a retreat goin' on in France? Not from the Follies Ber-gaire. Who gives a damn about the frogs and krauts, anyway, been fightin' each other for years. You want salted peanuts with that hot dog, lady?

She'd miss the girls, miss the rough-voiced barkers, miss the souvenir shops and Threlkeld's scones and Ghirardelli chocolate and quick-sketch artists and the college kids pushing old people around in chairs for fifty cents. She'd even miss the corn-fed couples out from Omaha, stars in their eyes, gasping at the colors on the Gayway at night, girl leaning into him, hair mussed, mouth waiting to be kissed.

Too young, too inexperienced, too much from Omaha.

Miranda rubbed the cigarette out in the Crillo's ashtray on the table. Maybe Pandora had been a small-town girl dreaming of the big city. Dreaming of something better than a dusty town and the boy next door, promise of her face and body a ticket to the Golden West.

Miranda looked out the window again, sun in her eyes.

All she could see was Spanish soil, Spanish sun, wine and tanned young men.

Johnny.

Before 1937.

When she was from Omaha, too.

San Francisco sunshine fresh, loud city, proud city, sparkled Sunday best, the kind they sold you on the radio and promised it could happen to you, too, if you bought the right deodorant.

Miranda walked down Mason and cut over to Powell on Sutter, past the Sir Francis and the St. Francis, bragging about how many honeymooners were in their beds that evening. Muscles in her calves were tight, and she stretched her stride, thin wool of her forest green skirt brushing her legs, pushing past tourists and factory workers and families back from church, headed for Treasure Island.

Cable cars panted, slow climb uphill, last gasp and a bell at the top, salesman from East Los Angeles hanging off the side while his wife holds the camera, kids chasing tracks down Powell Street.

She threaded through the crowds at the

turnaround, past Martell's Liquor, past the tourists lining up at a magazine stand to buy the perennial bestseller *Where to Sin in San Francisco,* by one Richard Guggenheim, sinner.

Three doors down on the left, mister, three doors down on the left.

Coffee was strong at the Owl counter, Chesterfield enhancing the taste. Poached eggs on toast, side order of bacon, and a genuine Florida grapefruit, broiled. Left a dollar and a quarter on the table for the straggly-haired blond waitress shouting orders to the short-order cook.

Walked upstairs and back to daylight, "Bei Mir Bist Du Schoen" playing on the Pig n' Whistle jukebox. Miranda inhaled the stick, then let it drop, crushing it.

Three cartons in the Owl bag should see her through the next few days.

The Monadnock was belching tourists, west, east, booking with Union Pacific. Trying to get to the two last World's Fairs before the end of the fucking world.

Shoved her way past a flower stand and a fat lady in a polka-dot dress. Gladys was busy at the counter helping a ten-year-old with a fussy grandmother.

She checked the newspaper rack, knew

better than to expect a story. Treasure Island was four hundred acres but still easier to control than a Chinatown murder.

Eddie Takahashi they buried. Pandora they'd wipe out clean.

New York Times headline screamed: GER-MANS PUSH DRIVE TO TRAP ALLIES IN NORTH. More fifth column jitters, Nazis in Mexico and South America.

Someone fed a nickel to the jukebox in the coffee shop, Tony Martin crooning "It's a Blue World."

She leaned up against the green-tiled wall, closed her eyes. A blue world without the Fair, without the money she'd counted on. The annuity from Burnett would help pay the office rent. She deserved it, too — her old boss had been a real bastard. But between the two phones at her apartment and new dresses from Magnin's, only two days, maybe three. Not much time for Pandora Blake.

It's a blue world without you . . .

Goddamn song. She'd seen the movie back in January, *Music in My Heart,* hard-on in my pants, same old Hollywood. Boy meets girl, girl meets boy, happy endings all around for Tony Martin and Rita Hayworth forever and ever and ever.

Miranda shook out another Chesterfield.

Tapped the stick on the wall, stuck it between her lips, opened her purse to look for the lighter. Fucking song wouldn't end. Blue, blue world, always had been. No Spanish reds, no Russian grays, no yellow orange mornings. Black and blue, no other colors allowed.

No other men allowed.

The flame flickered yellow in front of the cigarette in her mouth. She looked up into warm brown eyes.

Gonzales.

He smiled, teeth white, wrinkles at the corners. "Good morning, Miss Corbie."

She held his hand for a second, steadying the lighter. He looked less worried than the last time she saw him. Less like a cop.

"You heading somewhere, Inspector, or are things slow at the Hall of Justice?"

His throat muscles tightened when he laughed. Gladys, breathless, finally ran out from behind the counter, threw her arms around Miranda.

"Sugar, what are you doing here? Why aren't you at —"

"I got canned."

Gladys's mouth opened, bleached blond curls cascading into her eyes. She brushed them away impatiently. "What happened? Sally loves you —"

"Girl was murdered — nude model at Artists and Models. Dill's got a lot of little men in lawyer suits who don't like me much, called me a security risk." She shrugged. "Figured I may as well hang for a wolf."

Gladys looked back and forth between Gonzales and Miranda, her eyes lingering on his pinstripes. "Oh, honey — another whaddya-call-it — when you do those cases for free? Like the Jap kid —"

"Pro bono, Gladdy. Pro bono. I have a feeling Inspector Gonzales isn't here to buy a ticket on the Yosemite Railway. My office?"

He smiled again, brown skin buffed and smooth. Gladys gazed at him, letting a sigh escape, before squeezing Miranda's arm and running back to get some Rolaids for a middle-aged woman with an ugly scowl and even uglier hat.

"If you please, Miranda. I tried to call you this morning."

She didn't like the feeling in her stomach. Put it down to the Florida grapefruit.

"Slept late. Shall we go?"

The elevator was crowded. Didn't say anything on the ride to the fourth floor. Allen's office door was closed when they walked by Pinkertons.

Probably at the Fair. Everybody was at

the fucking Fair, everybody but her and Gonzales.

She fumbled once with the key but got the door open, stale air and cigarettes and a faint whiff of bourbon. Nodded toward the chairs in front of the desk, walked to the window and pulled it up with effort, room suddenly filled with the rumble of traffic.

"Sorry it's musty. I open the place once a week in the summer. Used to."

Miranda sank into the leather chair, thinking again how it was worth the commission she'd paid for it. Waved Gonzales down with the Chesterfield in her mouth. "Straight A's from Elsa Maxwell, Inspector, sit. Tell me why you're here, why you called. Or let me guess."

The inspector sat crowded on the least comfortable seat, too big for the small wooden surface. Light felt fedora in his lap. Smiling.

She twisted the stub out in the Tower of the Sun ashtray. Looked up briefly, meeting his eyes. Shook another stick out of the open pack, tapped it on the desk. Sparked the desk lighter and inhaled, waiting for the heat to hit her lungs and keep her hands still. Someone punched a car horn on Market, three-second screech and a shout.

He sat back with his legs crossed, nodded

toward the window.

"One way to start a street fight." Conversational.

"Get it over with. You're here to tell me to lay off. Eddie Takahashi all over again, except this time no newspapers, no family, no leads. No rope to hang myself with."

He took out a gold cigarette case from his inside breast pocket, placed one of the gold-tipped French cigarettes between his lips. Dug out a matchbook, struck it on his shoe.

"Enjoy those while you can. Hitler doesn't smoke."

He raised his eyebrows. "You think France will fall?"

"So hard it won't get up. Reynaud said he believes in miracles. The Nazis believe in tanks." She blew a stream of smoke toward the window. "Japan's got Asia and the Germans own Europe. The French and English armies are trapped. So yeah, Paris will fall. The whole fucking world will fall. Most of it's on the floor already."

Her fingers were tight on the arm of the chair. He bent forward again, dangling his hat between his knees. Ran his long brown finger along the inside brim.

"You didn't think so before, when you fought in Spain."

Dong. Church bells. Always goddamn

church bells.

"Long time ago, Gonzales."

"And yet you still carry the pistol."

Miranda pivoted to face him. "A good gun is a good gun, I've got a license, and what firearms I use are none of your goddamn business."

He laughed. "Same old Miranda. Looks like you are taking on another lost cause, are you not?"

She twisted in the chair. Watched the smoke curl its way out the window.

"I was an escort, Inspector. I know something about lost causes."

Gonzales smoked in silence for a few minutes, watching her. Miranda gulped the stick, then leaned across the desk and rubbed it out, half-finished.

"Japanese and Jews," he said softly. "A strange record for a woman who deals mainly in divorce cases. A woman for whom the world has been dead for three years. But then, for you, perhaps not. And perhaps not for the times. What was it you told me . . . you fight because you can?"

He rose from the chair in one move, elegant, athletic. Fedora falling to the floor. Walked to where she sat, open coat hanging loose. Stared down at her.

"I am not here on official business. I heard

about the murdered girl. Your name wasn't mentioned."

Miranda raised her eyebrows. "That would be a first." She busied herself with finding the key to the drawer and opened it. Lifted out a half-empty bottle of Old Taylor bourbon.

"Drink?"

He shook his head, smiling. She uncorked the bottle, smelled it, hesitated. Stoppered it again, shoving it across the desk.

Took a breath. Stood up and met his eyes.

"So why the hell are you here?"

He stepped closer, still smiling. She felt her pulse quicken.

"I almost broke your nose once, Gonzales. Second time's a charm. Are you gonna tell me why you're here or leave now?"

He reached out an arm and took one of her hands in his. Held it for a moment. Her voice was even.

"My reflexes are a little slow this morning. Better go while you can."

Gonzales opened his palm gently and turned it upside down. Her hand dropped awkwardly to her side.

"I am leaving, Miranda. I'm going back to Mexico."

Rush and roar, White Front, car door slam. Piano from the bar across the street.

Girl's laughter, long, low, flirtatious.

"You get fired?"

He shook his head. "No. I'm working with the House Un-American Activities Committee."

Her voice raised in surprise. "Martin Dies and his pack of Red-baiters? How the hell did you get mixed up with them?"

"They are not all Red-baiters, Miranda. The government is concerned about fifth column activities from the Fascists, too. So I'm taking a leave of absence — mutually agreed upon — from the San Francisco Police Department, and returning to Mexico. My family connection — my heritage — is a plus, for once."

She nodded, staring at the floor. He reached out a hand, barely brushing her shoulder.

"I came to say good-bye. I don't know how long I'll be gone."

"I'm glad for you, Gonzales. If this is what you want to do."

He tried to catch her eyes. "It is."

He fished out a small piece of paper in his breast pocket. Picked up her hand again and put the paper in her palm. His fingers were warm and dry.

"My information. My family's ranch. You can always reach me through them. I am not certain where I will be."

"Thanks." Her fist closed on the paper. She raised her eyes to his and held them.

"Thank you for saving my life."

He took her fingers in his, gently, brought them to his lips. Moved closer. Covered her mouth with his, hungry, warm, demanding, and Miranda shut her eyes, fingers digging in his broad back, blending, dancing, warmth and heat, desire and urgency, and she could hear the buzz of the fighters and the cannons booming in the dry hot sun.

"Good-bye, Miranda."

He pulled away and turned his back and strode from the room, coat billowing behind him.

The door shut slowly, soundlessly until the click. She picked up his fedora from the floor.

It smelled like sweat, leather, and French-tipped cigarettes.

She put it on her desk, sank into her chair, and stared at it.

She knew he wouldn't be back.

THREE

A fire engine screamed down Market. Miranda jumped up from the chair. She wasn't sure how long she'd sat, staring at a fucking hat.

She twisted the Bakelite knob on the old cathedral radio harder than she intended. Strung out the antenna line from behind the safe while she waited for the tubes to warm up, and then a crackle and then some imitation Boswell Sisters claiming that Everybody Loves My Baby and even if my baby is a sonofabitch, he doesn't love anybody but me. Only me.

She walked to the desk, uncorked the Old Taylor. Opened the filing cabinet, found a glass from Castagnola's and poured it half-full. Held it in her mouth a few seconds like Listerine, swallowed. Chased it with a Chesterfield, drawing the stick so hard the ash fell to the floor before she could flick it in the tray.

The singing group was replaced by a reedy-voiced bandleader and a hotel in the middle of nowhere, explaining the next number before he killed it. Miranda rose in disgust, turned off the radio. Stations all over the world, nothing she wanted to hear. Nothing but war news and *Pepper Young's Family* and Our Love Is Here to Stay.

So Gonzales was gone. So what? Made it harder to get information out of the bastards at the Hall of Justice. Made it damn near impossible to get near Pandora Blake. But she'd be all right. She was always all right.

She came out on the other side, through Dianne and Burnett and every sad-case Shriner from Pasadena who tried to sit her on the bed and pat her shoulder and run his hand between her legs.

Poor bastards. Almost as poor as their dried-up wives, waiting for their fat-breasted husbands to come rolling home, always with less money. Stuttering, stammering, hunting the magic mouth, the red lips, miracle cure, proof of manhood. Eyes wide and scared and angry, wanting. Always wanting.

Miranda rubbed the Chesterfield out in the tray. Fuck Gonzales. Too rich, too pretty, let him go back to his ranch in Mexico and raise blue-ribbon cattle.

She dialed the combination on the old

Wells Fargo safe, her fingers brushing against the holster of the Spanish pistol inside. Counted the money in the envelope: seventy-three dollars. Picked up his fedora from the desk and shoved it to the bottom, quickly shutting the safe again.

She was pouring more bourbon when someone knocked on the door. It swung open. Allen walked in.

"I heard you were here — came to see about lunch." He looked at the bottle on the desk. "Didn't expect to find you drinking it. What kind of mess are you in?"

The Pinkerton sat in the same chair as Gonzales. Frowned, got up, and moved to the wider one with armrests. Pulled out a pack of Camels, reaching for the One-Touch on Miranda's desk.

"Nothing I can't handle. Gonzales was just here, he's going back to Mexico." She set down the Castagnola glass with a thump, glanced up at Allen. "And I got fired. Peep show girl was murdered, and Dill and his cronies want it kept quiet. Seems I'm a security risk."

Allen chuckled, paunch straining against his shirt buttons. "So why the hush-hush? Public eats that stuff up. They'll make plenty of ticket money."

"Because whoever killed her wrote 'kike'

on her breast. In her own blood. And she was naked, getting ready for the opening act."

He raised his thick eyebrows, whistled. "Sweetheart, I don't know how you manage to be Johnny-on-the-spot, but Jesus Christ — try to stick to your Elks and Masons. No wonder they killed the story."

"Maybe *you* want a drink?"

"No, but I can't blame you if you do. What about Gonzales?"

She picked up the glass again, sipped the bourbon. "Gone. Sniffing out fifth columnists in Mexico for the Dies committee."

The Pinkerton tapped his cigarette in the ashtray. "You OK on dough?"

"For a while. Got anything to throw me?"

He shook his head. "Nothing. Slow season. War jitters. Husbands and wives rediscovering each other. Goddamn depressing business."

Miranda grinned. "Who are you kidding? You're a sap for your wife."

Allen's scalp turned red, and he took a final drag on the Camel before standing up. "How 'bout lunch? My treat."

She said slowly, "Thanks. No time, though."

He stretched, brushing some ash off his brown wool blazer. "We've got a file on some local Nazi lovers. Obvious ones like the Bund and Silver Shirts, some not so obvious. Might help."

"I appreciate the offer. The cops've got this shut tighter than a drum. Tighter than the Takahashi case."

The Pinkerton looked down at her, eyes worried. "You're a hell of a shamus, Miri, but you almost got croaked in February. A lot of crazy sonsofbitches in San Francisco. Some of 'em run around wearing swastikas and picking fights with Jews."

Miranda pushed herself up from the chair and stood, hands still on the desk. "I may have to drop it anyway — only got a few days before it's back to the Moderne and cheating husbands."

Allen grunted. "And they're no cakewalk." They walked to the door together, arm in arm, and he turned to face her, lines on his red face deep.

"I'll drop off a couple of mimeos. Make myself feel better. Be careful, Miranda."

Her mouth twisted up at the corner. "Always, Mama. Always."

He grinned and walked down the hallway, sound of his footsteps swallowed up by the laughter of a young honeymoon couple buying tickets to Niagara.

She phoned the papers, paid for the usual. "Can you trust your husband? Confidential, discreet." Two weeks, *Chronicle, Examiner, News,* and *Call-Bulletin.*

Reached for the phone again and dialed Meyer's home number. Opened another pack of Chesterfields one-handed. She was smoking too much, but she could give Life Savers a try some other fucking day.

"Mr. Bialik, please. I'm a client of his — Miranda Corbie." Tapped her foot, waiting for the housekeeper to deliver the message.

"Meyer? No — I'm in the office. Got fired. Sure they can. No, listen — uh-huh. Uh-huh. No, a security risk. Girl from Artists and Models was murdered — stabbed. Pandora Blake. And somebody wrote 'kike' on her breast. . . . Yeah. Yeah, I know. But they wanted me to sign a contract — yeah, I got a copy, didn't sign — saying I wouldn't investigate, would turn down the case if someone tried to hire me, all of it. Threatened to take away my license. . . . No, O'Meara."

She smiled at the explosion on the other end, tapped the stick on the ashtray. "Of course I am. Who else will? . . . Yeah. No,

I'm OK. Sally cut me a check for a week's worth of pay and Burnett's money takes care of the office rent. Ads'll run tomorrow. . . . Yeah, yeah. I know. . . . Hell, yes — if you hear anything let me know. . . . OK. I'll drop it by your office. Yeah. Pandora Blake. Let me know. Thanks, Meyer."

She dropped the phone, stared at it. Pulled out the desk drawer and rummaged for a Big Chief pad. Rubbed the cigarette out on the Tower of the Sun.

A church bell rang again, south of Market. *Dong. Dong.* Goddamn tolling bells.

She picked up the Esterbrook, blotted it. Wrote "Pandora Blake." Chewed on the end of the pen. Blotted again. Wrote "Who is Pandora Blake?"

Looked down at the wet ink. Reached for another cigarette.

She'd gotten as far as *"twenty-two, bleached blonde, pretty, parents? Jewish?"* and *"men?"* when the phone blared. Watched it tremble for a second, hand hovering over the receiver.

"Miranda? Tried to reach you at home. I heard."

Rick's lilt was missing, voice heavy with concern. It irritated her almost as much as the lilt usually did, Rick and his half-Irish bullshit blue eyes.

"What did you hear, Sanders? That I got canned or why?"

Grunt on the other end, punctuated by the clack of typewriters pecking out a letter at a time. "Christ, Miranda, don't take it out on me. I heard you got fired. Scat was iffy on the motive. Sam got back from Treasure Island this afternoon, glommed it from one of the barkers on the Gayway."

She gripped the Esterbrook, wrote out, "A&M barkers," on the Big Chief tablet. "Yeah. Iffy. They made Sally fire me because there's been a murder, and Dill and the whole goddamn board want it blacked out."

She could see him push his fedora back, leaning over the receiver so no one else would hear. "Give it to me, Miranda. I'll blow it wide open."

"I don't think you will. Girl at Artists and Models was stabbed, probably ice pick. Before the official opening. Somebody used her blood to spell out 'kike' on her naked body."

Exhale from Rick. *San Francisco News* room clatter got louder. "I'll badger Gleason — if they're clamping down that hard, he might buck it for an exclusive."

"They threatened my license — wanted me to sign a contract saying I wouldn't talk, wouldn't investigate. I've only got a few days to give this."

"So? What the hell's wrong with you? Bring me in on it. You usually do anyway, and all I get out of it is —"

"A hell of a story. You can shove the Little Boy Blue act."

A police siren screamed from somewhere up Market. Her stomach growled again. Miranda twisted the stick in the ashtray. They were satisfying a hell of a lot less than usual.

His voice held an edge. "Do we really need this dance, Miranda? OK, I could use an exclusive. Something sensational. But it's not like we're not friends . . . old friends. If you still even remember what the goddamn word means. What about the Takahashi case, Burnett's murder, New York? It's not like you don't call me whenever the hell you need some quick information or sometimes just a padded shoulder."

She set the receiver on the desk. Opened the drawer, looked at the pack of Chesterfields. Slammed the drawer shut again.

Rick and Miranda and Johnny. Old times, good times. New York times. Rick always there, watching her, trying to watch over her. Until he'd go away, leave for a while. Then back again, like a fucking stray dog.

She picked up the phone. "This is tighter than the Takahashi case."

"And I came through for you."

"You usually do. That's the problem."

Clack, clack, clack. Slow day in the newsroom. "Look, I don't know what the hell you're talking about, and it sounds like you started drinking a few hours too early. I'm coming over. Did you eat yet?"

"I worked through lunch."

"Jesus Christ — it's almost three o'clock! I'll take you out for a hamburger." He waited for a response, added casually, "And I wouldn't worry about the blackout — Gonzales should be able to feed you information."

Miranda said slowly, "He's not around. Got drafted for the Dies committee. He's off hunting fifth columnists in Mexico."

Pause. Rick's voice sounded like it had lost ten pounds. "I'll be there in fifteen minutes, tops. I may even have a lead for you."

She dropped the phone, willing the clang to pull her out of the verses in her head, calliope and cotton candy, red letters on a white breast. Gave in and lit a cigarette and inhaled until it glowed red. Until her lungs were numb again.

Miranda walked to the window and

pushed up the sill as far as it would go.

Sharpies in zoot suit trousers and wide-brimmed fedoras, waiting for the counter girl at the five-and-dime. White Front and Municipal Rail, match race down Market, bells clanging. Black coffee and diesel in the fog, twisted, gray, dancing like Lotta Crabtree, a whistle of wind, and the pungent tang of eucalyptus, straight from Marin.

It was always there for her, not always warm, but hard and fast and sure.

Her city. Where she was born.

Whore-mother, fickle nurse. Survivor.

Someone hit "Imagination" on the jukebox downstairs, Frank Sinatra crooning, spooning, floating to the fourth-floor window, to the woman with auburn hair leaning out the window, a cigarette between her lips.

"What'll it be?" Short gray hair, close cropped, small mustache. Bartender tough-guy act straight out of Warner Brothers, squinty eye and all.

"Scotch and water. Miranda?"

"Bourbon and water, up."

He grunted and turned his back, clanging glassware. A skinny man in his early fifties with a meat-juice-stained apron came around and asked if they wanted food.

"John's special. You, Randy?"

She winced at the old nickname and handed back the menu. "Rare sirloin and a baked potato. Come with green beans?"

The barman slid two drinks across to them while the waiter stared at her. "Peas, lady. Say — ain't I see you in the papers?"

"Yeah, bud, she's Rita Hayworth. Move it along."

He shrugged, disappearing into the kitchen. Rick looked at Miranda, took out a pack of Luckys and a Yellow Cab matchbook. Struck the match on his thumbnail and said: "OK, spill it."

The bourbon wasn't Old Taylor, but it was Old something and felt good going down. She swirled the highball glass, watching the bourbon melt the water.

"Pandora Blake. Worked at Artists and Models. You know the act — girls sit on a stage, and the so-called artists pay a quarter to take their picture. She was around for the last part of '39 and came back this season. Opened the act for the early birds. A loner. I only talked to her once or twice. None of Sally's girls knew her, figured she was stuck-up."

Rick lowered his voice. "What about the — the 'kike' thing? Was she Jewish?"

Miranda shrugged, reached into her purse

for her cigarette case. "Never came up. Tom found her before the show was even open — he works the lights, Fred handles the stage. Poor bastards got the third degree afterward, goddamn O'Meara looking for the easy out."

"What time?"

"Tom got me at about eight forty-five. People were sneaking through early to line up at Sally's or get on the Roll-O-Plane. She was stabbed with something long and sharp. Probably an ice pick. They sell the goddamn things as souvenirs. Word was written in her own blood on her right breast. The left one was where the stab wound was."

She swirled the bourbon again, took a long drink, holding it in her mouth before swallowing. Rick propped his arm on the counter, staring at Miranda, face red from the Scotch.

"This is one of those cases, isn't it? Where you go off on some mission like you're Sergeant York or Joan of Arc or J. Edgar Hoover. Get yourself in trouble, almost get croaked, till some knight in muddy armor like Gonzales shows up to save you." He shook his head, threw back the drink in one motion. "Well, honey, it won't be me. This isn't Spain. It's barely San Francisco." He raised his voice until the bartender couldn't pretend to be deaf.

"Another one."

It took four tries for Miranda to light the cigarette with his matchbook. The skinny waiter pushed his way through the kitchen doors with two plates. She pinched the end of the Chesterfield and left it in the tin ashtray, then dug into the steak, heaping some butter and sour cream on the baked potato and helping it along with pepper and Tabasco sauce.

She finished before he did, relit the cigarette. The bartender tried to pour more bourbon, but she put her hand over the glass.

"You asked for the information, Sanders. I gave it to you. So fuck the Drew Pearson editorial, and fuck you, too." She opened her pocketbook and took out a dollar coin and a bill, started to get up.

He swallowed a forkful of peas and choked, coughing over his plate. Reached for the Scotch and drained it. Wiped his mouth.

"All right, forget it. But Jesus Christ, Miranda, you were almost killed —"

"I'm not the goddamn princess on the glass hill. I earned my license. And yeah, I worked for Sally, but I took care of the whole Gayway, and Pandora Blake was killed on my beat. My watch. You can either help or get out of my way. Your choice."

She was breathing hard. Rick finally found her eyes. He cracked a smile, his voice softer.

"Same old Randy."

She glanced away. "This is business. Not auld lang syne."

He cocked his head, wide mouth turned upside down. "Forgive me, Miss Corbie. I was overcome by Scotch and the scent of your perfume." He dug in his pocket and slapped two dollars and fifty cents on the counter.

"I've got a lead — maybe. Let's go."

Miranda pushed a dollar coin toward the bartender. Downed the rest of the bourbon and water, wiped her mouth with the rough dinner napkin.

"What kind of lead? And where?"

"Trust me for once."

She shrugged, stubbed out the cigarette on the gold tin ashtray, and followed him out of John's Grill to Geary.

He led her up Webster Street, past the delicatessens and Japanese bakeries, past the faded Victorian boardinghouses. Radios blared from open second-story apartment windows, smells of tempura and pastrami and fresh-baked bread. A White Front chugged by on Sutter, where some Japanese and Filipino kids were playing marbles in a barbershop, pole spinning, cut and shave twenty-five cents. Miranda looked down Sutter when they crossed the street. No shoes from Mr. Matsumara today, no boarded-up Takahashi cleaners.

Hurried across Pine to California. Rick stood in front of a synagogue, squat Romanesque arches glowing pink gold in the dying sun. The sign read TEMPLE SHERITH ISRAEL.

He made a motion with his head for her to follow him. She walked through the middle arch into the dim, vaguely pink vestibule. An old man in patched overalls was kneeling on the cement with a can of strong-smelling lye soap and oily rags.

"Kike" was painted in large red letters on the inside wall.

FOUR

The old man ignored Rick's outstretched hand, groaned when his knees straightened.

Tall and thin, maybe mid- to late sixties. White beard stained with yellow, climbing in patches down his neck.

"You want something?" He looked from Rick to Miranda and back again.

Rick pushed his battered fedora off his forehead. "I'm from the *San Francisco News*. Got a call earlier about this." He gestured toward the wall.

A middle-aged squat woman in heavy shoes and faded red scarf shoved the main door open from the inside and stepped into the vestibule, holding on to a little boy. He froze when he saw Rick and Miranda, and clutched the woman's worn brown dress. She chided him in whispers, dragging him a foot at a time toward the last bit of sunlight filtering through the arches from California Street.

The old man murmured something in Yiddish. The woman nodded back, scarf around her head hiding any expression. She tugged at the little boy again. He stood firm, seven-year-old feet planted. Pointed to the wall.

"Schpin, Mame — schpin!"

Miranda turned around to where the boy was pointing. Above the other words, concealed in the growing shadows.

A swastika.

The woman muttered something else, and the kid started to cry. She bent down and picked him up, holding him tight against her, walking in a hurry toward Fillmore.

The old man said again, voice patient: "You want something?"

Rick scratched his head. "Yeah. I want to talk to someone about that." He pointed to the scrawled words, color of dried blood against the yellow surface. "When did it happen? Did anyone see anything?"

The old man sighed, rubbing his nose, and took off his cracked leather work gloves, hands like onionskin.

"Yah. Done last night, after evening prayer. We find this morning. I don't know who tells the policemen. Find three of these." He gestured toward the swastika, not looking at it. "I clean all day. You excuse, you talk to Rabbi Goldstein or Mr. Flamm."

He drew out a dingy yellow handkerchief from his pocket and wiped his face. Carefully fit the gloves on his hands again and braced himself against the wall, folding back to the ground like an aged crane.

"Where can we find them?"

He dipped a rag into the old Hills Brothers coffee can. "Inside. Office in back."

He wet the brick, then picked up a tattered piece of sandpaper. Back and forth, rubbing out the swastika. Wet again, rub again. Paint was fading, degrees at a time.

A yellow light clicked on in the vestibule, the old man's hands throwing garish shadows on the wall, his breath and the friction of sand on stone the only sound.

Rick said softly. "Don't you have help? Maybe somebody a little younger?"

He glanced up at them, faced forward again. "I take care of her. Been taking care of her for thirty-four years." He shook his head, dipped the rag. "No wife, no children. So I take care of her. Go look — you see." He gestured with a finger to the far corner of the vestibule, closest to the sidewalk.

They walked over. Through the worn stone, the patched pink and yellow. Traces of color.

Paint.

Red paint, black paint, thin, thick, fragments of letters. Layers of hatred built into the synagogue, scarred history of threat and violence, pain washed and covered over but never covered up.

Miranda ran her finger along a barely discernible black stripe. Asked him, "What does *schpin* mean?"

The old man turned his head and spat on the ground in reflex. Dipped the cloth, a stinging odor of oil and lye rising from the rusty can.

"It means 'spider,' lady. This is whole city of spiders."

He rocked back and forth, rhythmically rubbing the synagogue wall.

They walked through the auditorium, gazing up at the giant dome, light hitting the yellow arches and orange frescoed writing. Light was everywhere, almost blinding. It flooded the interior, sunset through the rose window, lifting the dome and making it seem weightless.

A few men sat together on benches, arguing about something. One looked up when they entered and walked over.

Big eyes, eager voice. "Welcome to the temple. Are you here for a tour? The building was built in 1905 by Albert Pissis, who also designed the Flood Building —"

"We're not here for a tour. We'd like to speak to Rabbi Goldstein or a Mr. Flamm, please."

It took a few seconds for his mouth to close and the fact to register. He scratched his head, fat stomach quivering a little, staring at Miranda.

"Sure, Miss. Thought for sure you wanted a history — lots of people come by to look at the temple. Abraham Ruef was indicted here on sixty-five counts of extortion after the quake — right here, they used it as the Hall of Justice. And —"

One of the other men spoke up from the benches. "Don't be such a rube, Ethan. Tell the lady and the gentleman where to find Flamm."

He looked toward the other man, back again to Miranda and Rick, face red. "Right this way."

He led them to a door beside the massive pipe organ, knocked twice sharply, opened it. Dark and narrow hallway, rooms opening to the side. Lamplight carved a triangle in front of an open door, and he walked into the door frame, making a harrumphing sound in his throat.

A deep voice rasped from the room, "What the — What do you want? I said not to bother —"

69

"I'm sorry, Mr. Flamm. Two people asked for either you or Rabbi Goldstein." He stepped awkwardly into the room, clearing the way for Miranda and Rick.

A man about thirty-five sat behind an old wooden desk, sharp face, good-looking, clothes tailored and too flashy. Pink display handkerchief, sateen navy lapels. His eyebrows rose when he saw Miranda.

"Hello, hello — afraid you're stuck with me. I'm Harry Flamm. Rabbi Goldstein's working on his book."

File cabinets lined the opposite wall, some of the drawers open and in disarray. Banker's lamp on the table, ledgers, receipt books. No photo frame. Brown Bakelite portable radio, latest model.

His eyes ignored Rick, focused on Miranda, quick up-and-down movement. Lingered on her legs.

She smiled, put a wiggle in it. Gestured toward the high-backed chair sitting crookedly in front of the desk. "May I?"

Rick pulled out the chair and straightened it. Said pointedly to Flamm: "I'll stand."

"If you'd rather. I can get another for you."

He shook his head, fingers brushing Miranda's shoulder. "Please don't bother."

Flamm leaned back, eyes on Rick, home

again to Miranda. Slow smile spread across his face. She met his eyes and smiled again, noticing two Tanforan ticket stubs under a stack of receipts. He opened a drawer of his desk, took out a pack of Viceroys.

"You mind?" His hand was already reaching for a matchbook.

Miranda shook her head, opened her purse. Took out her gold cigarette case and flicked it open. "Got a light?"

His eyes raked her again. "Sure — try this." Flicked the matchbook across the desk. She glanced at it. A restaurant on Montgomery. Long way from the Fillmore.

Rick moved to pick it up, but Miranda was already running the match along Flamm's desk, holding his gaze. Cupped her hands, lit the Chesterfield on the first try. Deep, slow inhale, breath out the corner of her mouth. Bent forward again to tap the cigarette on the cracked black ashtray. Two of the cigarette stubs were covered in lipstick.

Rick cleared his throat. Flamm looked up, amused, blew smoke in his direction.

"So — what did you want to see the rabbi about? You interested in joining the congregation?"

Miranda raised her arms above her head to adjust her beret, taking long enough to make sure Flamm noticed.

"I'm afraid not, Mr. Flamm. We're here about a friend of ours."

Flamm inhaled the Viceroy and finally noticed the fat man breathing hard and pressed against the wall. Condescending voice.

"You can go now. Shut the door behind you."

Ethan backed out, facing him. "Sure, Mr. Flamm. Thank you."

He turned to Miranda, making an effort. "I usually leave it open — gets like a morgue down here."

"I can imagine. What is it you do for the synagogue, exactly?"

Flamm puffed the Viceroy, flicking ash in the tray. "I manage the books for the rabbi, help him and the board run it. We got a big congregation here — Reform temple. I didn't catch your name, Miss . . . ?"

"Corbie. Miranda Corbie." Kilowatt smile, tilt of the head. Instinct told her to be careful with Mr. Flamm.

He nodded several times, opening the desk drawer, shutting it again. Finally found a pen on the desktop.

"I'm a busy man, Miss Corbie — so if you and your friend could get to the point . . ."

She craned her neck to look at Rick,

hovering behind her.

"Richard — would you mind waiting in the hallway? It would make it easier on me to talk about — you know . . ."

He looked over at Flamm, back to her. "Sure, Miranda. Whatever you say."

Flamm's eyes followed Rick out the door. He leaned back, shoulders relaxed, feet and legs spread wide apart in the chair. He picked up a half-dollar from the tip of a ledger, tossed it in one hand. Bargain-basement George Raft, straight out of *Scarface.*

He abruptly threw the coin to Miranda, who caught it in her left. He leaned forward, grinning. She set it down on the front of the desk with a slap, never leaving his eyes.

He laughed. "I figure you're not Jewish. If you're — interested — I'll leave you my number. So you can learn more about it."

He picked up the pen again, found a soiled business card in the desk drawer. Scrawled a number on it. Snapped the card into her hand, fingers brushing hers. Toothy smile, hair gleaming with cream, scent of patchouli and oak moss.

"Thanks, Mr. Flamm. I'll keep it in mind. I know you're busy, so —"

"Take all the time you need, Miss Corbie." He grinned some more, puffing the

Viceroy. "Call me Harry. I think we understand one another."

She nodded, looked down at her hands. "Does what happened last night — does it happen often?"

Flamm pulled his eyes back up. Alert. "What happened last night?"

"The vandalism outside. The paint. We spoke to the old man."

"Old Jabob?" Flamm's laugh caught a cough, and he ground out the Viceroy in the ashtray. "Sees Nazis around every goddamn — excuse me, every corner. That's not why you're here, is it? No — couldn't be, we never report that kid stuff."

"Don't you want to find out who's responsible?"

Flamm shook his head again, derisive smile twisting his coarse, good-looking face. "Miss Corbie — we could spend twenty-four hours a day tracking down people who hate Jews. All the synagogues in San Francisco get regularly attacked by morons with paint cans in one hand and some scare sheet in the other. So what? We scrape it off, get on with things."

"But surely the swastikas —"

"You think that's such a big deal? Listen, before there was Hitler there was Stalin, and before him there was the czar. Pogroms left, right, and center field. So there's new boys in town? So what? If we ran every time somebody called us a name, we'd run forever. And some do, but not here. Not at Sherith Israel. We take care of our own — period. That's enough."

Miranda slid the business card into her pocketbook. Picked up Flamm's matchbook off the edge of the desk and lit another stick, dropping the matches in her purse.

"But Hitler's not just another bully. The stories out of Germany and Austria after '38 —"

"Sure, sure." Flamm waved his hands around dismissively. "Everyone's out to kill all the Jews. People in the old country send hysterical letters. What do you expect? It's a different world, and they don't know how to get along. They're not educated. Not smart. They overreact."

He smoothed his hair down, lowered his voice. "Nothing for you to worry about, honey. Like I said, we take care of our own — make sure people who come to us are fed and clothed and have a place to stay. Beyond that, forget it." He looked at his watch, overplaying it.

"Now, you wanted to talk about something personal — a friend . . . ?" Glow in the eyes, leer in the voice, hard-on in the pants. He

75

picked up the half-dollar again, rolling it between his fingers.

End of the line.

Miranda leaned across the desk, rubbing her cigarette out in the ashtray, stain of her Red Dice lipstick bright against the stub.

"Friend of mine is half-Jewish on her mother's side. Never had any instruction, and would like to convert. Could she get instruction here?"

He tossed the coin on a *Chronicle* racing schedule. "The two of you came out here just for that? That's the big personal question?"

"She's worked in burlesque, Mr. Flamm." Miranda crossed her legs, leaned back in the chair.

Quick little nods. Big grin. Smoothed his hair, purr back in his voice. "To answer your question, she's considered a Jew if her mother's Jewish, and she could get instruction here. From me personally. We're Reform, Miss Corbie. Very modern." Eyes insolent now, hot and knowing. "You've got my number. You can . . . pass it along."

Miranda rose, holding on to the chair back. "Yeah. I think I do."

She pivoted to face him with her hand on the doorknob. "Maybe you knew her, Mr. Flamm. Her name was Pandora Blake. She

76

was murdered last night."

She pulled the door shut, stepping into the dark hallway.

She was alone.

Traffic on California was crowded with honking cars, fairgoers on the way home, welders back from overtime at the factory, heading for the Koffee Kup on Geary or Roberts at the Beach for a quick dance and maybe a hand job on Ocean Beach.

The WALK sign finally clanged, rose slowly. Rick stood across the street at California and Webster, waiting at the cable car stop, waiting for her. Arms folded.

"Jesus Christ, you could've told me —"

"Don't start. You said you had a lead and I acted on it. Harry Flamm's a minor league huckster with his hand in the till — probably gambling with synagogue money. You bothered him, and I made you go away."

She opened her purse, took out another pack of cigarettes, and peeled off the cellophane. Her fingers found the matchbook from Flamm's office.

"Besides, you know what I do for a living."

"Yeah, Miranda. I do. Doesn't mean I want to watch."

She exhaled, thin gray cloud against the

blue black sky. "Nobody asked you to. You've got your exclusive."

Someone turned on a car radio, Jack Leonard and Tommy Dorsey warbling "All the Things You Are" over the traffic. *You are the breathless hush of evening . . .*

"So I did. Did you get your lead?"

She shrugged. "Like I said — something's wrong with Flamm. Seemed agitated when I mentioned the murder. Maybe he's a single operator, maybe not. Smelled like low-grade gangster to me."

The cable car crawled up, bell ringer punctuating "Moderne" with two short clangs. She dropped the cigarette, rubbing it out on the sidewalk, found a nickel in her change purse and a seat on the inside bench. Rick squeezed between Miranda and a hefty woman in furs with a chest like a battering ram.

She looked down at the matchbook, still in her hand. The Black Cat Café, EXbrook 9511. 711 Montgomery. Squatty, nondescript dive on the poverty row end of the International Settlement.

Car started with a lurch, throwing her against Rick. His arm flew around her shoulders instinctively, lingering for a moment. Upside-down smile, hurt eyes. Goddamn fucking hurt eyes, all the fucking things you are . . .

She looked away, looked down, opened the matchbook. Thought about Flamm's face when she mentioned Pandora's name.

Eight matches left. Small writing, scrawled on the inside front cover in black ink: "Mickey wants to see you."

She dropped it back in her purse. And wondered who the hell Mickey was.

FIVE

Rick nudged her when they reached Nob Hill. "Mason's the next stop. You going home? Or do you want a drink? It's only seven — still early."

She turned around to look out the window at the Mark Hopkins entrance, doormen opening all four doors of a black Pierce-Arrow, blondes in silk and white fox tumbling out like bowling pins. Weak-kneed heir to a bottlecap fortune straightening his top hat, trying to two-step the entranceway. The cable car clanged and rolled past, tilting precipitously down the California grade.

"Thanks. I need to get back to the Island, see what I can find out about Pandora."

He grunted. "And I've gotta convince Gleason to run the story."

A three- or four-year-old Ford sedan in Cordoba tan sped up behind the cable car, then dropped back. Not passing. Not turning. Following since Leavenworth. The back of Miranda's neck tingled.

Up and down. Fast and slow. Two dark forms in the front seat.

Finally made a right down Monroe to Bush. She'd been holding her breath.

She opened her purse, pulled out a stick. Hand shook when she lit it. The cable car crawled to a stop at Montgomery, and Miranda stepped off, Rick behind her.

Financial district. Banks, skyscrapers, Russ Building towering over everything with the air of a maître d'. Dark canyon, office lights like little yellow eyes. North on Montgomery was the Hall of Justice. And the Black Cat Café.

"What are you looking at, Miri?"

Miranda blew a stream of smoke, watched it float over Montgomery Street. "Nothing. Let's go."

Rick insisted on walking her to the front door of the Monadnock, still packed with travelers, third and fourth floors lit in soft yellow.

Thickset man with a limp and heavy five o'clock shadow waddled out from behind a newsstand, plucked Rick's sleeve.

"You're Sanders, ain'tcha? News hawk for the *News*?"

"Yeah — what about it?"

"Nothing, gent. Name's Mike — usually work the corner 'cross the street. I seen you before, that's all, and heard some other fellas lookin' for you. Somethin' on account of this here." He pointed at the headline, extra evening edition.

Miranda grabbed at the paper. Rick dug out a quarter, told him to keep the change.

Headline read: EMPORIUM GIRL FOUND STABBED.

Rick ran for the number 8 White Front headed down Market, dodging another Municipal train and almost getting an arm cut off in the narrow clearance between the two. Shouted to Miranda that he'd let her know. She waved him on to Mission Street and the office of the *San Francisco News*.

She looked at the front page again. The *News* made it sound like Annie Learner kept too many boyfriends on a string, one got jealous, and knifed her in the apartment.

Miranda puffed furiously on the Chesterfield, skimmed the other papers. Gladys wasn't working the lobby stand tonight, and the redhead behind the counter was bored and tired, paying no attention to Miranda or the ten-year-old boy opening up packets of Chiclets while his mother read the latest *Modern Screen*.

Chronicle, page seven. *Call-Bulletin,* second page. *Examiner,* page nine.

Middle-aged businessman in a faded blue suit sidled next to her in the elevator, trying to read the headlines. She left him still curious at the fourth floor, taps on her pumps echoing in the hallway.

Crowds were finally thinning out. A couple waiting for the elevator stepped in, smiling over securing the last overnight to Chicago.

She paused in front of her office. The Cordoba tan Ford bothered her. Miranda shrugged it off, put it down to nerves left over from the Takahashi case.

Nerves. That's what the fucking Chesterfields were supposed to take care of.

She unlocked the door quietly, immediately hit the light. Exhaled, smiled at herself.

There was a large file folder on her desk. She picked it up, read the note from Allen:

Here's the dope on some dopes. Hope it helps. A.

Unlocked the bottom drawer of the desk, took out the Old Taylor. Found the Castagnola glass sitting next to the safe, smelled it, poured a shot of bourbon. Drank it down, wiping her mouth with the back of her hand. Poured another, set it on the desk.

The safe was always hard to open, thanks to a sticky combination and years spent protecting Wells Fargo gold. It finally swung wide with a squeal, and Miranda picked up the .22 from the lower shelf. Just in case.

She set the pistol on her desk, took the cigarette case and extra deck of Chesterfields out of her purse to make room. The Black Cat Café matchbook came up in her hand, and she stuck it in the cigarette pack, locking everything up again.

Checked the springs on the magazine, reloaded the gun. Took a deep breath.

Sank into the leather chair and faced the phone, dialing quickly. Girl's voice, bouncy. Must be the new shift.

No, Miss Corbie. No messages. Yes, Miss Corbie. Better get a paying case soon, Miss Corbie.

She threw back the second bourbon, grabbed her spare coat from the wardrobe. It was black wool and didn't match the green, but no one on the Gayway worked for *Vogue.*

She was halfway to the door when the phone rang.

"Miranda Corbie speaking."

"Glad I caught you." Rick, sounding far away, siren drowning him out. "I'm at the Hall. Listen, it wasn't in the papers, but this girl — the Emporium perfume clerk —"

"Yeah, yeah, tell —"

He cleared his throat, then paused for a moment, voice low.

" 'Kike' was written on her stomach."

She squeezed through the squeaking doors of the Last Chance Saloon. A well-dressed drunk catapulted out, hand on his crotch. Defense attorney blustered in after her, only a few rumples in the navy blue suit.

Silver hair, silver tongue, and I wouldn't turn down yours, lady, if you use it in the right place. Hips thrust against her side, eyes confident, up and down, hand in his own pocket for a change.

Miranda stared at him and he blanched, backing into one of the saloon's dark corners. Rick took her arm.

"Keep your head low and your mouth shut. Couple of boys from homicide on the other end of the bar."

She nodded, letting him steer her to the opposite corner. They crowded next to each other on the dark ruby leather wall bench while "In the Mood" played on the yellow-and-orange Wurlitzer and couples danced in between the small wooden tables. A Scotch and water balanced precariously on the cover of his notebook, half-empty.

"They figure ice pick again. Just like your girl. Not just twice, though — a couple of times. In the chest and neck."

Miranda plucked at a stained cocktail napkin barely protecting the table. Gray splotches and gauges marked the wood, marked the whole goddamn place. Just half a block down from the Hall of Justice, home of lost chances and last chances colliding in courtrooms, victims caught in between.

She folded the napkin like a fan, straightening the edges. Two uniforms at the bar were trading barbs and baseball scores with the plainclothes dicks beside them.

"Written with her blood?"

Rick nodded. Paused and downed the rest of the Scotch and water.

She opened her purse, took out a thick pencil and the *Chadwick's Street Guide.*

"Got an address for me? Relatives, boyfriends, any leads?"

He scratched his chin, fingers digging at the black stubble.

"Long list, according to the cops. They figure same M.O., same killer, but still keeping Pandora under wraps. I've only got tonight to break the whole story, by tomorrow every paper in the city will be on it. I only got as far as I did because Hoolihan owes me fifty bucks."

"I won't keep you. Just give me the address — I'll call if I come up with something."

"Drexel Apartments — 119 Haight, number eleven. No family in the city, but there's a sister and mother up in Walla Walla."

"Was she Jewish? Go to a synagogue?"

"Not often enough, according to some of the neighbors."

Miranda nodded. Shoved the napkin aside and stood up.

"Thanks, Rick. I mean it."

He pushed himself up from the narrow bench, juke crooning Miller's version of "Stardust." One of the secretaries from the police pool was draped all over a big Irish cop, eyes closed, moving to the music. His callused hands, freckled, rough, held her like a piece of blown glass.

Rick stared into Miranda's eyes. "Be careful, Randy."

She flinched. Said briefly: "I always am," and walked out through the doors of the Last Chance Saloon, ancient wood and hinges creaking, swinging into the night.

The cop at the turnstiles was too busy helping a stooped old lady and her middle-aged daughter in baggy tweed. Didn't know the dark-haired ticket taker by name, but he smiled and waved her through, and she pushed forward quickly, heading for the Gayway.

Loud applause erupted from the Cavalcade building, drowning the fragments of swing from the Dance Pavilion and the thin, reedy calliope beckoning children to the rides.

The sawdust underneath her feet felt almost as welcome as the faces that creased in recognition, patting her arm, Midget Charlie taking off his hat, bowing low, single leftover from the Village last year and now working for Ripley.

She headed straight for Artists and Models. No beat cop outside. Found Fred but not Tom.

His smile was hesitant. "I'm sure glad to see you, Miz Corbie. Tom ain't here, though." Swallowed hard, wiped his face with his arm. "They hurt him kinda bad."

"I'm here to help him — to help Pandora. Are there any girls who knew her better than others? Anyone I could talk to?"

"I — I think Lucinda mighta known her some. I seen 'em talkin' together before. The girls' hours was always gettin' moved around, dependin' on which girls Mr. Schwartz liked best."

"He like Pandora?"

Fred nodded. " 'Swhy she opened. He liked her a lot."

Max Schwartz was a flesh impresario that liked to preview the merchandise and buy what he could on the side. He owned and operated most of the shows that Sally didn't . . . Artists and Models, Candid Camera, Greenwich Village. She flipped open the notebook in her purse, took out the thick pencil and scrawled "Schwartz" on the page. Looked back up at the large man in front of her, his head bent forward in an effort to understand.

"Does Lucinda work tonight? It's ten o'clock," she added.

He scratched his ear. "Around midnight, maybe. Last show's at one forty-five, right before the Gayway closes."

"Can I go back to the dressing room, see if she's there?"

"Sure, Miz Corbie."

He led her through a small tunnel backstage, with a green room right off the platform where the girls waited before draping themselves in a not overly tasteful tableau.

Two more doors on the left. He knocked. Female voice answered, raspy and bored.

"Yeah?"

He opened it a crack. Another bleached

blonde, about thirty-eight, dressed in a cheap purple rayon robe and sitting at a World's Fair souvenir card table, playing solitaire. A younger brunette sat on a stool in front of a three-lightbulb mirror, rubbing Pan-Cake on her cheeks and face. They both looked from Fred to Miranda. The blonde's expression was wary. She stood up.

"What is it? Whaddya want?"

Fred muttered. "We was lookin' for Lucinda. This here's Miranda Corbie. She used to work for Sally 'cross the way — she's a lady detective."

The blonde picked up a pack of Camels lying beside the worn cards, shook one out, and lit it with a match. Blew smoke out the side of her face toward the brunette, who stared at Miranda.

"Lucinda's out stuffin' her face with a burger. Come back in a couple hours."

Miranda held the woman's eyes until the blonde made a noise and sat back down. The brunette took a step forward.

"You — you here with the cops, or what?"

Miranda shook her head. "The bulls want me out. Threatened my license."

The blonde leaned back in the folding chair, robe gaping open, most of her breast showing. "Then why don't you listen to 'em, girlie?"

Miranda turned to Fred and made a motion with her head for him to leave. He withdrew, face red, last glimpse of the blonde. Miranda shut the door behind her, listened for the click.

"I'm here to help Pandora Blake."

The blonde snorted while the brunette shook her head. "She's beyond help. Go home, lady. Nobody over here asked for you. Pandora can't use your goddamn charity, and Lucinda don't want it."

Miranda took out a Chesterfield, slowly, deliberately, lighting it with the Majorette. She leaned against the door, watching the women, and blew a smoke ring. The blonde looked up at her, then dealt herself another hand of cards.

The brunette was staring again. "Wait a minute — I know you. You're the one who used to be an escort, right?"

She snapped her fingers, turned excitedly toward the blonde, who was trying to ignore both of them. "Sheila — she's OK. She got fired from Sally Rand yesterday. I heard the boys talkin' about it."

Sheila dragged her eyes up to look at the younger woman, then back to Miranda. She glanced down, noticed her robe, and nonchalantly pulled the sides together. Yawned.

"So you're the broad who used to be an

escort. Sound too high-class for the job, but I guess you didn't work the corner of Turk and Eddy, huh?" She rubbed out the Camel on the top of the card table, then flicked it with two fingers to the floor.

Miranda didn't answer. The brunette took another step closer.

"Why do you wanna speak to Lucinda?"

"Because she knew Pandora. Not many people did."

The blonde snorted again. "Bullshit — I knew Pandora. I know who killed her, too."

She looked up at Miranda expectantly while the brunette's mouth opened, then shut.

Miranda took out her wallet, withdrew five singles and another five. The blonde watched her with narrowed eyes.

"Loretta, you should leave. I got business with this lady."

The brunette turned a frightened look on Sheila and gathered up an old *Photoplay* magazine spread out by the makeup bottles. Stuck her bare feet in a couple of ratty house shoes propped against the tattered dressing screen and slipped through the door, giving Sheila and Miranda last looks before shutting it.

Miranda dropped some ashes on the floor. "What do you know, Sheila?"

"How much you willing to pay to hear it?"

"How much do you want to stay alive?"

The woman opened her mouth and laughed, showing off a few missing teeth in the back. Got up to sit on Loretta's stool, studied her face in the mirror. Pinched her cheeks.

"I gotta go on soon, so don't waste my time. Nobody's gonna off me. I'm not a goddamn filthy Jew."

"Was Pandora Jewish?"

Sheila started to rub Pan-Cake makeup on her forehead, her skin darkening to a tanned bronze. "I ain't tellin' you a goddamn thing, lady, unless you come across with some scratch."

Miranda dropped the stick on the floor, crushed it with her pump. "You can either tell me or the cops. They'll call you up as a witness if you know anything. I'll give you five dollars, they'll slap you around. Your call."

The blonde eyed her in the mirror. "What I got is worth fifty."

Miranda's mouth twisted. "What you got, sister, isn't worth five bucks."

The blonde rose in anger, facing Miranda. "Listen here, bitch —"

"No, you listen. I don't have time for you. I don't think you know a fucking thing beyond whatever truck driver is going to get drunk enough to be rolled for a blow job. You're a middle-aged slut with no prospects and no future, and if you weren't a piece of shit of a human being, I'd feel sorry for you. As it is, my pity extends to five bucks. Take it or leave it."

Sheila backed up into the makeup counter. Sank to the stool, eyes venomous.

"Some do-gooder. How the hell do you know what we go through? Who the hell are you to judge?" Her breath came out in tattered heaves, and she grasped at the robe, pulling it tight. Dropped her eyes, dropped her voice.

"All right. Five bucks."

Miranda counted out five singles, laid them over the blue-backed cards. Sheila eyed the money greedily but didn't get up.

Miranda said. "What do you know?"

"Terrell Jacobs' place. One of the animal trainers. Name's Henry Kaiser."

"What about him?"

She walked over and picked up the money, sat back on the stool, and faced Miranda. "He's a fucking bastard, is what he is. A beater."

"Did he beat Pandora?"

"She went out with him. Came to work with bruises for the next week. They stopped

94

when she quit seein' him."

"How long ago was this?"

Sheila shrugged. "I don't know. Coupla months ago, maybe. She was smart enough so's it only took once."

Miranda nodded. "Thanks. I'll be back later to see Lucinda."

"She don't know any more than —"

"Then she won't get any more than you did."

"You're some cheapskate bitch."

Miranda turned back from the door, looked up at the blond woman. Spoke softly. "Fuck you, Sheila. And the eight goes on the nine of clubs."

She closed the door behind her and met Loretta's eyes.

Six

The brunette stared at her, half in awe. She was at least ten years younger than Sheila.

A tinny radio was playing "All the Things You Are" from behind one of the other doors. Miranda was sick and fucking tired of the breathless hush of evening.

"Well, Loretta? Got anything to tell me?"

The younger woman glanced down the hallway. From around the corner by the stage, a few whistles and whoops signaled appreciation for whatever model was posing.

She whispered. "Did Sheila tell you about — about Henry?"

"Yeah. When did you go out with him?"

Loretta looked down at the cement floor, kicked at a piece of pink chewing gum.

"Last year. Right before we closed up. He was workin' the Monkey Speedway part-time then, still with the Christy Brothers Circus." She glanced at Miranda, looked away again. "I tried to warn Pandora."

"And she didn't listen."

The girl nodded. Suddenly pulled down the terry-cloth robe from her left shoulder. "He left me with this."

The skin on her shoulder was puckered and scarred, a scaly pink.

Miranda put out a finger, touched it gently. "What did he do?"

"Tried to — to brand me. I thought he was playing around."

"Jesus." Miranda took a deep breath, pulled the girl's robe back over her shoulder. "Thanks, Loretta."

The brown-haired girl looked at her anxiously. "You won't tell, will you? I'm just — I'm so ashamed. . . ." Her lip quivered while she wiped the tears with the back of a Pan-Caked hand.

"I won't say a word, but don't ever let some sonofabitch hurt you and blame you for it."

The girl nodded, sniffling. She murmured. "My real name's Ethel."

Miranda patted her on the other shoulder. "Ethel, do you know if Pandora was Jewish?"

Large brown eyes flew open, surprised. "They said she was."

"Who's 'they'?"

"Oh, I don't know. Ben, the barker. We heard that's why she was killed, so she had to have been, right?"

"Does anyone work here who hates Jews?"

"Sheila hates everybody, says Jews and Communists are running the world. I don't know. I hear a lot of people talking about it. Some of 'em say President Roosevelt is a Jew. That don't mean they like Hitler any better. And it don't mean they would've killed Pandora just 'cause she was one." She looked up. "I'm sorry, Miss Corbie. I can't help you. Sheila and me think Henry did it, 'cause he's mean enough."

She shuddered, brushed past Miranda. "I'd better go in."

Her hand was on the knob, but she paused and faced Miranda again. "Lucinda really was Pandora's friend. If anybody knows anything, it's Lucinda. She won't talk to us."

"Where can I find her?"

Ethel/Loretta shrugged. "Maybe at the Ron de Voo Restaurant, down the Gayway. She tries to get dates to take her there."

She was still clutching the *Photoplay* from earlier and flipped through the pages. "Lucinda's kind of pretty, like Pandora was. Tries to look like Dorothy Lamour." She pointed to a photo of the actress.

Miranda slipped the five-dollar bill into the fold of the magazine. "Thanks."

"But I didn't ask —"

"Consider it a contribution to stenography school."

Her mouth opened and gaped at Miranda. "How did you know I want to be a stenographer?"

"You're practicing shorthand, aren't you?" Miranda pointed to the margins of the open *Photoplay.*

The girl smiled, her eyes and mouth falling back into tired lines as she drew the terry cloth around herself.

"Yeah. Funny way to make money. Thanks, Miss Corbie."

"Be careful, Ethel."

Miranda watched as the girl slipped behind the door.

First Lucinda. Then Henry.

It was going to be a long night.

Miranda clutched her purse, reassured by the outline of the .22.

The Ron de Voo sat at the far end of the Gayway on the south side, over by the shooting galleries and the snake show, close to Jacobs's animal exhibit and Henry Kaiser. The crowd in the long, narrow building was thick and chummy and loud, swing music strident, chatter brittle and trying too hard, wanting the blue and yellow neon words to live up to their promise before it was two A.M. and time to go home alone.

"We Three, My Echo, My Shadow and Me" floated above the chatter, skinny little Frank Sinatra singing for Tommy Dorsey and sounding about twelve. Miranda pushed her way past the music and through a curtain of blue gray smoke to the counter, where she threw a dime at a dishwater blond waitress with bags under her eyes and bought two rolls of Pep-O-Mint Life Savers. Unwrapped them quickly and popped two candies in her mouth at once. Leaned against the glass and surveyed the crowd. Tried not to think about a Chesterfield.

She still looked like an old twenty-five, but hell, new fucking wrinkles every day, and Nielsen told her the tobacco speeded it up, whatever magic cream or tonic she lathered on her body not holding back time, not keeping her from old-lady age and a bent back. And she was tired of the yellow tint to her skin after a long night at the Moderne, voice harsh and raspy, no breath for the San Francisco hills.

Face and body and license. All she had. All she was.

We three . . . we're all alone, living in a

*mem-o-ry . . . my echo, my shadow and
me . . .*

All she wanted.

Miranda reached across the chrome-and-
Formica counter. Grabbed a toothpick and
rolled it between her fingers. Thirty-five was
two years ahead, whole goddamn world
might be dead by then. But she didn't want
to go out needing a Chesterfield.

Looked over the crowd, light dim and
cloudy through the smoke. Corner table.
Under a painting of what was trying hard to
be an ocean sunset.

The woman threw her head back and
laughed, coral lipstick, dark makeup, long,
tapered nails to match the shade. Wearing
one of those sarong-type evening dresses
sold through the Montgomery Ward catalog
to housewives who would never go near the
South Seas and looked nothing like Dorothy Lamour, but who craved glamour and
hoped their husbands would do more than
roll over and grunt on a Saturday night.

Pretty in a cheap way. She'd be out of a
job in a year or two, once the tits started to
sag and the thighs got a little thicker.
Desperation oozed around the orchid-
colored sarong like Hawaiian dew, and she
laughed again, manicured hand draped on
the broad shoulder of a younger man.

He was tall, very well built underneath a too-loose and too-cheap suit, loud tie with yellow stripes, blue shirt stained with ketchup. About twenty-three, twenty-four. Nice-looking kid, red face crumpled, eyes sad. Cheeks a little hollow.

Miranda pushed her way past two sailors, brushing off the incidental hand on her ass with a jab of the toothpick. Shoved the dwindling Life Savers in the side of her mouth with her tongue.

"You're Lucinda? From Artists and Models?"

The dark-eyed woman quit trying to smolder the kid with how languid she was and breathed out a Kool, smoke slightly mentholated. Poured on a *Romance of Helen Trent* voice.

"And who is asking?"

Miranda grabbed an empty chair from a table hidden behind a potted palm frond, sitting down before the kid could figure out he was supposed to stand up.

"Miranda Corbie. I'm a private investigator."

The woman's high penciled eyebrows rose. She flicked some ash in the small glass tray. The young man leaned forward, eager.

"You say you're a private detective?"

"Yeah. I used to work security for Sally Rand."

The brunette pointed her cigarette at Miranda. "You're the one who got canned."

"Yesterday. After Pandora was killed. The brass wants everything kept quiet."

The young man opened his mouth to say something and the older woman held up a warning hand, looked at Miranda warily. "So why are you here?"

Miranda opened her purse and took out two more Life Savers. She sucked on them for a few seconds, trying to keep her hands still. Looked up, met the eyes of the kid.

"I want to find the sonofabitch that killed her."

The young man's voice rushed out. "They targeted her. Because she was my girlfriend. I was just trying to tell Lucinda —"

Lucinda grabbed his arm and said it through her teeth. "Shut up, Ozzie. We don't know who this broad is yet." Eyes like flint. "You got a license? You got ID?"

Miranda pulled out her wallet. Showed them both the license. Fought the urge to take out a stick, felt the sweat beading up on her forehead.

Lucinda stubbed out the Kool. The filter, stained with coral, still burned in the ashtray.

"So why do you care? It's not your job. Never was. You didn't know her."

"I don't like murder. I don't like what was done to her body. I don't like Nazis. If those reasons aren't good enough for you, I've also worked here since '39. Call it professional interest."

Lucinda tapped the nails of her right hand on the table. "OK. So you're Miranda Corbie, a broad and a P.I., and you slum down on the Gayway for two years, and you wanna solve a nudie model's murder. What's that got to do with me?"

Miranda looked from one to the other, the young man lowering his eyes to the table when Lucinda squeezed his arm.

"Maybe nothing. But I was told you were Pandora's best friend. Maybe only friend. Not a lot of people knew her."

Lucinda glanced at Ozzie. "Go away, lady. I already talked to the johns. You can read the police report."

The noise and the heat were starting to make her head hurt. The words came out sharp and staccato.

"Fuck the police report. You know something, goddamn it, you and this kid you're trying to protect. What you don't know is that another woman was killed today, just like Pandora. Same word on her body. I'm not getting anything out of this except a headache, and my patience is running out. Talk now or in court."

Ozzie shrank in his chair. Lucinda stood up to the onslaught, skin reddening. Miranda took a few deep breaths, trying not to choke on the remains of the Life Savers.

"I suppose big-mouth Sheila told you."

"Your friendship isn't exactly a secret."

"No. But . . ." She motioned with her head toward Ozzie "His was. Ozzie was Pandora's boyfriend. And he's a Jew." Lowered her voice. "Same as me."

Miranda turned to the boy. "Was Pandora Jewish, too?"

He shook his head. "She wanted to convert. Said she was always interested in it. Her family was Presbyterian." Eyes filled with water. "We were gonna get married when the Fair was over."

Lucinda patted his arm. "Ozzie's an Aquadonis for Billy Rose. He and Pandora met about six, seven weeks ago, after we started rehearsals. You know what young people are like." She smiled benevolently at Ozzie, shooting a warning glance in Miranda's direction.

Ozzie didn't pick up Lucinda's cue, and Miranda twisted her mouth into half a grin. She opened her purse, absentmindedly taking out the second-to-last Chesterfield from the pack still inside. It was in her mouth before she realized it. She shrugged, lit it with the Majorette. Grabbed the *Chadwick's Street Guide* and the pencil.

"I need your full names."

"Ozzie Mandelbaum."

Miranda looked up at the woman across from her.

"Lucinda Gerber."

She wrote it down on the William Rudko ad page and asked, "That your real name?"

Lucinda was defensive. "Certainly it's my real name."

"Did Pandora have any family?"

Emotion clouded the woman's hard face, softening it momentarily. "Poor kid. Came out here from Ohio. I think her mother's still back there — she used to get cards. Maybe a brother, too, but nobody out in California. You know how it is — came out all starstruck, figured she'd be the next Paulette Goddard."

Lucinda shook her head, stiff waves of her hair trembling flat against her scalp. "She was a good kid. A sweet kid. There's some real bastards on this island, but I can't think of anybody rotten enough to do something like this. Especially to Pandora."

"What about Henry Kaiser, at Terrell's place?"

"What about him?" Ozzie asked the question.

"I hear he likes to beat up girls."

Lucinda studied her nails. "Dumb animals and dumb women. No offense to Pan — she didn't know any better, and if she did, she wouldn't listen. Always picked the wrong kinda guy. He asked her out the first day we started rehearsals, about eight weeks ago, and she only went with him twice. A real sonofabitch. He might be rotten enough, but I don't think he's got the balls to kill somebody. He goes for the safe play, the ones who don't fight back. Pan was through with him before she met Ozzie."

The young man was holding his face in his hands. Miranda inhaled, making it last. Spoke to Ozzie, her voice gentle. "Anything else you can tell me?"

Face red, cheeks wet. Glanced at Lucinda, met Miranda's eyes. Deep breath.

"I got — I got a little packet of her things. She was staying with me to save money. I didn't want — didn't want to turn it over to the police." He wiped his eyes with the back of his hand, voice cracked. "It's all I got."

"Where do you live, Ozzie?"

"Hotel Shawmut. Jones and O'Farrell.

They didn't — they didn't much care if we stayed together, 'long as I paid a little extra for Pan."

"How about you?"

Lucinda was lighting another Kool, blew a stream of smoke out the side of her mouth.

"I got a shack of an apartment with two other girls. The La Salle, 650 Post."

Miranda recognized the name of a run-down building not too far from her own apartment.

"Ozzie . . ." He looked up. She tried to encourage him with a smile. "I understand why you didn't want to turn her things over. How did you do it?"

"When I found out — I — I left. Ran home. Kind of expected to see her there." His hands were trembling, but his voice held steady. "Of course she wasn't. I — I wandered around. Not even sure where. I'm off on Sunday until evening, and we were gonna — we . . ." He choked on the plural, wiping his eyes. Breath shuddered going down. Lucinda patted his shoulder.

The kid held his fingers over his red face until he could breathe again. "I knew they'd be coming — the police, I mean — so I bundled up a few of her things and came back here. Stashed them in my locker at the Aquacade. That's what Lucinda and I were meeting about tonight, to try to figure out what to do."

He was rubbing a spot on his hand, over and over, not looking at either woman. "God, I — I don't want to live anymore. But I want — whoever did this — I want —" He shook his head again, unable to continue.

"Ozzie — may I see them? There may be something there that will help."

He turned toward Lucinda, who gave him a small shrug.

"Maybe it'll help somehow, kid. Might be worth a chance. Cops'll just take it from you if they find out."

He hunched over the table, too-large blue jacket flapping open. "I'd need her things back, Miss Corbie."

She took a last draw on the Chesterfield and rubbed it out, making her voice as soothing as possible. "Of course. You have them in your locker now?"

He nodded. Stood up suddenly, pushed the chair back in, bent down to kiss Lucinda's cheek. "Thanks, Lu. You've been — been a real pal to both of us. I won't forget it."

He held out his hand to Miranda to shake. She grasped it solemnly. "Thanks, Ozzie. Let's go."

Lucinda looked up at Miranda. "Who was the other girl?"

"An Emporium perfume clerk. Annie Learner. You know her?"

Lucinda shook her head. "No. I was just thinking. If some lunatic is targeting Jews, maybe I'd better lie low for a couple of days."

"Anybody here know you're Jewish?"

"Sheila. And if she knows, everybody else does."

Miranda fished in her wallet for a business card, handed it to Lucinda. "Call me if I can help. Or if you remember anything else."

The other woman was reading the card, fingering the drawn-on beauty mark on her cheek, and accidentally rubbing some of it away. " 'Private — discreet.' Yeah, well, I hope you're all of those things, lady. And something else — smart."

She looked up at Miranda, worry in her eyes.

Seven

The exhibit buildings closed at ten, but there were families and couples and solitary people out and walking, trying to forget. About Monday, about their wives, husbands, children, the boss at the insurance firm, always picking, the same goddamn bus driver every morning, same grating voice. Old gossipy Mrs. Robertson down the hall and the young girl dating Davey who wasn't what she should be. Petty grievances of everyday life, of peacetime life.

A luxury made in America.

She popped two more Life Savers in her mouth. Turned to the tall young man standing in the colored light.

"Please do what I said, Ozzie. The bulls'll throw you under glass in a heartbeat. It's withholding evidence."

His chin was stubborn. "It's — it's all I got left."

She looked out at the dark smear that was

the Lake of Nations, cry of a night bird high overhead.

"I understand. But Pandora wouldn't want you to go to jail. Do it for her, Ozzie. Please."

Raised his face, eyes red even through the blue green lights. "I'd better go in, Miss Corbie. I got a key to the performers' entrance . . . some of the gang usually hang around after the last show gets out at ten thirty. I don't want them seeing me."

"Or me. How about if I wait in the Court of Flowers?"

"I'll find you."

She nodded. Ozzie blended into the night.

Miranda walked back through the giant Arch of Triumph, fountain gurgling in a syncopated rhythm.

Imitation Europe. Built to last another year, then tear it all down, make way for an airport. Maybe the real Europe would be torn down by then, too.

Flowers reflected in the spray, flowers everywhere. Fragrant reds and purples, framed in pastel and bright yellow lights, effusion, passion, love, and beauty, all screaming joy, joy and love forever, just like a fucking Miller song, like the teenagers sitting on a bench, like the old people arm in arm.

They wanted to forget the world, keep it

back. Make it stop.

She raised her eyes to the gold phoenix on the Tower of the Sun.

No stopping, not now. Fall, fall, fall, Humpty Dumpty and the goddamn eggshell earth, cracked and broken. Bombed and bloody.

Their heritage, their fate, their role on the stage. Out, out, brief fucking candle, but burning like a firework they were, the ragtime jazz-time we're in the money babies, conquer the world, conquer the Depression, make a utopia, Shangri-la.

Her generation. Their world.

Dying, dying, dead.

Ozzie found her standing by the pansy border. He held out a small parcel wrapped in brown paper.

"I'd like it back tomorrow, Miss Corbie. And then — I'll do what you said. I think Pan would want it that way."

She took it from him, her face in shadow. "Thanks. I'll bring it back tomorrow evening. Same time at the Ron de Voo?"

He nodded. "I want to help. Please let me."

She took a step closer, blue and green lights illuminating the half-smile on her face. "You already have, Ozzie. If there's anything else, I'll let you know. You got a phone number?"

"ORdway 4884. That's the hotel."

"All right."

She started to walk back toward Pacific Avenue and the Gayway, and he grabbed at her arm. "Wait — are you going to go talk to Kaiser?"

Anger, betrayal, shame. He hadn't known about the other man. Her voice was gentle.

"Ozzie, this is my job. Let me do it."

"But you might need —"

"I won't. Go on back to the Aquacade, find your friends. I'll see you tomorrow."

He hesitated, fists balled up, shoulders tense. Miranda said softly. "Go practice. I'll see you tomorrow."

Ozzie hung his head and walked away, dark outline finally disappearing through the Arch of Triumph and into the Court of Reflections.

She looked at her watch: 1:15 A.M. Henry Kaiser was waiting.

She walked past Monkey Mountain, animals trying to doze under the harsh bright light of the Gayway. A few stragglers, mostly drunks wandering out from one of the flesh shows, always lining up with their hands on the bars, making Tarzan noises, making faces at the chimps. Once in a while, one of the animals would throw a pile of shit at the tormentors on the wrong side of the bars, but satisfaction was short-lived. Defense qualified as misbehavior, and one of the so-called trainers would come outside with a strap.

Can't have monkeys act out of place, lady. They're losing us money, can't risk the show gettin' the boot. Goddamn dumb animals. Don't know any better, do they?

Man about five feet nine in a rumpled brown suit and no hat was starting to bang on the bars, shouting at the tired chimps. None of the workers in Captain Terrell Jacobs–branded overalls came out from the door in the back. No cops at this part of the Gayway, not now.

The act was locked down, deserted. Children's elephant ride closed for the night, the giant gray animals huddled in stalls on the inside of the building, their slow, gentle stamping a dull thump on the layer of straw. Old circus lions and tigers paced and panted in small dingy cages, endlessly roaming, endless quest for escape, toothless kings of the fucking jungle made by Ringling Brothers and Jacobs, step right up, folks, it's a thrill a minute for the brave wildcat trainer, armed with a pistol and a whip, step right up . . .

The smell of straw and urine carried on the cold, moist wind from the Bay.

Miranda chewed the Life Savers in her mouth and swallowed, walking over to the drunk, giving him a smile. He did a double take, made sure he wasn't dreaming. Leered at her, teeth yellow.

"Goddamn monkeys, look at 'em. I wanna see 'em swing or somethin', like the movies. How 'bout you, baby — you wanna swing wit' me?"

Her smile grew wider, and she leaned against the cage, Ozzie's package tucked safely under her left arm. "Me Jane, you Tarzan?"

He licked his lips, made a smacking noise, eyes small, piggish slits made smaller by the wide grin. "Yeah. Tha's what I had in mind."

She stood up straight. "You don't have a mind, asshole. You're just one big mouth." She gestured with her head toward the cage. "Leave the brighter boys alone."

He gaped at her a few times, face reddening. "What are you — some kind of man hater?" he hissed.

Miranda looked him up and down. "Since when are you a man?"

His breath in her face was short, hot, and stank like cheap beer. She stared into the small, stupid eyes until they dropped, and he backed away, muttering, finally turning around and yelling from the other side of the midway, "Fuck you, lady!" before disappearing into the games, weaving through Gayway leftovers.

The chimps retreated to the small wooden doghouse in the corner of the cage. One sat outside it, folding its long arms around its knees. Watching her.

Henry was still ahead.

She walked into the main building, underneath the huge letters proclaiming CAPTAIN TERRELL JACOBS'S AFRICAN JUNGLE CAMP. No one inside, except for a couple of men in work suits, standing over a bucket with a mop and talking in a corner.

The cats were locked up in small cages housed in the rear of exhibits advertising their savage ferocity. Nero or Samson, man-eating tigers and lions, death-defying courage, lady, only twenty-five cents for a thrilling show. . . .

Miranda could hear the animals pacing behind the plywood.

The men looked up when she entered, and the taller one spoke. About twenty-three, clean-cut, built like a fullback for a college team.

"We close before two, miss, so we can give the animals a rest. You're welcome to look around — Monkey Mountain is still open next door."

Her voice was dry. "I've seen it. I'm looking for Henry Kaiser, one of the trainers. He around?"

The second attendant nudged the first one with his elbow. The tall kid looked at him, then back at Miranda nervously. "I — I think he might be, Miss . . . ?"

She let the question dangle. "Just give him a description."

They looked at each other again. The shorter blond grabbed the mop and started in on a corner of the floor. The tall one hesitated, then nodded, sidling through a rear door.

She walked over to the blond. "You a regular, or just a summer job?"

He looked up at her, then down at the floor again quickly. "Summer job. Both of us go to Cal."

"Why didn't you try for a guide? Cleaner work."

He grunted with the effort of scrubbing a sticky spot on the floor. "We did. Not enough positions, and the ones who worked last year got priority."

She nodded, watching him.

"What do you want with Kaiser?"

"To ask some questions."

He straightened up, leaning on the mop. Wiped his brow with his arm. "What are you, lady? Inspector of some kind? Humane Society?"

She needed a cigarette. Hands were starting to shake again.

"You might say that."

The door opened, and the tall kid came out first. Slightly shorter but stockier man followed. About forty, wearing jodhpurs and a safari-style jacket. Red stains on his clothing.

His hair was closely shaved in the back, small pencil mustache, thick neck. He raised his eyebrows and smiled broadly when he saw Miranda.

"I understand you wanted to speak to me, Miss? Is this for the radio, perhaps, or a newspaper? It's a little late, but . . ."

She threw on the power switch. "Actually, it's regarding a — a personal issue, Mr. Kaiser. A mutual friend suggested I come see you. Can we go someplace — private?"

His eyes were careful. Teeth straight and shiny.

"Certainly, Miss . . . ?"

"Corbie. Miranda Corbie."

"Step this way, please."

He held the door open for her, making her brush past him to fit through into the narrow hallway. The two young men watched, no pretense of work. Once she was inside, Kaiser pulled the door closed with a loud clack, facing her with an ingratiating smile.

"My office is through here."

He led her past small doorways that entered the various cages before the cramped, dark hallway opened into a storage area. Left turn, past heavy sacks of grain, potatoes, and carrots and two large freezer units. Harnesses, collars, leashes, and whips hung on the walls.

Near the loading dock was a small Airstream trailer. He skipped up the three metal steps, took a key from his pocket, and unlocked the door, turning to her with the smile again.

She smiled in return but stopped short of pressing against him to get through the door. Gestured with her hand.

"After you, Mr. Kaiser."

Small sink, stove top on the left. Table big enough for two in the middle. And to the right, a trailer-sized sofa bed, pulled out. Sheets rumpled, gray wool covers on the floor.

He gave her an apologetic look as phony

as the jodhpurs. "I'm sorry it's such a mess — we had an emergency with one of the elephants today. Would you mind sitting at the table?"

Miranda nodded, squeezing behind the yellow Formica ledge and placing Ozzie's package beside her. Held her purse on her lap, underneath the table. Hands were trembling. Not the smartest fucking time in the world to lay off the sticks. She opened the clasp.

"Now then." He shifted his weight to his left hip, digging out a cigarette case from his pocket. "Do you mind?"

He thrust the shiny gold container at her. She shook her head. They looked like Parliaments.

"No, thank you."

He lit up with a matchbook on the table, waving the match to put it out, took a puff on the stick, and stared at Miranda through the smoke.

"What can I help you with, Miss Corbie? And who's the friend?"

"A mutual acquaintance. Her name is Pandora Blake."

Didn't flinch. Eyes narrowed, back stiff. Left hand closed to a fist. "Pandora was killed yesterday."

"I'm glad you noticed."

He leaned forward, voice razor edge. "Listen here, lady — what exactly do you want?"

Fuck the Life Savers. She reached into her purse and shook out the last stick in the pack, tamping it on the yellow Formica three times, watching his temple bulge. Lit it with the Vogel Brothers Meat Market matchbook.

"Just a couple of questions, Mr. Kaiser. For instance — you have a problem with Jews, or do you beat up Catholic women, too?"

His hand fell on the table with a thump, sweat dotting the small crevice above his mustache. He crushed out the Parliament in a cheap tin tray.

"You some kind of female cop? A peeper? What's your goddamn game?"

"I don't play games. I just ask questions."

"I'm not answering your fucking questions. Get out of here before I throw you out." He squeezed out from behind the table and straightened up in quick, lithe moves, surprising for his thick body. Banged open the trailer door. Fury poured off of him, the force pinning Miranda.

She fought to keep her breath even, tried to shrug, hands still trembling. Rubbed the Chesterfield out in the ashtray, dropped the rest of the stick in her purse. Picked up the package, tucked it under her left arm. Slow, deliberate. Sidled out of the seat and stood up, facing him.

"You're some sick bastard, Kaiser. Get your kicks from torture, is that it? Toothless old lions and naïve young girls, use your whips on whatever and whoever's too weak to fight."

He stepped forward, mouth a snarl. His feet and face froze when her right hand came up with the .22.

Miranda shook her head. "Uh-uh. I bite back."

A spasm hit her hand and shook the pistol. Her mouth twisted in a bitter grin.

"Not enough nicotine today. Better be careful. Now get the hell out of my way."

He backed up two steps into the small kitchen. "I didn't kill Pandora."

"Maybe. Maybe you didn't try to use a hot iron on one of the peep show girls, either."

"She asked for —"

"Is that what you tell yourself? They like it? They need it?"

Miranda's hand shook again, and he stared at it, transfixed. She stepped closer to the open door. He was groping toward a small cast-iron pot on the stove. Miranda took another step. She was now parallel with the door. She waved the gun at him.

"I'm a woman, remember. You wouldn't want me to get hysterical and put a bullet through your brain."

She moved sideways and took a step down, keeping the .22 trained on his chest. He gripped the edge of the yellow porcelain stove, eyes darting back and forth. Spittle sprayed his safari jacket.

"Whore — you'll beg me to kill you —"

She looked up at him. "I sure hope you try, Henry. I sure hope you try."

Miranda hopped down the final step, slamming the door shut with the back of her right forearm, fingers still clutching the .22.

EIGHT

Short gasps. Legs wobbly. She ran through the darkened warehouse, praying the hallway door wasn't locked, hoping the college kids were still in the main exhibit room.

Shoved open the door, eyes blinking from the lights. Felt a hand on her arm, and she threw it off, backing against the wall, hand in her purse.

One of the kids, the blond one. Stuttering.

"I'm sorry, Miss, didn't mean to frighten — you OK? Henry show you the lions or something?"

Miranda allowed herself a laugh, pressed up against the cold cement. Glanced back at the hall doorway, started to walk quickly to the main exit.

"Is the door open? I've got to catch the last ferry."

"I'll open it for you. But it's only two fifteen — you've got plenty of time. Last

125

boat's not until three."

He sprinted up to the large double doors, fumbling with the ring of keys on his belt. By the time she reached him, limping slightly, she could see the welcome darkness of the Gayway. Lights still on, but plenty of paths to shake a shadow.

"Thanks. Your friend go home for the night?"

"Went to grab a chili dog at Dinty's before they close."

She nodded, patted him on the arm. "Good luck with school."

He blushed at the contact, scratched his head. "You, er, work here, Miss? You ever get a night off?"

Miranda was already heading into the night, calliope gasping out a last, sad come-hither song, no children to lure, no cotton candy to tease, no Gayway until tomorrow morning. Smiled at him over her shoulder.

"You're sweet, kid. But try one of the Aquabelles."

She shivered in the cold moisture until the fog wrapped her like a blanket, hand reaching for the remains of the last Chester-field, buried somewhere under the .22. The blond Cal boy leaned against the door frame, watching her fade into black.

Second-to-the-last boat was crammed. Miranda tucked herself into a corner on an inside bench, too cold to face the wind. The small cigarette-and-magazine shop was still open, so she asked the middle-aged couple next to her to save her seat.

Rick made the front page, headline blaring, DOUBLE DEATH — MURDER OF PANDORA BLAKE, MODEL ON TREASURE ISLAND, LINKED TO KILLING OF ANNIE LEARNER. Nothing she didn't already know. Buried in the article, third paragraph from the top: "As yet, authorities refuse to confirm reports that the murderer wrote a word on the body of each victim, in her own blood."

Miranda rubbed the back of her neck, hands and fingers numb with cold. Dug around in her coat pocket, pulling out the gloves she usually forgot.

Artists and Models wasn't mentioned specifically, just a "girl show." That meant every flesh peddler on Treasure Island would be jam-packed tomorrow, sightseers lining up, asking to see the spot where Pandora Blake got murdered. Pandora would die a thousand deaths in a thousand spots all over the fucking Gayway.

She sat back, closed her eyes. Maybe someday Rick would be able to write full stories, someday when the press wasn't controlled by men who were controlled by big-budget department stores with large advertising accounts.

Wish upon a fucking star, maybe someday. Maybe someday her prince would come, too, except she'd lose him again, happily fucking ever after. Look in the Magic Mirror, lady, there ain't no one sitting next to you.

Miranda rubbed her neck again, gloved hands less cold but still trembling. She set aside the papers and woke up the counter girl, asking for a pack of Chesterfields.

She found a pay phone in the Ferry Building. Phoned Rick at the Hotel Empire.

He answered on the second ring, voice still alert.

"Miranda? You get anything?"

"Yeah. Congratulations on the exclusive."

"Just tell me what you got."

She tapped the ash and let it fall on the floor, gray blending in with the raised aluminum. Her left arm was stiff and sore from holding Ozzie's packet.

"Not sure yet. But there's someone you

can check up on, see if he has a record. Couple of girls at Artists and Models fingered him."

"Just a minute." She could hear him rummaging around his nightstand drawer.

"Name?"

"Henry Kaiser. Works for Jacobs's jungle exhibit. Tried to brand one of the girls with an iron, but that's strictly off the record."

Rick whistled, paused while writing. "Anything else?"

"More tomorrow, after I sleep."

She could hear him grinning on the other end. "What's wrong, Miri? Getting too soft for the business?"

"Go to hell, Sanders."

She hung up, pain in her right foot making her wince. Goddamn green pumps. She pushed through the chorus line of doors and out into the Embarcadero, foghorns belching mournfully, moon falling toward the horizon.

The package lay open on the kitchen table. Matchbooks, a pink-and-blue hanky from the Fair. Elephant train ticket, some postcards, photographs of Pandora with Ozzie, standing in front of *Pacifica,* in front of the *Evening Star* statue, in a swan boat on the League of Nations, arms around each other.

Powder compact, lipstick. A cheap rhinestone ring.

Mementos, trinkets, worthless bits, souvenirs of a life barely lived. Of a love never tested, except by death, and that's the test that every fucking body fails, because sooner or later someone else will come, someone else will stir up the old black magic, the smell of desire, the warmth in the loins, the heat. Somebody else.

Miranda swirled the Four Roses bourbon in the highball glass, watched the droplets cling to the smooth surface.

Somebody else. Death couldn't compete with life, no matter how hard it fucking tried, and it tried hard, mama, tried hard to suckle it all away, milk of loss, milk of desperation, milk of mourning. Milk of memory.

She got up from the chair, holding the glass, walked to the radio by the sofa. Turned the knob, waiting for the magic eye to open, to catch a signal from London, maybe, or Paris, resigned and waiting. From Buenos Aires and warmer climes, from rhumba parties in casinos, cigar smoke hiding the lovemaking in the corner, tango danced all the way to a bedroom with a canopy and silken red sheets.

Our love is different, dear . . .

Billie Holiday. A voice that knew pain, understood love, knew it was all the same thing.

Miranda drained the bourbon, twisted the volume up on the radio.

A love sent by the angels . . .

But of course the angels wore swords, God's soldiers, just like Lucifer, before he got demoted to private and left to form his own goddamn army. Hark, the fucking angels sing, hark, let's send some love that's true. Because our love is different. Isn't it, dear?

New York, 1936.

Cub Room of the Stork Club, thanks to Winchell, who slipped the word to Saint Peter that John Hayes and the girl with him were OK. And everything was grand and gay and beautiful, from the black ashtrays on the table to the white linen cloths, to the clinging backless evening gown that drew attention from everyone in the room, at least the way Miranda wore it.

Johnny didn't care. He liked showing her off, liked holding her hand, liked slipping the ring on her finger.

Lucius Beebe sat three tables down, and when the band started playing again, asked to cut in. Johnny shook his head, wouldn't let him. Beebe pretended to pout, gazing at Miranda while she laughed and Johnny clutched her tighter. Then he slipped a twenty to the orchestra leader, a thickset man who looked and sounded like Paul Whiteman, and who the hell knew, maybe it was Paul Whiteman, the champagne was flowing too fast to know.

And he cued the band, and the saxophones started first, and then the band singer, petite blonde, close to the microphone, mouthing the words, his song, her song, the song he liked to sing to her.

There's a somebody I'm longing to see . . .

And he held her hand in his, the one with the ring on it. Raised it to his lips, kissed it.

"I'll always watch over you, Miranda," he whispered, hips tight against hers, hot and warm, knowing and understanding every pore of her body, her being, who she was, where she'd come from. Where she was going.

She looked into his eyes. "I'm not lost in the woods. Not as long as I have you."

He gripped her tighter, spinning her until the lights made a bright swirl, until the laughter and the applause and the clink of the champagne flutes drowned out the beating in her chest.

Follow my lead, oh, how I need someone to watch over me . . .

They buried him near Madrid.

Too difficult to get his body out of the country, what was left of it. Too expensive. He was freelancing, the *Times* explained, we didn't make him go there. We can't bring him back.

Nobody could bring him back.

It was a hot July, and the roads were dusty. Someone gave her a leather wine flask, and she tilted it back until the red dribbled out of her mouth. She wiped it with the back of her hand and stared at the red clay, at the ramshackle coffin, at the doctor from the hospital and the nun from the church.

Johnny would've laughed. He'd gone to parochial school, where the nuns usually chased him with a stick.

The nun started to recite the Lord's Prayer.

Padre nuestro que estás en los cielos, santificado sea tu Nombre . . .

Splatterful of clay on the wood. The grave digger wiped his brow. The doctor looked to the north, eyes nervous.

Venga tu reino

Splat.

Hágase tu voluntad en la tierra como en el cielo

The nun threw in a paper flower she'd cut from a magazine somewhere. Two flies fought an aerial battle by the grave digger, and he rested on the handle of the shovel for a minute, hands futilely brushing them away.

Danos hoy el pan de este día y perdona nuestras deudas

Buzzing, not the flies. The doctor looked up, shielding his eyes from the glare. Made a noise, something Miranda couldn't hear, didn't understand.

Como nosotros perdonamos nuestros deudores . . .

He was pulling the nun by the hand, and the grave digger was already moving, already running. Their mouths were open, shouting at her, and finally the nun gave in, crossing herself, murmuring the last of the prayer running, her robes trailing the ground, filthy with dirt and blood.

Miranda couldn't hear them.

Finish the goddamn service, she was screaming, gesturing to the grave, finish the words, finish them, let him rest, make him rest, make it fucking stop . . .

The doctor and the grave digger dragged her to a broken wall, holding her down. She

134

was screaming.

The bomb dropped close enough to make the earth tremble, close enough for the grave digger to catch a piece of shrapnel in his throat. Blood spurted over all of them, the doctor unable to do anything but watch. No time, no time at all.

She couldn't hear anything. Didn't think she'd hear anything again. And finally the doctor moved off of her, nudging the body of the grave digger with his foot. And he motioned for Miranda to help, and she did, she and the nun and the doctor dragging the body to the grave, Johnny's grave. They heaved it in, and the corpse splayed on top of the coffin, a trailing red smear where his neck used to be.

The doctor grabbed the shovel, which was — mirabile dictu! — still standing, thrust in the grave. He quickly spaded a shovelful of earth, flung it over the coffin and the man. And then another. And then another.

And the nun started all over again.

Padre nuestro que estás en los cielos . . .

Miranda looked in the mirror. No memory box tonight; all she had to do was look in the Magic Mirror and her prince would come and watch over her forever and ever and ever. Princess on the glass hill. Cinderella. Snow White.

She raised the glass to the image, toasting herself.

The Lord giveth, and the Lord taketh away.

"Amen."

She dropped the glass and it shattered in the sink.

Miranda held her face in her hands.

■ ■ ■ ■

PART TWO:
EXODUS

■ ■ ■ ■

We can have peace and security only so long as we band together to preserve that most priceless possession, our inheritance of European blood, only so long as we guard ourselves against attack by foreign armies and dilution by foreign races.
— Charles Lindbergh,
"Aviation, Geography and Race,"
Reader's Digest, 1939

NINE

The phone woke her at nine. She groped
for it, tongue thick.

"Yeah?"

Heart was beating too hard, slowed down
at Rick's voice.

"Miranda? Did I wake you up?"

She struggled to sit up, rubbed her eyes.
"What is it?"

"I can't talk long — called you before
writing the story — you owe me —"

"Get to the fucking point!"

"They've made an arrest — for both murders."

She swung her legs over the side of the
bed. Fully awake.

"Was it Kaiser?"

Rick paused, *News* typewriters in the
background drumming like Krupa. "No, not
Kaiser. Someone else who likes to beat up
on women."

"Who the hell —"

"Your old friend. Ex-inspector Duggan. Arrested early this morning — no bail."

She said good-bye to Rick, shock making the words perfunctory and pleasant. Hung up the phone. Stared at the forget-me-nots on the wallpaper, periwinkle blue.

Gonzales. Gonzales told her Duggan had been demoted.

After the Takahashi case. After her bruises healed.

She was still staring at the phone when it rang again. Her hand hesitated before picking it up.

"Darling girl, this is Meyer."

Her lawyer wasn't typically an early caller.

"Rick just phoned me about Duggan — hard to believe they nailed one of their own."

He poured on extra oil, the kind of soothing delivery he usually saved for the closing argument. "It is, my dear, what Mr. Earle Stanley Gardner might call a 'frame-up.' "

She opened the drawer on her nightstand, found a pack of Chesterfields and a Yellow Cab matchbook. Miranda stuck the stick between her lips.

"Where'd you get the information, Meyer? It's good of you to phone me, but —"

"You should know by now I do precious little from the good of my heart. I'm calling you about a job."

"A job? I asked you for leads on Pandora Blake."

"And so you shall have them. The job is to work for me."

The bourbon and lack of sleep were making her tired and confused. She lit the cigarette, closing her eyes for a second.

"Meyer — you're my attorney. What's this about? And don't try any of your trial-style bullshit on me."

He laughed for a few seconds. "Exactly why I adore you, Miranda. All right. I want you to work for me because if you do, you will have a legitimate reason to investigate the murder of Pandora Blake and the other unfortunate girl, Annie Learner."

"What are you talking about?"

His voice was low, serious now. "I'm representing Mr. Duggan. And I want you to help me prove he's innocent."

Miranda cradled the phone in her hands, paying no attention to Meyer's muffled exclamations on the other end.

She finally held up the receiver. "You want to hire me to help defend Duggan. A dirty cop who nearly broke my face three months ago. Who hates my guts."

"You asked for a chance to work on the

Pandora Blake case —"

"Goddamn it, you're the one that nailed the bastard for what he did to me. You're the reason he got sent down. Why the hell are you defending him?"

Silence. Miranda ran a shaking hand over her forehead. Meyer let out a deep breath and finally spoke. "Because I believe he's innocent. And because he asked for me."

"He asked for you?" She wrapped an arm around her side, body stiff and sore. "I don't believe this. Duggan belongs in a nuthouse. They've arrested one of their own, for God's sake — they'll have damn good evidence."

"Precisely why he asked for me."

"I'm not so sure. There's no shortage of capable attorneys in San Francisco."

"My dear, you cut me to the quick. Why don't you come down to the Hall and interview him yourself? They've refused bail, but we're fighting it. We can all talk it over."

She reached across to the nightstand ashtray and gave the cigarette a vicious twist.

"Meyer . . . did you tell him you were going to hire me?"

The lawyer cleared his throat. "Yes. He made no objection —"

"Did it ever occur to you that he asked for you in order to get to me?"

"I'm not sure what you mean —"

Miranda shook her head and winced from the spasm, neck and shoulder muscles knotted and tense.

"I mean he's dangerous, goddamn it. And I wouldn't be surprised if he's guilty."

More silence. She looked down, picking at the tassels on the edge of the white cotton bedspread.

Meyer's voice came over the wire smooth and unperturbed. "I can only say I believe him to be innocent. At least of these crimes. Will you please come down for an interview? Speak to him, perhaps, before you make up your mind?"

Miranda closed her eyes. Duggan's face when he handcuffed her, when he slapped her, when he tried to break her. And then Pandora's body, kaleidoscope swirl, solidifying, red and white. Red and white.

Drip-drop. Drip-drop.

"Are the autopsy reports in? Would I have access to everything I need?"

"Yes. Their case is purely circumstantial, and the speed of the arrest itself proves —"

"Save the argument for the jury. What about the ethics of hiring me when you work for me?"

His voice relaxed. "I've taken the liberty of drawing up a contract. It stipulates that I have hired you as a temporary consultant who is to investigate the specific matter at hand, and that any legal issues resulting from the arrangement will be handled by Lattimore."

"He's junior."

"And a highly capable attorney."

She grunted. "I'll meet you at noon. On one condition."

"Name it, my dear — you know I have the utmost faith and —"

"Yeah, yeah, I know. Listen to me. If I agree to this — and it's a big fucking 'if' — I handle it my way. And if I uncover anything that corroborates the charges — anything — I turn it over to the cops at the same time."

He sounded surprised. "Reciprocal discovery of inculpatory evidence. We'll talk it over when you get here."

"You'll need to agree before we talk."

The lawyer blew out a breath in frustration. "Miranda, my child, you do want to find the killer, do you not? And you do need a source of income?"

"The bulls think the killer's in custody. I've got ads in the paper. I'll be back on my feet in a week. What I want to know is whether you're willing to stand behind Duggan all the way down the line."

Siren in the background, someone shouting. Meyer's voice gruff this time.

"Very well. You have my word — if you should choose to accept my offer. There are other private detectives, after all."

She grinned. "And my guess is you've had a hell of a time finding any who will touch this case, or you wouldn't have agreed to my terms."

Warm laughter poured out of the receiver. "Touché, my dear. I'll see you at twelve."

Miranda slowly hung up the phone. Her hand crept up to her left cheekbone as she remembered the last time she saw Gerry Duggan.

She took a long shower, lathering up with Lady Esther's latest soap. Rubbed Dorothy Gray Salon cream on her face, concentrating on the age spots of eyes, nose, and throat. Miranda looked at herself critically. Back on the chain gang at the Club Moderne soon and couldn't afford to look thirty-three.

Made a pot of Hills Brothers coffee on the small stove, wrapping up the package of Ozzie's treasures, still strewn on the kitchen table. Drank two cups quickly, large hands wrapped around a jadeite coffee mug.

Chose a conservative suit, gray jacket, white blouse, demure hat, last year's style, tilted on the left with a black net veil and plastic pearls bunched toward the front. Miranda checked the mirror. Respectably dowdy, like a girl from the typists' pool.

Roy was the doorman on duty, his Adam's apple bobbing as she waved hello and good-bye. Poor nervous bastard, still worried someone would see him down at Finoc-chio's, waiting by the stage door.

She walked up Mason to Bush, sensible and ugly black Cantilever shoes like silk slippers after yesterday's pumps. Two blocks to the Stockton Tunnel, down the steps to catch the F line, off again at Washington, and two more blocks to Chinatown and the Universal Café.

Two eggs, sunny-side up, and bacon, two hotcakes on the side. The coffee was black and bitter with grounds, no sugar to soften it.

A youngish woman in glasses and a se-verely tailored coat dropped a nickel in the juke, and "Blue Orchids" swelled until Mil-ler filled the counter and first dining room. Miranda wasn't in the mood for Hoagy Car-michael or fucking flowers of any color.

She picked up the morning *Chronicle* on the counter, relinquished by a middle-aged salesman with dandruff. Nothing new about Pandora or Annie Learner, and mention of an arrest but not Duggan's name or former occupation. Afternoon edition would be full of it.

Headlines blared that the Nazis were pushing on toward Dunkirk, already claiming Calais, the RAF squeaking out another day of survival for the trapped army. FDR assuring everyone in the fireside chat last night not to panic, defense was strong, but to beware the fifth column, the Trojan horse. She thought of Gonzales in Mexico and flung the paper aside.

The waitress pushed the order across with a smile, pouring more coffee, and Miranda looked down at the Buffalo China platter with the chip on the edge, covered in brown hotcakes, thick, crispy bacon, and perfectly cooked eggs.

Thought about what Gonzales said about Duggan. Tried not to think about Gonzales.

Good war record, used to be a good cop. Banged a lot of heads during Prohibition. Probably banged more than that, Miranda thought, and sipped the coffee.

Duggan was Irish and proud of it, tight family, and his brother died of syphilis. Lots of brothers in lots of cities died of syphilis, but he took it personally. Everybody knew that a woman who'd let you fuck her was a bad woman, not the kind you brought home

147

for corned beef and cabbage on Saturday night.

She took another sip of coffee, poured syrup over the hotcakes. The Chinese waitress smiled at her.

Miranda remembered his face when she drew her .22.

She didn't hold much hope for Gerald Duggan.

She walked down the hill on Washington, chased by the smell of freshly fried sesame balls and red bean cakes, past the Chinese Telephone Exchange and the green undulations of Portsmouth Square. Strode through the archway and up the inside steps on the Kearny Street side, down the marble halls of Tara, sure she wouldn't hear any harps.

A couple of uniforms passed her. One turned back, eyebrows knitted in an effort of memory. Riordan. She smiled until she got to the booking desk and found Collins sitting behind it.

He thrust himself forward, arms across the desk.

"Well, well, well. Miranda Corbie. Somehow I'm not surprised. Your pimp-lawyer said you'd be showing up."

She opened her purse and took out one of the Life Savers rolls she bought in Chinatown. Unwrapped the foil top with a white-gloved finger and opened her mouth, slowly placing it on her tongue and starting to suck it, not letting go of Collins's eyes.

Red flushed his cheeks, and he raised his voice. Slammed the fountain pen down next to the logbook, drawing the eyes of the two uniforms behind him and the bored secretary in the corner.

"He's talking to Johnson. Through the hallway, two doors down. You remember what the rooms look like."

Miranda tilted her head to the side, caressing tone.

"Thanks, Collins. You talk to Johnson, too? Or you just rub him a little?"

His mouth fell open and one of the uniforms in back snickered. She pushed through the partition gate, wood oily and black from the years of dirty hands on both sides of the divide. Held her fist up to the door, hesitating for a second, then knocked.

Lieutenant Johnson flung it open, looked her up and down with a frown. Meyer was sitting at the table. Closet-sized but equipped with an exterior window to Jackson Street. The arched glass and wood supports were thick with dirt and the dried bodies of dead insects.

Air was still stuffy, and Miranda loosened

the collar around her neck with a forefinger. Johnson motioned her in and closed the door, voice gruff without much effort.

"Miss Corbie. I understand you're going to be working for Mr. Bialik in an investigatory capacity."

She raised her eyebrows. "I haven't signed a contract yet, Lieutenant."

Meyer stood up, took her by the elbow. "My dear, we are between Scylla and Charybdis. The lieutenant here — who is heading the investigation — refuses to allow you to even speak to Mr. Duggan unless you have already signed the contract."

She looked from one man to the other, from Johnson and his shaved blond neck and food-stained uniform and red rectangle of a face to Meyer's ornate vest, duck's-head ebony cane, and black-and-white spats.

"Lieutenant — may I speak to Mr. Bialik privately?"

He shrugged slightly. "Make it quick. We need to transfer Duggan over to Quentin and out of County Jail." He closed the door behind him with a bang. She turned to Meyer.

"What the hell is going on?"

He held up a hand in pacification. Leaned closer. "I told you earlier. They're rushing this through. And Johnson, my dear, will use every hidebound rule in the book to get Duggan isolated and away as soon as he can."

Miranda rubbed her neck, pearls on her hat wriggling. Couple of teenage girls were walking up Jackson Street, eating fortune cookies from a paper bag. Laughing. She looked away from the window, staring into her lawyer's dark brown eyes.

Said heavily: "Give me the goddamn pen."

TEN

They walked outside through the north doors, down the sidewalk, and toward the alley that separated the jail from the Hall of Justice. Thicker building, ugly and brutal, hiding men who were the same way or learned to be. It crouched in the shadows of Washington and Dunbar, hiding behind the more respectable façade of its companion.

Miranda's hands were trembling again. She opened her purse and shook out a Chesterfield, lighting up with the Ronson while Johnson strode through the main hallway of County Jail Number One.

His long strides outpaced Meyer, whose cane taps were muffled by the woman in the torn wool coat with puffy cheeks, holding on to her sullen-faced son. More sobs from the main visitors' room, two hours a day to say, Goddamn it, I'm sorry, baby, it won't happen again, and Jesus, if I hear you're sleepin' around on me, I'll break your fucking face.

A couple of secretaries and a guard climbed in the elevator with them, making small talk about the Fair and Fiesta Days. Johnson was wordless, hands folded together, looking up at the ceiling as if it held stained glass.

Cigarette was three-quarters gone already. Miranda said, "What about the autopsy on Annie Learner?"

The door opened on three and the elevator emptied, the guard and secretaries sidling behind a partition in front of the thick steel gate that shut off the jail area. Johnson stood in front of the metal grid. Glanced down at her.

"Not completed yet."

"I thought Duggan was charged with both crimes."

Meyer took her by the elbow, bent pleasantly toward Johnson before the blond cop could open his mouth.

"I haven't been able to brief Miss Corbie yet, Lieutenant. We would appreciate a report on Annie Learner as soon as possible."

Miranda stepped toward the counter, where the guard from the elevator was now stationed. He stared at her, curious, while she rubbed out the cigarette stub on the wood. She raised her eyes to his until he blushed and looked away. Said with her back still turned, "I figured you wouldn't nail one of your own without the whole works, Johnson. You sure you got the right man?"

Meyer's smile was nervous. "My dear, we should save the questions for Mr. Duggan."

Miranda shrugged, pivoted, staring at Johnson, whose rectangular face was red and slipping into a trapezoid.

"If it's just a matter of pinning it on a dirty cop, you've got a lot to choose from."

Johnson's back stiffened. He nodded to the guard, who depressed a switch and walked around the counter to shove the gate aside, metal shrieking against metal. Meyer angled close, leaned into her. Whispered: "Why, dear girl, do you insist on making things more difficult?"

"I told you, Meyer — I do this my way or no way at all."

Johnson marched into the jail without looking behind him. Meyer sighed and gestured forward with his cane.

Duggan was sitting on his bunk, shoulders rounded, long arms dangling limp at his sides. Staring at the wall.

"You got fifteen minutes. As soon as the

marshal gets here, we're transferring him to Quentin. Foster is around the corner if he starts acting up on you." Johnson scowled down at Duggan before leaving, voice a rasp. "Goddamn disgrace."

Meyer spoke quickly. "Marshal? This isn't a federal affair, Lieutenant."

The blond cop stopped, slowly turned around. "Never said it was. But he was a part of this department for a long time. And I figured it would be smarter to ask a federal agent to transport him. Less to worry about."

He slid the stubborn metal shut, red, pulpy hands caressing the bars. Said it to Meyer, not looking at Miranda: "Fifteen minutes."

Meyer nodded. Turned toward his client. "Mr. Duggan?"

Miranda barely recognized him. Hair greasy, swept back, unkempt. Riddled with gray. Sunken cheeks. Duggan, sad-faced siamang, long hairy arms helpless, large hands, covered in scars, weak, white, empty.

Flare of energy when he met her eyes. Recognition.

Miranda sucked in her breath.

Misery, unspeakable pain. Anger still there, bubbling underneath the surface, but hurt sapped strength, too lethargic to strike

155

out. Too listless to hate.

His lips were dry and caked with last night's saliva. He wetted them with his tongue, pink length of it darting at the corners, mimicry of a smile. Flicked a glance to Meyer, thick eyebrows raised.

"So you got Corbie. Think a whore can save me? Or is she here to finish the job? She started it . . . her and that fucking Mexican." Spittle flew into the air. Meyer calmly reached into his breast pocket and wiped his face with a red silk handkerchief.

Miranda's hands reached for a purse that wasn't there. No cigarette, no Life Savers. She grabbed one of the rusty bars and held on, paint flaking off in her palm.

Deep breath. Get the voice under control. No weakness, not in front of Gerry Duggan.

"Gonzales always told me you used to be a good cop. Despite what you did to him. He was your best friend, you sonofabitch."

Her hands were sweaty on the cell bar.

Duggan looked at her once, then his eyes retreated, roaming the corner of the cell. He faced the wall again, animal sound in his chest, strangled sob. Trapped. Rubbed his hands, repetitive motion. Miranda noticed the palms were chapped, rubbed over and over, never quite coming clean.

She glanced at Meyer. He looked at her nervously and cleared his throat.

"Mr. Duggan, Miss Corbie will do everything she can to corroborate your alibi. She's the best there is at what she does."

Duggan was rocking now. Up and down, up and down. Mouth ground into a thin, bitter gash, jaw clenched shut, rocking, staring at the wall. Sudden spit of words streamed, anguish stretching them like a rack.

"Does best? Does best? I don't need her. I need — I need . . ."

Gerry Duggan's face crumpled up and then let go, unable to hold on. His eyes opened wide, as if seeing his cell for the first time. Covered his face with his hands. And kept rocking, drops of tears and sweat dripping through his fingers.

They didn't get much more out of Duggan. He stank of fear and urine and wet, warm tears, entrapment his only reality. He rocked and cried and growled, anger throwing off a spark or two, aimless and unfocused.

Another toothless tiger, pacing his cage.

No, he wasn't guilty. Wouldn't say if he knew Pandora, admitted he'd been there that morning. Walked into her dressing room, found her with the ice pick in her chest. Nobody else was there. Pulled it out, ran. Took a taxi from the Island. Cops found the cabdriver, who remembered the shaking Irishman with the darting black eyes clutching his stomach.

Couldn't remember what he did with the ice pick. The cops dug it out of a trash can over by Sunset Bridge, where he caught the taxi off the Island. Couldn't remember any writing, couldn't remember anything except her white, dead body, how the blood was dripping slowly around the hole and how the pick made a sucking sound when he pulled it out.

He crawled back to his apartment and tore out the phone. Got drunk and stayed that way until they broke down his door and handcuffed him.

Duggan talked to the wall, mumbling first, growing louder, more articulate. Wouldn't explain why he walked in on Pandora. They asked him about Annie Learner and he shook his head back and forth, not stopping. Eyes, moist and red, stared at the wall like a lost lover.

Duggan was in agony, and not just from the confinement.

She didn't speak to Meyer until they reached the steps of the Hall of Justice.

Checked her watch. Still early, just past one thirty.

"You see what I mean, Miranda. He isn't even fighting."

She blew smoke out the corner of her mouth. "Still doesn't mean he's not guilty. But I agree. Something's not right. And they've got a hell of a circumstantial case against him, Meyer. This isn't going to be easy, even if there's something crooked in it."

The lawyer nodded, staring at his spats, vest and demeanor both wilted.

"I'll send you a retainer by messenger along with the reports. Everything should be at your office in an hour."

"Thanks. I'll be in touch." She looked up at the older man, noticing the circles under his eyes, the yellowed skin. "Get some sleep. Jesus Christ, why are you even taking this case? What's Duggan to you?"

Meyer looked past her toward the gaily colored Chinese restaurants and shops along Washington Street. "Two years ago, Polish Jews were expelled from Germany. Left to rot on the border, unwanted by either country." His eyes dropped to his hands and the thick gold rings on each of them.

"I practice law. I earn a good living. I owe

159

it to this country — and to my father's country — to defend Gerald Duggan."

Miranda flicked the cigarette on the steps, rubbed it out. "You believe in him that much?"

He shrugged. "I believe he is innocent of these crimes, at least."

She shook her head. "You're a goddamn knight, Meyer. But this is a war we're in. And nobility can be fucking expensive."

He cocked his head and gave her a small smile. "I'll keep that in mind, my dear. And in the meantime, perhaps you can explain to yourself why you almost died for Eddie Takahashi. And why you just signed my contract."

Miranda opened her purse, lit another cigarette, then turned and walked down the steps.

She found No-Legs Norris on Grant and Commercial, propped against a wall next to Blind Willie and eating a liverwurst sandwich. Miranda dropped a dollar in Willie's rusty Campbell's Soup cup, and he smiled at her, no teeth, holding out a sharpened pencil. She gently pushed his hand away.

"Keep it for next time, Willie."

He folded his lips together, sucking on his bare gums. "Tha's wha' you always say,

Miss Corbie."

She leaned against the downside of the slope next to Ned, her back against the wall of the Far East Bakery. He pushed himself up straighter, weight resting on his powerful hands. She kept her voice low.

"Something's rotten."

"Nothin' new."

Half a man, and still fighting a war that left him that way. Face brown and lined with sun, mouth thin, eyes sharp. Good-looking as a boy, fresh from Flanders Fields.

Could've joined the sideshow, dancing on his hands, wearing a tux and driving a race car like Johnny Eck. But Ned turned down Ripley and all the cheaper impresarios that followed in his wake. He preferred to work on the streets in the city he was born in.

Miranda admired him for that.

"You hear anything about Pandora Blake or Annie Learner?"

He looked up at her, squinting in the sunlight. "I heard they arrested Duggan real damn quick. And I heard about the name, the Nazi connection. Goddamn bastards. My old lady's mother's side is Jewish."

Miranda raised her eyebrows. "I didn't know you were married, Ned."

He shrugged. "We been living together for a while. It ain't official." He winked at her.

"It's only my legs I'm missin', remember."

She grinned. Handed him a five-dollar bill.

"Any scat you hear. On Duggan, on Hitler lovers, on Pandora or Annie. Anything at all. I'll be around to check."

He saluted her, pocketing the money too fast to follow. Motioned for Miranda to bend closer. Whispered: "OK if I bring Willie in on it? I been tryin' to help him get around. And it's surprising what folks'll say around a blind man."

"There's plenty of money for both of you."

He turned to Willie, who was smiling vacantly. "You ready to scram?"

The blind man's voice piped like a baby chick's. "Anytime, No-Legs."

Miranda headed down Grant toward California. At Sacramento she turned around. Ned was pulling himself across the street one-handed on his plywood platform, holding on to Blind Willie with his other hand.

She walked into the Republic Drugstore at Grant and Sacramento, bought more Pep-O-Mint and Butter Rum Life Savers. Supposed to put spring in her step and pep in her back and take her mind off the goddamn nicotine withdrawal.

She looked to her left, up the Sacramento

grade to the Baptist church. Thought about Eddie Takahashi.

Telegram from Emily was still at the office. Miranda received it just a couple of weeks ago, while the Fair was in rehearsal, so she wired congratulations from the Western Union exhibit. The sales representative gave her a funny look. Guess she wasn't supposed to know anybody with the last name of Chen.

She unraveled the foil on the Pep-O-Mints and popped two in her mouth, staring at the vacant, shuttered shop on Sacramento Street. At the spot where Eddie lay dying.

And she thought about her life since February, about the flood of high-profile divorce cases that came her way, word on the underground circuit that the Corbie dame was good and good-looking besides, and that made it easier to get what you wanted, that grade-A divorce settlement, no Reno trip necessary. They were surprised when she turned most of them down.

She took on three cases. A bigamist — made the second one this year. Then a medical school case where the wife helped put him through it, and once he got the degree, it was *Young Dr. Kildare* time, tired old lines for the suddenly tired old wife.

You're such a drudge, Nancy. You never

take care of yourself, never meet me with a Manhattan after work and ask me how many lives I've saved. Nurse Rollins understands my work, understands a man has needs underneath his white lab coat.

Doctor who liked to play doctor. She enjoyed that case.

Then there was the most recent, the old lady who thought her husband was philandering on her. Took Miranda two weeks to convince her it was all in her head. Took her two weeks to convince the stubborn old bastard of a husband to buy his wife a new dress and take her out to the Golden Pheasant. Earned every fucking penny she made.

Miranda sighed, chewing on the Pep-O-Mints, and walked down Grant toward California, past Old Saint Mary's and her favorite admonition.

Son, observe the time and fly from evil . . .

Shoe taps on cement kept time with the images clicking by, slow-motion style, then fast, too fast to catch, to remember.

Pandora's body, sepia photo of her and Ozzie. Painted swastika on a synagogue wall, old man, blind man, legless man. Cruel man, strutting, brandishing a hot iron, harpy of a woman crowing in triumph. Perfume counter girl making eyes at a customer, Hitler's latest speech, spittle flying, Coughlin and Lindbergh on the radio, explaining why the Nazis were really fighting our war, the war against Communists and Jews.

And still they flooded her, overwhelmed her, until she had to stop walking and lean against the shaded brick of an apartment building on Pine, waiting for the film to unroll, the parade to stop.

For her hands to quit shaking.

Through it all, Gerry Duggan's eyes. Accused and accusing. In agony.

Miranda pushed on, walking faster. Finally turned the corner on Mason and was heading toward Bush when she saw it.

A Ford in Cordoba tan.

ELEVEN

Parked on Mason at the corner of Bush, facing downhill toward Union Square. One man in it, neck and shoulders bent. He straightened up with a cigarette, cranking down the driver's window, arm in a white linen suit resting on the door.

Miranda ducked into the shadow of a small redbrick apartment building, breathing hard, and not because of the walk from Chinatown.

Memory of the green Oldsmobile bearing down on her was still nightmare fresh, after the calendar pages turned and the bruises faded and Martini's grave was covered in ostentatious wreaths at the Lawndale Italian cemetery. She rubbed her right leg without realizing it, hand brushing against the thin dark wool.

She relied on Joe Merello to let her know if the Lanza and Lima families and their associates had her marked. Whether Gillio still wielded any power. Joe heard everything, either at the bar of the Club Moderne or behind the palm fronds and the little door in the back. Over a roulette wheel people talked, and Joe's boys listened.

He figured she was safe, they owed her a favor, since Martini was L.A.'s boy, pissing on territory that didn't belong to him, brought up at Gillio's invitation.

She wasn't so sure. And she didn't like the Ford sedan.

The man in the car looked at his watch. He was wearing a Panama, and it shaded his face. Tall, skinny build, with a long oval head to match, left wrist knobby even at a distance.

Miranda waited. Man in his late twenties, wearing overalls and carrying a box of tools on his shoulder. Ran down the apartment steps in a hurry, slowing down enough to get a look at her.

She smiled at him. He smiled back, no hat to tip.

"You need directions, Miss? Anything I can help you with?"

Shook her head, smiled again.

"No thanks. Just catching my breath before walking uphill." She gestured toward Pine. "I see there's an apartment vacant here. Looks like a nice building."

Eager voice. "Oh, it is, Miss, it is. The supe's a swell guy. Rent's fair, neighbors are all right." He looked her up and down again.

"My name's Albert. Albert Daniels."

The thin man in the Ford opened the car door, clambered out. Looked around the street and stretched. Miranda kept her eyes on him.

"If I had a car, I wouldn't have stopped to rest and we wouldn't have met — isn't that funny? I'm thinking about saving up for one. Maybe something like that."

She pointed to the Ford. The linen suit hung loosely off the driver while he walked across the street to the Cottage Food Shop. Albert glanced over at the sedan, shrugged.

"Fords are OK, Miss. Dependable. That one looks like a '38, good engine on it. Gets about eighty-five horsepower."

Miranda turned toward Al. "Do you know that car?"

The young man shook his head modestly. "No, can't say I do. Never seen it before. But I know my autos, Miss — I've got to." He pointed to the toolbox, gave her a grin. "I'm a mechanic."

She started backing down the hill toward Bush, sunlight making her squint up at Albert, smile fixed.

"When I get my car, I'll come looking for you."

"Hope so, Miss. Say — I never did get your name. And I thought you were headed up to Pine? That's where I'm going."

"You know, I think I'm just going to get a bite at the Cottage first. My name's Miranda."

He nodded, repositioning the toolbox on his shoulder, face a little crestfallen.

"Well . . . Miranda — hope to see you around." He called out to her when she was almost even with the Ford. "Personally, I like the Nash. A lot of power for only a few dollars more."

She waved. The mechanic stared at her for a few seconds, confused, then turned and trudged slowly up Mason.

Miranda crossed the street quickly, heading for the tan car.

Not much time. Skinny would get his pastrami on rye eventually and come back to the car, staking out her apartment.

If he was staking her. If she wasn't just wasting time she didn't have, worrying about nothing.

Car was clean inside. Passenger window rolled halfway down. Blanket in the backseat, nothing too unusual. Maps of San

Francisco, Oakland, and Los Angeles. Some coffee-stained napkins on the passenger side. Couple of matchbooks, Fisherman's Grotto Number Nine and the Chat Noir Café on Sutter.

Miranda wasn't sure what she expected. No bloodstains, no nooses, no blackjack. No gun visible, though he'd be wearing it, and the extra would be in the glove compartment.

She glanced over at the sunny corner of Bush and Mason. If she had any sense, she'd hightail it down to her apartment and pick up Pandora's packet, which was why she'd walked home in the first place.

Instead, she eased the handle of the door, checking to see if it was locked, grateful, for once, she was wearing gloves.

It was unlocked.

Quick look around.

Against the Storm was playing from the second-floor window of the apartment house across the street. Clang of a cable car bell on Powell a block away.

She bent down, pretending to tie her shoe, and quickly opened the car door, eyes still on the corner. Reached for the glove compartment.

It was locked.

Miranda cursed and quickly ducked out,

shutting the door more loudly than she intended.

Her hand was still on the handle when she met Skinny's eyes, across the street.

He stared at her while he crossed, waiting for a single blue Dodge to pass him on its way up the hill. She smiled, opened her purse slowly. Shook out a Chesterfield.

Nothing to do but wait. If the bastards were gunning for her, they'd know she knew it.

Paper bag in one hand, car keys in the other. Stooped, like a lot of tall men who were too skinny to stick out a chest and gloat.

She stepped to the hood of the car, keeping it between them, holding out her cigarette.

"Got a match? My lighter won't spark."

Six three, maybe six four. He kept his eyes on her face, dug around in the pocket of the linen jacket with the heavily padded shoulders. Couple of food stains on the lapel. Dark brown eyes, hollowed out, purple circles underneath that tunneled down to the bridge of his nose. Thin lips.

He held out a scratched-up lighter, flicked it once. She bent forward toward the flame, drawing down on the stick. Looked up at him again, showing plenty of teeth.

"Thanks. I was just admiring your car. I'm in the market for one myself. Didya buy it new, or pick up a deal on something used?"

His voice was slow, as if it took time and energy to travel up his long trunk and out the dry, pinched mouth.

"This here was a used model."

She nodded, running her gloved hand on the hood. "I hear good things about these sedans. Plenty of go for the size. Where'd you say you picked it up?"

He opened the door, threw the paper back on the passenger side, knocking one of the matchbooks to the floor.

"I didn't, lady."

Miranda backed up to the sidewalk while he turned on the ignition. She stooped down to the open passenger window, keeping the smile plastered on her face.

"Can't blame a girl for trying to find a bargain, can ya, Mister?"

He looked up at her. Slow, deliberate drawl.

"You'd gotta travel a long way. This car came from Los Angeles."

He let go of the emergency brake, and Miranda jumped backward, watching the Cordoba tan Ford pull ahead and roll down Mason.

■ ■ ■ ■

The Chesterfield couldn't keep her hands or legs from shaking.

Roy was back from lunch, sitting behind the desk. He brightened when she walked in.

"Didn't expect to see you so soon, Miss Corbie. A Pacific Telephone and Telegraph man was just here for you."

Her voice was sharp. "What did he want?"

"Just to see how your phone service was working, Miss Corbie, nothing important. He said he'd come back some other time. Left a brochure and everything, wanted to make sure you knew how to operate the phone."

He held out a pamphlet. Miranda grabbed it, looking it over carefully. Maybe she was being too goddamn anxious, seeing thugs around every corner. Maybe the skinny man with the Panama and the L.A. car was just some traveling salesman who lived in the neighborhood.

But she wouldn't fucking bet her life on it.

"What'd he look like, Roy?"

"Oh, I don't know, Miss Corbie. Kind of your average joe, I guess. Dark hair. Showed me a company card. I asked for identification, like you told me."

"That's good — thanks. Don't let anybody — I mean anybody — upstairs without me giving you the OK first. OK?"

She opened her purse and fished out a couple of dollars. Roy turned red.

"N-no need for that, Miss Corbie. I'm j-j-just doing my job."

She picked up his hand and put the money in his palm. "Take it."

He closed his fist around it and coughed, beet red.

"Did he leave a business card?"

Roy shook his head. "No, ma'am. He showed me a card in his wallet that said he was from PT and T."

"You remember his name?"

Roy shook his head again. "It was real quick. I think his first name was John."

"Thanks."

Miranda took a deep breath, started climbing the stairs.

Three months and three cases to try to knock her off, and no action.

Time to talk to Joe again.

Tonight.

She walked through every room, looking, sniffing, listening for any signs of intrusion.

The clock ticked, and it smelled the way it always did: warm wood, old coffee, cigarette smoke. A touch of Vol de Nuit.

Dug out a box of Arm & Hammer baking soda from the back of the cupboard, hoping it wasn't a solid rock of white. Shook it.

Still granular.

Set it on the counter and moved to the bathroom. Opened the shower door, plucked a long auburn hair off the wall.

Miranda picked up her purse and Pandora's package, held the baking soda with her right hand. Stepped over the threshold and set the packages down.

Sprinkled a fine layer of white on the inside of the foyer floor. Closed the door and locked it, carefully inserting the hair between the door and the frame so that it was held up by the lock mechanism. Stashed Pandora's package under her arm and walked downstairs.

"Keep this behind the desk for me, Roy. I'll be back for it later."

His mouth fell open. She handed the doorman the box of baking soda and stepped out into Mason Street.

She caught a number 2 White Front down on Sutter, riding in a packed car of chattering women, shoppers returning home to the manicured lawns of small Berkeley houses, comparing bath linen prices at the White House. Stared out the dusty window at the chrome of the Club Moderne, gleaming in the afternoon sunlight.

Checked her watch. Three o'clock. She'd promised Ozzie she'd meet him tonight.

First was the Moderne, and she couldn't talk to Joe looking like a reject from stenographer school. Left her a few hours to go over the facts, such as they were, and make a few phone calls. Two murders and Duggan. And the little matter of somebody shadowing her, most likely mobsters who wanted to get even for the filth she'd helped clean out of Chinatown.

She took off her gloves, dirty with soot from the Ford sedan, shoved them in her purse.

A spasm shook her hand. She unrolled a Pep-O-Mint.

Gladys was working the newsstand. "Hi, sugar! Got a couple of packs saved for you."

Miranda took out her wallet, smiled.

"I'll take some Life Savers, too, Gladdy. I'm cutting back on the Chesterfields."

The bleached blonde looked at her with horror. "Honey — you can't just quit. You gotta see a specialist or somethin'. At least take a vacation."

Miranda sighed. "Yeah. I'm just making 'em count."

She scanned the news racks while Gladys shook her head and wrapped up the purchases. No headlines about Duggan. Picked up an *Examiner,* coverage on page four. *Chronicle,* page three. Arrest of an ex-police officer, Duggan named this time. Still no mention of "kike."

Miranda frowned. "These the latest?"

"Fresh off the presses. We get the *Examiner* right away, you know, with the Hearst Building next door. The boys sometimes give me tips for Bay Meadows."

A couple in their thirties with three kids in tow pulled Gladys toward the jawbreakers. Miranda shoved a dollar toward her friend, while the couple's sons jostled each other and their little girl tried to decide between a peppermint stick and Necco Wafers.

Miranda walked quickly to the back of the large lobby and the front desk of the mailroom. Didn't recognize the attendant, who looked all of nineteen.

"My name is Miranda Corbie. I'm expecting a package. Messenger delivery."

The kid swallowed hard, Adam's apple bobbing underneath the cheap bow tie, and returned with a rectangular flat wrapped in brown paper.

"This arrived via Quick Way Messenger Service. From a Mister — Mister By-a-lick." He handed it to her.

"Aren't you forgetting something?"

His face ran from red to white and back again. "I — I'm sorry, Miss Corbie. What is it?"

"My identification. I've never seen you before — how do you know I'm really who I say I am?"

He relaxed his shoulders and grinned. "Oh, that's an easy one, Miss. We all know what you look like. The boys described you to a tee." His focus drifted downward and back up again, in a Little League attempt at a knowing look.

Miranda said dryly, "Thanks, Junior."

She grabbed the package and left him tugging at his collar. She'd need a better outfit for undercover work.

Meyer's package and Pandora's lay next to each other on her desk, along with her .22.

She unlocked the left drawer and set the file from Allen next to the two packages. Then pulled out the Big Chief tablet, flipping the pages back to where she'd last made a note.

Pandora Blake. Who is Pandora Blake? Twenty-two, bleached blonde, pretty, parents? Jewish? Men?

No goddamn answers. And two more names to add, different pages, more questions.

She turned over the rough paper. Wrote, "Annie Learner." Thought about it. Wrote, "Gerald Duggan." Stared at Duggan's name.

Miranda didn't give a damn about what created Gerry Duggan, what precise combination of malice and weakness formed his brand of bully. All she wanted to know was whether or not he stabbed two women with an ice pick and defiled their bodies with a dirty word. Whether Meyer was right and Duggan was a patsy in some way, set up by his own department.

Crooked cop, meet crooked cop. One of you is going to the gas chamber.

She shook out another Chesterfield, lighting it with the One-Touch. Savored the smoke, watching it curl toward the open window.

Miranda pulled over the heavy desk phone, dialed the operator.

Bright voice, cheery. Must be new.

"Operator — I need to find out if a PT

and T salesperson called on me this afternoon. He asked to wait in the apartment. . . . Uh-huh. Left a brochure with my doorman, no card. Would you? Thanks ever so. . . . No, a girl can't be too careful these days."

Miranda grinned, took another drag on the stick.

"Hello, Sales? . . . Yes — OK." She waited for a few seconds, looking down at the Big Chief tablet.

"Hello? Yeah. My name's Miranda Corbie. Drake Hopkins Apartments, 640 Mason. Number 405. . . . Very well, thank you. . . . No, can't say I do. Listen — the reason I'm calling is I need to find out if someone from your office came out to my apartment this afternoon. Said he wanted to see if I knew how to operate the phone properly. No, no card. Flashed ID at the doorman and left a pamphlet. . . . Uh-huh. Said his first name was John. Sure, go ahead."

She tapped the ash into the Tower of the Sun, took one more long pull on the Chesterfield before regretfully rubbing it out. The salesman came back on the phone.

"Uh-huh. Uh-huh. No — thank you. That's what I thought. Sure. Sure, I will."

She let the receiver drop on the cradle, not hearing the clang.

No record of a Pacific Telephone & Telegraph sales call to 640 Mason Street.

TWELVE

Miranda dialed Tascone's Coffee Shop downstairs. Chicken salad sandwich, lemon meringue pie, and coffee. Food would help blot memories, of speeding cars and a small, squalid bathroom on the edge of the International Settlement.

Unwrapped two more Pep-O-Mints, waiting for the pep to hit, and carefully untied the string around Ozzie's package.

Matchbooks, hanky, ring, photos, a couple of postcards, napkin from the Top of the Mark, lipstick still clinging to the soft white fiber. Scrapbook assortment, souvenirs from dates and dinners and time spent away from Artists and Models, nights when Pandora's dreams were just out of reach, shimmering on the debutante at the next table with the perfect manicure or reproduced in rotogravure on the cover of *Modern Screen*.

And the blond girl would sigh, walking down a dingy, dark alley to the one-room apartment, curling up in a wall bed next to Ozzie, Aquadonis and artist's model, sure they'd be discovered by some important Hollywood scout, smell of bougainvillea and sun-kissed orange orchards the next stop on their overnight to Hollywood.

Miranda flipped through the photos. All Pandora, small snapshots of her smiling, posing at the Tower of the Sun or in front of the Hollywood Show "Stage 9" at the Palace of Entertainment. Two with Ozzie in front of the *Evening Star* statue. The wind blew her hair while they held each other, dreaming of neon lights and movie premieres, of creaming ocean waves and beach houses, a chance to escape Ohio.

When you wish upon a star . . .

Miranda shoved the photos aside, plucking out matchbooks from Bernstein's Fish Grotto, Clinton's Cafeteria, and the La Fiesta Club. Dipped the pen, made notations in a separate small column by Pandora's name.

Two postcards. One was from Berenice Blake, 212 East 3rd Street, Lima, Ohio. Dated May 23, last year.

Dear Pandora, haven't heard from you. Are you alright? All fine here, Ben got a summer job at the refinery. Saw the

Frisco Fair at the newsreels. Write soon.
Your loving mother.

Miranda turned the card over. Lima Football Stadium, surrounded by green lawns and small houses. Edges of the card were worn and frayed, held and read over and over again.

The knock at the door made her jump, and she picked up the .22 before she remembered the chicken sandwich. Opened the door to a freckled teenager, silverware in his white coat pocket, holding a cup of coffee and the food on two Buffalo China plates, approximately as round as his eyes.

"Hiya, Miss Corbie. Sam says to just call us when you're done."

She nodded and he walked in, setting the food on the desk. Carefully pulled out the silverware, unrolling the napkin with a flourish.

"Anything else, Miss Corbie?"

She smiled at him, handed him a dollar. "Thanks. Keep the change."

He looked at the money. "Thank you, Miss Corbie . . . you sure?"

She gently pushed him out into the hallway. "I'll bring the dishes down myself."

"Oh, no, Miss — I'm happy to come back."

She shook her head, smiling, pulled the door shut. Leaned against it for a moment. Wondered about Berenice and Benjamin Blake, about the refinery job and the stadium and Lima, Ohio.

The family Pandora left behind.

She ate quickly, conscious of another church bell somewhere south of Market, of the sun's angle through the window. Too much mayonnaise on the chicken salad, but the pie was fresh and cold, coffee still hot. She finished the lemon custard and the crust, left the meringue, and lit another Chesterfield, relishing the taste.

Final item in Ozzie's treasure chest was another postcard, Nance's Hot Springs and Sanitarium in Calistoga. Unmarked, no writing of any kind. Description on back for "Hot Sulphur Water, Tub Baths, Volcanic Ash Mud Baths, and Colonic Irrigations."

Miranda propped her elbows on the desk, studying the card. Maybe Pandora took a day trip north, or maybe a roommate gave it to her and she kept it, planning to mail her mother.

Miranda dipped the desk pen, scrawled out, "Calistoga — Nance's." Gathered the artifacts back into a neat pile of memory.

What Ozzie wanted to remember.

He'd hold on to them for a year, maybe less. Try to forget about them while he kissed another girl, feeling her breath rise and fall. He'd lock them away, and they'd call to him when he woke up, arms beneath his head, staring at the ceiling, the girl next to him murmuring in her sleep.

And then he'd wrap them up and shove them in a closet or a drawer, buried in boxes or paper or clothes, heavy and leaden, memory of memory too strong, too fatal, and never really Pandora, because they were about him now.

His memory.

Not hers.

Then a year — or maybe sooner. And the matchbooks and the photographs and the postcards, the faded imprint of coral lipstick on a souvenir napkin with just a whiff of expensive cocktail, only the best for you, sweetheart, forever and always, would lie at the bottom of a garbage heap.

How fucking could you, my darling? How could you?

But dear, you're dead, fleshless, done, bones yellowed and dried, hanging mouth gaping forever at the satin lid of a pine box, only $2.99 extra and you get it in pink.

Ashes to ashes, dust to dust.

Past done with, finished, sound and fury

signifying nothing, thank you so fucking much for the Shakespeare quote, Father, or should I call you Professor?

Miranda's hand trembled as it raised the cigarette to her lips, burning forgotten between her fingers.

Time to move along, forget about lost loves, rediscover the vigor of life, life can begin at forty, especially if you use Pepsodent, and Jesus Christ, lady, when you gonna get over it, find somebody new? Bad things happen, people die. People fucking die.

Unless, of course, you're already dead.

She rubbed out the stick.

Stood up, passed a hand over her forehead, shoved the desk chair aside. Walked to the window and pushed the sill up wide, until the late afternoon Bay wind whipping past Lotta's Fountain curled and twisted and snaked to the fourth floor, until it stung her eyes and wet her skin, until her ears were full of the shouting and the honking cars and the music drifting from the Pig n' Whistle jukebox down the street, *for as the years roll by, you'll learn my love for you is true . . .*

Miranda stared into the San Francisco afternoon, hands grasping the window frame.

Lunch dishes were stacked over on the long file cabinet by the safe. Meyer's cash — no check, just three hundred dollars thoughtfully broken in twenty-dollar bills — inside, Meyer's file on Duggan — his deposition, the particulars of his relatives — open on the desk. Gerald Duggan had a mother living in San Francisco, three sisters, one local, one in Paso Robles, one in Seattle, and a brother, older, address in Livermore.

Graduated from St. Ignatius. Never married. Been living on a police pension and odd security jobs since getting kicked off the force two months ago. Current address the Del Rey Hotel, 352 Taylor.

Isn't that within a few blocks of the victim's address?

I don't know.

Did you ever go to the victim's residence?

I don't know.

Is it true you tried to get into the Hotel Shawmut and see Pandora Blake?

I don't know. . . .

Didn't look promising.

Miranda hunched forward, writing furiously. Dig deeper, scratch more than the surface of the Irish cop with the rolled shoulders and hard, brutal hands, the war record of bravery and the police record of brutality. Find out if he had friends. Find out about their witnesses, especially at the Hotel Shawmut, the kind of place where you could buy them for a fin and no questions asked.

She bit into the two Life Savers in her mouth and swallowed, reached for the phone. Tried to remember the number, frowned, thumbing through the well-worn Kardex until she found it. *San Francisco News.*

"Rick Sanders, please. . . . Yeah — Miranda. Since when does he rate a secretary, Marty? You know who the hell it is." She held the phone on her shoulder while she unrolled the last two Life Savers in the roll. "Yeah, I've got all day."

The peppermint flavor was starting to make her nauseated. Maybe variety helped with Life Savers, or maybe she should grab some Necco Wafers, or maybe she should just give up and smoke a fucking cigarette. She closed her eyes, listening to the siren somewhere up by Civic Center.

"Rick — yeah. A hell of a lot. I'm working for Meyer. He thinks Duggan's being framed."

She held the phone away from her ear and

189

winced at the reaction.

"Maybe I am — what's it to you? Look, if Meyer thinks . . . Yeah. Yeah, I know. But this way I've got access. . . . Yeah. OK. Listen — you say I never bring you in, and this time I'm asking. . . . Goddamn it, Rick, I've got two murders and Duggan to investigate — I don't know how long. He's on the track to the gas chamber, and if the sonofabitch is gonna pay for a crime, I'd like to make sure it's the right one. . . . Sure there's more. I'll tell you tonight, OK? Moderne. Nine thirty? OK. Yeah, anything in the morgue about cases, connections — Klan, Silver Shirts, Bund — yeah. Thanks, Rick."

She hung up the phone. Chewed the Pep-O-Mints, made a face, and opened the bottom drawer. Picked up the bottle of Old Taylor and twisted it open, wrinkling her nose, swig from the bottle, liquid heat hitting her stomach.

Miranda set the bottle in the drawer again, shut it. Thought about how that old bastard Dr. Nielsen would smile and nod approvingly.

"You must cut back on these bad habits, my dear," drone of a voice, solemn beard, but always ready to take a C-note to dry out her fucking father. "You don't want to wind up like him."

Fuck you, too, Dr. Nielsen.

It took more than a bottle of bourbon to make her father. Goddamn soulless bastard with a Ph.D., doctor of philosophy of myself, fuck everyone else, including her mother. The sonofabitch would never tell her where or when he drove her away, just that she was probably dead.

Uneducated girl, never his class, couldn't risk the association. Might hurt his chances at tenure, and then there was *emeritus* to think about. . . .

She shook her head to clear it, warmth of the bourbon flowing to her feet and hands. Reached for the phone again, dialed the operator.

"Oceanic Hotel, please."

"That will be SUtter 9764. One moment, please."

Miranda waited while the operator plugged herself in, sounding less human than Voder, the Machine That Talks.

She didn't know why Bente insisted on living in a dump of a hotel, except that it made her feel at one with the proletariat. Every bum was still a cause, every fat-cat mill owner a reason to bow to Lenin five times a day.

Bente Gallagher. Miranda's friend, maybe even her best friend.

Ringing finally stopped. Fumble with the receiver. Gravelly voice with accusation behind it, unsuccessfully lubricated by several bottles of something cheap and flammable.

"Osheeanik Ho-tel."

"Room 256."

"Jush — jush a minute."

She set down the phone, figuring on at least five. Sorted through the rest of Meyer's papers. Found the autopsy report on Pandora.

Still no answer. She drummed her fingers on the desk, started reading. Jumped a few minutes later when Bente's voice said: "What's cookin', Miranda?"

She pushed the report aside. "How'd you know it was me?"

"Who the hell else is gonna call this dump?"

"Can you meet me at the Moderne tonight?"

"You on to something rough again?"

"As a matter of fact — yeah. Remember the cop that beat me up during the Takahashi case?"

"That Irish bastard — I hope he drowns in a barrel of whiskey —"

"Bente — Meyer hired me to help defend him. He's been arrested for the murder of those two girls."

"The Emporium girl and the model on Treasure Island? Yeah, but . . . why the hell are you working for Meyer? Shouldn't you be at Sally's?"

She sighed, leaning back against the leather of the chair.

"Long story. They fired me, said I was a security risk. The girls were both — well, their bodies were defaced. Murderer used their blood to write the word 'kike.' "

Silence. Bente whistled. "Holy shit. You weren't kidding." Lowered her voice. "We shouldn't talk here."

"Nine thirty at the Moderne, OK? Rick will be there."

Bente snorted. "The old New York squad. Not exactly the International Brigades, but fuck — count me in. Sanders still making like a puppy dog with the big, sad eyes?"

Miranda picked up the fountain pen, drew a few dry circles on the Big Chief pad. "You know how it is, Bente."

"Yeah, I do. See you at nine thirty. Hope Jorge's workin' tonight. I could stand a good lay."

Miranda hung up with a grin. Stretched. Hands were shaking again, so she opened her purse and took out a Chesterfield.

Knock on the door.

Wall clock read 5:25. She let her hand rest on the .22, still on her desk. Said loud enough to be heard in the hallway: "Come in."

Allen crooked his bald head around the door.

"Thought I'd see how you're doing before I take the streetcar home to missus."

She waved him in. "Sit down and put your feet up. But not on the autopsy report."

He chuckled, sprawling into a chair. "How the hell did you get a report? I thought you're on the outs with the button boys."

She folded her arms, grinning at him.

"I'm official now, brother. I'm working for my own lawyer — digging up defense evidence for the same bastard cop that knocked me around in February. Gerald Duggan."

Allen almost rose from the seat. "You kidding me, right?"

He dug out a crumpled Camels packet from his coat pocket and a Bimbo's 365 Club matchbook stuck in the cellophane, flicking the match on his thumb. Shook his head.

"Goddamn tough way to get legitimate information, but I guess you know what you're doing."

"They're hanging one of their own out to dry. Must be something big."

He scratched the side of his chin, dotted with day-old stubble.

"And you always like to be in on the big stuff, sweetheart. Jesus." He pointed to the papers on the table. "So what does the autopsy say?"

She picked up a sheet of paper. "Looks professional. Right at the base of the neck, between the second and third vertebrae. Real Murder Inc. tactics. Then, when she couldn't move, couldn't speak, couldn't breathe, which was pretty much instantaneous, he stabbed her in the chest. Quickly, before the blood pressure dropped too much. Needed ink for his fucking finger."

She glanced away. Took a long drag on the Chesterfield.

"Know anybody in town that kills like that?"

Allen shook his head. "Nobody local. They like guns up here, an occasional knife, but nothing too exotic. And there's always the Bay. 'Dasher' Abbandando likes picks, but he's messier, too — sometimes throws in a meat cleaver. Besides, he's in New York and was convicted for murder four days ago."

He stood up. "Sorry I can't help you, sweetheart. But you're right. It's somebody who knows what he's doing. What about the second girl?"

"Autopsy's not back yet."

The Pinkerton raised his eyebrows. "And they still nailed Duggan on both charges? Hmm. Maybe you're on to something at that. By the way, I've got a lead for you on another anti-Semitic group. They're mentioned in the report as a fraternal businessman's organization, isolationist patriots and all that, but we just got word that they've been kind of slumming for the last three months. Been socializing with the Bund and Silver Shirts, not exactly country club material. Go by the name of the Musketeers."

"Anything else on them? Where they're headquartered, where they meet?"

He fished a notepad out of his pocket, crushing his cigarette in the ashtray.

"They've been meeting at a bar called Tonypandy, 51 Maiden Lane. Irish connections there, too — IRA, mostly. These Musketeer people are the kind with dough, not just hooligans wanting to play dress-up."

Miranda wrote on the pad. "Thanks, Allen. I appreciate it."

He grinned back at her. "With two murders and a dirty cop to clear, you'd better."

The Pinkerton walked back to the door, turning to face her with his hand on the knob.

"You sure you're OK, Miri? You not in

over your head?"

"Quit worrying and go home. I'm fine."

He took one more look around, eyes resting on the .22, then back up to meet her own.

"Keep your powder dry, kid."

She heard the door click, his footsteps fading down the hall toward the elevator. Miranda looked down at the Chief pad, stomach rumbling. Six o'clock. She could squeeze out another hour before heading home.

The phone rang.

THIRTEEN

Miranda picked up the receiver. Silence.

She said nothing, stomach tight. Held her breath. Sometimes long-distance calls took a long time, operators plugging in lines from here to wherever the hell a call came from, except she didn't know who would be calling her long distance, and she'd had enough of Pacific Telephone & Telegraph and Cordoba tan Fords for one day.

Counted to five. Sounded like breathing on the other end, not heavy. Listening.

Miranda hit the receiver, kept it down. Counted to ten, started over.

Line sounded clear. Hit it a few more times until an operator came on.

"The call that just rang my number — I couldn't seem to connect. Can you tell me where it was from?"

"I'll try, Miss, just a minute."

No use reporting trouble. You got more information if life and your phone service were just one swell party line and all that was on your mind was a missed phone call and who'd win *Major Bowes Amateur Hour.*

"Sorry, Miss — all I can get for you is the general exchange. It wasn't long distance — it was Fillmore."

"Thanks."

She replaced the receiver on the cradle and stared at the phone. Right about now she was supposed to run out of the building in a panic. Supposed to grab a taxi home, make sure the apartment was safe, run to a crowd, to somebody who could protect her from the big, bad bastards who were stalking her like a goddamn deer.

Fuck that.

Miranda opened her bag with a vicious twist, shaking out one of the Chesterfields. She lit it with the Ronson, which had risen to the top of the contents of her purse. Blew out a stream of smoke. Walked to the door, checked the lock. Walked to the old Wells Fargo safe, dialed the combination.

The door opened with a protesting squeak. Most of Meyer's money was on the top shelf. She reached toward the back, pulled out the Spanish .38 in the holster. Ignored Gonzales's fedora. Caught a glimpse of the pack of Chesterfields and the cigarette case she'd stowed last night.

She examined them while she walked to the desk. Took out the Black Cat Café matchbook that was still tucked into the cellophane. Opened it and read the words again.

"Mickey wants to see you."

Sherith Israel was in the Fillmore exchange.

Maybe it was time to pay another visit to Mr. Flamm.

One more shot of Old Taylor, she told herself. One more cigarette.

She couldn't figure out what Flamm or anybody connected with the temple would want with her. Unless Pandora was killed for reasons that had nothing to do with anti-Semitism. Unless the anti-Semitism was a cover-up.

But where the hell did that leave Annie Learner, about whom she still knew next to nothing?

Two murders, Duggan, and somebody shadowing her. Maybe wanting her dead. And she knew she needed to hurry, not much time left, but for what, she couldn't fucking say. Trust your goddamn instincts, Randy, never doubt yourself. Never doubt yourself.

She raised the Castagnola glass. Toasted

the dull yellow glow of her office. Toasted the moth fluttering around the one light bulb in her desk lamp, singeing its wings in a never-ending attempt to touch the sun. Shot of bourbon hit the back of her throat and burned down slowly.

Unforgivably.

Poor goddamn Icarus-moth. Blind to the torn screen and the open window, no matter how many goddamn eyes it had, blind to the darkness of San Francisco, where the neon bar signs danced a pink-and-green rhumba, where the roulette wheel spun forever, gleaming like new-minted money. Where the seagulls cried for each other, high above the blanket that wrapped the City tight, where men who worked all night at the steel plant crawled into bed with tired wives, one smelling like sharp, shaved metal and oil, the other like dirty dishes.

The De Young sign across the street carved a slice of white light across the floor.

Miranda looked down at Allen's report and started to read.

The Musketeers were like a hundred other groups, all fire and brimstone in red, white, and blue. Names like Defenders of the Christian Faith and the Paul Reveres. Raised money from selling memberships, selling hate sheets, but mostly raised it from good citizens like themselves, businessmen with families who thought Roosevelt was the Antichrist.

She remembered a drunk in the Moderne one night. New Deal — Jew Deal, get it, lady? Goddamn Roosevelt, he cried, he's the Red Jew Antichrist, he and his butt-ugly wife, goddamn nigger lover. *You kiss the niggers and I'll kiss the Jews, and we'll stay in the White House as long as we choose. . . .* Thigh-slapper, that one, until the ice cubes in her bourbon wound up in his face.

She sipped the Old Taylor, reading the rest of Allen's notes. The Musketeers were founded in '34, like so many of their ilk. By two professionals, dentist Dr. Hugh R. Parkinson and Samuel Brogdon, construction company owner, and described themselves as a patriotic service organization.

Patriotism and service — for the right people, of course.

These were men who dressed in ties and boasted about knowing the vice president of the bank branch, men who made sure their wives had a Negro maid. Men who played bridge with their neighbors and sold insurance policies. Who attended church every Sunday.

Solid, middle-class Americans. Contributing five and ten dollars a month to Father Coughlin and his brand of Social Justice. Men who swear by Henry Ford and *The Protocols of the Elders of Zion,* railing against Hollywood and Harry Hopkins and how the WPA is full of pansies and Reds.

Keep America for Americans, they brayed. Buy Gentile. Stay out of the Jewish war.

Miranda traced the leather on the holster of the .38 lying next to her. She'd seen where it could lead.

Spanish Republicans blown apart by Italian bombs.

Chinese women raped until they bled to death.

Black men hanging from moss-covered oak trees, calling card of the Invisible Empire, and Jews stripped of humanity. Stripped of life.

She sat back in the desk chair, gazing at the thin sheets of paper.

Her stomach was growling with hunger by the time she reached the apartment. Walked up the four flights, thick green carpet muffling her footsteps, old briefcase heavy with the .38.

Yellow light in the hallway was dim. She bent down to the keyhole.

Hair still there. No scratches, no signs.

She exhaled, took out her key, opened the door. Flipped on the light.

No footsteps in the baking soda.

Stepped gingerly over the white powder, setting the briefcase and purse down on the sofa. Locked and bolted the door, shoes tracking the white powder. Walked into the kitchen, opened the icebox.

Nothing except spoiled milk. Forgot to leave the bottle for the milkman again.

Miranda sighed, opened the cabinet, poured herself a small shot of Four Roses in a milk-glass coffee mug. Wiped her mouth, walked back into the living room.

The phone rang.

Double ring, wall phone on the kitchen, one in the bedroom. About a half second out of sync.

She reached toward the wall phone. Waited until midtrill, picked it up.

Faraway silence. As far away as the Fillmore exchange.

She drew a breath. "If you've got business with me, get it fucking done."

Click on the other end.

Silence.

Miranda wore the backless silk she bought at Magnin's last month, spring green to contrast with her hair. Velvet gloves up to her elbows, matching purse.

Raphael looked her up and down, gave her a grin.

"*Bellissima.* Good to have you back, Miss Corbie. You, how do you say it, jazz up the joint."

She smiled. A stockbroker from the society column leaned against the velveteen ropes behind Raphael, mouth open, gazing at her, waiting to get permission to walk through the chromium double doors of the Club Moderne. His crimped and manicured date elbowed him in the stomach, head of the fox stole flying in his face.

Miranda lowered her voice. "Joe's in tonight, right? Thought he might be up at the Mark, listening to Benny Goodman with everyone else."

The thin, high-cheeked Italian held his hand to his mouth, laughed wordlessly.

"No, *mia cara.* Joe's in the back, making money. That's the only sound he likes to hear. Well, one of them." He winked at Miranda, bowed, and made an elaborate gesture with his arm for her to proceed.

The gleaming door swung shut slowly, without a sound. She heard the stockbroker complain and Raphael's smooth, polished voice telling him he'd have to wait.

Joe Merello knew how to run a nightclub.

Make it swank, make it exclusive. Make the debutantes and shipping heirs beg to get in every night, Rolls-Royces, Grahams, and Cadillacs parked by a valet two blocks away in a garage, where plenty of light kept the rats in the corners and Joe made two dollars per car in profits.

Marie was working hat check tonight, sympathizing with the new cigarette girl. She brightened when she saw Miranda.

"Miri, sugar — it's been ages! I thought you'd be at the Fair, runnin' your fingers up Weissmuller's chest."

The cigarette girl, black-haired, about eighteen, wearing spangled shorts and matching halter, sighed. "You got a way to keep hands off, sister? I'm bruised all over."

"Keep one lit, and use it — on their hands."

The girl adjusted the tray around her neck and grinned. "I like the way you think."

She headed back through the phony marble columns to the dining and dance floor, wobbling on high-heeled spectator pumps that looked too small for her feet. Miranda turned to Marie.

"Bente and Rick are meeting me tonight — but I need to talk to Joe before they get here. Is he in the back?"

The blond girl shrugged. "I think so, Miri,

but you know Joe. He could be anywhere. In the back with Vicenzo, in his office counting receipts, or in the secret hideaway with his new canary. I think he's watching the roulette wheel, but Clark'll know for sure. How you been? Everything all right? You look good."

"Thanks. I'm OK. Working on an investigation — got fired from the Island."

"What? Sally would never —"

"Wasn't Sally — it was Dill and the rest of them. Got a little too close to a murder."

Marie pressed herself against the edge of the counter, blue eyes large enough to show where the liner wasn't straight.

"That Pandora Blake murder?" She lowered her voice to a whisper. "Was she a Jew?"

Miranda said sharply, "Where did you hear that?"

The blonde shook her head, took a step back. "Don't get testy, sugar, I'm not asking anything new. It wasn't in the papers, but you know — I hear things, working the counter. And people have been talking about this Pandora girl and the other one, what's her name — the Emporium clerk —"

"Annie Learner."

"Yeah — that's the one. Anyway, there's talk they were killed because they were Jewish." She lowered her voice again on the last word. Looked around, then back to Miranda. "Goddamn shame if you ask me. Too much of this going on, and we don't need San Francisco to turn into little Berlin."

Miranda met Marie's eyes. Put her hand over the hat check girl's, squeezed it.

"Thanks. Would you call me if you overhear anything important, any names or people who knew either of them?"

Marie looked down at the counter, straightened out the tip basket. Her face was solemn.

"I certainly will."

Miranda looked at her again, leaned forward impulsively, and whispered in her ear.

"Be proud of who you are, Marie. Joe won't care."

The blonde's hand shook as she moved it up to touch her lipstick, eyes filling, wide with surprise.

Clark seated her by her favorite palm tree at table twelve, where she could watch the few patrons who couldn't get in to see Benny Goodman applaud the thirty-five-year-old boy tenor. The band tried to swing into a Goodman tune, "Lilacs in the Rain," and a nervous redhead with big tits and a small voice grabbed the microphone.

Clark clicked his heels together in Teutonic precision, tuxedo spotless, hair just a little thinner.

"Shall I seat your companions when they arrive, Miss Corbie?"

"Yeah, Clark, thanks. Doesn't look like much of a house."

His mouth turned down in half a frown. "It's not much of an orchestra. The usual, or any special requests?"

"The usual, please. And a Singapore sling."

He raised his well-manicured eyebrow. "Not a blue fog?"

She shook her head. "If Jorge's working, can you send him over? My friend Bente —"

Clark rolled his eyes. "Yes, I know. Jorge moves with the grace of a matador. Unfortunately, he's resisted my every attempt to expand his repertoire. Will you be joining Vicenzo this evening?"

Miranda checked her watch: 8:25. "I'll eat first. Thanks, Clark. And one more thing — would you change these twenties for a single bill?" She opened her pocketbook and handed him five twenties from Meyer's retainer.

He nodded and spun around neatly, heading for the kitchen. Miranda's hands were trembling, and her head hurt like hell. She opened her cigarette case and took out a Chesterfield.

Lit the stick with one of the matchbooks on the table. Inhaled, eyes closed, feeling the gaze of the married man two tables down fastened on her décolletage. She opened her eyes again, met his. He cleared his throat, reddened, and turned to his wife.

A waiter she didn't know brought her a Singapore sling and a crisp hundred-dollar bill in a tray. She sipped the gin, thinking of phones and postcards and Cordoba tan Fords. The redhead warbled on.

When love forgets to smile, my darling, once in a while, remember April and lilacs in the rain . . .

She devoured the appetizer plate of mozzarella, olives, and peppers, the green salad with capers and Italian dressing. Jorge brought the steak and mushrooms over with a smile and wriggle of his eyebrows. Miranda blew a smoke ring before she stubbed out her cigarette, earning a scandalized look from a fat woman stuffed in a four-year-old evening gown.

Someone was playing games, trying to scare her. Wouldn't work, never did.

Not the bulls, they'd come out in the open. The Lima-Lanza mob would be more obvious, too, just like the cops. Maybe Gillio was back in town, through with hiding. Wanting to get even for February.

Not that the cops would care if he came back or not. The Takahashi case slammed shut once a Japanese shipping line got involved.

Miranda sipped the drink. Not in the mood for a blue fog tonight. Too close to working in one.

She looked around the half-filled club, lights artfully designed to make even the ugliest woman attractive. A few debutantes here and there, Junior League and Town & Country Club, with dates who couldn't get them into the Mark Hopkins or who didn't like the fact that Goodman played with Negroes.

Rice Bowl in February, Red Cross in May — can't get back to the Alps this year, darling, have to wait until the war's over. What's it all about, really — what's it all about?

Lives lived in rotogravure, reflected in crystal chandeliers. Right hair, right dress, polo in the summer, skiing in the winter, virginity lost over and over. Bruises from the one that drank, but darling, there are so few in our class . . .

Miranda pushed back the remnants of the meat and ravioli, downed the last of her Singapore sling.

Belgium was gone, France on her knees. Spain was lost a long time ago.

But there were two dead girls in the morgue in San Francisco.

She stood up from the table, gathered her purse, the red-haired chanteuse attempting another chorus of "I'm Nobody's Baby."

Time to place a bet.

FOURTEEN

Vicenzo was calling out the numbers for the latest spin on the wheel of fortune when Miranda sidled through the doorway, half-hidden by another potted palm. Dim light glinted off the golden wall lamps in the shape of seashells, smell of Shalimar and Chanel No. 5 mixing with perspiration and fear.

Crowded, hot. Tinkled laughter. Ceiling fan spun slower than the magic wheel, evenly distributing perfume and panic through the long, rectangular room.

Typical night at Joe's gambling den. Knock three times and know the password, lady, and you, too, can lose your money in a ritzy atmosphere.

Diehard gamblers looked for a hustle, upper lips moist, eyes darting between dice and cards and wheel before landing on their poison of choice. No cure, no antidote, except the occasional win.

On that they could fly higher than coke, pulses racing, throats hoarse, bodies trembling in an orgasm, faith redeemed, and confidence justified. Their win, their timing, their love affair with luck. Revival, children, come to the revival, lift up your shaking arms to Lady Luck and speak in her tongues, let her Holy Rollin' spirit possess you, because hallelujah, brothers, I beat the house.

Men or women, Luck eventually fucked them all. Left them dry and withered, lines of thirst around their eyes and mouth, photos of wives, children, and mothers smiling and forgotten in empty leather wallets.

Lose in style, lose with class. Lose at Joe Merello's Club Moderne casino.

Tourists were rubbing elbows with the top and bottom of the social register, shipping line heirs and bankrupt bankers, radio stars and phony European royalty. A couple of society girls sat in the green leather chairs, watching their dates burn through their allowance. It's your birthday, Midge, bet on twenty-three. . . .

The strawberry blonde held her head in her chin, nose still pink, fingers tapping on the table, eyes searching for something to focus on. She saw Miranda and fluffed her hair and called for a fresh martini. Her date saw Miranda and missed the next bet.

And the wheel kept spinning, the house hand at the blackjack table reached legal age, the fat man with the rented tux and the cheap toupee rolling snake eyes yet again.

Miranda pushed her way past the sequined gowns to the roulette table, dull light and piped-in warbles from the redhead onstage making it hard to see or hear.

Vicenzo's eyebrow raised about a quarter of an inch. She hadn't lost money at the Moderne in a long time, but she needed information. Dropping a C-note would guarantee the paternal treatment.

Miranda opened her evening bag, eyes around her envious, curious, and openly interested. She took a Chesterfield out of the gold case, the balding scion of a cane sugar refinery flicking his silver-plated lighter before the cigarette was in her mouth.

She glanced up at him, lit the stick, and inhaled. Blew the smoke out the side of her mouth.

"Thanks, sugar."

He showed a lot of teeth under a Melvyn Douglas mustache. Close to a million-dollar bank account and breath like rotten eggs.

"What's your money on, Miss?"

The strawberry blonde shot bullets at

Miranda while she sloshed her martini and tried to hold on to her high.

Miranda glanced up at Vicenzo, tucked her bag under her arm, and dropped the hundred-dollar bill on the table.

"Two fifties, please."

The tall, skinny Italian pushed two blue chips toward her wordlessly. He looked around the table, expertly spinning the wheel.

"Your bets, *signore e signori.*"

Miranda placed both chips on number thirty-six. The sugar heir added five red chips to the same box, still grinning like an idiot and trying to brush Miranda's arm. She ignored him, concentrating on the Chesterfield.

A produce dealer from Burlingame bet on red and even, a banker on odd and black, and one of the gamblers, a small man with a Vandyke and glasses and ash on his lapels, played the system and bet on zero, figuring Miranda was there to make a payoff.

"No more bets, *signore e signori,* no more bets, *prego.*"

Vicenzo kept his eyes on the wheel. It spun down slowly, the little silver ball dancing delicately in between the ridges, while the table held its breath and the strawberry blonde muttered imprecations on number thirty-six.

"Number thirty-six is the winner. . . . *La signorina* bet one hundred dollars on thirty-six straight up. Her winnings are three thousand, five hundred dollars."

Vicenzo plucked three gold thousand-dollar chips and one green five hundred from the rack at his side and pushed them toward Miranda with the rake.

"The winnings are with your bet down, *signorina*."

The croupier turned to pay the sugar heir, who was gaping openmouthed at Miranda. His date stood up, eyes narrow, mouth pinched, hand trembling and tugging on his arm.

"Come on, Edgar — let's go to the Mark. Goodman's there tonight."

His attention bounced between his pile of chips and the lines of Miranda's dress. He shook his head. "It's the first time I've ever won anything — I can't leave now."

The blonde stood rigid. She could flounce out by herself, dateless but dignified. Her eyes drifted to the door, table growing quiet. Then her shoulders slumped and she sank in a puddle of silver lamé, drowning her sorrows in another martini, more powder for her nose.

Not Elizabeth Arden.

Vicenzo checked the table. Miranda took a drag on the stick, glanced at the bald playboy and the hopped-up blonde.

Said: "Let it ride."

Edgar ogled her, pressing closer to her side. Figured he'd collect the winnings whatever money he won or lost. He signaled to Vicenzo to keep his money on thirty-six.

The Italian tugged at his collar, giving the pile of cash a nervous look. *"Mi dispiace, signore e signori,* I need to ask my boss. *Momento, prego."*

He spoke to a runner dressed in an ill-fitted tux, young man with a pockmarked face and easy grin. Italian was too rapid to follow. The young man nodded, sprinted off. Chatter from the other tables, desperate to see winners, pushed the wheel crowd forward, jammed up tight.

Band outside was swinging "Embraceable You" with a tenor clarinet lead, redhead numbing her vocal cords at the bar.

The sugar heir leaned toward Miranda with a toothy whisper. "We're a pair, aren't we? You've brought me luck once tonight — think you can do it again?"

Embrace me, my sweet embraceable you . . .

She exhaled a stream of smoke into the air, ground the Chesterfield in the gold

218

ashtray. Looked at him, his date, drifting into her martini and away from the white lines of powder.

"I think I'm going to cost you, sugar."

Loud noise from another hidden door at the back of the room. Joe Merello. Short, stout, in a white derby and vest, and with next week's band singer on his arm, this one a peroxide blonde.

The seas parted, and Joe shot a look at Vicenzo, saw Miranda and Mr. Sugar Plantation. No sign of recognition except a quick wink of his left eye while he grinned through his cigar, gestured toward the game.

"*Andiamo,* Vicenzo. The bet is OK, with me."

He waddled back toward the blackjack players, his stubby fingers glittering with rings, his laughter drowning out the restaurant band.

Vicenzo cleared his throat, aristocratic cheekbones a burnished red. Flicked the wheel. "Place your bets, *prego,* place your bets. *Prego, signore e signori — subito, subito.*"

The playboy stepped on Miranda's foot, his breath making her wince.

"Whatever happens — you've been grand. Might I see you tomorrow night?"

The wheel slowed, spin no longer fresh

and exciting, drama of decision hanging over the little silver ball and the red and black numbers. *Click-clack-click-clack,* crawling to a finish, bells tolling for the grocer with the mortgage, the lady with the old face and young body and the silver fox in the pawnshop.

Clack . . . click. Clack.

Collective inhale. Collective sigh of disappointment.

"Number fifteen is the winner, *signore e signori,* number fifteen."

Vicenzo discreetly raked the pile of chips from thirty-six while the grocer wiped his sweaty palms on his trousers and boasted to his table companions how his system never failed.

Joe appeared at the table, genie from a bottle. He bowed to Miranda.

"I am sorry for your loss, Signorina Corbie. But you are *bellissima stasera.* You are like *Venere, la dea d'amore.* I will buy you a drink." He extended an arm to Miranda.

The sugar heir grabbed at the glove on her other arm. She turned to face him.

"Sorry, Edgar. I warned you. Better luck next time." She gestured with her head toward the strawberry blonde, who was staring vacantly at the wheel. "You arrived with a date — remember?"

Panic, confusion. Red on his flabby cheeks. "But your name — I don't even know your name."

Miranda ignored him and slid through the crowd with Joe. The playboy stood looking after her. A man about fifty-five, wrinkled face, wrinkled blue suit, squinted up from his small stack of white chips.

"Don't you know who that was, son?"

The sugar heir shook his head. Older man nodded, face lost in a dream.

"That was Lady Luck."

Joe led her to the back and his soundproofed office. Shut the heavy doors behind him, smiling like a benevolent Roman emperor, then took his seat behind the giant mahogany desk. Miranda sat on the wine-colored leather chair in front, crossing her legs. Fought the impulse to light another cigarette.

He made an expansive gesture, arms apart. "What can I do for my friend, eh? You bring me luck tonight."

She grinned. "Vicenzo brought you luck. He knows I always bet on thirty-six."

Joe nodded, satisfied look on his round, chubby face. "*Sì, Vicenzo è molto intelligente.* He know that young man. Know he will bet with you, *bella.*"

221

He opened the top desk drawer. Drew out a hundred-dollar bill and tossed it toward Miranda. "You keep your money."

She waved it away. "No dice, Joe. I came here to lose it. Taking it back would mean I worked for you." She held her eyes on his until the Italian grunted and put the money away.

He pressed his manicured fingers on the desk, pretending to grumble.

"So working for me, Joe Merello, not so bad, not so bad. You know you got a place here, *cara mia.*"

She needed a cigarette. Italian rituals took too fucking long. She lit a Chesterfield with Joe's marble cherub desk lighter.

"*Grazie.* You are a good friend, Joe. I appreciate you letting me work out of the Moderne. Consider it rent."

He made a dismissive gesture. "I don't charge my friends. You bring me business." He smiled like a little boy. Shrugged. His voice was soft.

"I trust you, *bella.*"

Trusted her not to find out where the strawberry blond snowbird got her coke, trusted her to play. Miranda knew Joe was clean, one reason why she worked through the Moderne as her club of choice. But sometimes the customers came in dirty.

A matching white marble cherub on his desktop held up a small tray stained gray with ash. She tapped the Chesterfield. Her voice was careful.

"I appreciate that, Joe. And I trust you, too. Tonight, I need your help."

The subdued light in the milk-glass lamp caught a glimmer from one of the gold rings on his fingers. Brown eyes stared across at her, warm but shrewd.

"*Farò qualsiasi cosa, bella.* How can I help?"

She took a last hit on the stick, rubbed it out in the tray.

"Somebody's tailing me. Tried to get in my apartment. Skinny bird, Cordoba tan Ford." She leaned forward. "If Tony Lima's trying to bump me off, Joe, I need to know. Maybe Gillio's back in town. I figured after the Takahashi case he'd try something, anything."

Joe Merello's fingers tapped lightly on the desk, his mouth turned down like Pagliaccio in the second act. He glanced up at her, then back down at the reddish brown polished wood.

"Lima owes you, *cara. I concorrenti* — how do you call it — competitors. You helped get rid of them. I told you I never do business with Gillio's boys. Too hard, too rough.

223

Sono stronzi. Life's too short, plenty of money to make in better ways."

He pivoted the chair to fully face her, shrugged again. "I do not hear everything, *hai capito?* But I never hear Lima or the Lanza boys say nothing about you. *Niente.* They got problems of their own."

"Like what?"

Joe stuck a chubby finger in his ear and wiggled it. His round faced creased with pain. "*Maledetto!* Goddamn ear." He sighed. "*Allora, bella,* Gillio is still in Chicago. Lima is busy with other men who betray him."

Her voice was dry. "Any of them trying to kill me?"

Joe looked past her to the soundproof doors. Then he stood up, lines on his face deep. Waddled to where she still sat, legs crossed in the chair. Put his hand on her shoulder and lowered his voice to a whisper.

"*È possibile, cara.* I do not know much, you understand. *Non di certo.* But I hear things. *Un cugino di Martini, quel figlio di puttana,* making trouble for Lima. *Un traditore,* making his own *famiglia,* new family. Lima has more friends, better friends, in Los Angeles, he brings them up to San Francisco. For what, *non lo so — non domando, capito?* But this *cugino, questo culo,* he makes trouble, refuses to work with Lima's new friends. *È possibile* he wants to, to *vendicarsi* — to make revenge on you for his cousin. You know?"

She laid her gloved hand on Joe's, still on her shoulder. Squeezed it. Said heavily: *"Grazie sempre, Joe. Come si chiama?"*

The short, stout man bent over to whisper in her ear, smelling of Chianti and cigars. Dots of red wine marred the white of his gold-buttoned vest.

"Benedetti. Angelo Benedetti. He came out from Chicago when Gillio ran away."

He patted her shoulder and straightened slowly. Memories of Martini and a brain-splattered bathroom flooded through Miranda, her stomach clenched, drowning her in fear. Took a deep breath, closed her eyes. When she opened them, Joe was staring down at her, face in shadow. Worried.

"I have not heard anything against you, *bella,* you understand? Nothing. You have not been mentioned. If someone says something and I hear, I tell you. They don't try nothing in my club, don't talk around me. My boys let me know."

She squeezed his hand and tried to smile. Stood up.

"I'd better get back to dinner. I've got friends coming."

225

Joe took her by the arm, led her to the door. *"Qualcos'altro. Questi bastardi sono furbi e cattivi, molto cattivi."*

He grasped her shoulders and turned her to face him, voice driven by urgency. *"Fai attenzione, cara mia, guardati. Capito?* They're not like me, not even like Lima or Gillio. *Sono fascisti.* They are Fascists."

Miranda's eyes widened. She stared at Joe. Picked his hand off her shoulder, kissed his palm, and stepped out through the thick silver doors.

FIFTEEN

Bente was waiting for Miranda at the table, whispering something to Jorge while he replaced her gin fizz. Still no Rick.

"Bourbon, Jorge. Neat."

The waiter smoothed his hair, shiny with oil, curled his lips at Bente, and danced toward the bar, hips narrow, waist tapered, lithe and smooth.

"What's wrong? You look like a goddamn Irish ghost, all white and green."

Miranda opened her evening bag and took out her second-to-last Chesterfield, lighting it with one of the Moderne matchbooks on the table. Her whole body was trembling.

"I already ate. Order whatever you want."

"Don't avoid the question. What the hell's happened?"

"I'll tell you what's happened. Belgium's through. King Leopold's surrendered."

Rick sank heavily in the chair on Miranda's left as Jorge sidled to her other side and deftly set down a shot glass.

The reporter looked up at Jorge, stony-faced. "Scotch and water, and make it a double."

The waiter bowed low, retreated.

Miranda took a deep drag on the cigarette, blowing smoke toward the palm fronds and phony marble columns, incandescent sparkling streamlined colors of the well-bred and well-to-do.

She almost felt sorry for them.

Couples swaying to the music, pressed together between tables. Singer warbling "The Way You Look Tonight," scent of It's You and Blue Grass and Shocking.

Drink while the French were still making champagne, chatter about the Riviera and Sun Valley, fuck whomever you wanted to fuck and marry your kind, café society, toast of the town, because your kind won't last forever.

Your world is ending, masque almost over, goose-step, swastika, and blitzkrieg coming.

Better learn to march, not rhumba. Sold American.

Belgium lost, so much smoke. France next, and how much time could Britain hold out, tiny green island with twenty-one miles of water to cross. If Gertrude Ederle could swim it, the fucking Nazis could launch an armada across the Channel like a kid skipping a rock.

Miranda swallowed the bourbon until it bit her throat. Set down the glass, crushed the cigarette in the ashtray. Looked across the table at her friends.

"Au revoir, Belgium. *Tot ziens.*" She said it softly, raised her glass. "It was a beautiful country."

They were both staring at her. No crooked smile from Rick, no Irish lilt in his voice. Crumpled clothes, cigarette ash, mustard on the navy tie. No display handkerchief. Bente eyed him with distaste.

"Looks like you're the one that surrendered, Sanders — don't you believe in dressing for dinner?"

"As much as you believe in Rockefeller. Pray, forgive my sartorial faux pas. The goddamn Nazis are overrunning Europe and I forgot to dress for the occasion." He gave a mock bow to Bente.

Miranda drained the rest of the bourbon, gazed at the glass in her hand.

"Belgium died yesterday. Died in '38, when Hitler marched into Czechoslovakia and nobody did a goddamn thing to stop him."

Bente sipped her gin fizz. "Whole world's on the ropes. What I want to know is why you walked out of Joe's casino room looking like shit. White as a southern governor."

"You're not my goddamn mother, Bente."

"No, but I am your goddamn friend, and so is Sanders. You going to tell us what's going on, or do I ask that fat salesman at the bar if he'll be a fourth for bridge?"

Bente Gallagher. Short-tempered, big-breasted, body like a Viking goddess. Half-Norwegian, half-Irish, all red, from hair to politics. Saw Spain, saw the '34 strike, saw her brother get killed by strike breakers. Found hope in Lenin and Trotsky, enough to keep her breathing, keep her believing in something beyond *Reader's Digest* and Jimmy Dorsey and whether hats were full on or off the face this season.

"I need your help."

Jorge appeared with Rick's Scotch and fresh drinks, dinner menus. Bente opened the bright yellow-and-green covers, glanced at the pages.

"Hamburger steak and dinner potatoes. And chilled tomato slices. All together, not in courses, please. Meat medium rare, Jorge. Make it tender."

The waiter grinned. Rick said in a clipped voice, "Roast leg of lamb dinner. Baked potato, cauliflower au gratin. Sliced tomatoes. All at once."

Jorge glided toward the kitchen, throwing a last wriggle of his eyebrows and ass toward Bente. Rick leaned over the table.

"OK, what's up? Asking for help isn't exactly your style, Miranda."

She held the small glass tightly, right hand warmed by the brown richness of the bourbon.

"War nerves, I guess. This case — these cases — I don't know. Feel like I walked into the middle of the third act."

Bente shrugged. "Whatever I can do, Randy. There's been some trouble at the meetings — all this fifth column bullshit. People think every Party member is sending out invitations to Stalin."

"Can you blame them? He signed a treaty with Hitler, remember —"

"Yeah, Sanders, but not every Party member is a Stalinite. I dropped the bastard a couple of years ago. Now he's trying to kill the only good leader we've got left, poor old Trotsky down in Mexico." She shook her head in disgust. "He's like Hitler with a better mustache."

Rick removed a crumpled pack of Lucky Strikes from his jacket pocket.

"Whoever's behind it, the fifth column's not just hysteria. Check the *News* tomorrow. Some red-blooded American flew a swastika over the University of Idaho today. Reports are coming in from all over the country — swastikas on buildings, Jews threatened."

His eyes drooped with tired shadows, mouth stretched downward in a wide, thin line of disgust.

"Another synagogue like Sherith Israel, Miranda, this time no swastika — just the word. Beth Hamidroth on Turk Street. And the police radio called in a fight on the corner of Arguello and Lake in front of Temple Emanu-El — a couple of Bund members in uniform singing 'Deutschland über alles.' "

He shook his head, looked over toward the long chromium bar across the room.

"Like I said when I came in — Leopold surrendered. Rolled over and let the Nazis take Belgium without so much as a 'Fuck you' to the French and English. And it's only going to get worse."

"On that cheerful note, Sanders, why don't we ask Miranda what she needs?"

Miranda sipped the whiskey, body still cold. Dabbed at her lips with the dinner napkin, Red Dice lipstick leaving a perfect print on the white cloth.

"Pandora Blake was a starstruck girl from Lima, Ohio, looking for fame, fortune, and an MGM contract. What she found was work at a nudie show. Artists and Models at last year's Fair. Dated Henry Kaiser when she was rehired on for '40. He's a lion tamer for the jungle show, a sadistic bastard who likes to brand his girlfriends like cattle."

Bente's face reddened. "I volunteer to use a whip on the sonofabitch."

Rick ground the Lucky into the glass ashtray. "I checked on him, Miranda — one arrest for assault, two ex-wives. Moves around a lot. Assault warrant was in Bakersfield, working with the Christy Brothers Circus."

Jorge sashayed toward the table with the busboy, who placed fresh drinks in front of all of them while Jorge served the food, bending down to make sure Bente's napkin was in her lap. The redhead grinned at him, and when he turned to leave, she lightly slapped his butt. The busboy blushed, bowed, smiled. And backed away.

Miranda's voice was wry. "Keep it up, Bente, and none of the waiters will turn their backs to you."

Her friend shrugged. "I like a good piece of tail. What's wrong with you, Sanders?"

Rick was choking on a piece of cheese-covered cauliflower. He reached for a glass of water, swallowed. Caught his breath.

"I should know better than to eat with you."

Bente snorted. "You're a reporter. You don't have a reputation to worry about."

"All right, you two, listen. Kaiser was on the spot, but other than jealousy I don't have a motive. Pandora's most recent boyfriend was Ozzie Mandelbaum, a Jewish kid and an Aquadonis at the Aquacade. She moved in with him — they were going to get married."

Rick wiped his mouth. "Is that the Jewish connection?"

Miranda sighed. "I don't know. Ozzie said she wanted to convert. And that's it . . . I need more information. On both Pandora and Annie Learner."

"I've got some for you."

Rick dug a reporter's notebook from his side pocket and flipped it open.

"Annie Learner knew Pandora Blake. Pandora's address was found in her address book — Hotel Potter. Different one than now, so it's before she started living with the Jewish kid. No update in the book, so maybe they weren't in touch very often."

Miranda's left hand closed in a fist, knuckles white. "That's no fucking coincidence. Someone targeted both of them."

"But only Annie was Jewish. Doesn't

make any sense." Bente's tone was sober.

Rick shifted in his chair. Picked up his fork, said it carefully.

"There's something else — something important. I got this just before I left, from a cop who was on the scene when they went over her apartment. Annie knew Duggan. Her address book was full of a lot of names — a lot of men — and Gerald Duggan was one of them."

Miranda took out the last Chesterfield. Rick dropped his fork and lit a match. She inhaled deeply, holding his hand. Blew the smoke toward the ceiling, met his eyes again.

"Thanks, Rick. That changes a few things but not everything. Meyer believes Duggan's innocent. I don't know what I think." She looked down at the fluted shot glass, shook her head.

"Why did a U.S. marshal escort Duggan to Quentin? Why no bail? I don't trust Johnson. I don't trust how fast they moved — complete hush-hush to immediate pinch. Doesn't jibe."

Rick drained his Scotch and water, pushed away the white china plate.

"You sure you just don't want to admit the bulls are right for once?"

"No, goddamn it. Sure, at first I thought

he was guilty. He's a real bastard, a crooked cop. And yeah — he hates women. Get in line for that one. I can see him shadowing Annie, losing his temper. Killing her in anger. Sudden, explosive, like a grenade. But stopping to write that word on her body — no. Not his style."

Rick cleared his throat. "Not necessarily, Miranda. You asked me to dig up some information — connections with other groups. Duggan wasn't suspended from the police force just because he's a dirty cop who got found out."

Miranda stared at Rick, rubbing the cigarette out in the ashtray.

Bente shifted in her chair. "What the fuck are you waiting for, Sanders? Tell us."

"He's trying to persuade me to leave the case alone, Bente. You should know Rick's methods by now."

Their eyes locked, unmoving. Blue irises searching hers.

"I appreciate your help. But you don't own me. No one does — and no one will."

He fell back to the table, cheeks red. She cared about the half-Irish bastard, maybe even loved him in a way, loved him like a lost memory, a grade-school kiss. But he wanted more, always did. Always looking up to Johnny, Johnny's stories, Johnny's writing.

Johnny's girl.

Bente kept her eyes on her food. Rick said heavily: "Duggan attended some IRA meetings. That's the Irish Republican Army."

Miranda swirled the bourbon in her glass.

"The IRA isn't known to be anti-Semitic — I mean, maybe some of them are, but that's never been part of their platform. Some of them fought with us — you remember, Bente, the Connolly Column."

No one spoke while Jorge and the busboy returned with a silver dessert tray. Bente picked the strawberry shortcake. Rick waved the tray away.

The orchestra tried to mimic Goodman on an arrangement of "Blue Skies."

Blue skies, smiling at me . . .

"Maybe the IRA explains the federal interest in Duggan, the protection. Maybe they've found common ground with the Fascists — both groups supporting Germany against England."

Rick threw his napkin on the table, face twisted. Eyes pleading and angry.

"Goddamn it, Miranda, Duggan's probably guilty, you've said it yourself. But if you want to defend a murderer, I guess that's your business."

Bente opened her mouth to say something and Miranda made a motion for her to keep quiet.

He stood up, shoved the fedora on his head, got his breath under control.

"You don't need me, Miranda — you're official. You work for Duggan's attorney. But for the record, two more pieces of information. I checked the files on Harold Flamm. He squealed on a bookie to get charges dropped for illegal gambling. This was three years ago. He's been clean since — or not caught."

She raised her chin. "And the other?"

His voice rasped, mouth contorted.

"Make sure you get the autopsy record for Annie Learner. It'll be released tomorrow. She had an abortion — and was sterilized."

He pushed his way quickly through the nightclub crowd, tall and straight from the back, one end of the belt on his soiled trench coat dragging across the gleaming floor.

"Holy shit. You think that's got anything to do with the murder?"

Bente knew better than to talk about Rick.

Miranda wriggled one of the long green gloves on her hand.

"No motive. Women get charged in abortion cases, too, so blackmail's out. But the sterilization . . . reminds me of the Ann Cooper Hewitt case a few years ago."

"Heiress, right? Sterilized by dear mother so she could control the trust fund or something?"

"Her share passed to her mother if she didn't have children. So when Ann needed an emergency appendectomy, her mother had her sterilized without her knowledge, claiming she was feeble-minded. She sued her mother when she turned twenty-one and got an indictment, but the case was dismissed."

Miranda pulled on the other glove, stretching her fingers into it until they touched the ends of the cloth. Bente was watching her.

"What do you want me to do, Randy?"

Half a smile. "Things just got a whole hell of a lot more complicated. I need some breaks to fall my way, get some clarity. Get some answers." She lowered her voice. "There's a fifth column group called the Musketeers — they meet at a bar in Maiden Lane. Tonypandy."

The redhead raised her eyebrows. "As in the Tonypandy riots? Typical example of worker exploitation — Churchill's never lived down sending in those troops."

"So why would a Fascist organization meet in a Welsh bar with labor sympathies?"

Bente snorted, slapped her hand on the table.

"Well, now you've got my curiosity up. Unless it's a front, I don't get it. Or unless it's like what you were saying about the IRA. Maybe Left and Right want to bury the hatchet in England's back, fucking Stalin and his nonaggression pact leading the way."

Miranda shook her head. "Who the hell knows. But now I need to concentrate on Annie Learner. Can you check on Tonypandy, see if you can catch something?"

Her friend's voice was brisk. "Count on it. I'll call you tomorrow. If I can't get you at home or the office, I'll leave a message with the service."

"Thanks, Bente." Miranda reached for one of her friend's hands. "And be careful, OK? I may have to take a trip out of town in a day or two — just not sure if I've got a lead yet."

"Follow your instincts. They're usually right."

Miranda looked at the uncharacteristically sober redhead for a few seconds, brown eyes meeting green, then picked up her handbag, tucking it under her arm. "You could use my apartment. Get away from the Oceanic. Jorge would probably appreciate it."

Bente laughed, waved her hand.

"Him? Fucks like a mink. Doesn't care where, and doesn't much care who." She winked. "But sister, he's damn good at it. Try him sometime."

Miranda grinned, stood up from the table. "No thanks."

Bente's eyes focused on her friend. "Honey, I worry about you. Sometimes all we can expect out of life is a well-cooked steak and a good fuck. That's what men are after, and it's high time women started following suit."

She shoved the remaining piece of strawberry shortcake in her mouth, saluting Miranda with the fork.

SIXTEEN

She left the Moderne in a hurry, looking for sharp-faced men in expensive clothes. Kept in crowds, kept with strangers, the kind who weren't wearing .45s.

Taxi outside, bored man about forty-five, two-day-old beard, listening to the *Swing Quiz* on KMPC from Los Angeles. He hurtled down Sutter and then a left on Mason to Post, past Francis, saint and sinner, past Union Square and Alma Spreckels stretching her hands to the sky. Past the Mechanics' Institute, past the Hallidie Building, warm gold of streetlamps reflecting like Christmas lights in the cool curtain of solid glass.

Dropped her by Lotta's. He grunted at the tip, turned the radio back on, and sped down Market toward Van Ness.

She walked quickly between a Municipal and a Market Street car, clanging bells and racing to see who'd get to Third Street first.

Crossed all four rail tracks without getting her heel caught.

The Monadnock was nearly empty except for Tascone's. Wurlitzer blared "In the Mood" while army men sat in a row at the counter, eating pie and ice cream, double or triple date. Gladys wasn't working, and the brunette at the cigarette counter didn't bother to look up from the *Photoplay,* Ann Sheridan posing coyly on the bright cover. Miranda bought a pack of Chesterfields and another roll of Pep-O-Mint Life Savers, the girl grunting a mumbled thanks while the cash register clanged.

Slow elevator, creaks and groans. Miranda wished the Monadnock still used operators. She used to enjoy conversations with the old man on the stool, wink and a smile, tell her to call him "Pops" like something out of an Andy Hardy movie.

A year ago. A year was a long time.

Off on four, heels echoing down the hallway, then deep breath and her office.

No hatchet men with smiling faces and cheap aftershave. No note under the door about her legs or even a simple, scrawled promise to kill her.

She opened the bottom drawer of the desk, uncorked the Old Taylor, swallowed a shot from the bottle. Left it on top of the desk, then back to the safe, left-right-left, got it the first time.

Grabbed Ozzie's package. Grabbed the .22 and her handbag, .38 too large and back at the apartment. Looked down at her gown. Fuck the matching green evening purse.

Poured another shot of bourbon and flung up the sill, chilled wind from the Bay stinging her awake, eyes wide. No Cordoba tan Ford chasing streetcars down Market Street, no gangly tall man standing outside the blinking light of the bar next to the De Young Building or waiting for her at Lotta's Fountain, braced against the cold bronze.

She sat in the darkness and sipped the Old Taylor, beats of reflected neon her only illumination. Wind slacked, suddenly changed, and blew elsewhere. Gray tendrils, gentle and reaching out, crept through the darkness to touch her face.

Like a mother's touch.

She shut the window with a clatter.

San Francisco was waiting.

The *Yerba Buena* pulled up, one minute overdue. Passengers held on to their hats in the Bay wind, men grasping the arms of their wives. Roar and embarkation, excited chattering, Ferry Building full and smiling again, purposeful. Temporary victory over the gray and orange spans choking her life away.

Miranda inched forward with the rest of the crowd, lady in an ermine coat on her left, sailor on her right, his arm around a giggling blonde. Stood on the upper deck, cheeks cold and wet, facing the Island. Dance of colors, pinks and yellows glinting off the gold phoenix, aerie on the Tower of the Sun.

Mythical bird, mythical city. Veneer of gilt as thin as the respectability cloaking Pacific Avenue and the former Barbary Coast.

Empty promises whispered by the Gold Rush town, City of Hope and City of Hopeless, full of sin, shine, survival. Beached ships sunk into sand, build a house, sell supplies, serve some liquor and girls and dancing for the men in the mines, dreams broken up on the sharp ragged rocks of El Dorado.

She dropped the cigarette stub and crushed it, brushing against two office clerks flirting with a bus driver and a milkman on his night off. Laughter high and shrill, mixed with the baritone beat of the foghorn off the Headlands, white wool blanket on the way, muffled lights, wispy ghosts, forever dancing the tarantella down Market Street.

Live through another quake, San Francisco. Climb your green hills, make your babies, build your schools. A hundred years from now you might be docile and domestic and fit for the families, magic gone, gamblers no longer welcome. You might tame your people, might be the lady you pretended to be.

But Miranda didn't think so.

The City, 1912.

Steamships and sailing ships, pale billows puffing on wind ripped through the gate, more green than golden. Muddy streets, horse manure. Hammer and saw, hammer and saw. Cement trucks and bricklayers, dusty, gray hands, Barbary Coast glittering, casinos and electric lights. San Francisco whores spilling into pools of blood on Market Street, cops fighting over which one gets the payoff.

Abe Ruef's city. Not for children, though plenty roamed the streets and worked in the factories, and twelve-year-old girls with bound feet leaned against the bricks of Ross Alley, two bits a throw.

I'd rock my own sweet child to rest . . .

Seen and not heard, especially in the corners of hotel rooms and back alleyways, men with bristling mustaches and small, sick eyes offering a bonus for virgins, young

246

and tender. Boys learned to fight, learned to run, unhampered by the long skirts and the forced petticoats, trapped in hands too rough to escape.

Sleep, baby dear, Sleep without fear . . .

Not sure if it was memory. Something to hold on to when Hatchett locked her away in the dark, shuttered room or her father came home surly, boots muddy, school papers not in order, hands trembling but quick to strike, not yet numbed by rum or gin or whatever bottle was waiting for him.

I'd rock my own sweet child to rest . . .

She sung the words to herself, dreaming of a dark-eyed and dark-haired woman holding her close, melodic, lilting, and the woman would sing it again, in an English made sweet by the sound of her voice.

She'd sing it over and over, clutching herself and rocking, waiting for her father to fall asleep, for Hatchett to nod in front of the fireplace. Dark night, fog her friend, muffling any sounds. Creep downstairs, slip out into the night. Invisible and alone.

Sleep, baby dear, Sleep without fear . . .

Lotta's Fountain gave her water, smell of steak and onions and fresh-baked sourdough bread. Dodge the carriages, sometimes get a free ride on a cable car if the conductor rubbed his red nose and waved her on. One tipped his hat once, made her feel like a lady, despite the old calico dress that was too short and too thin for the thick, cold wrap of summer fog.

I'd put my own sweet child to sleep . . .

Head for the blazing lights of Pacific Street, Terrific Street, gin joints and gambling halls, swing of hot ragtime pouring out of Purcell's, where handsome men with black skin played music that wasn't so sweet as her lullaby but stirred her soul just the same. Sometimes one of the women in feathered hats and red dresses would call her over, feed her champagne, roast pork, and potatoes, talking about Sophie Tucker and the Pantages circuit, and how Mary Lewis was packing them in at Taits, and how Al Jolson owned the town.

She knew better, of course. San Francisco didn't belong to anybody but her.

And the memories or make-believe blended, swirled, combined. Mother's lullaby, protected and made safe, running and knowing how to run from the men with the funny eyes, knife fight behind the bar, held-out hand with the gold piece in it. She'd sing it to herself under her breath, back away, run back to the closet where they locked her up. Because she'd get out again.

Nothing to hold her, nothing to be scared

of. No one to own her.
Sleep, baby dear, Sleep without fear . . .
Mother is here with you forever.

Miranda walked straight down the Gayway to the Ron de Voo, gaudy lights and constant patter buoying her past the jungle exhibit and the tired chimpanzees. Crowds were thicker than usual around the peep shows, brought out by curiosity and crime, murder the brand-new, never-before-seen attraction for the Fair in 1940.

Still a line at Sally's, drunk trying to weave his way in. Probably just to unbutton his pants and press himself against the glass the girls worked behind. Plainclothes cop grabbed his arms, dragged him off the wooden stage while he protested in a loud, slurred voice. Rest of the line tittered, moved on.

Ralph, the old bald barker at Greenwich Village, winked at her, voice hoarse from one too many "Nothing vulgar, ladies and gentlemen, purely educational, nothing objectionable here, folks, from the top of her beautiful head to the tips of her toes . . ."

Smell of hot dogs and buttered popcorn, cotton candy and sweet, baking bread from the Maxwell House coffee Doughnut Tower, neon tubes glowing red and yellow along streamlined curves, almost as enticing as the steaming coffee and old-fashioned doughnuts, fresh from the oven.

Same old Gayway. She was surprised she missed it so much.

The Ron de Voo was only half-full. Ozzie and Lucinda huddled in a corner, no sarong this time. Tailored street clothes and angry lips made her look older, thinner, less exotic. Ozzie was playing with some French fries on his plate. Saw Miranda and jumped up from the table, face stretched by a big, eager smile.

"Miss Corbie — we didn't think you'd come."

Lucinda looked at her wristwatch as if she'd never seen it before. "You're over an hour late."

Miranda slid into the chair by the rubber plant, set Ozzie's package on the table.

"I got here as soon as I could."

The dark-haired woman grunted, glanced over at Ozzie. His hair was slicked back, still wet. He gazed at Miranda, puppy eyes.

"Thank you, Miss Corbie. Did — did it help?"

She smiled. "Yes. Thank you. I've got a few more questions for you both."

Lucinda shook out a cigarette from a package of Kools on the table. "Why? I thought this was over. Cops arrested some bum bastard already. Why're you still interested?"

"I work for the defense attorney. We don't think he killed Pandora or Annie Learner."

Lucinda blew smoke over Miranda's left shoulder. "You think it was somebody else? That the killer's still out there? Goddamn it — I was gonna sleep so good tonight."

Sarcasm couldn't drown the fear in her eyes.

Miranda opened her purse. Found a Butter Rum roll half-finished, popped two in her mouth.

"Look. It's late. I appreciate you meeting me. Let's just get to the point, OK? Lucinda, you met Pandora when — last year?"

The other woman nodded, inhaled sharply. Miranda could smell menthol in the blue smoke from the Kool. Her right hand trembled, and she held it under the table, clutching her purse.

"I met her in '39. She got hired when the Fair opened, not before."

Ozzie was staring at the package, voice low. "Wish I'd met her then."

Lucinda squeezed his arm. "Me too, kid. Didn't know you'd be Mr. Rose's star Aquadonis a year later, didya?"

She turned to Miranda, ferocity in her

small face. "Ozzie's got it — real pizzazz, real star stuff. He's already grabbed a feature role in the Aquacade — no tellin' where this boy's gonna wind up. Don't he look like Tyrone Power?"

The woman's eyes fell on him with a mixture of maternal pride and desire, lingering on the strong set of his shoulders and perfect tapered waist.

Ozzie blushed. "Cut it out, Lu."

"Anyway, he's talent. He's going places. The coppers didn't even wanna talk to him, but the *Chronicle* did — got a big write-up tomorrow." She pointed the cigarette at Miranda.

"So don't fuck up his life any more than it has been. Dreams are goddamn hard to live on, lady. He's still got a few that can come true." Lucinda ground out the cigarette with a violent twist.

Ozzie was hesitant. "Lu, I wish you wouldn't —"

"What? Care so much? Can't help that, kid. You're the tops." The dark-haired woman swallowed, looked away, then up at Miranda. "What else you wanna know?"

"Did Pandora miss any time at work — like a weekend — ever mention going to Calistoga?"

The brunette opened her mouth, closed it

252

again. "Pan missed more than a weekend. She was gone for about six weeks last year starting in April — only a coupla months or after from when that prick Schwartz hired her. Maybe she mentioned Calistoga. I don't remember."

Miranda nodded. "You sure? Might be important."

Lucinda shifted her weight in the chair. "Yeah. I don't know."

"All right. This might upset you, Ozzie, but — how many men did Pandora see on a regular basis?"

Lucinda reached up to straighten her hat. "Whaddya mean, 'regular basis'?"

"Steady. No one-shots."

The brunette's hands fell on the table with a slap, face red.

"Listen, sister — Pan was no easy number. She didn't skate around, like most of the broads in this joint." Agitated glance over at Ozzie. "You don't have to listen to this stuff."

He picked at the strings around the brown paper–wrapped package. "Yeah, I do. If it helps Miss Corbie, it'll help Pan." He raised his face, high cheekbones burnished with red, eyes on fire like Ronald Colman in *A Tale of Two Cities*.

"Tell her, Lu. I want to hear."

253

Lucinda stared at him. "OK. But Ozzie, take it from me — she didn't love anybody but you."

Teeth bright, white smile. Then his face dropped back to its customary grief.

Miranda said. "Make it simple — who, and how many?"

Lucinda counted off on long red nails. "Some bird with dough. Started going with him right away — caught her act in the morning, took her out that night. Lasted maybe five, six weeks. Poor kid thought he was her dream man, come to take her away to some castle in Burlingame. It was after he ditched her that she went away."

"To Calistoga?"

Lucinda shook her head. "Uh-uh. I already said I don't remember."

Miranda grinned. "OK. Who was next?"

The brunette shrugged. "Nobody on the Gayway for the rest of the year, not until Kaiser. She went out a few times with some customers . . . a sailor, some army joe. Nobody serious, maybe one or two dates apiece, probably five or six different guys."

"No names?"

"I don't remember names. Pan probably didn't either. I'm tellin' you, nobody serious."

"What about Kaiser?"

"That bastard." Lucinda shook her head in disgust. "I warned her, but she wouldn't listen. He grabbed her up first time we got here to set up for the Fair — back in March. I told you what happened."

"Yeah." Miranda looked across the table at Ozzie. Made her voice gentle. "When did you decide you'd get married?"

"After two weeks." He turned toward Lucinda. "We didn't tell anybody, not until later. Pan wanted to keep it a secret, just us two."

He laid his hand on Lucinda's shoulder. "She said she wanted to — to — get married and have babies, right away. Give up on acting, on being a star."

His voice was heavy, cracking with emotion, as his eyes fell to the floor. "Said she wanted my babies more than anything." Tears rolled down his cheeks, his forehead dotted with sweat.

Miranda stood up. "I'm sorry, Ozzie."

She studied the woman with the stiff, tight curls under the wide-brimmed hat, the handsome young man with the wet cheeks, hand still on her shoulder. Lucinda raised her chin and glared.

No more information — not tonight. Miranda nodded and left, Lucinda bending over Ozzie and murmuring consolations.

She threaded back through the Gayway, strung bulbs crisscrossing the fading sideshows, glaring orange, lighting up old Madame Marie's crystal ball and not much else. Passed a row of games, a guess-your-weight gimmick, shooting gallery. Didn't know the wizened barker, "Try your skill, folks, win a gift for the little lady — you look like you can handle a gun, fella. . . ."

Miranda pivoted suddenly, looking to her right.

Sharp metallic crack.

Burning, goddamn burning pain, left arm. Push and a shove, get down, Randy, goddamn it, hit the fucking dirt, and sawdust under her, boots and work shoes and cheap leather pumps making a fence, backing away.

Gasps. Screams, running feet kicking up the sand, *thud-thud-thud* on the midway.

Police whistle.

Knees in the dirt, knees and one hand, green silk dress hiked up too high. Eyes all around. Cigarettes and bottlecaps, napkin from the Chinese Village crumpled up, soy sauce drenching the white paper.

Voices shrill, hysterical. *Thud-thud-thud,* more running feet.

No music, no barkers. No calliope.

Someone held out an arm and helped her

up, middle-aged man with a black fedora and blue eyes.

Left arm was numb. She touched it, watched as her palm filled with dark red. Stared at her green glove, viscous liquid brushing the velvet, pattern like a Japanese watercolor.

Running again, more whistles. The man with the kind eyes searched her face.

Said: "Lady — you need a doctor. You've been shot."

■ ■ ■ ■

PART THREE:
SACRIFICE

■ ■ ■ ■

To-day's your natal day,
Sweet flowers I bring;
Mother, accept, I pray,
My offering.
And may you happy live
And long us bless;
Receiving as you give
Great happiness.

— "To My Mother,"
Christina Rossetti (1842)

SEVENTEEN

"You're a lucky girl, Miss Corbie. Getting grazed by a bullet isn't such an easy thing to do."

She didn't know the doctor on call. Tall, thin, a young forty with the prerequisite graying temples. He dabbed more iodine around the elongated gash on her left arm. Gillespie stood with his arms and mouth folded, shaking his head. Too late for Grogan to be on duty. Lucky again.

"A .22, Doctor?"

He glanced up at the cop. "I'm not an expert on gunshots — most of the cases we get in here are heatstroke and sore feet. Judging from the wound, the bullet was small-caliber. We're just lucky it didn't hit someone else. Have you found the shooter yet?"

"Got a line on a skinny guy who ran. Haven't been able to track him, but we will."

Miranda winced as the doctor wrapped

the bandage tight. "I doubt it."

The patrol cop reddened. "You were fired, Corbie. Maybe you'd like to tell me what the hell you're doing on the Island?"

She tried to shrug, grimaced. Dr. Kildare chided her gently.

"You'll have to wear an arm brace, Miss Corbie. Try not to use your left arm or shoulder — the wound will be painful for at least a week. And you'll need to change the bandage twice a day."

"I remember how to change bandages."

He tied the brace around her neck and shoulder, letting his hand linger on the lower part of her arm.

"What made you turn? Twisting toward your right probably saved your life."

Miranda shut her eyes, wishing for a goddamn Chesterfield.

"I thought I heard someone call my name."

Gillespie cleared his throat and asked, "I can question her now, Doc?"

The physician nodded, last look at the patient. Closed the door of the small examination room. She stared at Gillespie, stony-faced.

"What the hell do you want? I've been shot at and I'm tired and I want to go home."

"Why are you on the Island?"

"None of your fucking business. It's a free country."

Gillespie gave her a hard look, fleshy rectangle of his face tired, skin unnaturally yellow in the overhead light. Then he cracked a grin.

"All right, sister. I won't write up in the report that you're investigatin' the Blake murder, which — for the record — is closed. Truth be told, a few of us miss ya around here. Used to brighten up the place."

She couldn't hide the surprise. "Thanks, Gillespie. I always suspected you were a human being." Miranda hopped off the examination table, flinching when the motion made her arm move.

He said nonchalantly: "Don't expect much action on the skinny bird. Most of us had to calm the crowd down, scared the bejesus out of 'em. Too many people, too much noise. He got away clean. But then, I figure you might know him anyway."

She looked up at the tall, beefy cop. "Maybe."

He held out his arm to steady her. "C'mon, I'll drive you home. I'm goin' off duty, and you'll be missin' the last ferry."

She hesitated, then took his arm. "I could

use a ride."

She looked down at her bedraggled Magnin's dress, silk ruined, while he draped her coat around her shoulders.

"I don't look so good."

"Better than the dames I usually give a ride to."

She raised her eyebrows and smiled. Stopped at the door.

"Gillespie — why the sudden concern? I'm not usually a favorite with the button boys."

He grinned at the understatement. "Well, it's like this. We know you're workin' for Duggan. Surprised the hell out of us. But some of us figure that's a good thing."

She looked up into his brown eyes, age spots and freckles dotting the sagging skin along his cheekbones.

"Surprised the hell out of me, too."

They walked out of the examination room together, Gillespie gently guiding her toward the stairs of the administration building.

They didn't talk much on the way to Mason. Gillespie asked her if she'd heard from Phil; she said no. Silence after that, until he pulled off the Bay Bridge and turned toward downtown, mentioning how he knew Duggan when he worked vice, that he was a decent cop who got broken by circumstance. Miranda nodded, pain in her arm and the bruises on her knees and body making it hard to concentrate on anything other than making it home.

Gillespie drove up the hill, threw on the emergency brake to hold the heavy police car on the grade. Mason was quiet, bedroom lights from a couple of windows and the top floor of the Drake Hopkins.

"Can you get out OK, Corbie?"

He leaned over to help open her door, saggy eyes blinking at the bright light from the apartment lobby. She fumbled with the handle and climbed out on the curb, picking up her bag from the floorboard. Poked her head back inside.

"Thanks, Gillespie. I appreciate it."

He grunted. "Yeah, well. You ain't such a bad shamus." He started to put the car in gear.

"Say, Gillespie . . ."

"Yeah?"

"You hear anything about Duggan and the IRA? Irish Republican Army. I heard that's why the brass discharged him."

He frowned, staring straight ahead over the steering wheel. "You oughta know why they broke the poor bastard — though you weren't the first woman he couldn't handle, not by a long shot. Kept himself to himself, Duggan did, but we all knew when he was on a tear. No, if he was involved in somethin' political, I never heard it."

He revved the motor and slipped the car into first. "Be seein' you, Corbie."

"Yeah, Gillespie. Thanks."

She watched the police car crawl up the steep hill and turn right on Bush. Two steps to the entrance, struggle to open the heavy glass door of the Drake Hopkins Apartments.

Old Leo was sleeping, mouth open, false teeth put away in his blue overcoat pocket. Breath easy in, easy out, faint sinus trill.

Goddamn elevator still out of order. New goddamn building and fucking elevator broken most of the fucking time. . . .

Miranda readjusted her arm in the sling, tears of pain in her eyes. Climbed the carpeted stairs, pausing at each landing to rest, breath ragged, each exhale sending an electric shock through her arm and shoulder. The .22 in her bag felt like a fucking cannon, useless goddamn weapon when somebody tries to shoot you in the fucking back.

Finally reached the fourth floor, almost tripping and falling against the door, legs and body trembling in shock and exhaustion.

Flicked on the light and dragged herself inside, scattering the already dispersed baking soda. Wriggled out of the coat, biting her lip. Long gash in the thick wool on the left side. She stared at it for a second, dropping it on the couch.

Wobbled into the kitchen and poured herself a coffee cup of Four Roses, downed it in two gulps. Grabbed a satin comforter off the bed and dragged it into the living room, where she nestled under it in the overstuffed chair. Brought in the bottle of bourbon, placed it at her fingertips.

Dreamed of bright flashing lights and the roar of mortar shells, smell of oil and cordite bitter and overwhelming.

The ringing woke her before the pain did.

Gray light filtered through the pale yellow curtains, and she sat up, swearing at the knives twisted in her left arm.

Miranda pushed herself out of the armchair, staggered toward the bedroom phone. Sank on the bed, waiting for a voice.

"Miranda? My child, are you all right?"

Squeezed her eyes together, opened and blinked. Goddamn blue forget-me-nots. Stretched her neck backward, wondering if

267

she'd ever feel better again.

"Yeah, Meyer. Give me a chance to wake up. What time is it?"

"Eight o'clock. On Tuesday. What happened? Was the shooting connected to Mr. Duggan in some way?"

"I don't know. Maybe." The edges of the room started to sharpen. She looked down at the beautiful spring green silk, stained with blood, scuffed and torn on rocks and Gayway garbage. "You owe me a new dress. And a coat."

"City of Paris, top of the line. Just tell me what is going on."

Miranda yawned until it hurt too much. The pain was becoming sharp and localized, but her entire body felt like a green-and-yellow bruise.

"I was walking through the Gayway — main strip — and somebody took a shot at me. Grazed my upper left arm. I'll be all right."

Reproving silence. "I'm your attorney, my dear. You should tell me everything."

"You're not my attorney right now, Meyer. I'll be all right. Let me handle this in my own way, OK? I'm a big girl. I've been shot at before."

Nonverbal noise of disagreement on the other end. "You could have been killed —"

"But I wasn't. Let it go." Softer tone: "I can't use my left arm for much, so I've got to work smart and fast. I need you to send me Annie Learner's autopsy report — it's supposed to be released today, and Rick got an early peek. Did you know she'd been sterilized?"

His voice came out slow and shocked. "No. No, I didn't."

Miranda pulled open the nightstand drawer, rummaging until she found a packet of cigarettes. Half a Chesterfield still inside. She shook it out on the bed.

"An abortion, too, apparently. Find out everything you can from the M.E. about this, would you? Whether the two operations were simultaneous, whether they were professional, estimation on how long ago they took place. It's important. They've been sitting on this information too long."

"I'll call the coroner immediately, and ask for a copy to be delivered to your office."

She clicked the small silver lighter with the Tower of the Sun stamped on it and drew down on the cigarette. Exhaled gratefully, placed the stick on the small glass ashtray next to the .38, still propped beside her lamp. Picked up the phone again.

"Thanks. Something else. Annie Learner knew Pandora Blake and Duggan. I'm heading over to Annie's apartment this morning. Rick got it from a cop who said both of their names were listed in her address book. That's physical evidence that you should have seen already, processed and booked and in a locker at the Hall of Justice."

She could hear him breathing.

"I hope to God you didn't keep this from me, Meyer."

His voice was quiet. "You should know better than that."

"Had to ask. Find out what else they've got. Tear into the sonsofbitches. Don't play along."

"In other words, use your tactics?"

She started to shrug, yelped from the pain in her arm. "Yeah. They work so well. I'll call you later today from the office. OK?"

"Take care of yourself, Miranda."

"I always do." She hung up the phone, took a deep drag on the cigarette.

Blew smoke at the pale pink wallpaper. Stared at the forget-me-nots.

Ripping off the bandages on her arm made her grind her teeth, so she threw back another shot of Four Roses. Took an hour and a half to shower and get dressed.

She called downstairs, and Roy ran to the drugstore at the St. Francis, bringing a package of gauze, tape, iodine, and Chester-fields up to the fourth floor like a dog with a prize duck. She tipped him a dollar, his blue eyes watery and blinking and worried, Adam's apple bobbing nervously.

"You need anything, Miss Corbie, you just ring me up. Oh, and here's your baking soda."

She took the box and smiled. "Thanks, Roy."

Miranda stood in front of the bathroom mirror. Bruises on her legs, skinned knees, strained right wrist, and above all an ugly puckered rip on her upper arm that would leave a scar.

So much for bathing suit season.

She dowsed the wound with iodine, holding one end of the gauze in her teeth. Wrapped it around, not too tight, the way they'd taught her at the Red Cross, and picked up the pieces of tape she'd cut earlier, securing the bandage. Let her arm slowly hang down until she couldn't stand the pain, then brought it back to a more rigid position.

Fuck the arm sling.

They'd hear it didn't work, hear the shot went wide. So they'd follow her, waiting for another chance, make it good the second time, put the Corbie broad on the slab, goddamn whore who killed Sammy Martini, bitch who thought she could compete with a man, thought she could win in a man's world, fight a man's war.

Miranda studied her reflection, practicing how to hold her arm.

Looking like a crippled woman wasn't a goddamn option.

She ate breakfast at the St. Francis, splurging on atmosphere. Eggs Benedict and a broiled grapefruit, enough coffee to take a bath in. The hotel was full, soldiers and ex-soldiers and families in town for Memorial Day, laying a wreath in the Presidio cemetery, remembering boys lost in Belgium. Last war, not this one.

In Flanders Fields the poppies blow, between the crosses, row on row . . .

Miranda rubbed her forehead. Tried not to make her disability as obvious as it felt, not to show the pain on her face when she moved the wrong way or flinched at the sudden backfire on O'Farrell. Asked the middle-aged waitress for a *Chronicle*, remembering the pride in Lucinda's voice from last night.

Local news, and a full half page on Ozzie Mandelbaum, Aquadonis. She smiled at the photo of Ozzie next to Weissmuller and Esther Williams, at short, bald, and fat Billy Rose standing in front of his swimming pinups.

No mention of Pandora. Closed case, Gillespie said. Official.

Ozzie grew up in a lot of places, from Boston to Amarillo, where he worked for his uncle the chiropractor, helping little old ladies with back problems. Saved enough money to come west, try his luck in show business.

California, here we come. Right back where we started from.

Fame and fortune, name in lights, you oughta be in pictures, lady. You can give my regards to Broadway, but hooray for fucking Hollywood, where any shopgirl can be a top girl with a producer underneath.

The waitress pushed back a gray hair struggling out from under the white hat of the uniform, smiling wanly at Miranda while she poured more coffee. Miranda set the platter aside, lit a Chesterfield.

Climb a stairway to paradise called Los Angeles. Movie stars and movie palaces and wide boulevards with even wider cars, weather always an even seventy-two degrees.

Names in neon lights, lines at Grauman's. Duck hunting with Gable and bridge with Colbert. Love and adoration, what every-

273

body fucking wants, writ big, writ large, filmed in Technicolor with music by Max Steiner and gowns by Edith Head. Live forever, admired, envied. Just make sure DeMille directs.

Until they got lost. Until the boulevards dead-ended in small, cramped hotel rooms off Wilshire. Vast, empty. All make-believe.

A desert disguised as paradise.

Better you should stay in Kansas, little girl. Live in a real city, where the predators can't promise you eternal life, forever young. Forever beautiful.

Miranda folded the paper and left it on the table with a dollar.

Walked outside into the fog, already starting to burn off above Powell Street.

Annie Learner's apartment was next.

EIGHTEEN

Miranda stepped off a number 7 White Front, looking quickly to her left and right.

No thin man with a Panama. No tan Ford. Couple of teenagers walking toward Market Street, hand in hand, boy in his father's suit, girl in a carefully pressed calico.

She adjusted the wide-brimmed fedora, smoothed down the scalloped edges of the tailored navy jacket. It was pretty, feminine, and a little large, good disguise for her .38 when she needed to wear it. Hoped the jacket would make her look more mobile than she felt, hide the stiff way she held her left arm, bent at the elbow, pressed against her stomach.

No gun today. Nothing but a demure handbag, too small for anything other than her Baby Browning, and that was back at the office.

Click. Clack. Boom. Polka dots, red and pink on white. Martini's brains splattered on a bathroom wall.

Three months ago she killed a man. She wasn't sorry.

Miranda dropped the Chesterfield on the sidewalk. Stared up at the two-story Edwardian, cream colored, brown trim, one of a series on this stretch of Haight. Old houses huddled together, comparing scars, dreaming of a single family again, servants' quarters downstairs and men with handlebar mustaches shouting for more port.

The Drexel Apartments looked purpose-built for the trade, larger and deeper than its neighbors. She climbed the short row of steps, examined the call buttons. Annie Learner's name was still on number eleven, neat writing, faded blue ink.

Peered through the dusty glass door. Long, narrow corridor, stairway to the left. First door on the left marked MANAGER.

Her blue-gloved finger held the button down for ten seconds until she saw the door crack open, parchment thin hand snaking out around the edge.

Old lady, seventy or older. Wrinkled, bent, white hair curly, framing a face with a generous mouth and small, pointed chin. Blue eyes still clear. She'd been pretty once.

Miranda plastered on her best Sunday school smile, glad she chose a conservative suit. The old lady surprised her by moving quickly, neck craned upward to compensate for her crooked back.

Eyes roamed Miranda, looking for a fault and unable to find one. Another White Front car rumbled by, nearly drowning out the old lady's rasping voice.

"No vacancy. Best try the Seville Apartments down the street." Up and down again, lingering on the navy pumps. "They ain't so particular."

She started to close the door when Miranda reached for the handle. The old lady cocked her head, gathering her pink quilted robe tighter. Shuffled forward. Peered at Miranda.

"You ain't lookin' for an apartment."

Miranda opened the door wide with her right hand and propped herself against it, trying not to wince from the stabbing pain in her left arm.

"No. I'm here to ask you some questions about Annie Learner."

The old lady looked her up and down again. Eyes rested on the handbag.

"Whaddya got?"

Miranda sidled inside the dim foyer, letting the door shut automatically behind her with a soft click. Interior smelled like mothballs, camphor, and chicken soup.

She looked down at the shrunken face, cheekbones still dotted with rouge from when women wore bustles. Miranda grinned.

"Depends on what you got. Let's start with five and work our way up."

The old lady nodded, false teeth loose enough to make a clacking sound. Turned to her doorway.

"Come in. Name's Edwina Breckinridge."

"Mine's Miranda Corbie."

The old woman craned her neck, looked back at Miranda. "I know."

Miranda raised her eyebrows and followed the shrunken form of the old lady into a dark, cramped apartment, overcrowded with burgundy velvet, dilapidated Victorian furniture, and scandalous paintings of a woman in a skimpy stage costume.

Gnarled finger pointed up proudly. "That was me. Turned quite a few heads in my time."

A sensual smile still promised the kind of pleasure that lured randy young dandies to backstage doors and sent their wives to lectures on the decline of morality. Curling, flame-colored hair fell over a bloodred costume that showed off her thighs.

"You were an actress?"

The old lady walked to a walnut desk bigger than she was and fished out some keys.

"One of the best. Played all the circuits, had me beaux aplenty. Money, too. Threw it away on that sonofabitch Breckinridge, may his soul rot in hell."

Miranda was still looking up at the portrait. "Why'd you marry him?"

Mrs. Breckinridge sighed and clutched her robe, glanced up at the painting.

"Ain't got time for tall tales. You wanna see her apartment or not?"

Miranda nodded, following the old woman down the dingy hall to the back of the building. Mrs. Breckinridge turned the key in the lock, faced Miranda. Wrinkled palm up and out.

"Cops told me not to let anyone in, a' course, but I know who you are. Lady detective. Saw your picture in the paper. You can call me Edwina. Where's the five bucks?"

Miranda transferred the purse to her left arm, holding it gingerly while she opened it with her right. Took out her wallet, opened it one-handed, and pulled out a five-dollar bill.

The old lady snatched it from her fingers. "Whaddya do to your arm?"

"You mind if I smoke?"

Edwina shook her head. "You got somethin' worth smokin', I'll join you."

Miranda replaced the wallet and plucked out the deck of Chesterfields. Offered them to the old lady, who took three.

Miranda grinned, stuck one in her mouth, and lit it with the Ronson. Passed it to Edwina, who shoved two sticks in her robe pocket and lit another, smacking her lips as if she were eating the tobacco.

"Not bad. Not as good as the cee-gars I used to get from France, but not bad. What's wrong with your arm?"

Miranda looked down at her over the cigarette tip. "I got shot at last night."

"D'ya find the bastard?"

"Not yet."

The old lady grunted. "Hope you do. All right, in you go. You find anything in there worth more than five bucks, you know where I live. Thanks for the smokes."

Miranda asked. "So why'd you marry him?"

Edwina curled her neck back around, peering up at her. " 'Cause he could fuck like nobody's business."

She watched the old lady's bent back and small, crooked legs scurry down the gray corridor, finally disappearing into her own room.

■ ■ ■ ■

Annie Learner's possessions were meager and already pillaged by the cops. Her address book — along with anything else obviously linked to the case — would be down at the Hall. Miranda was left with the detritus, everyday junk the bulls overlooked, ordinary bits of an ordinary life that ended in an unordinary way.

Small, dingy, dark. Corner room, would've been quiet enough for the liaisons Annie supposedly had, nights when the perfume counter closed, maybe hoping to score a rich husband or at least a boyfriend who could take her to the movies and treat her more like a lady.

Girls who worked perfume cultivated an air, a radio voice, necessary to sell women on the idea of allure through scent and to persuade men that buying it for their wives would make them smell and look like the woman who sold it. Miranda hadn't seen a photo of her, not yet, but she knew Annie was pretty and could sweet-talk her way to a commission.

Came with the job.

She stubbed the cigarette out on the door handle, dropped the remaining half in the

Chesterfield package.

Walked to the tiny closet, riffling through the clothes. Mostly Emporium, mostly on sale, one or two pieces from the White House or City of Paris, last year's models. No Sears, no Montgomery Ward. Looked up at the hat boxes on the closet shelf.

Grabbed a hanging umbrella to knock one of the boxes down, tumble of cardboard on the wooden floor. Jarring sound in the still, small apartment.

Newest hat box held last year's style, medieval side affair with a feather.

Impractical, and definitely a luxury for Annie Learner.

The bedroom was more like a closet itself, barely large enough for a single bed, small dresser, and vanity. She squeezed between the footboard and the vanity stool and sat down, looking in the mirror.

Annie must've been a few inches shorter than Miranda, about five three. Perfumes strewn on the blond wood were mostly high-end samples, makeup Elizabeth Arden with a few less expensive brands mixed in.

Cheap red lacquer jewelry box sat crookedly behind the bottles of fragrance. Miranda opened it. "Always" began to play on a tinny little music wheel, rotating ballerina dancing jerkily to the music.

I'll be loving you, always . . .

Tink. Last note. Ballerina frozen, mid-pirouette.

Costume pieces, inexpensive rhinestone, and a very small silver ring, minuscule diamond. Miranda squinted at the inside, couldn't find a mark. Tried to put it on her smallest finger.

Wouldn't fit.

She held it in her palms, fingers closing on it, and dropped it in the inside flap of her purse.

She stood up, grimacing, arm jostled from the smallness of the space. Stepped into the living room, toward the oak desk that stood in the farthest corner from the door, under a ventilation shaft thick with dust.

Portable brown Bakelite radio sat on the edge, dial turned to KFRC, last year's phone book propped beside the phone. Miranda riffled through the pages, looking for Pandora Blake.

No listing.

Tried the Hotel Potter, bent closer to the paper in the dim light. Faint penciled checkmark next to the number and scribbles in the margin of the page, nothing legible. She flipped back through to the Ds.

Gerald Duggan's name was circled in black ink.

Unblotted, ink bleeding through several pages, edges blurred and furry. More scribbling in the margins. A few words: "tonight, 8 pm, the Fox."

Miranda felt her face muscles pull tight, and she closed the book, thin pages making a whooshing sound as they fanned shut.

Next to the telephone was a small heap of papers. Postcards, stationery, photos, and souvenirs, careless pile made by careless cops.

On the top was a postcard from Nance's Sanitarium.

Message scrawled in pencil on the back. No stamp, no postmark, never mailed.

Don't want you to worry. You're always so sorry after you get mad. Just need a few days off to think about everything. I'll write soon.

Love always, your Annie

P.S. Don't lose your license again, you might need to come get me.

Date was hard to read. Looked like "April 8, 1939."

Miranda held the card in her hand, pain in her arm forgotten. Remembered the same card in Pandora Blake's pile of memories, unmarked and unsent but still kept, gift or souvenir.

Pandora missed six or more weeks of work at Artists and Models last year. Sometime in April, Lucinda said. She remembered the brunette's snappish evasion on the subject of Calistoga, just last night.

She needed to talk to Lucinda.

Miranda carefully placed the card inside her *Chadwick's Street Guide*.

Picked through the pile, unearthing a couple of small snapshots, one in front of the main entrance to the Emporium, another laughing and gesturing toward a bottle of Soir de Paris on her perfume counter.

Smiling girl, dark-haired. Pretty.

Another postcard, corner bent. This one advertising "The Hollywood Show 'Stage 9,' " running one full hour, two to ten P.M. daily, only forty cents for the secrets of a Hollywood soundstage. Neil Hamilton and Marian Marsh beaming fame and happiness against a red star background.

Miranda flipped the card over. Careful, curly writing, this time in blue ink. Dated Monday, May 15.

I wanted to let you know that I'm back to work. I don't think I could have come back without your help. We are more

285

than sisters.

I know we agreed never to tell anyone and to try to forget, and I want to do that more than anything now. No one will know about what happened, not even my mother. But if you ever need to talk, Annie, you know where to find me.

No signature.

Miranda combed through the pile, looking for more postcards, heartbeat pounding in her ears.

Nothing.

Map of the Emporium, an Owl Drug Store menu. Matchbook from the Riviera restaurant. Small box of Hanukkah candles, half-empty. Go-a-Graf brochure on events for New Year's, a '39 guidebook to the Fair. Municipal Railway ticket. Ghirardelli chocolate wrapper from Treasure Island. Coupon for a dime off a new Max Factor lip crème.

Souvenirs of average, everyday existence, individual shreds of receipts and coupons adding up to one life, her life, Annie Learner's. Kind of paper junk that gets thrown out every three or six months when it's no longer useful and the memories attached no longer vivid enough to take up the room.

Small square envelope, thick and still sealed, caught her eye. She plucked it out from under the stern face of *Pacifica,* glaring from the cover of the Fair guidebook. Small typed letters at the bottom read GOLDEN GATE INTERNATIONAL EXPOSITION.

She recognized it as one of the mail envelopes for oversize souvenir matches, the kind that read A PAGEANT OF THE PACIFIC and were painted with an orange-and-purple scene of San Francisco.

Penciled writing scrawled across the envelope, different, rougher hand than the postcards.

Happy Dreams, Annie. P.S. Found my license, too.

She held it between her gloved fingers, film scenes unrolling, spiral of images, spinning, speeding, goddamn kaleidoscope, it's the wheel of fortune, ladies and gentlemen, where she stops nobody knows, and thirty-six, thirty-six is the winner.

Of swan boats and straw-covered Roma wine bottles, fights and late nights and squeaking bedsprings, sweaty backs and damp sheets, sweet and pungent. Smell of diesel from Market Street, liquor sign flashing red against the clothes on the floor.

Of a swelling stomach and worries about

money, fear and the stench of stigma, mud baths in Napa Valley, time to think, time to plan.

Of trust and a fuck and an ice pick at the neck. Of a finger dipped in blood, last act of humiliation.

Raped with words.

Miranda lifted a trembling hand to wipe the sweat from her forehead.

Goddamn room was too stuffy.

She picked up one of the photos and the matches, placed them next to the two postcards inside the *Chadwick's.* Shut the door quietly behind her.

Edwina opened her door as though she'd been waiting by it.

"So? Got any more for me?"

Miranda squeezed past her into the cramped room. "An extra ten, if you answer some questions."

The old lady gestured toward the old-fashioned horsehair sofa. Miranda perched on the end. Musty, heavy curtains and dark wood and burgundy, knick-knacks and scrapbooks. Felt like she was drowning.

Edwina picked up two cut-glass tumblers, still cloudy with evaporated liquor. Walked, uneven and crablike, into the small kitchen, door swinging behind her. Brief sound of running water. Came back with something clear inside each.

"All I got is gin. You want some?"

Miranda nodded, didn't look too closely at the glass. The old lady sat down, swallowed by an enormous red velvet chair, circa 1900.

"Ask your questions, girlie. My program's comin' on in a few minutes."

"You follow the case in the papers?"

Edwina sipped the gin, grunted. " 'Course I did. They was wrong, the goddamn flatfoots."

Miranda crouched forward, left arm stiff against her stomach. "What makes you say that?"

The blue eyes were shrewd and calculating. "I'm old, girlie. But that don't mean I'm stupid. I know this city, I know my tenants. Just like I knew my cues back before San Francisco decided to get religion. Goddamn quake scared the bastards somethin' bad, you know how hard it was to get a good job afterward? Sure, Pacific Street was OK, but unless you was George M. Cohan you couldn't get a goddamn booking, not for any decent money. . . . Where was I?"

"You said the cops were wrong."

"Yeah. Well, let me tell you somethin'. Annie Learner wasn't no tramp like they made

289

her out to be. She liked a good time, who don't? I didn't give a damn if she was a Jew — back in my day, we didn't care what you were, Jew, Mohammedan, or a Hindu princess, so long as you knew your lines and when to raise your skirt for the can-can."

She swallowed a large gulp of the gin, shaking her head. "Kid worked hard. Sure, last few months she's been seein' a lot of men. Who can blame her? She weren't gettin' any younger. Figured she'd find her Breckinridge, God help th' poor little thing."

The gin tasted like Prohibition hootch, and it was making Miranda's eyes water. She set the glass on an ebony end table. Time to play a hunch.

"Edwina — was Annie gone last April for a week or so?"

The old lady snorted. "Week? More like five or six. Sent her boyfriend over with the rent on time, though. Surprised she kept her job, but them Emporium people are OK. Goddamn understanding, if you ask me."

Miranda tried to keep her voice deliberate, unexcited. "She had a regular boyfriend back then?"

Edwina sputtered gin on the pink robe. "I thought you was a detective, lady. 'Course she had a boyfriend. The poor bastard they

got locked up in San Quentin. Gerry Duggan."

NINETEEN

Miranda's hands were trembling. She reached into the purse and shook out the half-smoked stick from earlier. The old lady watched, adding, "That ain't a bad idea," and held out her palm for more. Miranda gave her the rest of the pack. Edwina slid them into her robe pocket.

"How long did they see each other?"

The old lady pulled out one of the cigarettes, lit it with a matchbook from the Bonita Meat Market on Fillmore. Tossed the used match and the matchbook back on the side table.

"They was serious. Figured they'd get married, though I told Annie not to get involved with cops. Went together maybe four, five months, off and on. Arguin', fightin', then makin' up again. You know how it is. That Duggan fella's got a bad temper. Slapped Annie around some. I advised her to throw the bastard out, but she weren't gonna listen to an old lady like me."

"Why don't you think he killed her?"

Edwina coughed in the middle of an inhale, waving Miranda back and glaring at her.

"Siddown, dearie. I just ain't used to these cheap smokes."

Coughs racked the old lady's thin frame while her stiff fingers and overlarge knuckles clutched at her robe like talons.

"Duggan's a mean bastard, no good and rotten, but he ain't a killer." She stopped, trying to catch her breath. "When Annie came back from Calistoga, she dropped him like a hot potato. I figure she got some sense — 'bout time, too."

Edwina shook her head, clearing her throat with one last guttural rasp. "No, he ain't the one. Threw him over last year, and if he was gonna do somethin' about it, he woulda then."

The old lady swirled her glass and tossed the rest of the gin to the back of her throat. Belched softly.

"Came around with his hat in his hands a coupla weeks ago, lookin' for her. I told him where he could go." She frowned. "Maybe I weren't so smart."

Miranda spoke quickly. "Duggan came by here?"

"Beat me all to hell. Figured they was over and done with. I knew they were finished on her end." She raised her face, patchwork pink and white, pointed chin softening a little. "Bastard looked about as sad as an organ grinder's monkey, poor goddamn slob — long, hairy arms an' all."

Information was coming fast and thick, overwhelming her. Duggan as brutal, dirty cop she recognized. Duggan as lover would take more than a glass of ten-year-old gin to make sense.

"Edwina . . . could you tell me what happened on Sunday?"

The old woman took a cautious puff on the Chesterfield. Gray ash dropped off on the Oriental carpet, nearly monochrome with stains and age.

"Mrs. Jenkins from number nine comes round, crowin' at me about Annie again, she ain't heard Annie go to work, Annie's got too many fellas, Annie's this and Annie's that. Goddamn busybody." Flashed a glance at Miranda. "Nosin' in Annie's business is the best time she's had since her husband died."

The old lady stared at the stick burning between her fingers. "Found her lyin' there on the bed. Called the cops. Took me down to the Hall with 'em to identify her."

Tiny bed, cramped room, smell of *Soir de Paris*. Pretty girl, dark hair, red splotches spreading, staining the torn-off dress from the Emporium sale.

Drip-drop. Drip-drop.

The landlady coughed again, deep rattle. Pinched out the cigarette, dropped it on the table next to the matchbooks.

Miranda asked: "Why'd she stop seeing Duggan?"

Edwina shrugged. "Annie wouldn't tell me. Got some ideas, though. This trip she made — he didn't know she was up at Nance's. He let that out when he came to pay her rent. She told him she was goin' to see her mother in Walla Walla."

Miranda looked up sharply. "Why? What's wrong with Nance's?"

The wrinkled old woman raised a partially bald eyebrow. "Nance's? Resort for high-falutin slobs that wanna wallow like pigs in mud. Not the place for the kind of people Annie was."

Edwina rubbed her nose, veins standing out like a road map. Leaned forward, narrow shoulders hunched, blue eyes sharp on Miranda.

"She was there for weeks. So where the

hell did she get the money, huh? And why go at all? Figure that one out, girlie. Figure that one out."

Edwina tilted the glass so that any remaining drops of gin would trickle down her throat. Miranda stubbed out her cigarette in a shell-shaped ceramic ashtray, faded gold sticker reading MADE IN SAN DIEGO. Laid her business card on the couch. Counted out a ten and five singles.

The old lady's eyes shone with pleasure. "You ain't much of a detective, honey, but you're a real lady. Thanks."

Wry smile. "I'm working for Duggan's lawyer."

"Yeah? Well, I hope you get him off. Like I said, the poor bastard was crawling around here a few weeks back."

"You think she went up there to meet someone else?"

Edwina looked up at Miranda, voice pointed. "My program's comin' on, dearie."

Miranda stood up. "Thanks. I'll let myself out." The old lady nodded, her mind on NBC Red. Turned the knob on the Philco.

"Did you tell all this to the police?"

Edwina was staring at the radio as if the tubes would warm quicker that way.

"Hell, no. I just answered what they asked me — if Duggan were sniffin' around and if he knew Annie. And I ain't heard a word from 'em since, 'cept to keep the place locked up. Which I do, exceptin' for lady detectives, a' course." She threw a grin up at Miranda, her eyes falling back to the radio with a shake of the head. "I guess her mother's comin' down to fetch her things."

The creamy tones of a soap seller started to ooze through the speakers. Edwina bent forward, back hunched and round like the seashell ashtray on the ebony table. Miranda closed the door behind her softly.

Noon sirens were hitting a high note. Edwina's gin was still burning in her stomach.

Miranda walked to Market and Gough, couple of streetcars rumbling by the McRoskey Mattress building across the street. She yawned, staring at the beds in the window. Yellow neon gleamed dully across and down Market, beckoning her to Page.

The Bohemian Garden boasted twenty-four-hour service and beer on draft — the "kind you like." Bright, colorful paintings of happy-go-lucky Czech maidens dancing against a snow-covered backdrop decorated an exterior wall.

She walked under the green awning into a long, low restaurant, dark counter crowded with beefy men in work clothes drinking flat lager out of glass mugs. Some of them looked up when she walked in; some of the eyes lingered. One of them clambered off the stool with effort and waddled over with intent.

"You want somethin', Miss?"

She held his eyes up. "Yeah. Lunch."

He grunted, waddled to the counter, and shouted to the double doors at the far end, "Millie — customer!" then crawled back on his stool, work done for the afternoon. A tall, gaunt peroxide blonde with two messy braids hurried out from the kitchen, tomato sauce on her chin. She saw Miranda, grabbed a menu. Gestured for her to follow.

The odor of stale beer chased them to a small table with a faded, flowered tablecloth. The waitress slapped the menu down, looked up without much hope. "We got a special today."

"Other than beer?" Miranda looked around the empty dining room.

Millie shoved a braid behind her shoulder. "Roast pork, potatoes and sauerkraut, beer or coffee, apple pie for dessert. Thirty-five cents."

"Make it a special. Coffee, please — strong."

The blonde nodded, relieved that Miranda

wasn't going to demand anything she couldn't give her.

One of the men in dungarees and a hard hat got up from his stool and dropped a nickel in the jukebox. Andrews Sisters warbled out from the speakers. *Roll out the bar-rel, we'll have a bar-rel of fun . . .*

"Beer Barrel Polka." Only thing Bohemian in the joint.

Miranda picked at the pork, more boiled than roasted. The food explained why they depended on the beer. The beer couldn't explain anything.

Coffee was black enough to matter and helped melt Edwina's gin. She could use a couple of shots of bourbon right now, but she and her arm would have to wait for the office bottle.

Miranda shoved aside the blue-striped lunch plate and plunged a fork in the apple pie. Doughy in the middle, but the filling was sweet and tasted good with the coffee. She stared ahead into the dark greenness of the restaurant, at the faded Czechoslovakian flag still flying above the door.

Opened the second and last pack of Chesterfields in her purse and shook out a stick, lighting it with a pack of green-and-white matches on the table.

She thought of Nance's Sanitarium and the pencil check next to the Hotel Potter, the postcard, unsigned, from the Hollywood Show in Annie's desk.

I don't think I could have come back without your help. We are more than sisters.

Thought of two women, both missing from work for a few weeks. Same time, maybe same place. One, a blond dreamer from Lima, Ohio, eyes on *Modern Screen* and the Beverly Hills Hotel, working in a peep show on Treasure Island. The other, a young woman from Walla Walla, Washington, another dreamer in her way, this time of marriage and settling down and Hanukkah candles in her desk.

Miranda blew a stream of smoke, watching it curl and drift toward the open door. Rubbed out the cigarette, dug out fifty cents for Millie.

Hotel Potter was on the way back to the office, at Ninth and Mission.

Where Pandora used to live.

Run-down neighborhood. Cheap hotels and apartment houses squatting around the corner from the Civic Center, symbol of

San Francisco resilience.

The Hotel Potter was a three-story brick building, no uglier than its neighbors. Couple of little boys were sitting on the stoop of a single-story wood house, paint peeling, smell of cabbage curling out the window and turning her stomach. They stared at her, no curiosity.

She dropped the Chesterfield on the sidewalk. Walked under the faded awning into a dark closet of a lobby, making her way to the hotel desk. Thin, middle-aged bald man in a sleeveless T-shirt sat on a stool behind a scarred wooden counter, reading *The Saturday Evening Post*. Air was still and overly warm. He looked up when she entered.

"Help you with something, Miss?"

Eyes were rheumy and moist and dropped down in little bags on his face. A Fatima burned between his lips.

Guess she didn't look like a customer. First compliment she'd gotten all day.

Miranda opened her wallet and pulled out two singles, slowly enough for him to notice, though her only competition was a wall calendar with a girl on her tiptoes who apparently didn't realize she was wearing a see-through bathing suit.

"I'd like to ask you about a former tenant.

Blond girl, pretty. Name was Pandora Blake."

The baggy eyes narrowed, forming deeper pockets on the bottom rim. "You a cop?"

She shook her head. Lifted up the two dollars. Rubbed them together.

His mouth turned upside down, eyes flicking back and forth between Miranda, the money, and a door on the left. Probably the manager. He was worried about a split.

She said smoothly: "If you can tell me what I need to know, I don't see why I'd need to talk to anyone else."

His shoulders relaxed a little. One more glance at number three before gesturing with his head toward a side office, on the right behind the counter.

Miranda followed, protecting her arm when she squeezed through the wooden gate.

The office was an extension of the exterior, drab, dingy, dirty. A small safe stood in the corner, couple of mismatched chairs tilting unevenly in front of a wooden desk.

She looked up at the ceiling, high enough to provide some air and maybe even thoughts of escape. Hope might have lingered for a time at the Hotel Potter, lost in a corner, buoyed by innocence and backstage bouquets. But eventually it would die from what they used to call a wasting disease, consumed by the dead air and the dead flies, the dead eyes of the man behind the counter, and the smell of cabbage from the house next door.

He scratched a pimple on the side of his neck, keeping an eye out on number three. Said nervously: "Whaddya wanna know?"

Miranda laid a dollar on the desk. "How long did Pandora live here?"

He eyed the money, made no move. " 'Bout a year. Apartment 5C. It's rented out again, so's I can't show it to you, so don't ask."

"She not show up for a while? Say, last April?"

The skinny man coughed, chest heaving. "Goddamn Fatimas — always do it to me." Caught his breath, stared at Miranda. "Funny you know about that. What'd you say your name was?"

"I didn't. But it's Miranda Corbie. I'm a private investigator."

He cracked a smile, back of his cheek sinking in on the right side where he was missing some teeth.

"You? A dame? Yeah . . . I think I've hearda you, at that." He glanced down at the dollar, voice more confident. "You can do better than two bucks."

Miranda flicked the second dollar on the table. "You're lucky to be getting this. I could look up the information for myself." Glanced toward apartment three. "Maybe the hotel manager would appreciate the money."

"Not so hasty, lady." He coughed again, spit up something in a soiled yellow handkerchief yanked out of his back pocket. Glared at her over the cotton. Snatched the bills and stuffed them in his pocket along with the handkerchief.

"OK, so the girl's gone for a few weeks. What's it to me? That fat slob Mertz gets all hot and bothered about it, not me. I figured she'd be good for the dough, what with the sharpie who was takin' her out nights."

"Steady joe?"

"Slick-lookin' egg he was. All pinstripes and pressed pants, smelled like a skirt, real sweet. But he didn't pay, no sirree. Pandora sent a friend around, some other dame, hootchy-kootchy brunette."

He tried to leer. "Like you, sister. Nice to look at. Not that Pandora weren't, but hell, she kept the stars in her eyes, poor kid. Even with this crooked gee she was seein'."

Miranda fished out one more dollar, tossed it on the desk. "You got a name?"

"Yeah. Walter Lodges. You can call me Walt."

Her lips curved in half a grin. "I meant the name of Pandora Blake's boyfriend, Walter."

He scratched the thin wisps of hair still clinging to the back of his scalp, mouth turned upside down in an effort to remember.

"I remember laughin', 'cause I figured he wasn't no good, and his name rhymed with somethin' funny . . . what was it? Something about leaving town." Scratched his side again, smell of perspiration making Miranda's nose wrinkle. "Can't remember so good. Maybe I can call you, if it comes back? Maybe get a little somethin' for it?"

She flipped a card. "Call me any time your memory comes back, Walter. There's an extra five in it if you can jump-start it by tomorrow."

He picked it up, reading the words aloud. " 'Private — Discreet.' " Looked up and grinned, tapping a freckle on his bald head. "Save me a sawbuck, sister — by tonight I'll be Mr. Memory."

Miranda nodded, feeling his eyes on her back as she hurried out of the Hotel Potter, odor of cabbage and sweat following her down to Market Street.

Twenty

She caught a number 8 White Front in front of the still grand and stately Hotel Whitcomb, former seat of government after the quake and fire. It looked benevolently on San Francisco's Civic Center with an aging pride, the prerogative of old architecture, while a party of tourists strolled out, dressed for Los Angeles and shivering. One of the wives was describing the scene in *San Francisco* when the dome crumbles, hoping to find Clark Gable.

Politicians and attorneys drove by in long, low cars, on their way to meetings with developers and factory owners to figure out who was next in line to get his. City Hall gleamed with old money, new money, money any way you liked it, testament to the city of the phoenix, the city that rose from the dead and came back twice as rich.

SAN FRANCISCO, O GLORIOUS CITY OF OUR HEARTS, THAT HAST BEEN TRIED

AND NOT FOUND WANTING, read the inscription inside the rotunda. GO THOU WITH LIKE SPIRIT TO MAKE THE FUTURE THINE.

Or at least make money thine. Before '34, the like spirit was the kind you could drink, not so holy. And plenty of money was made, O Lord, liquor and gambling and easy women, the eternal foundations of San Francisco, shake the rest down, O Lord, and those will remain.

Silver may come and silver may go, but sin is everlasting.

Just ask the Lima and Lanza families. And a man named Benedetti.

Car was about half-empty. Two extra pennies were still hard to come by, especially when you could ride a Municipal Rail for an even nickel, but Miranda liked the Market Street Railway cars. They were made in San Francisco, seemed tougher and more durable than their city-owned rivals.

She sank into the first empty seat. Man in a soiled brown fedora behind her leaned forward, tapped her on the shoulder.

"You're smart to ride the White Fronts, lady. You hear about the hullabaloo with the Municipals this morning?"

She could tell he was a talker, but there

weren't too many stops between Ninth and the Monadnock, and maybe he could take her mind off the pain in her arm. She gave him an encouraging look.

"What happened?"

He preened under her interest, yellowed teeth bared in a gloat of appreciation. About forty-five, thick mustache, dirty fingernails. Still figured he was a ladies' man. Smelled like stale rye.

"These posters on the cars. Market Street Railway's got a few, too, but the city cars got 'em all over. There was some who was figurin' it's propaganda, especially with Belgium and France an' everything. They been protestin'. Slowin' up the cars — you never get nowhere fast."

The car rolled to a stop at Sixth Street and a couple of young women with shopping bags from Hale Brothers stepped inside, arguing about what shoes to wear to the Fair on Saturday.

He folded his arms on top of her seat, gave her a slow eye up and down. "You look like a smart dame, sister. Extra two cents saves you time and trouble."

"What do the posters say?"

He rubbed his nose. "Somethin' about the Yanks not coming, patriotism and peace, an' all. Couple of committees sponsored 'em."

"They are sponsored by the San Francisco Youth Council and the San Francisco Coordinating Council for Peace."

Miranda looked up into the red face of a stout, middle-aged dowager with horn glasses and a beard. A pale woman dressed in a loose-knit sweater sat beside her, hands folded. She gave a vague smile to Miranda.

"Patriotism *is* peace. What happens overseas is none of our business, and those people complaining are a pack of warmongers. Just like the president." She raised her lips, revealing a set of large false teeth. "I hope you'll both be coming to the Memorial Day Peace Meeting on Friday."

The man slouched in his seat, cowed. Mumbled something about a job out of town.

Miranda tugged on the wire to signal her stop. Turned around and studied the woman, from the bulky black dress to the chin shoved forward, bristling with a few gray and black hairs. Brown eyes, flat and cold behind the glass, full of righteous and unwavering certainty.

Miranda stood up. Spoke softly.

If ye break faith with us who die

309

We shall not sleep, though poppies grow
In Flanders Fields.

The dowager snorted, double chin trembling, as she jerked her head toward the opposite window. There were tears in the eyes of the small, pale woman beside her.

Miranda stepped off the car in front of the Monadnock. Trembling again, goddamn it. Sighed and relit the cigarette she'd saved from the Bohemian Garden.

Scanned Market Street, from the giant Mobile gas sign down through the Harvard Billiard Parlor on Kearny. Her eyes rested on the DR. WILLETT — CHIROPRACTOR sign across the street on the De Young Building, "Free Examination" lit up in yellow. Made her think of something, but she couldn't remember what. Someone inside the Harvard fed the juke, and she could hear the Andrews Sisters swinging "Billy Boy," most of the chorus drowned out by the streetcars and car honks on Market Street.

Oh, where have you been, Billy Boy, Billy Boy . . .

Billy Boy's pinned down at a beach called Dunkirk, Ma, can't bake him that cherry pie after all. Guess he didn't get the memo about the Memorial Day Peace Meeting, guess he didn't catch the lecture at the Tower of Peace and Temple of Religion.

But then Billy Boy's not American.

Billy Boy's a Frenchman, watching his farmland raped by tanks and gutted by bombs, impregnable Maginot Line, pride of the peacekeepers, failing, failing, crushed in thunder and lightning and rain of the blitzkreig.

Billy Boy's a Belgian, tiny country overrun, king fled, crown no longer golden but a tarnished, baser metal.

Billy Boy's a Pole, last stand of last century's cavalry, men and horses charging tanks on a lush flat Polish field, green-and-red slaughterhouse. Stink of burned flesh, horses and men mangled, horse and rider one. Victims of a new century. A new war.

Poor goddamn patriots.

Patriots all.

Hoist the flag and let her fly, like true heroes do or die, send the word, send the word, over there . . .

Over there.

Miranda dropped the stub on the sidewalk, rubbing it out with the toe of her navy pump, steam from the sewers spewing street-level geysers in the cold summer air. She watched it disperse, swirling out over

Market Street, drifting across the blinking neon of the billiard parlor and the bars, surging and stretching through flower stands and taxi queues and into the monochrome gray above her. Gray canopy, dome on the city, her city. Her battlefield.

Over here.

Johnny, get your gun, get your gun, get your gun, and Johnny listened, and he left her, left her in her own war three years later, left her to watch the world crumble under black leather jackboots, and she warned him, begged him, fought him, but he died anyway, left her to the beetles and the maggots and the flies, always the flies.

Left her to make her own way.

No one to watch over her.

And Johnny didn't finish his goddamn job, didn't matter if it was in Spain or San Francisco, you start something, you finish it, she learned that from the farmworkers she taught to read English, learned it from the Italians waiting for Dungeness crab to fill their pots and make a good catch, learned it from the Chinese women laboring over intricate lace dresses in the tailor shops on Grant.

She'd finish it for him.

And she was a good soldier.

■ ■ ■ ■

Gladys was busy helping a portly man buy pipe tobacco while a couple of teenage girls combed the movie magazines for pictures of Tyrone Power.

Miranda surveyed the newspaper rack. There was an article about Duggan in the *Examiner,* about his supposed murder spree, about the "love nest" he violated, about his uncontrolled rage and jealousy.

So much for O'Meara, Larson, and Dill, fucking Winken, Blinken, and Nod.

Nothing about her shooting accident. Murdered nudies packed 'em in all right, good for business, make the Chamber of Commerce happy happy happy, with all those couples and families coming out to see the West like they did in '39. But gunfire on the Gayway was too much like the goddamn war overseas, and they could hear about that for free. Besides, someone might get hurt and sue, Fiesta Days over, end of *Pacifica*. No more chimes for the Tower of the Sun.

Duggan was sixth-page material, sharing space with a paragraph describing the discovery of a body in the Bay, this time a thirty-year-old man named Eduardo Scorsone. No report of foul play, no specifics.

Gladys was still trying to please the fat man in the derby, sounding weary from pulling down tin after tin of tobacco. Miranda noticed how he ogled her friend's hips and ass, mouth open, sweat on his forehead, as she reached for the dusty tobacco on the top shelf.

She walked over while Gladys set a big blue tin of Edgeworth Tobacco on the counter, wiping a wilted blond curl off her forehead.

"Heya, Miri. Be with you in a minute."

The fat man cleared his throat, looking down nervously at the array of tobacco tins, square shape, round shape, rectangular, lined up in a row. Licked his lips. Peered back up at Gladys and asked in a hopeful voice, "You got any more?"

"Benedaret's Tobacco Shop is right down the street. 564 Market." Miranda leaned against the counter, facing him, and tapped the metal cover of the Edgeworth with her gloved finger.

"You want something better than this, I suggest you try Benedaret's."

He raised his eyebrows and made a puffing noise, eyes darting between the two women. Gladys grinned, sat back on her stool with her arms folded.

"Surely you don't speak from experience, Madame."

The "Madame" hurt, and so did her arm. Her lips curved in a dangerous smile.

"Plenty of experience. You want a cheap thrill, mister, go pay a quarter to Sally Rand. Otherwise buy your fucking tobacco and drift."

Red, white, red again. He dug out a cracked leather billfold from his back pocket, dropping a receipt and a ticket stub. Wordlessly threw a dollar on the counter, bent over to pick up his pocket contents, mumbled something about "keeping the change." Slunk quickly out the main doors. Gladys was shaking her head.

"Miri, you got nerve. I kinda figured he was clockin' me, but you know what they say — the customer is always right."

Miranda set the afternoon papers on the counter, wincing.

"The only people who say that never worked retail. You're selling magazines, candy, and tobacco, Gladdy. Nothing else."

The blonde brought over change from the five, peered into her face. "What's wrong? You hurt or something?"

"I'm OK. Got shot at last night on the Gayway."

Gladys's hands flew to her face, red nails

bright against her skin. "Jesus, Miri — I knew this was gonna be bad business. Are you really OK? Shouldn't you be in a hospital or somethin'?"

Miranda smiled. "I was lucky — got a graze on my upper arm."

Gladys shook her head. "Sugar, why can't you stick to the divorce cases? They're good bread and butter, and philandering husbands don't generally come at you with a gun." She cocked her head at her friend, her mouth stretching into a horizontal line of disapproval.

"I worry about you, Miri, I truly do."

Miranda squeezed her hand. "Likewise. You better ring me up for four rolls of Life Savers — Butter Rum."

Meyer's package was delivered as promised. She stepped into the elevator and ripped open one end, pulling out the cover sheet for Annie Learner's autopsy. A short, well-built man in a trench coat was trying to peer over at her reading material. She frowned, folding it in half.

Miranda got off on four with a young couple and two kids, boy and girl, and the man in the coat. She paused, popping two Life Savers in her mouth. The family turned to the right, and so did the trench coat.

Allen's door was open about a foot. She was glad to skip the formal routine, the well-bred, well-moneyed Pinkerton front office, country club of private investigation, secretary drenched in Chanel No. 5 and answering the phone like Norma Shearer. Plush carpet, detailed files on everything except Pinkerton himself, and probably more dirt than even Hoover could vacuum up.

Knocked on Allen's door. Not protocol to see him this way, but he didn't give a rat's ass about protocol.

Gruff voice answered "Yeah?" to the knock.

"You know it's me."

The door swung out. Allen was leaning back in his green leather office chair, leg still outstretched from kicking the door open. He grinned, shoved the cut-glass bowl of lemon drops toward the front of his desk.

"Have one. Helps the thinking process. How's the case coming? The papers make it sound not so good for your old friend Duggan."

She fell into the opposite chair. "Hell of a lot going on, Allen. Maybe too much. I got shot at last night —"

The Pinkerton half rose, and she waved him back down. "I'm OK, just got grazed on my left arm."

"Because of this Duggan case?" Allen's face rumpled into lines of concern that stretched all the way up to his bare, bald head, freckled and weathered like old leather.

Miranda crunched and swallowed the Life Savers. Plucked out two lemon drops.

"I don't know. Somebody doesn't want me nosing around. Or maybe just wants me dead. Martini's got a cousin from Chicago, Angelo Benedetti. No fucking angel, either, supposed to be splitting up from the Lanza mob."

"Christ, Miranda, you make more enemies in a year than most gumshoes do in ten."

She smiled. "It's a gift. I'm on a lead, though, a good one. You ever hear anything about Nance's Sanitarium up in Calistoga?"

Allen smoothed a hand over his scalp. "Doesn't ring a bell. Should it?"

Miranda frowned. "I don't know. It's a connection with Pandora Blake and Annie Learner."

His thick eyebrows rose higher. "That's a hell of a coincidence. Calistoga, huh? Plenty of bootleggers up there a few years ago. Wine, mostly, squirreled away in Napa and the Alexander Valley. What the hell have you gotten your nose into, Miri?"

She laughed and stood up. "Nothing I

318

can't handle, Old Mother Hubbard. If your encyclopedic files extend to any references on Nance's, I'd appreciate them."

Miranda turned to leave when the Pinkerton called her back.

"You ever follow up that Musketeer tip?"

She shook her head. "My friend Bente's going out there tonight. Don't have enough time to do it myself, and wish I did. Goddamn case keeps sprouting legs."

Allen grinned. Leaned back in his chair, hands behind his head. "Just cut 'em off at the knee, sister. But tell your friend to be careful. We got a tip that something's gonna pop around Memorial Day."

Miranda's voice was quick. "That's the day after tomorrow."

"Yeah, I know. I'm not workin' it, only feeding you what I hear. Stoolies are singing about Memorial Day and 'Onward, Christian Soldiers.' Looks like the Musketeers might be trying to unite the other swastika boys. So be careful."

"Thanks, Allen."

Miranda plucked three lemon drops from his bowl and slipped back into the hall of the Monadnock.

TWENTY-ONE

Angry horns screeching on Market outside, bass rumble of the trains. Ray Eberle and "The Nearness of You" drifting up from the Pig n' Whistle jukebox. Fragments of laughter, anger, anticipation. Low, soft cooing of pigeons.

No tan Ford. Just a gray white curtain. Bright white and fog blind.

Oh no, it's just the nearness of you . . .

Miranda's heel taps hit the floor with angry clicks. She started to pace.

Annie's abortion was anywhere from nine months to a year and a half ago, based on the scars, and that was a guess, the M.E. insisted. Meyer's note said he wasn't happy about being cornered, but fuck, they never were.

Tubal ligation at probably the same time, only possible if the pregnancy was early but still a bigger risk, especially since one of the operations was legal and the other one wasn't. Both were expensive. And both meant time in a hospital or at least a bed.

Miranda unwrapped two more Butter Rum Life Savers and picked up the M.E.'s report on Pandora. Read it twice.

Walked toward the window and back to the door, sucking on the Life Savers, siren screaming somewhere by Battery or Front, pigeons still cooing, sound of wings.

Dropped the papers on the desk, pages fluttering apart. Sank in the chair, holding the postcard addressed to Annie.

I wanted to let you know that I'm back to work. . . . We are more than sisters. . . . But if you ever need to talk, Annie, you know where to find me.

Woman, young enough to be Annie's sister, back to work and presumably on Treasure Island, since the card's from the Hollywood Show, happy fucking endings on the hour.

I know we agreed never to tell anyone and to try to forget, and I want to do that more than anything now.

Only thing you try to forget is pain. Happy memories are too goddamn hard to come by. Pain, misery, loss. Secrets and shame. Keep secret what you're ashamed of, what can get you in trouble. Deeper the pain, more quiet, more secrecy. More guilt.

Miranda took a deep breath, fought the urge to stick a Chesterfield in her mouth. Postcard was shaking in her hand.

No one will know about what happened, not even my mother.

Girl has a mother, evidently close to her, "even" my mother. Promise, not a threat, a pledge, an oath, and she's making Annie a sister, more than a sister. Depth of trust, sacred pact.

I don't think I could have come back without your help.

Goddamn it.

Miranda set the card on the desk, closed her eyes. Come back physically, come back to work, come back home, come back from some fucking prison of an abortion clinic run out of Calistoga and hiding behind bubbling mud baths and massages and physiotherapy? "Results in Health," the postcard claimed. What kind of fucking results for Pandora Blake?

She flipped quickly through the papers on

the desk until she found Annie's other postcard, the one from Nance's. Never sent.

So different from this one. No escape necessary.

Don't want you to worry. You're always so sorry after you get mad.

Edwina said Duggan smacked Annie around. And Miranda knew what he was capable of.

She closed her eyes again, saw Duggan with the sad monkey face scrunched up tight, red rage, red remorse.

Sorry, so sorry, he'd sniffle, and maybe mean it, maybe she was different from the whore that killed his brother, from the women he arrested down on Turk Street or Hyde, the whores that serviced him in Chinatown alleys, blow job if you keep me out of the can, mister, and sometimes he'd take them up on it, confession afterward, three Hail Marys, Gerald, and you're done.

Maybe Annie was different.

P.S. Don't lose your license again, you might need to come get me. Love always, your Annie

Miranda shoved a newspaper aside and

stared down at the souvenir matchbook from Annie's apartment.

Happy Dreams, Annie.

Same man? Same Duggan? Same dirty bastard who tried to break her last year? Same man squatting in a San Quentin prison cell for murdering Annie Learner?
Back to the card.

Just need a few days off to think about everything. I'll write soon.

Not the words of a woman looking for an abortion.
Not the words of a woman who'd never be able to have kids.
Miranda shook her head and held the card up in the daylight from the window, examining the writing. No sign of a hurry, no evidence of dictation. Just a postcard Annie kept but never sent, preserving a memory.
Why? Why didn't she mail it to Duggan if it was an innocent vacation, time away from a lovers' quarrel? And why fucking preserve it if it memorialized the loss of a child, loss of all potential children? What the two women shared was something not to be spoken of, not to be told.

Sisters in pain. Nothing to be remembered.

Miranda passed a shaking hand over her forehead. Gave in and opened her desk drawer, found a half-empty package, and shook out a stick. Lit it with the desk lighter, drawing deep. Stared straight ahead, unblinking.

Reached for the phone.

"I don't give a fuck whether he's the head M.E. or not, Meyer. If Fortescue autopsied Pandora Blake, he either overlooked something or neglected to add it to the report. Something like an abortion. Lucky for us he wasn't the M.E. on Annie."

Her attorney grunted. "Annie Learner and Pandora Blake, both missing from work for the same period, proven to know each other, both sharing a painful event, both murdered. We'll need more than postcards, Miranda."

"I'm driving up to Calistoga this afternoon. What I need from you are bank receipts and phone records and some goddamn information about whether Pandora's body showed signs of an abortion."

Meyer sounded tired, usual jaunty verve conspicuous in its absence. "I'll see what I can do. Mr. Duggan's arraignment is next week. Brady won't entertain a plea bargain of any kind."

"Why should he? He's got Duggan where he wants him — and the bastard's cooperating in his own destruction." She tapped the Chesterfield in the ashtray, frowning at the postcards.

"Pandora and Annie were in contact recently, or why else would Duggan go to Artists and Models? He was trying to see Annie — and probably approached Pandora because he found out about what was between them, what they shared." The cigarette wasn't helping her hands or her arm or her goddamn nerves. She rubbed it out on the tarnished spot and left it in the tray.

"I'll arrange for any records to be sent over. But why not visit Mr. Duggan and speak with him first?"

"Not until I know more. Duggan's in a frame and he doesn't want out. I think he blames himself for Annie."

Meyer made a noise. "The charges make no sense. Where is the second murder weapon? He admits to picking up the ice pick and dropping it in a trash can. And if it's a *drame de la jalousie,* as the papers would like us to believe, then how did Mr. Duggan happen to find another ice pick and

Fucking when Irish eyes are smiling, and they only smiled when dreaming about her, shoving her in a corner, making her something she wasn't and never could be, not his fucking wild Irish rose or anyone else's.

She glanced at the clock: 1:37 P.M. Lowered her voice, tried to make it businesslike.

"I've got a lead. I think Pandora and Annie were at Nance's Sanitarium together. I'm hiring a driver and heading up there around four. From my office. If you want to come, meet me here."

Silence on the other end, machine-gun beat of typewriters in the background.

She said it evenly. "Or not. Your choice. Take care of yourself, Rick."

The phone clanged when she dropped the receiver in the cradle.

Miranda stood at the window, smoke curling into Market Street from the Chesterfield in her hand. Ran her fingers through her hair, glad not to be wearing a hat.

She remembered how they smelled, furtive eyes, sweat on their necks and in their palms when they looked at her. She your best escort, Mrs. Laroche? Want the best, gotta look good to the board, don't you know, and please make the bill out to my business address only.

Lick of the lips, quick breaths in and out. Anticipation. Send her up to the Ritz, to the Huntington, to the Top of the Mark.

And Dianne's voice would purr back, hint of southern aristocracy, Spanish moss, and mint juleps dripping from her tongue. Anything you need, gentlemen. Anything you need. "Mrs." just a suggestion, an honorific for the tearoom, Earl Grey at four P.M., gentlemen, though I'm sure you'd prefer the countess.

Laughter all around. Franklin, clear the tea china, it's time for dancing. Black man served, watched, and waited, Howard graduate, knowing his lines.

Then cleared throats, startled, and some of them turned away, couldn't stand to look in her eyes. Others would ask her to dance, pressed close, her body bruised from over-size bellies, crushed against her, thighs and what was between them desperate for contact.

And one of them would choose her, not minding the eyes, relishing the challenge, enjoying the pain. Sometimes they'd be tall enough, young enough, fit enough, to make her forget, to get lost in acceptance, in reception, to drift away for a time, unheeding, because it wasn't her, and what happened didn't matter.

Never touched her. There was nothing to touch.

And then there was Phil, who felt sorry for her, wanted her too much, and wanted to protect her. Couldn't go out with Phil, could dance with him, serve him tea, but he was a cop and a decent man who drank too much and wanted her too much, and that was all he'd ever be.

She remembered when she saw Rick. First time after New York.

Lotta's Fountain, where survivors meet.

She remembered how he made her feel. How he made her remember.

The next day she quit Dianne's.

Miranda closed her eyes and inhaled, holding the smoke in her mouth, feeling the nicotine course through her body, finally exhaling in a stream through the fourth-floor window.

The answering service listed four messages, two of which were responses to her ads. One from a Mrs. Beringer, shrill voiced, forty-five, worried that her husband was unfaithful, another from Mrs. Dalton, missing a Chinese jade parure. High-toned Boston accent and a past spent in Pittsburgh.

She wrote down the names and numbers, hoping to string them along for an appointment next week, after she'd proven Duggan's innocence and found the murderer and incidentally rescued the fucking British Army.

The other message was from Rick. Last one was from Lucinda.

"Read it to me again, please."

Girl working for the Teleservice Answering Company spoke slowly and carefully, despite the swollen adenoids.

"Yes, Miss Corbie. Here it is. 'Need to talk. Am confused. Please call. Lucinda Gerber.' "

Miranda blew out a deep breath in frustration. "It's not like a fucking telegram, she doesn't have to pay per word. . . ."

"Sorry, Miss? I didn't quite catch —"

"Nothing. Thanks." She slammed the receiver in the cradle, bell jangling in protest. Her hand poised above it, waiting for the connection to break.

Picked it up again, hitting the receiver until an operator came on. Pawed through her purse contents for her *Chadwick's Street Guide*, ignoring the sharp sting in her arm, and opened it to the William Rudko Valet ad in the back.

"Lucinda Gerber, please — any number at the La Salle Apartments, 650 Post?"

The operator was about fifty, probably the

supervisor, with a tone that presumed it was always correct. "I'm sorry, Madame, but there is no one listed by that name and that address."

"You mean she doesn't have her own phone number."

Raised voice, peevish, as if Miranda were hard of hearing. "I'm sorry, Madame, as I said, no one is listed by that name and that address."

"Just give me the number for the La Salle, then."

"One moment, Madame." Frosty silence while the operator dwelled on how much easier her job would be if only people paid attention. "I'm sorry, Madame, there is no phone listed at that address."

Miranda swore, and the operator immediately clicked off. Miranda kept hitting the cradle until another one came on.

"Is there a number for the Artists and Models concession on Treasure Island?"

This one sounded less like the Legion of Decency, circa 1692. Still, Miranda didn't hold out much hope. Schwartz was a cheap bastard. Even the Nude Ranch paid for a phone, just dial FAirgrounds 1224 and breathe hard.

The operator came back on. "I'm sorry, Madame, but —"

"Yeah, yeah, I know." She thought of Ozzie. "How about the Aquacade?"

Billy Rose needed phones to keep Tanforan and Bay Meadows in business. The woman at the switchboard sighed, and Miranda could hear her paging through paper, then, "One moment, please," while she plugged in the right line.

Ringing. Brooklyn accent picked up after five or six times. Out of breath.

"Yeah? I mean, Billy Rose's Aquacade, how may I direct your call?"

Miranda grinned. Wondered what she'd been doing when the call came through.

"I need to speak to Ozzie Mandelbaum, please. He's an Aquadonis. It's urgent."

The girl on the other end yawned. "It always is, sister, 'specially if you're an Aquabelle. Hold on."

Miranda waited, hoping Ozzie was at practice early today. Lucinda knew something about Calistoga, whatever Pandora told her when she asked her friend to go to the Hotel Potter with the rent money, the exotic brunette, impressing Walter with her "hootchy-kootchy" looks.

Miranda picked up the autopsy report on Pandora again, reading over it until Ozzie's voice made her jump.

"Hello? Hello?" Sounded as though he'd

been running.

"Sorry, Ozzie, it's Miranda Corbie. Didn't mean to worry you."

She could hear the smile on his face. "Oh — Miss Corbie. I'm so glad it's you. What can I help you with?"

"Lucinda doesn't have a phone at her apartment, and I need to speak with her. Is she there?"

He sounded surprised. "I don't know, Miss Corbie. I haven't seen her all day, if that's what you mean. Lu usually meets me at night, before or after one of her shows."

"Listen — can you have her call me, please? I'll be out of town tonight, but tell her to leave me a number where I can reach her tomorrow morning. It's important."

"Sure thing, Miss Corbie." He hesitated, somber again. "Is this — is this about Pan, Miss Corbie?"

Miranda reached for the pack of cigarettes on her desk. One more stick.

"I don't know, Ozzie. Don't forget — have her call me."

She could hear girls giggling in the background and what sounded like the receptionist yelling at Ozzie for dripping water on the floor.

"All right, Miss Corbie. And thanks."

She hung up and frowned, staring at the phone.

Sharp knock on the door.

She opened the bottom drawer and lifted out the .22, slipping the safety off with her thumb. Rubbed out the Chesterfield. Cradled the .22 in her lap.

Said in a voice loud enough to be heard: "Come in."

The door opened wide enough for a man to walk in.

Short, well built, and in a trench coat.

TWENTY-TWO

Man from the elevator, the one nosy about her reading material. He stood in the doorway, smiling, gray fedora dangling from his fingers, crooked red feather stuck sideways in the ribbon. About thirty-eight, thirty-nine. Small brushy mustache. Glint of gold on his ring finger.

She forced a smile on her face. "What can I do for you?"

He held the hat outstretched, gesturing to the chairs in front of her desk. "Mind if I sit down, Miss Corbie?"

Her fingers clutched the .22 in her lap.

"Can't say until I know why you're here. I usually don't accept walk-in cases."

He chuckled. Ran strong-looking fingers through curly dark hair flecked with gray. Sat down on the hard chair in front of her. Body compact and muscular, around five nine. Twirled the fedora back and forth. Smiling.

"My name's David Fisher. Inspector David Fisher." He opened the trench coat, flashing a city-issued .38 in a shoulder holster, red suspenders, and a white shirt in need of starch. Pulled out a brown leather wallet crammed with business cards and old receipts and opened it to show his badge, eyes on Miranda. He smelled like cigarettes and Ivory soap.

She let out a breath, shoulders relaxed again, electric shocks through her arm. Lifted up the .22 and set it on her desk. He raised his eyebrows, smile still in place.

"You expecting other company, Miss Corbie?"

Miranda reached for the Chesterfield pack on her desk. Empty. She unraveled the last two Butter Rums.

"Excuse me, Inspector, but why are you here? The Pandora Blake and Annie Learner case is closed . . . and we're working opposite sides of it."

He nodded, coat still open. Pulled out a pack of Old Golds. Phil's brand.

Said, "Mind if I smoke?" and she shook her head.

He lit the stick with a matchbook. "Want one?"

"No thanks. I'm still waiting for an answer."

He drew down the stick, looking toward the open window. Church bells chimed twice south of Market. He cracked a smile, blew the smoke out through his nose and mouth.

"Those homicides are considered closed, yes. But some of us don't like how it's been played. Second reason, Miss Corbie, is that you were shot at last night. In case you didn't notice, that's illegal in San Francisco. Hell, it's illegal in the whole state." He grinned, leaning forward, tapping ash into the Tower of the Sun ashtray.

"I think in my case the department will make an exception."

He broke out into actual laughter, right hand resting on his knee, left still dangling the hat. Miranda wasn't used to cheerful, merry cops, and the Life Savers tasted like shit.

She walked to the safe. Shook out two decks of Chesterfields from the carton she'd stashed, shoved the rest toward the back, and slammed it shut.

He smiled, reached into his coat pocket, and threw her a matchbook. She caught it in the air with her right hand.

He said easily, "Light 'em with that."

She looked down at the matchbook in her hand.

Black Cat Café. Same as Flamm's matches in her safe, "Mickey wants to see you . . ."

Miranda yanked her head up to Fisher, eyes narrowed.

"What's your goddamn game, Inspector? Because right now, I don't like it so much."

He sighed. "I've been accused of dramatic flair. Maybe that's not the best approach. Cards on the table?"

Miranda sat down behind the large oak desk, Weinstein's special, big enough to buy time with bad customers and cops with a fairy tale to sell.

"You're the one who's dealing."

"Fair enough." He deposited more ash in the tray, eyes darting toward the papers on her desk.

Miranda reached across with both arms, fuck the shoulder, gathering most of the documents in a lopsided pile, anchored under the .22. The cop watched her, smile growing. Then leaned forward, lines on his face falling downward, more serious.

"A man named Eduardo Scorsone was shot and killed last night with a .22." He nodded toward the pistol on her desk. "Body was found on the rocks below the parking lot on Treasure Island. He was carrying a .22 pistol, from which two bullets had been fired."

"Let me guess — not the pistol that killed him."

Fisher nodded again, crushing the Old Gold stub in the ashtray. "But we think one of the two fired was aimed at you."

She settled back in the chair. "Lucky for me, only a graze. What's your point?"

"Miss Corbie, don't you want to know who shot you?"

"Sure, Inspector. I'd like to know who shot me. I'd also like to know who stabbed Pandora Blake and Annie Learner, and why our oh-so-noble crusading D.A. is railroading Duggan straight to the Quentin gas chamber. While we're at it, I wouldn't mind knowing how the goddamn Maginot Line turned into a picket fence, and if the Allied army's gonna live past Memorial Day. Let me know if you come up with any fucking answers."

She ripped open a deck, lit a stick with the One-Touch. Waited for the smoke to warm her lungs. Grabbed her shaking left arm with her right hand and braced her back against the padded leather.

"They told me about you. They were right."

"I was an escort, Inspector. I've heard all the lines."

Fisher hunched at the edge of the wooden

seat, hat dangling between his knees.

Reminded her of Gonzales.

She blew a stream of smoke toward the opposite corner of the room. Waited.

He took a deep breath. "OK, here it is. There's been some talk that maybe you killed Scorsone."

Her lips curved upward. "After I was shot or before? I was in the hospital with Gillespie after the bullet hit me. He drove me home. Before that, I was working on the case I was hired to work on. Which was the only reason I was there."

She tapped some ash in the tray.

"Of course, maybe somebody thinks I shot him and then he shot at me. And then he dragged himself across the entire Gayway to the parking lot, where he threw himself on the rocks, waiting for the waves like the fucking Little Mermaid."

Fisher threw his head back and erupted in laughter again, dropping his fedora. Miranda raised an eyebrow, wondering if this was some sort of new police interrogation tactic. He bent down to pick up the hat, still chuckling.

"Actually, Miss Corbie, some people would like to think you killed him and then were shot by one of his confederates. Scorsone is — was — a dropper from Chicago."

Goddamn it. Chicago.

She pointed the cigarette at him, smoke curling from the bright red tip.

"Who's trying to set me up?"

He held up his hand as if waving her back. "It's just talk, Miss Corbie. I'm not here to arrest you."

Another tremor passed through her arm as she brought the stick to her lips. Her eyes never left the cop.

"Talk can kill people, Inspector."

Fisher nodded, looking down at the fedora and twirling it around his finger, red feather split and splayed against the dirty black ribbon. Stopped abruptly, almost crushing the hat between his two large hands.

"That's why I'm here. Some of us think Duggan's getting a bum rap. Pressure, Miss Corbie. Some of it's aimed at you."

"I'm used to it."

"We think this time it's because of Duggan."

Miranda surveyed him critically. "Who's 'we'?"

He shrugged. "Gillespie. Regan. Gonzales." Noticed her look of surprise. "Gonzales stays in touch — keeps his options open."

Fisher looked up, then away, then found something to examine on one of his fingernails.

"Phil, too. He still plays poker Friday nights."

Miranda felt the blood in her face, kept her eyes steady. She blew a smoke ring, watching it unravel like a spiderweb, torn apart by wind off Market Street. Sound of wings from the open window. Cooing.

"I worked with Inspector Gonzales on the Takahashi murder in February. And I've known Phil a long time. He helped me with one of my first cases as a detective."

"Yeah — the Incubator Babies. I've been reading up on you."

The Chesterfield was burning her fingers. She dropped it in the tray.

"All right, Inspector. I appreciate the fact that a small group of San Francisco police officers believe I'm innocent. Relatively speaking, of course. I still want to know why you think Scorsone has anything to do with me — and why you're here."

Fisher nodded, thinking it over and taking his time. Sat with his back against the hard wooden chair and crossed his legs, shaking his foot up and down like a fidgety kid. Eyes roamed the office, coming back to rest on Miranda, on the papers in front of her.

"I'll lay it on the line. Scorsone is part of the Angelo Benedetti mob, minor class, but vicious. They operate on the South Side,

344

out of Harvey and Dixmoor, and they're wanted by HUAC, which is why Gonzales is checking in about it. Seems they've got some connections to Il Duce that make the government itchy."

The detective paused. Met her gaze dead-on.

"Benedetti is Sammy Martini's cousin. He and his gang rode the *City of San Francisco* out here in April. Guess they decided the fresh air and crab cocktails would do 'em some good, because they've stuck around. We figure Tony Lima invited them . . . or maybe they invited themselves. We don't know. And we don't know how their politics fit in, if they do. But we're worried."

No more cooing. No pigeons, unless she was playing one with the cop across her desk.

Miranda said slowly: "I've been shadowed. Silent phone calls, somebody dressed as a PT and T salesman tried to get in my apartment. I figure Benedetti wants me dead, and if Scorsone was a button man, it makes sense. What doesn't make sense is how he wound up shot and killed."

Fisher heaved a sigh, brushed some dust off his fedora. "Yeah. And with you on the spot . . . well, just keep your nose clean, Miss Corbie. That's all I'm saying. Whatever you're doing for Duggan is upsetting more people than just Benedetti. And he's got his own reasons to rub you out."

Her eyes flickered over the muscular face and high, burnished cheekbones.

"Thanks. And call me Miranda."

He grinned. "Sure. Miranda. Nice name."

He patted his pockets, searching for the Old Golds. Found the deck and stuck a stick between his lips, match on the finger-nail trick to light it. Favorite of tough guys and cops.

"I worked with Duggan last year — bunco case, old lady got killed. Maybe you remember it? Anyway . . . he changed. Oh, he was always rough and not exactly by the book, but something made him mean. Resentful. Made Gonzales' life hell."

Fisher took a long drag on the cigarette. "He always treated me OK. Like a human being. No whispers, no funny looks at Christmas. No remarks about my nose, my name, my politics. Wish I could say the same about some of the others."

He exhaled, blowing smoke in a long stream. Looked up at her, mouth taut, jaw set.

"Duggan's innocent. Whatever he is, whatever he became . . . he'd never kill those girls. You learn to spot 'em, Miss Corbie, the ones who call you names or the ones who whisper behind your back. The ones who wait on a street corner in a gang, until they drink enough courage to beat you up." He shook his head, disgust etching deep lines around his mouth. "He's not the type."

Fisher was still leaning forward. Face darkened by memory, staring ahead. Staring at nothing.

She busied herself by opening the bottle of Old Taylor, setting out the Castagnola glass and a dirty coffee cup. Swabbed the cup with an old flour sack towel draped on the file cabinet, poured the bourbon in her glass. Fisher was watching her. She looked up, question mark, bottle poised over the cup. He nodded. She finished pouring and handed him the cup, both of them savoring the bite of the bourbon. David Fisher was a man she could work with.

"Anything else you want to talk about? Black Cat Café, maybe?"

Mood broken. He passed a hand over his face, a thumb across his mustache. Flashed a smile.

"You don't miss much. There's another group of organized hoods in town, up from L.A. Lanza mob's weak, especially after you got through with 'em. We got word these Hollywood boys are setting up a laundry outfit at the Black Cat, and I don't mean the kind you take your furs to."

"What needs cleaning?"

"Bookmaking dough, mainly. We're hearing about wire services set up, maybe some girls on the side, but mostly gambling. Lots and lots of gambling. Sugar's getting cleaned and we'd like to know how."

"You a vice cop?"

"Used to be. Only Jew in homicide. Six of us on the force. Fisher the laughing Jew, they call me. Haven't had much to laugh at lately."

Miranda sipped the Old Taylor. "Why come to me about it?"

He drained the coffee cup, reached across, and set it on her desk. Scratched the five o'clock shadow on his chin.

"Found your card at one of the small wires we cleaned up in the Richmond district. Same L.A. bunch. That card didn't go down so well with Chief Dullea. Figured you should know."

Her arm was burning. She finished the bourbon. Leaned back and stared at him, rocking the big leather chair.

"So the department thinks I killed a Chicago assassin and work with an L.A. gang of gamblers. Tell me, Inspector — does Dullea think I invaded Belgium?"

Fisher laughed for the third time, long and hard. Wiped his eyes, looked at her appreciatively. "You're a pip, Miss Corbie. A real pip."

Miranda glanced at the clock again. Pushed back from the desk and stood up.

"Inspector Fisher, I'm going to do something I'm not used to doing. I'm going to trust you."

She held out her right hand. He jumped up, shook it up and down, grin lighting up his face.

"I figured we could work together."

Flamm's smirk and the two Tanforan ticket stubs on his desk unrolled in her mind like the Pathé newsreel. Miranda said slowly, "I don't know anything about who's tailing me other than it's a tall, skinny bird in a Panama hat and a Cordoba tan Ford, '38 model. Something else, too — lion trainer over on the Island — name of Henry Kaiser. He's got a connection to Pandora Blake. Real sadistic bastard. Tries to brand his girlfriends."

Fisher's eyebrows climbed into his scalp. "Kaiser, huh? He a German national?"

"No accent. I don't think so. Anyway, he threatened to kill me."

The inspector grinned. "You certainly make an impression."

He dug out a card from his overstuffed wallet, coffee stain on the corner.

"Anytime. Even at home. The wife knows what the job's like."

"Inspector . . . why did you walk down the other hallway a while ago? You obviously knew who I was."

Fisher shoved his fedora back on, palm finessing the rim. He looked embarrassed.

"Oh, I figured you might need some time to yourself. The way you ripped that package open." He met her eyes. "Call me anytime." He grinned and slipped out into the hall.

The door swung closed. She stood up and locked it from the inside. Glanced at the black-and-gold letters staring at her from the glass.

MIRANDA CORBIE — PRIVATE INVESTIGATOR.

TWENTY-THREE

Only three rental companies in the phone book who offered drivers. Last time she used one she spent the whole goddamn trip keeping his hand out of her lap. Arm or no arm, she'd drive the car herself.

Miranda puffed furiously on the Chesterfield, running a finger down the page. Berry-U-Drive at 655 Geary Street offered special rates on long trips and advertised the latest 1940 Plymouths, DeSotos, and Packards.

She was in no mood for a Ford or Oldsmobile.

TUxedo 2323 answered on the third ring. Gruff voice, cigar between the teeth.

"Yeah? Berry-U-Drive, we deliver."

"How much for a coupe with good horsepower I can take to Calistoga?"

She could hear him sliding the cigar around in his mouth. Cleared his throat and tried to sound less like Wallace Beery and more like William Powell.

"Well now, lady — you thinkin' of takin' a car up them steep roads off 101, you need something with a little get up an' go, know what I mean?"

He laughed, throat rattling, held the phone to his chest, and spit.

"So how many in the party?"

Miranda tapped her foot, glancing at the clock. "Two. That's why I asked for a coupe."

"All right, little lady, all right. Glad you know the difference 'tween a seedan and a coupe. So it's seven cents a mile, ten dollars a day for a brand-new Plymouth, and that comes with a radio and the in-surance. 'Case you and your fella get in any trouble in them mud baths."

She could hear him winking on the other end. Miranda gritted her teeth.

"I need a goddamn coupe with six cylinders and at least a hundred horsepower and good brakes, and I need it by four P.M. today. Give me a model and a price, and tell me whether or not you can get me the fucking car in an hour and a half."

Dropped his cigar. Mumbled curses from off the receiver, then back on, coughing, William Powell forgotten.

"Gotta 1940 DeSoto S8 Deluxe Business-man's Coupe. Plenty of room in the back for luggage, three-speed manual transmission, hydraulic drum brakes on all four wheels. Radio, heat, and dee-frost. Six cents a mile, eight dollars a day, fifty-dollar deposit. Insurance included."

"I'll take it. Three days, Cash payment in advance. Deliver it to the Monadnock Building, 681 Market Street, four o'clock sharp. My name's Miranda Corbie."

He grunted. "Show your license to the driver, lady. An' don't get so tetchy."

He hung up the phone. Miranda looked at the receiver in her hand, grinning.

Couldn't reach Bente through the Oceanic Hotel, couldn't trust the clerk to take a message.

Almost 2:45. Still needed to grab a quick taxi to her apartment, pack a bag, and change the bandage on her arm. She clicked the receiver until an operator came on.

"Sailors' Union of the Pacific, please."

Middle-aged woman on the other end yawned. "Sorry, Miss. Connecting you now. Number is EXbrook 2228 for your reference."

"Thanks."

Miranda waited until a receptionist answered, asked if Bente Gallagher had been in yet. No, Miss, sorry, Miss, no one here by that name, Miss, sorry I can't help you, Miss.

Goddamn it.

Tried the operator again, this time for the Communist Party offices. Cold voice, clipped and severely disapproving.

"UNderhill 9335, Miss. Please dial direct next time."

Miranda slapped the receiver down with her right hand. Dialed the number herself and reached a young man on the fourth ring.

"Hello? I need to leave a message for Bente Gallagher. I'm a friend of hers."

His voice brightened. "Bente? Haven't seen her. But she'll probably be in later, we've got a meeting at five."

She exhaled. "Good. Please give her this message, from Miranda: 'Wait on Tonypandy. Too dangerous.'"

"Is Bente in trouble, Miss? Can I help?" Excited and eager, playacting politics.

Sounded about nineteen. Sandy-haired college boy, believing Lenin had all the answers, that communism somehow made people better than they were.

Not young for much longer, his generation. Not for much longer.

She tried to make her voice gentle. "You can help, Junior, by giving her the message.

354

And — just stay out of trouble."

Miranda grabbed her coat and hurried out of the office.

Carefully printed sign on Gladdy's counter read BE BACK IN 5 MINUTES. Miranda tapped her foot, hand on her hip, hoping it would be more like three. Bent down to look at herself in the mirror behind the counter. Repositioned her fedora. Goddamn thing wouldn't stay straight.

"Miss Corbie?"

Looked toward the rear of the lobby. Mailroom kid with the Adam's apple, red-faced.

She pushed through the elevator line to the counter, brushing by a stout lady wearing summer white and waiting to collect a package. "What is it?"

He held out a postcard, face like a beet. "I — I knew you'd want this right away. Got a stamp from England on it. Postman brought it earlier, and I forgot to give it to you, 'cause it's addressed General Delivery. . . ."

She didn't know anyone in England. Not anymore.

Miranda snatched the card from his fingers, stared down at a photo of Westminster Abbey.

Flipped it over. It was postmarked March 23, 1940, and addressed to Miranda Cor-

bie, General Delivery, San Francisco.
Blue ink, firm writing. Feminine.
Just two lines on the card.

Would like to meet you. Your loving
mother.

She didn't know how long she stood, holding on to the edge of the counter.

Mailroom boy's voice droned insistently, summer wasp or yellow jacket, and she tried to block it out, run away, run down to Pacific Street or to the nickelodeon on Market, run from the apartment on Turk, run from her father, from Hatchett, and find her mother, somewhere, one of the women, maybe a pretty one, fine ladies in bustles and carriages, maybe, or the ones that laughed and spoke with the singsong voices, made her smile just to hear them.

You OK, Miss Corbie? Wanna sit down, Miss Corbie? Miss Corbie?

Miranda blinked. Card still in her hand. Her fingers closed around it, and she pulled her eyes up to the nervous kid in front of her, his cheeks alternating in splotches of white and red.

"Thank you."

She turned away, hobbled like an old woman, blind, feeling her way on one good arm and two strong legs and not much else. Her hat was crooked again, and she could see Gladys waving at her, smiling. She headed for Gladys, whose smile faltered when she got a look at Miranda's face.

"Sugar — what's wrong with you? Look like you've seen a ghost."

Concern poured from her friend, concern for her, Miranda Corbie. If Miranda Corbie was who she was.

Miranda Corbie, who took her mother's name, who never knew her mother, who tried to find her mother, who figured her mother was dead.

Gladys put two arms out, held Miranda up by the shoulders. Shooting pain through the left one, but it didn't matter. Nothing mattered.

Nothing.

Mattered.

The blonde propped Miranda up on the counter, staring at her, then stretched to reach her coat, draped on a stool behind the cash register. A dyspeptic old woman with a nose that nearly touched her chin was tapping a roll of Tums on the counter, and Gladys waved her away, the woman stalking off and angrily denouncing labor unions. Gladys pulled out a flask. Miranda wrapped her fingers around it.

"Drink it, sugar," the voice said, urgency behind it, like the women from the bar who used to make her eat. She obeyed.

The liquid felt like silk in her throat until it started to burn. She swallowed, feeling it course through her body.

Gladys was urging her to drink again. She tilted back the silver metal with the engraved initials, finished whatever was inside.

Good girl, Miranda. You're a good girl. Good girl, Randy. You're a good girl. . . .

Her arm started to hurt.

And she remembered.

Girls stabbed to death, bodies mocked. Japanese boy dying in her arms, gangster, smooth and hot as the liquor in the bottle, using women, abusing women. Killing women. Trying to kill her, red and white, red and white, brains splattered on a bathroom wall. Dead friend, dead escort, left to rot like garbage. Vicious cop, still capable of love.

Red-haired friend, kind heart and fierce politics, bald detective escorting her to the Pickwick and the Rusty Nail, equal in his eyes, respect. Newspaper reporter, always there, always there for her, wishing she could love him, and a Mexican cop with eyes like fire and a mouth that tasted like Spain. . . .

And Johnny, how she missed him, how she wanted him, how she wanted to be nothing else, do nothing else but belong to him, swallowed up in all he was, but she was her own woman, and he helped make her who she was, who she'd been all along.

Opened her eyes and looked at Gladys. Tears streamed down her face.

Her left hand still clutched the postcard.

She whispered: "Thank you, Gladdy. I've got to go."

She ran out of the Monadnock, her friend calling her name.

Roy stuttered out a greeting when she walked through the door of the Drake Hopkins, and she waved, grateful to see the automatic elevator working for once. Doors sprang open with a clang, and she stepped inside.

She closed her eyes for a moment and the elevator obligingly chimed again, reminding her to step out at the fourth floor, and she thought of Abe, the old colored man with bright white false teeth always stretched in a smile, and how he used to greet her in the mornings when she left for work.

Miranda opened her apartment door, not really giving a damn if Benedetti or his men were waiting inside. No time to worry about it. No time.

Looked around, deep gulps of air. Yanked open the side closet by the foyer and took out a small tan suitcase. Toted it into the bedroom, weight on her right arm. Unlocked the hinged halves.

Her hands were shaking like her father's when he couldn't find the bottle of gin.

She flung open the drawer of her nightstand, pulling out a pack of Chesterfields, shoved one in her mouth. Lit it with a Moderne matchbook from the drawer. Inhaled until the trembling stopped.

Picked up the .38, Spanish gun, and laid it in the suitcase. Let her fingers caress the leather.

Found two dresses that would work for hot weather, another for nighttime, working clothes for the Club Moderne. Opened a highboy drawer too fast and the wood squeaked in protest, and Miranda grabbed underwear, slip, bra, nightgown, cotton socks, and silk stockings, down to two clean pair, and when the hell are you going to do any laundry, Miranda, can't run around San Francisco in dirty clothes, go back home to your da, little girl, you ain't gonna get nothing here for 'im. Don't sell no liquor on credit.

She shook her head, took another puff on

the Chesterfield.

Shoe tree in the closet. Picked sensible black walking shoes, one pair of high-heeled open toes for dancing, and some rubber soles for tennis, or at least to look like tennis.

Shit, tennis. Stooped down to the bottom drawer of the highboy, pulled out a folded-up tennis outfit of shorts and short-sleeved shirt and underneath it a one-piece bathing suit.

Laid everything in the suitcase. Wrapped the pistol up in her nightgown, stuck it in the middle.

She was in the hall closet again, digging for the small makeup case, when her phone rang. She swore, fingers touching the handle, and she yanked it out, covered in dust and cobwebs. Set it on the floor and ran to the bedroom.

"Hello?"

"You were right, my dear."

She was out of breath and sank on the bed. Brought the cigarette to her lips, body shaking again.

"Pandora had an abortion?"

"Fortescue didn't think so. He was predictably irritable on the subject. Of the opinion that since the girl was no better than she should be, any information related to her sexual activity was unnecessary."

"Fucking puritan." Miranda's voice was steady. "What happened to Pandora?"

Meyer spoke in a whisper. "I'm still at the Hall. Tried to call you at the office, but you'd already left. The young woman had a tubal ligation, possibly as long as two years ago and as recently as eight months ago."

"She was sterilized."

"Yes."

Silence on Meyer's end while she finished the cigarette. Miranda said: "I'm packing for Calistoga now. I'll call you if I find anything."

"Miranda . . . please take care of yourself."

"There's a homicide cop who came to see me — Inspector Fisher. You might want to arrange a meeting. Seems I'm the new fair-haired girl for some of the blue boys."

His voice was delighted. "But my dear, that's wonderful!"

"Don't get too excited. I'm still target practice for most of them, especially the ones at the top. Dullea wants to trip me up on that body they found out by the Treasure Island parking lot. Turned out to be a member of the Angelo Benedetti gang, and Benedetti is Sammy Martini's cousin. Figure he wants me dead. Listen — I've got to go. I'll fill the rest in for you later."

Her attorney was sputtering. "Miranda — if someone is trying to kill you or frame you, don't you think you should tell me? I'm your attorney!"

She smiled at his outrage. "You're also my client. Bye, Meyer."

She hung up the phone.

She stood in front of the mirror, studying the wound on her upper arm, stained red from iodine and blood that oozed out from underneath the wrapping.

Miranda poured on more iodine, directly from the bottle. Just the way you like to drink it, right, mister? Oh, 'scuse me, it's "Doctor," ain't it . . . sure can't fix the pain in my leg, though, can ya, mister? Y'can talk pretty. Talk real pretty, kinda like singin'.

She bit her lip and waited for the wave of pain to pass. She was used to pain. Miranda couldn't remember when she'd ever been without it, her only companion, fuck the Echo and the Shadow. Pain kept her company, one kind or another, either the bruises on her face or the growling in her stomach or the knowledge that she'd never be one of those fine ladies in a bustle and carriage, never be anybody but that poor bastard girl of the professor's, scrounging for nickels so her pop can get his gin.

She picked up one of the pieces of tape she cut, anchored the fresh bandage in place. Made a neat, perfect square around the wound, like a goddamn yard around a goddamn house, with a mother and a father and a white picket fence, fucking Andy Hardy and the perfect goddamn family, only pain you had to worry about was solved in seventy-five minutes and summed up in a moral at the end of the story.

Outlasted everyone, pain did, and they were on intimate terms, and she was jealous with it, not willing to share it with other people. Suffer alone, guard it well, it's your life, sum and total, all your goddamn days.

Miranda looked into the mirror.

Roy dragged her suitcase and cosmetic case downstairs and called her a taxi. She left him a dollar and told him not to let anyone at all up to her room for any reason and gave him Meyer's telephone number.

Taxi got her to the Monadnock without conversation and within five minutes. She tipped him fifty cents. He smiled shyly behind the heavy beard, drove off in the direction of the Ferry Building.

Three thirty. Church bells behind Market. *Ding dong. Ding dong.* Then the jukebox started up again, sermon over, sin back on the spinner, Bea Wain warbling "Deep Purple" for Larry Clinton and His Orchestra.

Gladys was waiting on another customer when she saw Miranda. She flung change and a *Liberty* magazine at a lady in black crepe and rushed out behind the counter.

"Honey — what happened? I thought you were going to faint, and that's not like you. You looked really bad. And you were crying. You all right?"

"Thanks for taking care of me, Gladdy. I'll tell you all about it later, OK?"

Her friend stared into her eyes as though she expected to find signs of a concussion. Made a dissatisfied noise, walked back behind her station. Miranda picked out five rolls of Life Savers: variety pack, Pep-O-Mint, and Butter Rum.

Gladys rang up the sale without a word. Miranda pulled out two dollars, and when the blonde tried to protest, she said, "Gladdy — that was a whole flask of rye down my throat. Please — keep the change, sugar. I really appreciate it."

Gladys's eyes welled with emotion. "OK, Miri. But you've got me awful worried. And that nice Inspector Gonzales isn't here to help you out of a jam."

Miranda squeezed her friend's hand. "I'll

be all right. I'm going up to Calistoga for a couple of days."

Gladys's face lit up like Independence Day. "Sugar, that's the best news I've had all week! It's about time you got away from this nuthouse and had a real vacation."

Miranda smiled. "It's a working vacation. But don't worry." She hugged the blonde and promised to write if she stayed longer than a couple of days.

Her watch read 3:45. Fifteen minutes.

She got in line for the elevator behind an arguing family of six, rode up hugging the left wall, and walked straight to her office.

Opened the door. Still smelled like Fisher's Old Golds.

Locked the window, unlocked the safe. Counted out one hundred and eighty dollars from the money left out of Meyer's retainer. Reached in the back and pulled out the Baby Browning.

Miranda sank into the padded leather of her desk chair. Checked the magazine and firing mechanism, the hinges and clasp on the slightly oversize gold cigarette case she concealed it in.

Four inches long, about twelve ounces. Saved her life in February. A .25-caliber can kill just as easily as a .44, especially up close.

She owed Gonzales for bringing it back to her.

Miranda ran a finger along the silver metal, tracing the *FN* intertwined on the handle, the *Fabriques Nationale d'Armes de Guerre Herstal Belgique* on the barrel.

Not the first pistol she'd killed a man with. Not the first time.

Miranda straightened her shoulders. Loaded the Browning, six bullets, and cradled it in her palm, thankful for the large Scots-Irish hands, the peasant hands she'd been taught to be ashamed of.

Her mother's hands.

No time to think about it, she told herself. No time.

Miranda closed the gun in the case and slipped it into her purse. Took out the .22, along with the postcard of Westminster Abbey.

Would like to meet you. Your loving mother.

Stared at the writing, at the postmark from London.

What else do you fucking say after thirty years?

Miranda shoved the .22 in the safe, set the card on the top shelf.

Looked up at the wall clock. Five minutes. She should leave now. The call to her father would have to wait.

Instead, she sat down and closed her eyes, head cradled against the back of the chair. Her breathing was ragged, halting, and she let it wash over her, let it drown her, Pandora's blood and Annie's blood, and the blood in Spain, Johnny's, red earth wet from shattered bodies and all the blood, God, all the pain, pain of childbirth and children, never knowing that pain, that joy, that sharing. Only pain leading on to pain, never birth. Only death.

She laid her head in her arms. There was a knock at the door.

Miranda looked up and answered, "Come in."

Rick stood in the doorway, battered fedora in his hands. His voice was rough.

"Your car's waiting downstairs. Let's go to Calistoga."

■ ■ ■ ■

Part Four:
Sin

■ ■ ■ ■

It is better for all the world, if instead of waiting to execute degenerate offspring for crime, or to let them starve for their imbecility, society can prevent those who are manifestly unfit for continuing their kind. The principle that sustains compulsory vaccination is broad enough to cover cutting Fallopian tubes. . . . Three generations of imbeciles are enough.
— Oliver Wendell Holmes, from the formal opinion of the U.S. Supreme Court in the case of *Buck v. Bell* (1927), legalizing compulsory sterilization.

Twenty-Four

He said nothing at first, grin gone, eyes grim and staring straight ahead. He jerked the radio knob, and the afternoon news roundup blared over the speakers, H. V. Kaltenborn speculating on how long France could last.

They reached the toll plaza and drove onto the Golden Gate.

Rick said: "Wanna get one thing straight, Miranda. I'm here because you're good copy. And that's the only reason."

She nodded and looked out the window toward Alcatraz.

"Best way is to take 37 and some farm roads northeast to 29. Mostly paved, or at least oiled. And 12's too goddamn steep out of Santa Rosa. It might be easier to go through Oakland and Vallejo, but you said you wanted 101."

"Thanks, Rick."

He grunted, both hands on the steering

wheel of the DeSoto, eyes on the road.

Rick kept the DeSoto at the 45 mph speed limit, coasting down the grade toward Sausalito. Afternoon sun was bright and hot, no fog in Marin. Undulating bluffs stretched on either side of the highway, yellow gold with summer grass, small birds diving for flies and crickets.

Gold in these hills all right, farmland, ranchland, divided by decrepit wooden fences and tall stands of ancient eucalyptus, planted when ranchos ruled the West and Vallejo traveled on horseback, lowing of cattle in the parched dry dirt, music of mandolins drifting from the adobe.

Brown-and-black herds whisked flies and ambled toward the widespread shade of live oaks, gnarled from drought, only shelter from the relentless sun. Weathered barns rested in hillside cracks, small windmills pumping precious water in troughs, farmwives wiping hands on an old soiled apron, calling the field-workers home.

Miranda felt the warmth on her face from the open window, closed her eyes. No vaqueros, their day, their land, no longer. No song, no guitar, no clink of spurs on wooden floors. Only the missions remained and the memory of their names.

Wild grass rippled by the side of the road, drowning the noise of the car motor. San Quentin stretched toward the mainland, pink like a shell, like a delicate blush, never seen by the men who stayed locked inside. Lights of the city always just out of reach.

They climbed again and dropped into San Rafael, cafés and motor inns lining the road, raucous laughter of men off work filling the bars and roadhouses, car horns and jukes playing "One O'Clock Jump," smell of tortillas and beans from a Mexican place drifting through the open window.

Little towns, little California towns. Fishermen and lumbermen and ranchers, skinny men in overalls climbing ladders in fruit orchards, families of five or six picking fruit, peaches and plums, living in one-room shacks or canvas tents pitched close by the railroad. Take them to the next town, look for work, any kind of work.

California gold, no Oklahoma dust, golden state, full of promise. Foreman stares at the woman's breasts, nipples outlined under the thin cotton print, youngest pressed against her legs. Lick of the lips, maybe got some day work for ya, honey, then the husband walks up. Clears his throat, waves his hand. Depression here, too, folks, move on to the valley. Move on south.

Turned off 101 to 37 east, crossed the Petaluma River. Barge passing underneath them, eggs and butter to market, heading for San Pablo Bay.

Wetlands stretched on either side of the river, reeds and marshes spotted white and gray, egrets and heron. Summertime hot, blue sky, no clouds, only blots of black, inked by factories, eastern shores. Men with dirty faces and oily clothes, home to tired wives and children dressed in parochial school clothes, altar boys still learning catechism.

Northeast to an oiled road, wrapped around foothills green with grapes. Old wines, old vines, planted by the first Italians, Tuscan hills no match for California. Waiting for fall, for the purple sweet juice to run from the press. Prayers spoken, candles lit, barrels stained like blood. Prohibition drove some of them away, but most of them stayed, tied to the earth, deeper blood of the vine.

Railroad again, old coal burner, group of little boys with sticks walking beside the tracks, grasshoppers jumping just out of their grasp. Chickens squawking from a small house by the road, old Rhode Island Red rooster sounding the supper call, men and boys still in the fields, baling the hay, crows and red-winged blackbirds darting in and out of the yellowed stalks.

The land and the road opened, and Napa Valley stretched out to the bay. Cows, sheep, and grapes, ranches and orchards, mines in the mountains east, geysers in the ground north. They turned off on 29, heading north.

Car rumbled past lush land, Napa State Hospital, 1,900 acres and a 250-acre farm, three thousand people declared mentally unfit for anyone's company but their own. They passed the city of Napa, vineyards and tanning factories, then Yountville and Oakville and Rutherford, prune and peach, olive and fig groves. More wineries and orchards, old cellars of St. Helena, and finally, the top of Napa Valley. Sun was setting, yellow orange light slanting long shadows on the small, narrow road.

Little town of geysers and sanitariums and healing water, nestled tight against the orchards and grapes, shadowed by the mountains, fed by tourists and health seekers, can you help me, Doctor, can the waters cure me, make me live longer, make me younger, prettier, bring me back my husband, my boyfriend, my wife. My life.

Calistoga.

And Nance's Sanitarium.

■ ■ ■ ■

Rick pulled off a side road by the old pioneer cemetery. Turned to face her, fedora pushed back on his forehead, face softer in the sunset.

"So both of the women were sterilized and one had an abortion. And you think it happened here, and that it somehow ties in with why they were murdered."

She watched a dragonfly flit across the gravel road. "It ties in somewhere."

He shook his head and lit a Lucky, striking the match on his thumb. Rolled the window down a crack.

"Christ, Miranda — sure, abortion's illegal, but sterilization isn't. Even compulsory sterilization. And it doesn't just happen."

She shifted around in the seat and met his eyes.

"Something happened here, Rick. At least the start of something. Rural California's not exactly known for the United We Stand campaign."

Miranda took a breath. Looked out at the green, placid meadow across the road, orange in the failing light.

"A bunch of upright Sonoma County

citizens almost killed a Jewish farmer in '35. Lynched, beat, tarred, and feathered. They were acquitted."

Her nails were digging into her palms, and she slowly unclenched them. "Sol Nitzman's crime was being a Jew. And supporting the migrant apple pickers . . . on strike for thirty-five cents an hour."

Rick studied her for a minute. Waved smoke toward the window, shook his head again.

"Still a hell of a lot to pin on a couple of postcards."

"If I'm wrong, I'm wrong. I'll pay for your hotel. You'll be able to scare up some kind of story."

Rick sighed. "Yeah. I always do. So are we posing as a married couple, or what?"

"Unmarried. And I'm pregnant."

He turned toward her, sweat dotting his forehead from the heat. "You're gonna hint around for an abortionist, aren't you? Goddamn it, Miranda . . ."

"You drove me here. You're the helpful type. We've been going out for a year." She laid her hand over his. "We'll say there's bad blood on my side of the family, if you want. You check into another hotel, I'll stay at Nance's."

The reporter squeezed her fingers without

looking at her, opened his palm. Took a long puff on the Lucky.

Said heavily: "All right. Anything else? And how long are we here?"

"Tonight and tomorrow. Gotta get back before Memorial Day."

"For reasons related?"

Miranda sighed. "Who the hell knows, Rick. I'm chasing one shadow at a time. But that reminds me — I'm Jewish. So keep your story straight."

"You want us both to be?"

"No. You sound too much like County Cork. Like I said, you're just the loyal, helpful type." She gave him a smile, unrolled two Life Savers, and popped them in her mouth. "Easy acting."

Rick snorted, shoved the hat brim down over his eyes, and pulled the DeSoto back on the road to Lincoln Avenue and downtown Calistoga.

He parked in front of Nance's and walked into the office with her, hat in his hands. Clerk behind the counter was about twenty-five, blond, and obviously a fan of Ginger Rogers, judging from the way she'd drawn the fake mole on her cheek. She stood up, gave Rick the eye before moving on to Miranda. Tried to sound like Ginger putting on a refined voice but only managed to sound like a blond hick trying to sound like Ginger Rogers.

"May I help you?"

"I'd like a room, please. Oh, and the full treatment — waters, mud bath — and if you have a consultant on duty, I'd —"

The phone rang. The blonde held up her hand as though she were stopping traffic. "Just a minute, please."

Miranda and Rick glanced at each other, then around the room. *St. Helena Star* on a chair, some brochures on the Fair, the Petrified Forest, and the geyser over on Tubbs Lane. A small rack on the counter held medicinal pamphlets that looked left over from the days of corsets and Lydia Pinkham, and next to them a stack of the same familiar postcard. Miranda took one of everything. The room was small, painted white with red trim, and just clean enough, like a no-frills motor inn with business guaranteed.

The clerk hung up, eyes darting at Rick again. Miranda was getting annoyed. "As I was saying, Miss . . ."

"Yes, Madame. You'd like a room, full treatment. We close the plunging pool at nine P.M." She glanced at her wristwatch. "That leaves you a little over an hour. I can send someone over to talk to you about the baths and the kinds of corrective massages we offer." She looked Miranda up and down critically. "Posture bothering you, Madame?"

Miranda's voice was short. "No. How much do I owe you?"

The blonde raised her eyebrows, looked back and forth between them. "Isn't the gentleman staying with you?"

Rick spoke for the first time. "I'm, er — I don't want all the baths and such. Is there a regular hotel in town?"

The clerk gave him what she thought was a knowing smile. "Sure, mister — the Mount View is right down the street, past the old depot. Can't miss it." She added archly, "Place downstairs is good for a drink and dancing — it's called Johnny's."

"Thanks." Rick threw a glance to Miranda. "Miri, I'll wait outside for you."

She nodded, still staring at the blonde, whose eyes followed Rick out the door. The counter girl sighed a little, then rummaged in the back.

"You're in cabin four." She held out a key to Miranda. "Just go out the door, turn left, and turn left again. There's a row behind this main building. That'll be four dollars, tonight and tomorrow, everything included.

You can tip the attendants extra."

"Thank you," Miranda said dryly. "Isn't there a register I'm supposed to sign?"

"Oh, yeah. Here you go." The blonde lifted last month's *Photoplay* off the cover of a large registration book.

Miranda opened the book. "Do you have a pen?" The blonde stretched her lips flat and poked around on the desk. Miranda turned to the front page. Goddamn it — only went back to last August.

The clerk held out a green fountain pen, and Miranda signed her name. She hesitated, then spelled it "Korbe." Looked up at the clerk. "Could you send someone by my cabin in about twenty minutes?"

Ginger shrugged. "Sure. I'll find someone who can show you the ropes. Cora ain't here, but Gracie's around." She opened the *Photoplay,* indicating the conversation was over.

Miranda walked outside, blinking her eyes to adjust to the dark. Rick was leaning against the car door, illuminated by the neon sign advertising Nance's.

She beckoned him with her head, and he followed her to cabin four, situated in the back of the complex next to a large cement building, probably for the mud baths. The door swung open easily, and they found themselves in a small, dark room with a hot plate and a radio, along with the standard dresser, chair, and bed. A landscape of an old mill hung above the bed, which gave an alarming creak when she sat on it.

Miranda took out her wallet and thrust some money at Rick, speaking in a whisper. "For expenses. Just save me the receipts."

He pocketed the money, mouth turned downward. "You want me to stay at that Mount View place?"

She nodded. "Yeah. And I want you to pump that blonde for information. See if you can get her to give you a look at the register for April '39 — this one starts in August. I don't think Pandora or Annie had anything to hide when they came up here — they'd have used their real names."

"What do you want with the blonde?"

Miranda leaned back on the bed, smiling, bracing herself on both arms until her left started to burn. She sat up. "Use your charms, Rick. Find out whatever you can about who works here. Especially doctors, nurses — any medical personnel. She's willing to come across, and not just with information."

The reporter grinned. "Maybe she likes my baby blue eyes."

"Be careful."

"That's my line."

"Ginger Rogers is supposed to send someone named Gracie to come see me soon, and I'll go from there. You figure a way to get that register, ask her out to that club she mentioned."

"Johnny's."

"Yeah." Miranda tilted her wrist until she could read her watch in the dim light. "It's almost time. Meet me here around one and fill me in. If you can tear yourself away from the blonde, that is."

His eyes crinkled at the corners. A soft lilt came back to his voice. "Blondes aren't my type."

Miranda stood up and pushed him toward the door. "They are tonight, Romeo. See you in a few hours. And Rick . . . thank you."

He flashed his crooked grin at her before disappearing behind the cottage door.

Miranda barely had time to unpack her bathing suit and nightgown when a loud rap struck the door hard enough to make it shake. She hurriedly threw a dress over the .38 in the suitcase and opened the door.

Gracie was a lumbering woman with brown-and-gray hair bound in rolled braids on either side of her head. Taller than Miranda, maybe five eight. Could stop Red

Grange from getting a touchdown and cracked her knuckles as a hobby. Somewhere between forty and forty-five, with an unexpectedly high-pitched voice and a sly, narrow-eyed smile. Her teeth were caked in tartar and her canines chipped, but she could choke you to death long before biting you. Miranda tried to smile.

"You must be Gracie."

The woman nodded, looked her over. "Mary said you got some questions."

Miranda bit her lip, lowered her voice to a whisper. "Would you mind coming in for a moment?"

Gracie shrugged, showed her teeth again. "Whatever you say, lady. But you ain't got much time left tonight for the plunge." She pushed past Miranda, filling the door frame and the little room, then settled herself in the chair, eyes curious.

Miranda sat gingerly on the bed facing her, suitcase within arm's reach. She summoned up a blush, glued her eyes to the floor.

"I — I've got a — a — problem."

The large woman's voice was bored. She studied her fingers and cracked one knuckle.

"We all got problems, sister. Mud and a massage can fix your back, not much else. We got water to drink for gland problems, water to clean you out if you're irregular, water to soak in for any female troubles. An' that's about it. Anything else, you best see a doctor."

Miranda didn't say anything but reached for her purse, which piqued Gracie's interest. She pulled a ten-dollar bill out of her wallet and held it between her first two fingers like a cigarette. Still kept her eyes on the floor, away from Gracie. Took a deep breath.

"I need your help, Gracie. I'm — I'm in trouble. Someone told me once that Nance . . . that I could come here for help."

"Who told you that?" Squeak of a voice was sharp around the edges. Miranda looked up this time, met her eyes.

"Girl I met a few months back. Annie Learner."

Gracie exhaled, long and slow, and her dull brown eyes flickered, catching some green from the Hamilton dancing between Miranda's fingers.

"She tell you to see me?"

Miranda shook her head. "No. Only that I could find someone to help me at Nance's."

"You talk to her when?"

"About a month ago. I've been . . . well, I've been out of town. Just got back in this weekend."

The woman exhaled, satisfied, look of alarm replaced by desire and greed. Her eyes were trying to add up how much Miranda might be worth. Held out a paw for the ten-dollar bill.

"You're lucky I'm workin' tonight, lady. Cora's normally here on Tuesdays, and she couldn't help nobody with nothin'."

Miranda dropped the money in the woman's outstretched hand, which closed into a meaty red fist around the sawbuck. For the first time, a smile creased Gracie's heavy features. She ran an expert eye over Miranda.

"You sure ain't showin' yet. How long?"

"Two — two months."

The heavy woman grunted again. "All right. You need to meet the doctor. He ain't here — an' he don't work outta here. But you make it worth my time — an' I don't mean nickels and dimes, lady — an' I'll set you up an appointment with him tomorrow. He's a busy man, so you better come across."

Miranda gave her voice a quaver. "What if — what if I don't want to go through with it after all? What if I change my mind?"

Gracie raised her thick eyebrows. "That's 'tween you and the doctor, sister. Alls I do is get you to him. But he ain't cheap —

leastwise, not normally — so better come across, like I say."

"You say he's not here — do I have to go to another sanitarium? Can't I stay here?"

The woman's short, high-pitched laugh made Miranda shudder inside. "Sure, you stay here, get a mud bath tomorrow morning, the works. He can't get up here till later, 'long about six or so. I'll take you to him when he's ready."

She pushed her large body out of the chair, smoothing the braids down on the right side of her head.

"An' that's another thing. Doc likes to know somethin' about the women he helps out of a jam. I'll bring you along a little form, save you some time fillin' it out before you see him." Gracie turned to leave, added over her shoulder, "Tomorrow I expect the rest of the fifty you owe me, lady."

Miranda murmured, "Of course. Thank you, Gracie."

She shut the door and chained it, bracing it against her back. Took a long, deep breath.

Annie was a shot in the dark, but she'd struck home.

You could get a hell of a lot more than a mud bath at Nance's Sanitarium.

TWENTY-FIVE

She checked the lock on the suitcase. Heat made her feel trapped, goddamn pacing lion, like the ones Henry Kaiser chained and whipped.

Stuck the stick between her lips and shrugged into a summer coat with big pockets. Needed a coat to hide the Spanish pistol, even if it was fucking ninety degrees outside. Gracie would search the room as soon as she left it, and a loaded .38 in the suitcase of a pregnant woman might look a little out of place. The thin black twill of her right pocket sagged, but no one would notice in the dark.

Miranda looked behind her one more time. Made a show of shutting the door, for anyone out by the pool or the mud baths or lurking by the utility shed, waiting for her. She headed toward the still lit swimming pool.

Blue green water lapped against cracked

and broken Spanish tile, mineral smell. An old lady lay back in a wooden pool chair, lap covered in a cheap cotton towel. Yellow light of a heat lamp make her flabby skin look jaundiced, and the lamp made a sizzling sound, old wires and the suicide flights of insects. The old lady snored, oblivious.

A younger woman sat next to her, gazing at the blue water. Frowsy thirty-five, probably younger than she looked.

Miranda looked around brightly, trying to make conversation. "Good evening. Nice out, isn't it?"

The woman nodded, hair as colorless as her personality. She sat tensed and hunched forward, as if waiting for the old lady to wake up and unsure of what to do until she did. Miranda tried again.

"I just drove up from San Francisco. Much warmer here."

Snort and a gurgle, and the old lady opened her eyes, sitting bolt straight. Wrinkles crashed back into gullies and crevices, deep enough to hide any sign of kindness. She blinked round eyes at Miranda, mouth pinched. The younger woman's hands fluttered around her like the wings of a wounded bird.

"You lookin' for somebody?" Voice as gruff and bearded as her face.

Miranda inhaled the rest of the Chester-field, then dropped it on the cement and crushed it with the toe of her navy pump. The old lady watched silently, disapproval and sweat oozing from yellowed pores.

"No. I'm staying here, thought I'd see what the pool is like."

The noise was a dismissive harrumph. She turned to the younger woman.

"Quit flappin' your hands, Jane. Why didn't you wake me? I told you I wanted some hot cocoa . . . I declare, you can tell your mother I'd just as soon leave my money to the church. Family is as family does, and you've shown me no 'ppreciation 'tall for bringing you along. Why, if it weren't for me, your ma woulda put you in the Sonoma Home for Feeble-Minded Chil-dren. . . ."

Her harsh voice dwindled with her crouched and shrunken form, helped along the dim path to another cabin by the woman she was berating.

Miranda checked her wristwatch: 9:10. Her stomach growled, and she headed southwest on Lincoln Avenue, toward the pink and yellow neon lights of central Calistoga.

Commerce in Calistoga revolved around the

health resorts, but a small strip of businesses catered to both locals and tourists, offering more than odd-tasting water to take your mind off your troubles. Bars glowed in yellow neon, the Johnny's sign at the bottom of the Mount View Hotel blinking on and off, sounds of laughter and a piano wafting out through the open doors.

Miranda walked past the old railroad depot, past a late night pharmacy, two teenagers sitting at the counter, sharing a vanilla malt. Jukebox inside sang out with "In the Mood," and the kids tapped their feet on the chromium bar, soda jerk in a little white hat smiling like Cupid.

She turned the corner and walked down Washington. Passed an Italian restaurant despite her empty stomach, heading for bright lights and loud singing from a big complex off Franklin Street. A lit sign proclaimed DR. AALDER'S SANITARIUM, NATURAL SULPHUR AND MUD BATHS.

Aalder's was larger than Nance's, with a whole series of cabins radiating from a center pool. More privacy for the cabins probably meant they rented by the hour, judging from the peroxide blonde and the drunk she was reeling in. He stumbled up the two steps into the cabin, trying to finish a chorus of "I'll Be Glad When You're Dead,

You Rascal You."

Miranda turned back to the café. Ordered some ravioli and a bottle of homemade red wine, made mostly, according to the attentive young waiter, from a grape called Sangiovese, "Blood of Jove."

She smiled at him but refused to tell him her name, and he finally gave up, though she could still feel his eyes on her while she sipped the garnet-colored wine. Food was delicious, the ravioli light, filled with cheese and mushrooms and fennel-flavored sausage.

She declined the free homemade cheesecake and a suggestion that she try Dr. Aalder's sulfuric baths or meet the slick-haired waiter for a treatment of any kind. Walked back down Lincoln, past the now closed and shuttered drugstore, fingers in her right pocket lightly touching the Spanish pistol.

Johnny's was still open. She stopped and lit a cigarette, staring at the sign. Hoped Rick was inside with Mary, the hard-mouthed blonde. Tried not to wonder why every goddamn hole in the wall of a town had to have a bar named Johnny's.

Kicked at the gravel on her way to the cabin, trying to make noise. Gracie should be long finished with the search. Miranda pushed open the door with her left hand, right still in her pocket.

Her suitcase was moved about a foot from where she'd left it near the pillow. Third drawer of the dresser hung open half an inch.

On the floor, as if it had been slid under the door . . . a typewritten piece of onionskin.

She found a pencil in the drawer of the nightstand, next to a tattered, leather-covered version of the Doré Bible. Crushed the cigarette stub in a chipped glass ashtray by the radio; ran an eye over the typed list of questions.

Any disease in your family? Which sides? How far back in generations? Any mental disease? What was your father's profession? Your grandfather's? How long has your family lived in America? Were you born in the United States?

Hell of a lot of information for an illegal operation that could land both doctor and patient in jail.

Handy multiple-choice list right after name, age, profession, and level of education. Check one: "I am employed, unemployed, married." Check one: "I am Catholic, Protestant, Communist." Check one:

"I am an American, a Negro, a Jew."

Miranda wiped her forehead. Started to fill out the form.

She was dreaming of men in white coats and stethoscopes, holding her arms down and smiling, one stuffing a pillow over her mouth. Her mother was beside her, faceless except for long black hair and a smile, murmuring her name over and over.

"Miranda, my child. . . . Miranda . . . Miranda . . ."

She sat upright in bed, gasping. Scritching sound at the door.

Glanced at her watch: 1:20 A.M. Blinked, turned on the lamp by the bed, padded to the door in her bare feet.

"Rick?"

"Let me in — it's cold out here."

She opened it a crack and Rick pushed inside, flinging himself in the chair next to the bed.

"Jesus, I'm bushed."

Her mouth curved upward. "Blonde beat you up?"

He grimaced, tossed his fedora on the bed. "Only on the dance floor. And on the way up to my room. Had to tell her it was all too soon, I still wasn't over you yet, and besides, you weren't feeling well. But hell,

I'll pass her along to some of the boys in the newsroom, for them she'd be worth the trip." He hitched up his pants and tightened his belt, shaking his head. "Not exactly the hard-to-get type."

Miranda sat on the bed facing him. "I hope she was as easy with the information."

Rick fished out a Lucky Strike from his pocket, lit it, and waved the match out. Inhaled, nodded. "Saw the register for April '39. She opened a safe and took it out for me. Told her it was for a bet, and I wound up having to kiss her for it. I never kissed a woman that tasted so much like fucking cod liver oil. Anyway, Annie was here on the twenty-first, Pandora on Saturday the twenty-second. Interesting thing, though — neither one checked out."

Miranda leaned forward. "No date at all? Any notation?"

"Just one word in both cases — 'Aalder's.' Mean something to you?"

Her eyes opened wide. "There's a Dr. Aalder's Sanitarium just about a hundred yards from here. Looks like they rent rooms — or at least mattresses — by the hour."

Rick rubbed the shadow of beard on his chin. "You think Annie and Pandora moved there?"

"Nance's is a small-time outfit — not

many places to hide. Maybe Aalder's is where this doctor works. Maybe it's Aalder himself who performs the operations."

Rick yawned. "I'm awfully goddamn tired, Miranda. You'd better fill me in."

She told him about Gracie, showed him the form. He made some noises, pinched his nose. Shook his head.

"You think it's Aalder?"

"I don't know. Gracie said he couldn't 'get up here' until six. Makes it sound like he's in the City, or someplace south."

Rick grunted, rubbed the cigarette out on the arm of the chair. "She's not exactly a reliable source."

"Did you ask the blonde about Annie or Pandora?"

"Yeah. Mary said she couldn't remember, people come and go all the time. I did find out that a head attendant named Cora usually works weekdays and the big one you talked to takes weekends. She said there's no doctor affiliated with Nance's — just a couple of local kids they pay to mud people down and water them off, plus the two women. Place started up about fifteen years ago with an old claw-foot tub and a bucket of mud. I tried to hint around about services that weren't on the books, but the only service she was interested in was in my pants."

Miranda chuckled. "Sorry to send you to the Wolf, Little Red Riding Hood."

He pushed himself up out of the chair. "I've still gotta walk back to the Mount View. What's on for tomorrow?"

"Not much until six. I'll be watched, definitely by Gracie and maybe by your blonde. I'll sit in the sun, try a mud bath, go for a swim. There's a tennis court on the other side of the pool."

"What about me? I didn't bring a bathing suit."

"Find out what you can about Dr. Aalder's. Find out if there even is a Dr. Aalder. Poke around town. And call Meyer, tell him what's going on."

He stared down at her, blue eyes into brown. "What is going on, Miranda?"

She was silent for a moment. Then turned back to the nightstand drawer and opened it. Took out the .38 and its shoulder holster.

Rick said: "That's John's gun."

She held it out to him. "Be careful with it."

He took it in both hands for a few seconds. "I'll have to adjust the holster to fit me."

"I know."

He met her eyes again. "You've got your .22?"

"My Browning."

He nodded, satisfied. "So they're taking you someplace at six o'clock."

"That was the impression. We should meet for meals — breakfast at nine thirty at the drugstore, let's say. Stake out a place where you can watch this cabin and follow me when the time comes."

He clenched the Spanish pistol in one hand and with the other one reached out a finger to touch Miranda's cheek. She flinched.

"I'll be OK, Rick."

Widemouthed grin, upside down. Hurt behind the eyes.

"You always are, Miranda. See you tomorrow."

She laid a hand on his arm, stood on her toes to brush her lips against his.

"Thank you, Rick."

He held up two fingers and placed them against her lips. This time she didn't move.

Rick squeezed out of the small, overly warm cabin and into the cold high-valley air of Calistoga. Miranda held the door open and watched him through the gap, walking straight-backed down the gravel path, milky light of a million stars raining silver on his battered fedora.

TWENTY-SIX

The alarm clock woke her early, seven thirty. Miranda groaned, rolled over on her left side until a dull pain made her sit up in bed.

Shit.

Tennis, swimming, mud baths. She'd forgotten about her left arm.

Clambered out of bed, slight shiver. Air filtering in from under the door was cold, fresh, sweet smell of wet wild grass mixed with the tang of volcanic earth.

Miranda winced as she ripped off the bandage. Climbed in the small bathtub, stooping slightly so she could fit under the corroded showerhead. Ran an eye along the tile for any peepholes, then washed quickly, toweled off, and changed her undergarments.

Arm was green, blue, and purple, with some yellow on the outside edges. Still stiff and sore to the touch. She dowsed it with some iodine she'd packed in her cosmetic case, rewrapping the wound with gauze and first-aid tape.

The mirror above the sink was sprinkled with white paint from the last time they ran a coat over the room. She angled for a better look at her skin. Circles under her eyes. Fit the job.

Picked out the tennis clothes from the suitcase and the rubber-soled shoes that matched. More vain than active, exactly what she wanted.

Looked at the arm again. Maybe say she tripped and fell, scraping it in an accident, but tell it like she's hiding something, probably a fight with her boyfriend.

Miranda smiled wryly. Rick wouldn't like the backstory, but it would fit, just in case anybody caught a glimpse of him with Johnny's gun.

She repacked everything. Folded the onionskin and stuck it in her purse. Took a deep breath and smoothed down the tennis shorts. She'd lost weight in the last few months.

Squared her shoulders. Stepped into the bright early morning sunshine of Calistoga.

Gracie was nowhere to be seen; neither was Rick's blonde. A few hardy souls were try-

ing the mud baths inside the main building
— gasps and squelching sounds, earth hitting fat, accompanied by the sour, acrid
smell of peat and minerals, wafting through
the propped-open double doors.

It was 9:05 and she was early for Rick, so
Miranda walked through Nance's complex,
passing another large white building with
lockers and small, therapeutic pools.
Headed across an old farm road leading to
a vineyard, then over the abandoned railroad
tracks, behind the former depot.

She could glimpse Dr. Aalder's from
Nance's, just southwest on Gerard and
Washington.

Miranda approached it from the opposite
angle, coming upon a long row of connected
cabins, along with a double column of
freestanding units surrounding a Roman-
style plunging pool. The bath building was
more grandiose than Nance's, but there
were chips in the stone mosaic work and
green paint peeling on the backs of the cottages.

Opened her purse and popped two Life
Savers in her mouth, barely tasting the
cherry and pineapple. A couple of teenagers
were wheeling old people around in chairs,
and women with fat white legs lay prone in
the morning sunshine under big straw hats.

Seemed innocuous enough, but then there was the blonde and the drunk from last night and the notations next to Pandora's and Annie's names.

She strolled up to the office, smiling at the women and old people, at a middle-aged man in swim shorts who shadowed his eyes for a closer look.

A small bell tinkled when she walked in, the counter cleaner but otherwise almost identical to Nance's. Same gamut of brochures, with the addition of an advertised tour of the Beringer winery.

The door on the right opened, and a heavyset man about fifty-five walked in, gray hair in a grizzled ring around a shiny bald spot. He wore a dirty smock with DR. AALDER's embroidered on the upper right corner and looked her up and down, mouth stretched wide in a toothy smile.

"May I help you, Miss? We don't offer tennis, but there's the Napa Valley Country Club, for golf . . . you look like the type of lady who could get in, if you don't mind my saying so."

His teeth pulled back even farther, showing white pink gums in a ferocious leer. The pudgy hands on the counter were black under the fingernails, spots of mud still clinging to the tufts of hair on the back.

She threw him a smile. Said sweetly, "Even with a last name of Korbe?"

She pronounced it as though it were Russian. The man's smile faltered, turned into a grimace.

"Well, now, that I wouldn't know."

He held up two fingers to his lips and whistled. A skinny high school kid with a freshly shaved neck slammed through the door, skidded to a stop. Looked around from the bald man to Miranda.

The older one gestured with his head toward Miranda.

"You help the lady, Walter. See what she wants."

He looked her up and down again, rubbed his nose, and slid past the counter through the same door.

The kid looked back and forth between them, mouth open. Then back to Miranda. Cleared his throat.

"What did you want here, Miss?"

She shrugged. "How much is a room?"

He licked his lips, still watching the right door. It was open a crack.

"We're, uh, we're full up, Miss. High season, you know? Sorry, but try Nance's or Pacheteau's."

Miranda said slowly: "I see. Thanks for your help."

The kid laughed nervously, relieved she didn't question the row of keys on the pegs behind him.

"You, uh, you hurt yourself, Miss?" He pointed to her arm.

She looked at him thoughtfully. "Accident. As a matter of fact, I'd love to see Dr. Aalder about it. He in?"

His eyebrows shot up to meet the short brown hair, and he shook his head.

"There ain't no Dr. Aal—"

A loud cough came from behind the doorway, and the teenager flushed red. Glanced at Miranda, then eyes to the floor, voice low.

"Sorry, Miss. Dr. Aalder ain't here. Best try one of the doctors in town." He looked up at her, his eyes confused and almost pleading. "Anything else you want?"

She stared at him. Said: "Thanks, sonny. Got everything I came in for."

Wrenched the glass doorknob and stepped down the three cement steps, feeling the sun on her back.

And two pairs of eyes.

Miranda ordered one egg, sunny-side up, bacon, and rye toast. Waiter at the counter was a thirtyish man with a small mouth and lank brown hair, not the cherubic soda jerk she'd noticed the night before. He wiped the glassware with a faded cotton cloth over and over again, eyes flickering up and down the linoleum counter. She kept her voice low.

"Let's meet again at one. Italian restaurant, corner of Washington."

Rick nodded, legs pressed close to hers. The tennis outfit was drawing more attention than she liked, and Miranda felt exposed sitting on the small stool, her feet touching the chromium bar below. Rick reached for the Tabasco sauce, liberally dousing his scrambled eggs and sausage.

"I called Meyer. You want me to phone that cop you talked to?"

She drained the coffee cup, pushed it toward the front of the counter for a refill, and nodded. "Inspector Fisher. Find out what you can about Dr. Aalder's, and get a list of all the doctors in Calistoga."

The counter waiter poured fresh coffee, glancing up at Miranda a little too long. She waited until he walked to the other end to ring up a man in overalls and muddy work boots.

Held the thick china cup in both hands, staring at the glass case filled with apple, peach, and rhubarb pies.

"There's something wrong here."

He shrugged. "There's something wrong with every small town, Miranda. And every big city."

A truck driver dropped a nickel in the juke, punching "Loch Lomond," Martha Tilton swinging with bagpipes and Benny Goodman, *By yon bonnie banks, and by yon bonnie braes, where the sun shines bright on Loch Lomond . . .*

They parted outside the drugstore, Miranda heading straight back to Nance's, Rick toward the office of the *Weekly Calistogian,* counting on brotherly love among the fourth estate.

She clutched a brown paper bag with a new Big Chief tablet inside, trying to ignore the stares and occasional low whistles from the farmworkers and truck drivers that filled the town with morning hustle.

Walked into the motel office. Blond Mary was back on duty, bored and reading the same *Photoplay.* She looked up when the doorbell jangled, raised her eyebrows at Miranda's arm.

"Mornin'. You hurt yourself?"

Miranda summoned up a flush. "While ago. It, uh . . . it was a car accident."

"Huh." The blonde just stood and stared, birthmark smeared and in a different place.

She gestured to the clothes. "You lookin' to play tennis? Thought Gracie was gonna do you up with a mud bath."

"Later. Have you got any rackets?"

Mary wiped an eye, nodded. "Ask Leroy. He'll get 'em out of the lockers for you, out by the pool."

Miranda said: "Thanks. Gracie around?"

The blonde smirked. "Gracie's always around. Cora's back today, but Gracie said she was gonna take care of you personal. She likes you. Ain't you lucky?"

Miranda looked into the girl's eyes until the blonde faltered and fell back in the chair, holding up the *Photoplay* and reading the ads in the back of the magazine for how to revive fading sex hormones. According to Rick, she didn't need any help.

The court next to the swimming pool was empty, net frayed and sagging with a hole in the center. Miranda looked around. Old lady and the browbeaten niece, more middle-aged women, and one young couple in the pool, trying to pretend it was Miami or Havana.

Not a whole hell of a lot to do in Calistoga. No tennis, no golf, just sit around and watch the fucking mud dry.

A weedy young man in a work suit dotted with wet clay walked out of the mud bath building.

"Excuse me — are you Leroy?"

He stammered, looking down at her legs. "Y-yeah, Miss. W-what can I h-help you with?"

"How about a tennis racket? You play?"

He shook his head, aghast. "We ain't allowed to play with the customers, Miss."

She murmured. "At least not tennis."

He looked confused. "Excuse me, Miss?"

Smiled, double bright. "Nothing, Leroy. I'd like a ball and two rackets, please."

She lit a cigarette while Leroy searched through lockers for the rackets. The young couple climbed out of the swimming pool and toweled off, throwing glances in her direction. She walked over, gave them a vacation smile.

"Either of you up for a game of tennis — provided our attendant can find the equipment?"

Her question was punctuated by a cacophony from the locker room. They all laughed, easy way of young people on holiday. Woman was around twenty-three, slim, and pretty, hair almost jet-black. Boyfriend — no ring on her left hand — ex-collegiate type, Berkeley or Stanford, maybe thirty. Both pasty and white, like they didn't get outside much.

Leroy came out of the main building holding two rackets unused since Helen Wills Moody won a gold medal in Paris. The girl stuck her hand out, Miranda shook it.

"My name's Nancy. We picked this place because it's called Nance's — funny, huh?"

"I'm Miranda."

Her boyfriend touched Nancy's arm, said, "I'll watch."

Looked up at Miranda. Eyes flickered. "Ralph's the name."

Miranda nodded, crushed the stub of the Chesterfield.

Nancy was a talker. Boyfriend was a banker in Oakland and she was at Cal, earning a master's degree in accounting. Miranda concentrated on the ball and tried not to trip on the uneven, neglected court. Played one-handed, left arm sore and stiff, but still managed to win the set 6–4.

She could feel Ralph's eyes on her. Wondered if he'd seen her somewhere, recognized her. Not a client at Dianne's, not a customer of Burnett's. She wiped her brow.

Gracie moved into her view and watched them play, meaty arms folded across her chest. From the mud bath building another woman emerged, short, smiling, dumpling shaped. She joined Gracie, watching the game. Must be Cora.

Miranda faulted on her serve, and the old lady with the niece shouted from poolside, calling Cora, who waddled over, dragging Gracie behind her. Miranda's breath came easier.

She won the second set in four straight games, Nancy getting bored and making eyes at Ralph instead of paying attention. Miranda called Leroy, told him they were finished. Waved good-bye to Nancy. Caught eyes with Gracie, gave her an imperceptible nod.

By the time she unlocked the cabin and wrapped two twenty-dollar bills inside the folded onionskin, Gracie was at the door.

Miranda opened it wordlessly, handed over the packet. Gracie unfolded the paper, shoved the money in a pocket of her dirty smock. Her eyes darted over the form. She looked up sharply.

"You Jewish?"

"Does that matter?"

The large woman sucked her teeth for a moment, staring at Miranda.

"I'll come for you about six."

She turned her back and stomped off down the gravel path.

Miranda took a deep breath.

■ ■ ■ ■

She showered and changed back to street clothes.

Ralph worried her, especially with Nancy's mouth attached.

Sat propped in bed and wrote in the Chief tablet:

Dr. Aalder
Dr. (abortion) — City? North?
How much $$?
Kaiser connection? Shot on Gayway?
Pandora's boyfriend?

She stared at the words for a while, lips pressed together, eyes troubled. Thought about the form she'd filled out, about Aalder's this morning, about the baby ring in her goddamn purse.

Picked up the pencil and scrawled in big capital letters:

EUGENICS.

Fuck.

It all pointed one way, Ann Cooper Hewitt and California law. Doctors in white, doctors and scientists trying to save the race, Aryans in America, Nazis in Germany. Science, fucking science, better living through chemistry, especially if your chemistry was white, Anglo-Saxon, and as Protestant as a clapboard church in New England.

Miranda shook her head. Ripped out the piece of paper and shoved it in her purse.

Dark waters in Calistoga, hellish with more than the smell of sulfur.

Weather was in the eighties, and most of Nance's patrons seemed to be soaking in the pool. Rick was waiting for her, small table in a corner, away from the window.

He handed her a list. She ran her eyes over it, stopped at Parkinson, frowning.

"Dr. Hugh Parkinson. Goddamn it, I've heard that name. He's only here part-time?"

Rick nodded, twisting a forkful of spaghetti. "Offices at 450 Sutter in the City, here two days a week. He's a dentist. Father was some political muckety-muck twenty years ago."

"Wish I could remember . . ."

She shook her head as if to clear it and reached across the table, laying a hand over Rick's.

"Meet me back here at four thirty. I think I know what's going on."

He chewed and swallowed. Said: "Mind telling me?"

She held his eyes.

"I don't know who, and I don't know how. But somebody's sterilizing Jews."

Twenty-Seven

Rick almost spit out the water. His cough drew eyes, and Miranda waited impatiently for the attention to subside.

"I told you. Sterilization is perfectly legal in California, whether you're Jewish or Catholic or Prot—"

"I'm not talking about elective surgery, Rick."

She leaned forward. "Annie didn't want an abortion. Sure, maybe she thought about it after a fight with Duggan — but goddamn it, she came up here for the same reason most people do — rest, relax, get away from the city. And Pandora wasn't even pregnant."

Miranda looked down at the white tablecloth, play of shadows from the tree outside making macabre patterns on the linen. She spoke low, as if to herself.

"Those women wanted children. Wanted to be able to have children with a man they

414

loved. Somebody sterilized them against their will."

Rick shoved aside the spaghetti, shook his head.

"Miranda, even involuntary sterilization is legal, if you've got the consent of certain people. I don't know the ins and outs, but —"

"Find out what they are, OK? Before five o'clock."

He rubbed his nose. "I'll try. But look — Pandora wasn't Jewish. And if a doctor sterilized them only to murder them later, why not do it on the operating table?"

"I don't know. I don't know how it all fits, don't know all the answers. But I know what I know." She unclenched her fists, knuckles on her thick fingers pale against reddened skin.

"I can't do anything at Nance's, just sit and wait. Aalder's involved, and if I could just remember where I've seen Parkinson . . ."

Her eyes grew wide.

"Jesus Christ, Rick. It's the fucking Musketeers."

She paid the bill, and they headed around the tree-lined corner of Washington, within view of Dr. Aalder's. Rick was already sweating in the hot afternoon sun. She grabbed his arm, tugging him toward the shade of the largest oak.

Miranda braced herself against the tree. Rick shoved his hat back on his head, stood close enough to smell her hair.

"We're safer in the open. Let people think we're necking."

Rick's lips brushed against the side of her head. "OK. Talk."

"Hugh Parkinson cofounded the Musketeers with a construction company owner, Samuel something. Fraternal businessman group, isolationist, hate Jews and FDR, love Hitler and Henry Ford. Meet at a bar in Maiden Lane called Tonypandy. They're growing — recruiting more roughneck members, probably as storm troopers."

Rick grunted. "Parkinson's a dentist, not a surgeon. And a lot of these big-mouthed bullies are just that — all talk. Christ, Miranda, you're accusing a prominent dentist of doing what even the Nazis haven't done."

She was trembling. Opened her purse and plucked out a Chesterfield. Rick stepped back, snapped his lighter. She held his hand and lit it, meeting his eyes over the stick. Deep inhale, long stream of smoke.

"Eugenic scientists in America are inspirations to Hitler — that's on the record, according to the Fuehrer himself. Or maybe you think all those 'sick' people they've been euthanizing are really sick."

She leaned back, tree bark digging in her back. Voice was even, controlled with effort.

"Sure, concentration camps are more efficient, but we don't really know what the hell the Nazis are doing. What about the Jews trapped in Lodz? What about the Jews in Belgium, now that Leopold's rolled over for the Wehrmacht?"

She brought a shaking hand to her lips, quick puff. Looked past Rick to the corner of Gerard and the dilapidated cottages of Dr. Aalder's Sanitarium.

"Right here and now we know this: Somebody paid for those two women to get tubal ligations. Somebody paid, somebody operated. Maybe a doctor on that list you gave me — a doctor that knows Parkinson."

Rick moved close to her again. Hand brushing her arm, eyes worried.

"I'm just a city beat reporter, Miranda, not Eddie Murrow or Bill Shirer. I'm holding my breath like everybody else. I'm here in a little town in Napa Valley trying to help a friend, and I'm telling you — all this talk about conspiracies and sterilized women and anti-Semitic killers sounds like some kind of goddamn plot drummed up by Warner Brothers."

Miranda watched the smoke curl up between the leaves of the tree, watched Rick's face flush red, smell of perspiration and scent of bay rum on his skin.

"Annie and Pandora were sterilized. Against their will. Then murdered a little over a year later, by someone who hates Jews. And a cop in San Francisco was railroaded, a medical examiner withheld evidence, and the U.S. Marshal's Office got involved, along with Hoover for all I know. That's no Saturday matinee."

He stepped forward, long body pressing against her, voice a rough whisper.

"Mary's walking down Lincoln. She just saw us."

"Pretend like we're arguing." Half a smile. "Won't be too hard."

Rick suddenly bent down, kissing her hard on the lips, heat and pressure from his body smothering her. Her hands balled into fists at her sides, and she shoved him back with both hands, breathless, wiping her mouth.

"What the fuck are you —"

"Shhh. She was watching us. Just walked into a bakery across the street." He grinned down at her, lipstick on his mouth. "Helps the cover, Miri."

She slid away from the tree trunk. Dropped the stick on the cement, rubbing it out with the toes of her sensible and ugly black walking shoes.

"Your goddamn cover is safe enough, Sanders. I'll see you at four thirty. Ask around about Parkinson and the Musketeers. And keep your ears open about Memorial Day."

"You really expecting trouble?"

"Allen said so. These groups aren't known for their peace rallies, unless it's peace with *der Vaterland*."

He pulled the fedora low over his forehead. "I said I'd meet the editor of the local rag for drinks. I'll ask him about Parkinson."

"Wipe the lipstick off your chin. You got enough money?"

"Flush enough. Just — well, goddamn it, be careful. Even if this isn't what you think it is."

"I'd better get back. You coming?"

"Yeah." He shook his head. "I still think it sounds nuts, Miranda. We're not in Berlin."

Miranda shielded her eyes against the bright sun, staring down Lincoln Avenue, small-town shops and corner cafés, smell of peach trees and grass and table wine grapes, rooster crowing from a farmhouse a few blocks away.

"No, Rick. Berlin's come to us."

She turned away from him, walking quickly down the Calistoga sidewalk.

Miranda kept to the stuffy, one-room cottage for the rest of the afternoon.

She was worried about Ralph and how he'd looked at her earlier, recognition flitting behind his eyes. Worried about Benedetti, too, still a target in Calistoga, always a target until memories of Martini could be scrubbed clean of brain and blood, like the dirty bathtub in the run-down house on Cordelia Street.

No goddamn evidence to speak of. What the fuck kind of detective was she, anyway, postcards and rings and matchbooks, the words of dead women, and they'd never hold up in court.

Promiscuous, the papers would say, attorneys with a snide, knowing look, wink and a leer at the jury. Whore-slut, spread her legs for a cheap cloth coat, new hat, bottle of French perfume.

Besides, ladies and gentlemen of the jury, Annie Learner was a Jew. Christ killer, Communist, no morals, why all you have to do is look at Hollywood to see what they've done to us. To US, to U.S. of A., to America the beautiful, America of spacious skies and no room at the counter for your kind, black, brown, yellow, red in lowercase or upper-. Poor and white, poor and anything.

It's a goddamn holy sin to be poor, Father, make your confession, say your Hail Marys, pray to Our Lady of Perpetual Help for some fucking perpetual income and a job that doesn't lay you off and make you spend company money at the company store.

Poverty's your own goddamn fault, and if we could just keep you slovenly dirty bastards from multiplying . . .

She ran a wet cloth under the dripping bathroom sink.

Drip-drop. Drip-drop.

Back to the sagging mattress, cloth on her forehead.

Miranda lit a cigarette and closed her eyes, head against her pillow.

She met Rick at four thirty, shadows starting to stretch tall under the leafy oaks lining the sidewalk. Italian restaurant again, waiter from last night, hand slicking his hair back, eyes challenging the man she walked in with.

"You don't look so good, Miranda."

"Health resorts don't agree with me. You find anything?"

He shoved the fedora off his forehead, still beaded with perspiration. Lit a Lucky Strike, nodded.

"Maybe. Parkinson drives up here on Mondays and Tuesdays. Drove back to the City this morning. I left a message for your pal Fisher, told him he might want to check on it."

Rick paused, drawing down the stick. Hunched forward, propped his elbows on the table.

"Got something interesting from Dewey Scott — editor I told you about. He knows Parkinson vaguely and has heard of the Musketeers. Businessman's organization, secret initiations, Masonic stuff, you know the type. Knew Parkinson was involved, and knows Parkinson doesn't like Jews — the good dentist doesn't make a secret of it."

Furrows around his mouth grew deep. Rick inhaled until the end of the cigarette was glowing bright red.

"Now Monday night, Scott saw Parkinson talking to a couple of other men at Johnny's. Scott was at the bar, nursing a Scotch like good newspapermen do, and they didn't notice him."

The waiter appeared suddenly at their table, eyes caressing Miranda.

"Your ravioli, signorina. And your spaghetti, signor." He bent forward, voice a purr. "Wine, signorina? We have more of the Sangiovese."

She shook her head, gave him a smile. Rick said in a louder voice. "Thanks. That'll be all for now."

The waiter tossed him a contemptuous look, stalked off toward the counter.

Miranda sipped her water, looking at Rick over the rim.

"Your cover holding up all right?"

"Don't you worry about my cover. Listen — that night — Monday — Parkinson threw around a lot of money. Scott saw a couple C-notes change hands. He was curious because the men with Parkinson looked like stir-birds, not the vest pocket, country club kind of company he normally keeps."

"Your friend's got good eyes. How're his ears?"

Rick grinned, crushed the Lucky out in the tray. "He caught a couple of words that made him curious: 'government place' and 'rocket's red glare.' That last bit is what really made him listen, since he said they weren't the type to be singing 'The Star-Spangled Banner.' "

Miranda made a note in the back of her *Chadwick's Guide*. " 'Government place'? You sure that's what they said?"

"That's what Scott said he heard. Why?"

She poked at the ravioli with her fork. "I don't know, Sanders. Memorial Day's got me worried. Whole goddamn thing reminds me of that Christian Front mob in New York. The trial's going on, not getting much coverage out here, and the defense attorney's making a joke of bomb plots. Not such a joke to the Jews getting beat up on the subway. I need answers, goddamn it, and all I come up with are more questions."

Rick sprinkled Parmesan cheese on his plate and rolled up a forkful of spaghetti.

"I'm not saying I'd bet on you, Miranda — you're too much of a long shot — but you do have a way of closing in the last furlong."

She smiled. "Thanks. I think. As long as that means I'm Seabiscuit and not a nag you lost a week's salary on."

He reached over, picked up her hand, and held it. Eyes blue, crinkled at the corner. Goddamn lilt back in his voice.

"You'd be worth it."

She pulled her hand away. "I know you don't like cheap blondes, but I don't think she's in the restaurant. You find anything else? Anything on Aalder's?"

He studied her for a moment. Dropped his eyes to the plate.

"Used to be Iacherri's. Something else before that. Nobody's ever seen a Dr. Aalder, and Scott said it's owned by a corporation. That's all anybody knows."

She nodded, writing it down next to "government place" and "rocket's red glare." Looked down at the words and sighed, deep and long.

"I'd better be getting back."

He gestured to the uneaten plate of ravioli in front of her. "You forgot your dinner."

"I'm not hungry."

He leaned forward. "Listen, Miranda, if this is even close to what you think it is, there's more than one man involved — hell, it's a wholesale indictment. I did some checking — California's sterilized more people than any other state in the country. The Department of Institutions replaced the old Lunacy Commission almost twenty years ago, and all the state and private hospitals pretty much run things how they want. As long as the board of trustees signs off with a psychiatrist, the operation's perfectly legal."

Her eyes fell to the clumps of red sauce and mushrooms on the abandoned ravioli. She stood up, shoved the chair in.

"Try parking at the old farm road across from the train tracks. Be seein' you, Rick."

425

He looked up at her, mouth tight. "Be seein' you."

Rap on the door at 5:45. Heavy, coarse hands. Gracie.

Travel cases near Miranda, packed and ready. Gracie stood in the doorway, eyed her up and down. Voice high soprano, body a gross non sequitur.

"You leave that here. I'll bring 'em, if'n the doctor decides to help."

"Any reason he wouldn't? I brought money."

The big woman chuckled, ran the scales up and down like fingernails on a chalkboard.

"He don't need money, girlie. I'm the one like that."

Gracie wrapped a beefy hand around her upper left arm, and Miranda flung it off, angry.

"Don't touch me."

The woman paused, sneer stretching her fat face.

"From the looks of things, you ain't used to sayin' that much. All right then, lady — come on."

She turned her massive back and headed down the gravel path, twisting left.

They crossed the old farm road, poppies

shut tight for the evening, drooping bright orange. Miranda hoped Rick was watching with the car. Crossed the railroad tracks, stepping through the overgrown thistles grown up between the wooden slats.

Same way Miranda walked earlier, on her way to Dr. Aalder's Sanitarium.

Gracie unlocked one of the freestanding cottages lining Gerard Street. Second from the end, dilapidated, paint peeling. Miranda's nose wrinkled from the smell of mildew. She turned to Gracie.

"This is where I meet the doctor?"

The attendant rubbed her hands down her muddy smock and nodded.

"You wait here. He'll be along directly."

Gracie shut the door behind her, and Miranda heard the key turning in the lock.

So much for any change of mind.

Sagging single bed, ancient coverlet, one dresser with the wood veneer peeling off, one nightstand with a lamp, one wingback chair with torn upholstery. No radiator, no hot plate, no radio. Made Nance's look like fucking Biarritz.

She flung open the drawer of the nightstand. No Bible, no papers. Tried the dresser and found old newspapers lining the bottom, dating back to '35.

Miranda sank on the bed. Lit a Chester-field, hands shaking. Another knock on the door.

Punctual. Six o'clock even.

Key turned in the lock, and she expected to see Gracie. A well-dressed man in an old-fashioned high collar stood on the cracked cement, hatless, oiled brown hair receding and faded gray at the temples. Slight double chin, full lips, careful blue eyes.

He murmured: "Miss Korbe?"

He gave it the Russian accent she'd pronounced it with at Aalder's that morning. Miranda nodded, stepped back. He walked into the room, one hand in a vest pocket. Checked his pocket watch.

"I like to be on time for my patients. Please sit down."

She sat stiffly on the edge of the mattress. "Thank you, Doctor . . . ?"

He smiled, dimples making indentations above his jowls. " 'Doctor' will be fine. You can understand, Miss Korbe, a man in my position must be very careful. And yet — cases such as yours interest me very much. I believe we are given gifts to help how we can, where we can."

"You'll — you'll perform the operation, then?"

He nodded, still smiling. "There's a recovery period, of course. That will take place here at Aalder's, though" — he looked around the room with distaste — "perhaps not in this cabin."

"You haven't mentioned money, Doctor. I'm afraid I don't have much."

He waved soft, pudgy hands in the air, fingernails long for a medical man. A silver signet ring gleamed on his middle finger, left hand.

"As I said, we are given gifts to help, not to profit. I'm interested in helping you out of your, er, dilemma. One hundred dollars should be sufficient. Do you have that much?"

She opened her purse. Counted out one hundred dollars in tens and twenties, thrust it at the doctor. He held up his hands.

"Oh no, not here, please. You can pay my associate in my — in my office."

She mustered up one of those brave little women, Olivia de Havilland–type smiles.

"I don't know how to thank you, Doctor."

He patted the knees of his striped pants, benevolence oozing from every manicured pore.

"I'm happy to help. And now it's time."

She looked around the room in phony dismay. "Surely, not here . . ."

Small, professional chuckle. "Of course

not, Miss Korbe. You'll be driven to a safe, sanitary environment." He stood up, held out his hand. She took it, pretending to notice his ring for the first time.

"That your class ring, Doctor? Mine begins with an 'M,' too — graduated from Mills."

Soft, damp fingers squirmed like fat maggots.

"I won't be in the same car, you understand. Grace and another assistant will be driving you. Wait here."

She nodded while he opened the door, glanced to his left, and shut it behind him. Key in the lock again.

Deep breath, in and out, one Mississippi, two Mississippi, three Mississippi . . .

Miranda counted thirty-seven Mississippis before the unmistakably heavy hand of Gracie rapped on the doorway again.

She opened the door. Gracie and the kid from Aalder's stood in front of her, holding her luggage. Gracie gestured with her head, growled: "Come on."

Miranda picked up her purse and followed them. Walter was nervous, his shaved neck broken out with acne, head wobbling back and forth like a carnival doll. Led her to a black Plymouth two-door sedan, at least five or six years old. He slid behind the wheel, and Gracie squeezed in next to Miranda in the backseat. Car started up after four tries, the boy licking dry lips and muttering to himself.

He finally backed out of Aalder's parking lot. Headed down Lincoln past Nance's, turning south down a narrow gravel road. She craned a quick look behind. Clouds of yellow brown dust in between the poppies and mustard weeds, Plymouth kicking up gravel.

No sign of a car. No sign of Rick.

Twenty-Eight

The road was long, dry, bumpy. Parts raw dirt, furrows still caked hard and deep from the rivulets of rain washing down from Mount Saint Helena and the Vaca Mountains in early spring. Miranda smoked three Chesterfields, one after the other. Tried to talk to Gracie.

The big woman looked out the window, grunted answers, while the kid sweated for twenty miles, the old Plymouth shocks bouncing them up and down on the seat. No Rick, no other cars except twenty-year-old farm trucks and a couple of tractors.

Not a road for tourists. Red-tailed hawks swooped down on field mice crouching in the tall grass, and birds warbled over the rumble of the car motor, rattle and clank of rocks and gravel rolling under the high rubber tires.

Miranda tried again. "Say, Gracie . . ."

Grunt.

"Did you suggest the doc to Annie or did Annie come to you? She never told me."

The fat woman's eyes narrowed into folds, skin mapped in pink and red across her cheeks. Braids were still in place, though her hair was oily and coated with dust and grime.

"What's it to you?"

Miranda shrugged. "Just tryin' to pass the time."

Gracie looked out the window again. "She your friend, 's up to her to tell you. I ain't gonna tell you nothin'. Leastwise not for the fifty bucks you gave me."

"Just trying to pass the time, like I said, but I figured you should get the credit more than Annie. Figure on making her a present, soon as all this is behind me."

The big woman snorted. "You lookin' to give out presents, lady, you should start with me. Your friend din't know up from down till I told her 'bout the doc. She just wanted to lay around and mope, like most of them big-city broads do when they come up here, whinin' and cryin'."

Hard smile, and she cracked her knuckles, popping each of them in turn.

"I'm the one to set her up. I'm the one to give her the idea. An' I'm the one to make sure she goes through with it when she tries to back out."

Her face fell together and flushed, wishing the squealed words of triumph back inside the fat red mouth. Darted a glance toward Miranda, who pretended not to notice anything.

Miranda said, unperturbed: "Well, I'll make a present to you, then, Gracie. You've been a big help."

The big woman shoved an elbow into Miranda's wounded arm. "Make sure you remember that, lady. Jus' remember it."

Miranda held on to her left arm with her right hand, looking through the dusty window. Wouldn't show pain, not in front of the woman beside her.

For the hundredth time, she wondered what the hell happened to Rick.

They finally reached the junction for 28 but turned east instead of west, rolling across another gravel road for twelve miles, heading toward Davis.

Walter tried to turn on the radio, couldn't hear anything but static and the tires vomiting up rocks behind them. Gracie refused to say anything else. Miranda kept checking her watch and the rearview mirror, hoping to see the outlines of her rented DeSoto. Caught eyes with the pimply kid. He looked scared, eyes darting back to the road, lamps of the old Plymouth bumping up and down the pitted surface, fighting the dusk.

They finally crawled to a paved road at the 37 junction, turning south toward Vallejo. Twilight almost over as the land opened up toward San Pablo Bay, fields of wheat and cattle stretching out on either side of the road, cars and trucks keeping the Plymouth company. They passed a sign for Imola.

Still no Rick.

Reached a small paved road and a hulking stone archway, illuminated by a light post and the headlamps of the Plymouth. The road beyond the gate was long and led into what looked like a fairy-tale castle, turrets and towers, tall, leafy trees lining the road. A California bear flag flew beside the pale stone arch, rippling in the steady wind.

Miranda caught a glimpse of the signpost as Walter swung the Plymouth through the arch. Gripped the handle on the passenger side of the car.

Stone plaque, etched with words.

NAPA STATE HOSPITAL FOR THE INSANE.

The kid pulled the car around a sweeping driveway to the back of the castle, to what looked like a service and delivery entrance

435

of a mammoth country estate. Only the bars at the brick arched windows suggested you wouldn't find the Duke and Duchess of Windsor at home.

Miranda tried to control her breathing, tried to think ahead. Rick told her psychiatric hospitals and homes for poor people performed most of the sterilizations in the state. Napa was one of the largest, almost completely self-sufficient, with something over two thousand acres of farm, orchards, cattle, vegetable gardens, and a bakery. Easy place to lose more than your mind.

Gracie motioned her out of the car, and she barely had a chance to look up at the fairy-tale turrets before the woman's fat claws dug into her elbow, propelling her toward an open door and through a huge kitchen and pantry, white and yellow tile, smell of vegetable peelings and disinfectant. A car door slammed and Miranda craned her neck backward to see Walter drive toward a large gray garage about fifty yards from the house.

Pale-eyed women with straggly hair and tired mouths were peeling potatoes along a long tiled counter on the left, while on the right two men in baker's hats mixed dough for the next day's bread. No one looked up at her.

Gracie pushed her, sudden and hard, through the end of the kitchen area into a dim passageway. Miranda nearly lost her balance, threw up her arm in a windmill, and whirled to face the fat woman, teeth clenched.

"I told you once — keep your goddamn hands off me."

Gracie shrugged in her dirty smock, braids gray from the dust on the road. "Doc ain't got all night to take care of the likes of you. Move."

Miranda's arm was on fire, breath quick and shallow. She needed a cigarette. She needed a fucking plan.

She quickly followed Gracie through the corridor, rooms on either side of the passage double-bolted, occasional droning voices, more machinelike than human, filtering through the thick painted white wood and the small barred windows at the top. A man with a thick southern drawl was reading the Bible, and a woman's raspy voice shrieked in protest from a room across the hall.

I applied mine heart to know, and to search, and to seek out wisdom, and the reason of things, and to know the wickedness of folly, even of foolishness and madness . . .

The woman's scream choked in a rush of

words, angry, incoherent. Powerless.

A burly male attendant about thirty-five and dressed in a dingy white uniform walked toward them down the passageway, face bored. Gracie nodded to him, crooked a finger. He stopped, staring at Miranda. The woman in number 114 started to sob. The reading continued, male voice and its twang sounding pleased with the reception.

And I find more bitter than death the woman, whose heart is snares and nets, and her hands as bands: whoso pleaseth God shall escape from her; but the sinner shall be taken by her.

The woman flung herself at the door. *Thump-thwack. Thump-thwack.* Sound of flesh on wood, no caution, no care for injury. Rhythmic, regular, like a goddamn metronome, door shuddering with each attack. No cry of pain.

Gracie was murmuring something to the attendant, both of them oblivious. Then the scratching started, audible even over the heartbeat in Miranda's ears, pounding in her chest. Fingers and nails digging gutters in wood, small, gouged channels where the blood from broken skin would flow, blood from whatever part of her body she could hurt, maim, kill. Repeated syllables, over and over. Something about the Bible, snares and nets and traps. Twisted, distorted, her own language. Recited like a litany, rosary of pain.

"Can't you do anything to help? She's hurting herself."

The attendant shrugged, looking her up and down, mouth curled. "Like she hurt her own five-year-old daughter? Maybe you'd like to hold her hand, lady — I wouldn't."

Gracie motioned with her head for Miranda to follow, triumphant smile stretching her fat cheeks.

Miranda stared at them both. Straightened her back and walked through the rest of the corridor, chased by the madwoman's strangled sobs and the peculiar, sadistic croak of Ecclesiastes as recited by the man in number 113.

Gracie gestured to a room on the third floor, and again the key turned in the lock. Said she'd be back for the money.

The room was small. Looked like the cubbyhole of a law clerk, chipped ecru-colored paint fading down to dark red wainscoting. No pictures on the small oak desk, no certificates on the wall.

Not his real office, Miranda thought. Dr. Jowls would be close by, though. Not the kind of man who liked to be inconvenienced.

The air smelled like old carbon paper. Better than the passageway, with the cotton candy odor of ether floating like a threat, no Gayway smell, no popcorn, no loud, raucous laughter, at least not the kind you hear on Treasure Island. Goddamn it, the place unnerved her, cold eyes of attendants and staff, dead to the world they controlled, more inhuman than the sick bastards they were supposed to be taking care of.

Miranda jumped off the wooden chair, lit a cigarette to take away the smell. Kept the case in her hand, stick calming her down enough to try the file cabinets.

No luck. Tried the desk. Last year's calendar, pocket Bible, blank paper. Not a goddamn thing.

Key turned in the lock outside, and the doctor stepped inside the small room, face flushed to his scalp, expression grave. Gracie scowled, small piggish eyes glaring like coals.

Something was wrong.

Gracie moved to flank Miranda from the right side. The doctor walked toward her slowly, sorrow drooping the jowls, deepening the dimples. Looked like Hoover after the Bonus Army march.

"Miss, uh, Korbe . . ."

She leaned backward against the small desk, Chesterfield between her fingers. The smoke curled up and around the dingy yellow light globe on the ceiling, forming a question mark.

"Yes, Doctor? I'm ready with the payment whenever —"

He sighed, shook his head. Gracie took a step closer, beefy arms folded across her chest.

"No need."

The eyes that met hers were large, blue, liquid. Full of reproach.

"We've just received a call from an associate. It seems you are not the woman you claim to be."

Fucking tennis bastard at Nance's. Recognized her from somewhere, probably some jerk-off sonofabitch she tossed out of Sally's.

She shifted her weight. Purse was under her arm, still open. Tried to hide her shaking hands.

"What bothers you the most, Doctor — that I've uncovered your little eugenics lab or that you lost a chance to sterilize another Jew?"

The fat woman made a motion toward

Miranda.

"Wait, Gracie."

She halted like a trained Doberman, mid-step. He ran a puffy white hand over his sweaty forehead. Voice was matter-of-fact, sure and certain.

"You're a private investigator, Miss Corbie. And, I understand, a prostitute. Thank God you're not pregnant — you'd be an unfit mother of morons and criminals. In a moral world you would never have been born." He shook his head. "Your kind are why this once great nation is floundering. All the strength and virility sucked out of our country by radicals. Degenerates."

Miranda brought the cigarette to her lips, slow inhale. Stared at the yellowish whites of his eyes, the flushed cheeks. Blew a stream of smoke over his right ear.

"I'm sure you know all about what degenerates suck, Doctor."

His skin flamed red up to the distinguished gray temples and pink, shiny scalp. Gracie interjected a squeal.

"Let me do her, Doc. I can shoot her up with somethin' — dump her over on the river wharf. Nobody round there this hour."

He looked at Miranda thoughtfully.

"No, Gracie. Too many questions. I think it would be far better to make Miss 'Korbe'

— or Miss Corbie — disappear."

Miranda's stomach clenched. He read the whitening of her skin, and his full lips stretched in a prim smile.

"Indeed, Miss Corbie. You'll be admitted under a Jane Doe. Simple case of nymphomania and an unsuccessful operation. I'm sure I'll find you have enlarged sex organs when I operate."

His eyes fell to between her legs, and she felt soiled, violated beneath the light summer dress.

"You've interfered in a noble enterprise — something bigger than merely my profession or reputation." He shook his head again. "No. I consider this a correction of nature's mistake."

He and Grace moved in coordination, stepping toward her.

Miranda's eyes darted back and forth. Could only tackle one. He removed a pair of handcuffs from his coat pocket. Three feet. Two feet. Her right hand was poised over the cigarette case in her open purse.

"Nature's mistake. Like rocket's red glare?"

Shot in the dark.

He stopped midstride, hands outstretched with the open cuffs. Consternation now, surprise and anger.

"What do you know about it?"

She shrugged, kept her elbows close, trying to control the trembling racking her legs, her body. Still clutching the cigarette.

"Enough."

He looked back and forth between Miranda and the disappointed Grace. Barked a command to the heavy woman, handed her the cuffs.

"Lock her up and sedate her. I need to make a phone call."

"Glad to, Doc."

He cast one look back, warning to Gracie.

"No marks on the outside."

The door closed softly behind him. Key in the door again. Gracie turned to face Miranda, gloating smile. Her fat fingers played with the handcuffs.

"I knew you wasn't right from the beginning. Askin' 'bout that girl."

"The one you killed?"

The beefy woman made a face. "We ain't killed nobody. Jew bitch got more than she counted on, but we ain't the ones who killed her. You're the first, sister. A real honor."

She took a lumbering step toward Miranda.

"I been lookin' for some fun."

The Chesterfield was almost gone, but a quick puff lit the ember at the end. Miranda pivoted right so her left hand was over Gracie's thick, pulpy fists, and she slammed the stub into the fleshy part of the fat woman's arm. Gracie let out a yelp, face convulsed. Miranda took two steps backward, yanked out the thick gold cigarette case. Her purse hit the floor, drawing Gracie's eyes, and when the other woman lifted her head, she was staring into the muzzle of a Baby Browning.

Miranda's breath was ragged.

"Last time I used this I blew a man's brains out. Set the cuffs on the desk."

She moved sideways around the fat woman, pushing the tiny gun against the back of Gracie's skull. The big woman let out a Donald Duck squeal between her lips. She tossed the cuffs on the small oak desk, and they landed with a loud clatter, sliding toward the other side.

"Move to the chair. Slow."

Gracie swung her head like a pendulum, one step at a time in a half-circle around the desk. Miranda ground the Baby Browning tight enough to leave red gashes in the back of the fat woman's scalp.

"Face the door and sit in the chair."

Miranda pushed past the filing cabinets and storage boxes, making sure no obstacles were in her way. Gracie sat down, her

445

breathing heavy. Miranda stood behind her.

"Sit on your hands."

Gracie complied, shifting her bulk from left to right and back again, while with her left hand, Miranda leaned over her and reached for the cuffs.

No goddamn time. She expected the sound of the key in the lock at any second.

"Now clasp your hands together on the top of your head."

The large woman leaned forward, some bravado coming back into her voice. "Doc'll fix you up real pretty for this, lady. He'll make you feel it 'fore you go."

Miranda twisted the barrel harder. "Shut the fuck up and put your hands on your head."

Gracie locked her pudgy fingers together on top of her grimy braids. With her left hand, Miranda snapped one of the cuffs on the fat woman, the steel barely closing over her wrist.

"Goddamn bitch — that hurt!"

Snapped on the right cuff while Gracie complained again.

"You jus' wait — you think you're so smart, Miss Private Detective, some kind of goddamn Commie is what you are, just like your goddamn Jew friends —"

Miranda stood up straight, deep breath.

Quickly cradled the Browning in the palm of her right hand and slammed it into the back of Gracie's skull with as much strength as she could muster. The large woman slumped forward, out cold on the oak surface.

Miranda checked for a pulse, found one. Reached around Gracie to the pockets of her smock. Plucked out a rack of keys. Picked up the cigarette case and purse off the floor, tucked everything under her arm. Took several gulps of air, smoothed her skirt, brushed her hair back. Kept the Browning in the palm of her hand.

Time to find the doctor.

TWENTY-NINE

She bent forward over the lock, listening for voices outside. Nothing.

Skeleton key on the set from Gracie's pocket was filed to work on more than one lock. She tried it, holding her breath at the click of the tumbler, listening again, pushing the door open a crack.

Browning was still in her right palm, damp from the sweat of her hand. She flicked the safety back on with her thumb.

Miranda slid out into the dully lit hall, keeping her back to the open door while she pulled it shut, scanning the corridor. When it clicked, she turned around and locked it again, checking from right to left down the empty passageway.

The room was at the T nexus of another corridor. She'd walked up that direction from the stairway and the labyrinth of cells off the first-floor kitchen. Too much exposure, but the doctor could be right or left or even down the passage toward the stairs. Her eyes landed left on a door marked LAUNDRY.

Footsteps up the corridor. She hurried toward the laundry room, tried the knob. Door opened and she squeezed inside, small dark space, smell of sweat, piss, blood, and vomit hanging heavy in the still air. Left knee banged into a wood-and-metal laundry cart, and she bit her tongue to keep from crying out. Froze, listening.

Voices outside with the tap-slide of footsteps on the tile floor. They were near the file room.

One was the doctor.

Other voice was deep, guttural, unpolished. "It's all set, Doc. You don't got to worry."

Nasal, whining noise, not the sure surgeon from a few minutes earlier.

"I'm expecting a call from the old man anytime now. We need to get this — this thing solved. I'd planned something — something easy and clean —"

Two more sets of footsteps, two voices, male and female. Whispered "Hush" by Jowls, grunt from the guttural man. Words more clear as the feet approached. Something about the patient in number 114.

Younger male voice spoke. "Good evening,

Dr. Gosney."

"Dr. Richardson."

So Gosney was the bastard's name. Miranda leaned against the door, breath shallow.

"Number 114 tried to gouge out her eyes with her thumbs. Nurse Hill here arrived in time to prevent it, but I'm not sure if we'll be able to restore her sight. I know you were interested in ordering a lobotomy on the woman. . . ."

"Yes. Excellent candidate. Not until her injuries heal, of course. We can send her to Toller over at Stockton. He's the most experienced."

The younger doctor made an agreeable noise. "Well, I'll keep you updated. Someone told me they saw a woman come in through the kitchen — another Jane Doe?"

Nervous chuckle from Gosney. "Another sex case, Dr. Richardson. We do get our share, don't we?"

"Certainly seem to." Pause, then: "Go on, Hill, change your gown. Can't let the patients see that blood."

The nurse replied meekly, "Yes, Doctor."

Footsteps toward the laundry room.

Miranda backed up, and her left hand struck another knob. Closet.

She squeezed through the door and fought her way to the hot, humid corner, behind muslin and wool, uniforms and smocks on thick wooden hangers, smell of mothballs and ammonia threatening to make her sneeze. Held her breath, eyes watering.

The light flicked on, shone pale yellow through the half-inch crack at the bottom of the door. She was in a wardrobe filled with white-and-blue uniforms.

Hill was still in the outer room, grunting as she removed the bloodstained clothing.

Footsteps again.

Closet door flung open.

Look up, lady, not down, don't rummage in the corner, don't spot the black walking shoes, the bulge behind the last row of smocks. White flash, like a gunshot, like a cannon blast, like dust and dirt along the ancient olive groves in the little hut, bombs dropping from German planes, mangled flesh scoring the red Spanish earth with more red, more blood, more life. Goddamn it, Randy, stay where you are, don't run out like a goddamn bunny rabbit . . .

Miranda closed her eyes. The nurse shut the light, shut the door with a click.

Miranda nearly fell, knees buckling. Grabbed at a hanger, clatter of wood against wood.

Light in the outside room shut off. Hill was gone.

Didn't know how many seconds she shrank back in the corner, holding her breath. Blinked her eyes, still sore from the sudden light. Crept out of the closet, groping with her left hand, right arm cradling the pistol and pressing the purse against her side. Picked up the voices in the hallway again.

Guttural voice. ". . . never know what hit 'em. Got everything planted during the celebration." Tone rose a little, boasting. "Won't be no opening ceremony next week. Not after tomorrow."

"Keep your voice down, Ralph. All right. I'm sure she was bluffing. I still need to wait for Parkinson. Why don't you search for that man she was with . . . report back to me with any information."

Grunt. "Office, Doc?"

"327. You never remember."

She could hear the rough-voiced man grin. "Yeah, but I do the important stuff. Ain't my fault I get the numbers backwards."

Heavy footsteps strode off down the perpendicular hall, back to the stairs and the kitchen.

Gosney sighed, took a few steps. Probably

paused outside the file room door. Steps moved on. She let out another breath.

Miranda straightened up, groped her way back to the closet. Felt on the hangers until she found a loose smock. Set the purse down on her feet and wrapped the jacket around her, too big, but in company colors.

Picked up the purse, tucked it under her arm again, and carefully made her way out of the laundry room and into the hall.

Deep gasp of air, fight the knot of fear in the gut, impulse to run like hell.

She knew what Gosney and Parkinson and the Musketeers were planning.

June 7, a week from tomorrow, was the dedication of the Federal Building, address Government Way on Treasure Island.

Tomorrow, May 30, Memorial Day. They were going to blow it up.

The file room was unnumbered. Gracie still out cold, no sound from behind the door. Miranda glanced down at the Baby Browning in her palm. Made a handy blackjack.

Her legs were starting to shake, and she hurried down the corridor on the other side of the file room, direction of Gosney's footsteps.

Two nurses were walking up from the stairwell, laughing. She was in front of them.

Slowed down, normal walk. Held her right arm pressed to her side. They came up the corridor, turned left toward the laundry room.

Breathe again, steps quick.

Dr. Satterthwaite. Dr. Douglas. Break room, with lockers. Number 317. Unmarked. Dr. Roland Bennett.

Light under the office door for number 327.

A young male orderly was stomping down the corridor carrying a tray with covered dishes, whistling under his breath. He gave her a curious look, and she met his eyes, smiled, checked her watch, and strode purposefully toward the office door. Held up her hand as if to knock, then dropped it, waiting patiently.

He craned his neck, last glimpse, "Stardust" shrill and out of tune. She counted the footsteps as he walked away, turning left down the hall toward the stairs and kitchen.

Silence again. Except for the voice through Gosney's door. The doctor sounded distressed, voice higher pitched.

"Goddamn it, Hugh, I did what I thought best. I still think we — Yes, yes, I know. I know you've pulled all the strings. . . . Of course I don't want to see your son endang —" Pause while he listened. "All right. . . .

No — perfectly legal. I can set it up in Peta-luma. We've got boys on the force . . . not ours, Silver Shirts. Uh-huh. All right. No, we can use her real name. She was a whore, for Christ's sake. She'll be on the operating table tomorrow morning and just won't wake up."

Pause again. Miranda inched closer, look-ing up and down the hallway.

"It'll go off. Ralph's got everything under control. Show those sonsofbitches who the real Americans are. . . . Yes, Hugh, I know. I am. I am calming down. . . . All right. I'll start setting it up with Petaluma. Yes — don't worry. You won't have to pull any strings with this one. Yes. G'bye now."

Miranda took a deep breath.

Flung the door open.

His mouth gaped like a fish. Beads of sweat dotted his forehead, the full lips and cheru-bic cheeks flushed and discolored.

She shut the door with her left hand. Slid the safety off and aimed the Baby Browning at his chest with her right.

"Keep your hands on the desk where I can see them."

He blinked a few times, denial, shock. Slowly splayed the fat, wormy fingers on the polished walnut surface, gray and brown hairs on the backs of his hands pricked upward by nerves.

"How — how did —"

"I want two things from you."

He swallowed a few times. Nerve was coming back. "And if I don't comply? Shoot me, and you'll be committing yourself here or Tehachapi."

"You were going to kill me anyway. I'm not afraid to die. Are you?"

Miranda trained the pistol on his chest. One of his hands slid toward the right.

Eyes narrowed, focused. Good soldier, Miranda. Good soldier.

"The bullet's already chambered. Move again and I'll blow your hands and kneecaps off before I get to your head."

He sucked air in through his teeth, slid the hand back. "What do you want?"

"Medical records on Annie Learner and Pandora Blake. Proof of what you did to them — before you had them murdered."

Big eyes, bloodshot. He sputtered, "I — I didn't order anyone to be killed. You were the first one — forced to it —"

"First but not last, is that how it works, Doctor? Or don't you think your little 'bombs bursting in air' exercise is going to hurt anyone?"

Blood flared into his face again, back

straight. Wrong tactic, never argue with a fucking fanatic. The Browning was slipping a little in her palm, and she shifted her weight, arms and legs tingling from the pressure, tense and tight.

"We're taking back America for Americans. This country's diseased, sick, needs to be purged before it can be healthy again. Jews, niggers, wops, micks — breed like flies — running the government, squeezing out taxpayers, taking our money. Getting us in a Jew war — Hitler's got the right ideas about how to make a country strong —"

"Like sterilizing the people you object to. And blowing up the Federal Building on Treasure Island." Her stomach knotted with anger, overriding the fear and pain. Grip tightened on the Browning.

"Get me the goddamn files."

He rose slowly from the chair, hands in the open. "I have to look inside the file cabinet. Names?"

"Learner and Blake. One was a Jewish girl whose pregnancy you aborted before you sterilized her. The other one was her friend. She wasn't pregnant, and thanks to you, never would be."

She took two steps forward, gesturing with the small pistol, disgust and fury keeping both gun and voice steady.

"Be careful, Doctor. I'm degenerate enough not to need much excuse."

He was shaking as he turned his back to her, bent over, and unlocked the middle cabinet.

"When?"

"Around April of last year. Through your hatchet man Gracie up at Nance's. Girls came looking for an escape and wound up in your little recuperation ward at Aalder's, hating themselves. Then they wound up dead."

He riffled through green and manila hanging folders, sweat from the back of his neck making a ring around the high collar. Fetid smell of fear, clinging like cologne.

"We had nothing to do with that."

"Maybe. Maybe you had your boss Parkinson get on the phone with the D.A., drop a few hints not to look into it much and pick up a quick fall guy, somebody with a connection to one of the girls, with a bad record and questionable politics."

He froze, body awkward and stiff. Slowly spun to face her like Annie's music box ballerina, two green folders in his hands. *With a love that's true, always . . .*

He whispered: "I knew you were dangerous. I should have just killed you when I had the chance."

"Drop the fucking folders on the edge of the desk, Dr. Gosney. And back up."

Blue irises quivered back and forth, never leaving her face. He stepped backward until he was standing against the still open filing cabinet drawer.

"Very good. Now sit down and call Parkinson. Tell him the bomb plan's already blown."

Flame lit behind the eye, and he raised his chin. "I'd rather you shoot me."

She reached out and picked up the two folders, transferring her purse to under her right arm, Browning up and aimed high. Stared at the doctor, stout, sleek, successful, wrapped in a fantasy, American hero. Deciding who was clean enough to live. Killing children not yet born.

Her eyes started to water, and his face blended into that of Father Coughlin and the "Christian Front Boys" on trial in New York. Wavered again, and now he was a Nazi soldier with shaved hair and a laughing mouth, setting a synagogue on fire in 1938, screams, desperate wails, pounding, flailing fists on the wooden doors.

And still it swirled like the merry-go-round on the Gayway, calliope playing the Horst Wessel song, sound of jackboots marching over Spanish soil, sound of German bombs dropping on Guernica. Shriek of women, blood and brains smeared on rags.

Clutching dead husbands. Cradling dead children.

The Browning spit fire and blew a hole in his stomach.

He fell back into his office chair, shock on his face, red swirling from the center of the small wound.

Miranda fled down the hall.

Footsteps. Doors slammed on either side. Somebody hit an alarm.

Headed down the corridor toward the stairway, met three men and two women dressed in uniforms coming straight at her.

She ran up to them, breathless. "Was that on this floor? I was on my way to number 114 when I thought I heard a shot."

One of the shorter men nodded. "We're checking all the rooms. You see anything unusual, anybody who shouldn't be here?"

She wrinkled her brow as if in thought. "Y-yes, now that I remember. I was coming from the break room around the corner — about half an hour ago — and saw a heavy-set woman with braids wandering the halls. Thought she was a visitor."

He nodded. The other four were already

sprinting ahead. "Go on down to the first floor. The alarm will bring security."

She gave him a brave smile, walked quickly to the landing. Three more staff, a doctor and two nurses, running upstairs.

"Security here yet?"

The nurse brushed past her. "No. We need to go ahead and seal off the floor."

Miranda nodded. "I'll make sure the kitchen knows. Whoever it is wouldn't dare try the front."

The middle-aged doctor showed his teeth to her, quick glance at her legs. "Just getting back on duty?"

Mustered a Moderne wriggle, kilowatt smile. "Wouldn't you know it?"

Miranda took two steps at a time down the stairway, folders under her left arm with her purse, Baby Browning damp in the palm of her hand.

She made it through the kitchen quickly, staff there too frightened to speak to her. They huddled near the stove and a block full of butcher knives — just in case.

Walked about twenty feet through the back door before she weakened, gasping for air, evening cold and clear. Moon not out yet, stars and the Milky Way bright enough to make out the garage. Where the kid parked the car, if he hadn't left with it.

Miranda crept to the back of the building, found a side door. Tried Gracie's passkey, wriggled it around in the lock until the tumblers fell away. Pushed open the door, peeling paint sticking to her damp palms.

A bus, three farm trucks, two cars. Shit. No rickety Plymouth from Aalder's.

She sighed, set down the gun, purse, and folders on top of an old black Ford farm truck. Threw off the white smock. Too goddamn easy to see in the dark.

Ran in between each of the cars, checked for keys. Nothing.

Slid the folders inside her dress and under her slip, paper cold and sharp against her bra and skin. Picked up the purse, thumbed the safety on the Browning.

Footsteps outside, flashlights.

She waited until the beam passed through and over the high window spanning the length of the garage. Voices carried on the still night air, floating from the front of the house.

Miranda slid through the back door. Headed for the dense shadows of a grove of oak and eucalyptus flanking the front of the castle, like the grounds of an English estate. More voices, more lights from the front of the house, and now they were circling toward the back entrance again.

Must have found Gosney.

She started to run. Only one goddamn chance, or they'd fucking lock her up, his word against hers, and she'd use the Browning on herself before she'd let that happen. No lobotomy for Miranda Corbie, life wasn't worth much but it was fucking worth more than that.

Made some distance. Out of breath. She stopped, panting, dropped the purse on the dark ground, rustle of dry leaves. Cattle lowed somewhere nearby. Two thousand fucking acres, and she hoped the forest would keep her near the road.

Coyotes were yipping, maybe heard the cows.

Fuck.

Miranda picked up her purse, ran again, pushing herself, fell, goddamn fucking ankle on a goddamn fucking rock. Pulled herself up, limping, knees skinned and bruised, sharp stone dug into her cheek. Groped for the purse in the dark, grateful she'd slid the safety on the pistol.

Not coyotes.

Dogs.

Left ankle still wasn't right, not after February. She limped as fast as she could, desperate for a glimpse of light other than the fucking starlight, star bright, first star I see tonight, wish I may, wish I might, for a fucking car and no fucking hunting dogs howling and ripping my throat out . . .

Gee whiz, Mother, look at that woman in the cage, regular freak, can't talk, can't speak, can't move, just like the picture show, gave me nightmares, it did, and they said she used to be pretty once . . .

Breath was shallow, coming faster. Barking was getting closer.

Mother. That's a fucking laugh, isn't it, Miranda? Thought she was dead, and hell, maybe she is, maybe that's a phony postcard, but you'll never know, because you'll have to blow your own brains out or wind up at Ripley's or in one of the little rooms with bars, where they can all stare at you, use you if they get bored enough, brain's dead, not what's between her legs . . .

She gripped the Browning tighter, dragged her left foot behind her, trail of dirt and eucalyptus bark. Clearing up ahead, too goddamn fucking scared to care, just find the goddamn road . . .

She limped out into a lawn. Tall stone arch raised itself to heaven, praying to a God whose name she'd never know. Miranda took a gasping breath, ran across the grass and onto the main road.

Bright white light struck at her like cannon fire, and she froze, moth in flame, burning, dying, dead.

A voice said: "Thank God — get in the car."

Rick.

■ ■ ■ ■

PART FIVE:
REVELATIONS

■ ■ ■ ■

Perishing things and strange ghosts —
   soon to die
To other ghosts — this one, or that, or I.
                — Rupert Brooke, 1887–1915

THIRTY

Miranda fell into the DeSoto, Rick running around to the passenger side, slamming the door shut. Sirens were starting to sound from the Napa State Hospital.

Smeared white face from the bright car lamps, slits for eyes, mouth a gash, and he clashed the gears together and spun out into the paved road of State Route 37.

"Jesus Christ, Miranda — should get you to a doctor —"

She clutched the Baby Browning in her hand, holding her purse on her lap, ankle sending sharp, wrenching pain through her leg and back, arm numb, hot and searing. Leaned against the seat. Started to laugh, rasping bark, like the dogs through the trees, like the cough of dying women in white hospital wards.

Croak of carrion crows, cawing out truth, truth, truth, don't you know that's what Corbie means? Carrion crow, picking at the dead, trying to put them back together again . . .

Salt ran in streams down her cheek, stinging the gash where the rock cut her cheekbone, and she held her Baby and held her purse, rocking back and forth, until the laughter went away, Mama, oh yes, the laughter not the pain, and she rocked and she rocked and she rocked herself to sleep.

Rock-a-bye, baby. Rock-a-bye.

Moon was finally dangling in the sky, inky black, white spots, made of Spanish Manchego, taste like tangy sheep's milk, bottle of Cava empty, rolling, rolling, rolling down the clumps of earth next to the crater.

"Miranda?"

"Hmm."

"Wake up. We need to figure out what to do."

She blinked. Opened her eyes. Rick's face, worried, creased, upside-down clown.

"Where are we?"

"Outside Geyserville. Figured we'd be tailed — headed north to throw 'em off. Been traveling back roads for a couple of hours. You've been out cold."

She tried to sit up straight, winced. "Goddamn ankle."

She plucked a Chesterfield out of the

Browning case with shaking fingers. Rick shifted to the right, dug out a matchbook from his left pocket. Struck it on his thumb. Held his hand with both of hers while she gulped at the stick, his skin hot and dry against the cold clamminess of her palms.

"Need to get to a phone."

"There's a bar on the south side of town."

"All right."

He started the car and pulled out of the dirt road and out from under the embrace of an old eucalyptus tree, sharp, clean odor of the leaves reviving her.

She groped in the dark for his hand. "Thanks, Rick."

He squeezed back, didn't say anything. Pulled the DeSoto into a graveled lot next to a yellow neon sign advertising CARLO'S PLACE. Piano blues, Kansas City style, banging through the open door, moths and mosquitoes dancing a jitterbug in front of the cold yellow light, hum of electricity audible whenever the piano paused for breath.

Rick turned to face her. "You don't look good. Better let me go inside and call — don't want any questions."

"Fisher first. Tell him the Musketeers are planning to blow up the Federal Building on Treasure Island. Already laid in the

471

dynamite or whatever they're using. Supposed to go off tomorrow — today — Memorial Day."

He opened his mouth to say something — changed his mind, jaw clenched. Nodded.

"What else?"

"Meyer. I got the files on Pandora and Annie. Dr. Gosney — he's a Musketeer, friend of Parkinson — abortions, sterilizations. I'll know more soon as I read these."

She reached under her jacket and inside her dress, drawing out the bent and crumpled manila file folders. Rick twisted his mouth into a smile.

"You always get the goods, Randy. Be back in a minute."

She was reading the report on Pandora by the light of her Ronson Majorette when he climbed back in the DeSoto.

"That's done. Fisher's going over personally. Said O'Meara won't like it."

"Fuck O'Meara."

Miranda looked up at him, mouth grim and exhausted.

"Gosney claimed Pandora was a nymphomaniac. Targeted because she talked about what she did for a living, proud of it, proud to be an artist's model. Adding 'Jew' on her form clinched it. You can read it all here . . .

472

how they offered her corrective therapy, how her 'sex organs' were 'abnormally large.' 'Steps taken to prevent further manifestation of obvious nymphomania.' "

Took a deep inhale on the stick, eyes not seeing the papers anymore.

"Woman looking to abort is already a criminal. He can do whatever he wants, she can't tell the cops. Woman who undresses in public, automatically sick, wrong, diseased. No voice for either of them. No way to speak out."

Miranda shut off the lighter with a click and shoved the records back inside the manila folder, Shell sign and Carlo's the only lights in Geyserville, her face half-bathed in reflected neon. She stared into the dark, surrounding vineyards and prune orchards, quiet and cool.

"That's what he was going to do to me. My record would speak for itself, and I'd die on the operating table."

"He can't touch you, Randy. You know too many people. Me, for one."

She glanced at Rick, sadness in the smile. Her hands were shaking again. She pinched out the end of the Chesterfield.

"Didn't think I'd see you again. What happened?"

Rick pushed the hat off his forehead,

scratched his ear. "Got a Mickey Finn."

"Your blonde?"

He nodded sheepishly. "Thought I was smoother than that."

"Don't blame yourself. I played tennis with a girl — think her boyfriend recognized me, probably from Sally's. Mary must've been suspicious and didn't get a chance to tell Gracie until they phoned from the hospital. How the hell did you figure out I was at Napa?"

"Asked Scott who Parkinson liked to hang around with locally — he's a big shot in the City, you know, friends with a couple of supervisors. Turns out he's real chummy with a gynecological surgeon at Napa. I figured everything fit."

"Lucky for me."

"I was waiting until midnight. I wouldn't let them hurt you, Miranda."

She looked into his blue eyes, lit green by the yellow neon, worry lines deep around his mouth. Lifted a hand to caress his cheek, brown stubble pricking her palm.

"Thank you, Rick."

He looked at her until she broke it off. "We'd better get back to San Francisco. Straight to the Hall of Justice, and try to take any road around Petaluma you can. Cops down there are in Parkinson's pocket."

He nodded, started the car. "You sure you're all right?"

"I'm OK. Better shape than Gosney."

"Why? What happened?"

She rolled down the window, inhaling the cool, fruitful air of the Alexander Valley. There was rain in the night, rain to dampen the dynamite on Treasure Island, rain to help wash the blood on her cheek. A gentle rain from heaven. Like the rain in Flanders Fields, like Shakespeare's mercy, the mercy no one bothered to show Shylock or the woman in number 114.

Piano music started up again, "St. Louis Blues." Her voice was even.

"I shot the Nazi bastard in the stomach."

She convinced Rick to drop her off at Portsmouth and go home, phone the paper, hint of dawn rising behind Twin Peaks, rain falling like tears on the green grass, the tenements of Chinatown.

The smell of *jool* and pork buns wafted from iron stoves in cramped backroom bakeries, red banners waving across Grant in the Bay wind. Fishermen trudging toward the Van Ness pier with long poles and tackle boxes, others toward shrimp boats on the wharf, looking for tonight's dinner, for next week's rent, faces battered by sheets of water, one with sky and sea.

Metal doors screamed open as men and women swept the fronts of produce markets and flower shops, eddies of rainwater swirling incense sticks down the gutter, while downstairs, tiny, fine-boned women hunched over ancient sewing machines, patiently threading beads on an elaborate evening gown, rain hammering like gunfire on the cheap tin roof.

Early morning Chinatown. Miranda limped into the Hall of Justice.

Mostly quiet before dawn, except for a raid on Pickles O'Dell and her girls from the International Settlement. Pick your hair color, mister, all types except gray, and no coiffure was by Marcel.

Some worked as B-girls in the Conga Club, shaking hips on the dance floor to bop-bop-bop-bop-BA-bop, Guatemala Marimba Band posing in puffy orange sleeves and coconuts, maracas out of tune.

No complaints from the pros, just saved their throats for better pay, lit up a cigarette and watched the cops, taking bets on which one would be knocking on the door at Pacific Street next week. Tears from the young, girls in a literal sense. Fifteen and big eyes, runaways from Utah or Oregon, bruised by the big city, count to ten and out. Most wouldn't get back up again.

Pickles was slipping, dealing in underage meat. She usually left veal to the big boys, the ones Miranda tried to take out of business in February.

Meyer met her, took her by the hand, helped her to a hard wooden chair that kept her awake, along with the chatter from the B-girls, one on top of a nearby desk, fat legs kicking back and forth in fishnet stockings.

Miranda swayed and teetered, ankle swollen to the size of a grapefruit, cheek bruised and gashed, and her attorney-cum-client was dressed hurriedly and without suspenders or vest, like a john rousted by the blue boys' call on the International Settlement.

Numb, exhausted, smoked all the goddamn Chesterfields on the way down 101, bummed a Camel off a cop.

Lawyer kept asking her if she was all right. Right as rain, Meyer, I gut-shot a fucking doctor at a crazy house, had to do it, had to get away. They were going to kill me, and that was if I was lucky, they ice-pick people in the brain there, that's what they do, set 'em up real nice in these little cells where they gouge out their own fucking eyeballs. Yeah, mental hygiene, they call it, fucking mental hygiene, and he sterilizes Jews and loose women, and you get a bonus off the fucking pinball game if you're both.

Shhh, Miranda, calm down. Not so loud. No bulletin from Napa County, no one's chasing you. They don't want the publicity, you're safe, my girl, safe.

Safe. Just don't go to Petaluma or Napa or Calistoga for the rest of your fucking life. Someone with a framed degree might call you crazy, might call you diseased, might say you're better off without your fucking ovaries or even your fucking life. . . .

Fisher's waiting for us, he's back from the Island, let's go, Miranda, let's go.

Kept slipping backward, chest still hurting from the laughter. Laughs like swallowed razor blades, and fuck, maybe she was crazy, but she'd fix it herself, all by herself, that's what she did, me, myself, and I, Miranda Corbie. Miranda Corbie, who had a mother, maybe, somewhere in the world, if only she could meet her. If only she wouldn't be ashamed.

Johnson was strutting in and out of the background, red-faced, self-important, slamming doors. Fisher was typing next to her, one key at a time.

"OK, Miss Corbie. O'Meara's gonna have some questions for you about how you found out —"

"Not gonna answer them."

Fisher chuckled to himself, rubbed his eyes. Stretched them open, looking like one of the Ritz brothers. "It's almost dawn. You OK?"

One of the girls screeched. Wished people would stop asking her silly questions. Miranda blinked, yawned, desperate for air. Wrenched open her purse, took out two Life Savers. Didn't give a fuck about what flavor they were.

"I'm taking Miss Corbie home as soon as we're done, Inspector. You can see she's not feeling well — girl needs to see a doctor."

Too tired for the laughter, but it welled inside her chest, wanting to explode. Explode like the bombs on Treasure Island.

Fisher cranked the knob and cleared the paper, holding it in front of him, running an eye over it. "I'll call you if we need follow-up, but as I say, it'll be O'Meara. I'm just involved because you called me."

Meyer leaned forward, hand on her elbow. "You sure they got everything?"

He nodded. "Setup was clear. Dynamite, hidden in trash receptacles and mail slots, coordinated attack. Doubt they could've blown up the whole building with what they had, though."

"How're you releasing the information?"

He shrugged. "That's up to the chief and

479

the D.A. Johnson brought in the feds. Got to with fifth column cases, and this being tied to the Federal Building and coming on Memorial Day . . ."

In Flanders Fields, the poppies blow . . .

"It's the fucking Musketeers, and the fucking D.A. plays fucking golf with the fucking head of the organization. You busting the gang at Tonypandy? You bringing in Hugh Parkinson, doctor of dental science? You fighting the fucking war?"

Shhh, Miranda, shhh. She's really not herself tonight, Inspector. I'm sure she'll want to talk to you later about how this may impact our client. I understand her investigation has yielded some information that we hope will help exonerate Mr. Duggan.

Man to man. Back and forth. Both looking at her, both worried. *There's a somebody I'm longing to see . . .*

Meyer helped lift her out of the chair. Fisher stood up. Miranda blinked, remembered.

"Dunkirk . . . what's happened at Dunkirk?"

Looks again. Quiet voice, the kind used for children and hysterical women.

"British are trying to pull off a miracle. All the little boats — fishermen, pleasure craft — crossing the Channel, saving the

480

men. They're working, Miranda. They're fighting."

The floor was dirty. Cigarette wrappers, soot, boot prints. No jackboot on England. Not yet.

She tottered, closed her eyes. Opened them again.

"Be seein' you, Fisher."

Meyer led her out through the wooden gate and down the cavernous hall, hoarse laughter from one of Pickles's girls bouncing against the marble walls, chasing behind them.

THIRTY-ONE

The phone was ringing.

Hand snaked out, groping for the alarm clock. One eye, bruised, focused over the pillow.

Fuck. Eleven already. Still Memorial Day.

Miranda groaned, crackling lights in her eyes from the sharp pain shooting through her ankle and leg.

Knees, face, arm . . . everything hurt.

The phone wouldn't stop, so she reached out and answered it.

"Yeah?"

"You OK?"

Rick. At work. Typing in the background, somebody cursing at the copy boy.

She sat up, wincing. "Yeah. Glad you've still got a job."

"I dropped the car off for you. And listen . . . been monitoring the police reports from Napa and Sonoma. Nobody reported a shooting."

"I didn't report an attempted murder, either. Guess Gosney and I are both remiss."

Silence on the other end. He cleared his throat. "Miranda . . . I gotta turn the story into a fluff piece on Calistoga. Orders."

She reached out and pulled open the nightstand drawer. Grabbed a pack of Chesterfields, groped for a matchbook.

"Yeah? And who ordered the orderer, Rick? Parkinson? The D.A.? City's always been corrupt, but this smells like Goebbels."

Exasperation flaked off his voice, tired, thin, stretched too tight.

"You don't have any proof, Miranda — it's your word against theirs. Stalemate. You don't have any evidence except for the records on Pandora and Annie. Those might prove a point of interest to the jury — at least spread some doubt Duggan's way — but they don't convict Gosney of anything except abortion — if he even mentions it, which I doubt. You didn't tell me."

She stared at the cigarette between her fingers. "It's not in Annie's file. Only the sterilization."

"See? They covered themselves. And you can forget about digging anything else up. You think other women will step forward and straight into a prison cell? Why the hell should they? No, Miranda, listen to me.

Maybe they killed those two girls, maybe they ordered it done. But you can't prove it, and you can't even prove that they're doing anything illegal. Or wrong."

Deep gulp on the Chesterfield. Blew a stream toward the window, watched the smoke unravel and curl, small gray ghosts disappearing in the sun.

"Miranda? You still there?"

Her voice was heavy. "I'm still here, Rick. Bring the Spanish pistol back later, OK?"

He sounded puzzled, almost hurt. But then Richard Sanders, Esquire, friend of John Hayes and Miranda Corbie, reporter of secondhand scandals and lonely hearts columns, always sounded hurt. Fucking world hurt him, and where it didn't, she did.

"Yeah, Miranda. Whatever you say."

"Thanks, Rick. Be seein' you."

She hung up the phone. Stared into the air of the bedroom. Listened for the whine of plane engines, sound of bombs falling on San Francisco.

Wanted to get dressed as fast as she could, but her limbs wouldn't work, and she said fuck it and took her time, taking a long shower, steaming hot, examining the gash on her cheek. Hoped it wouldn't leave a scar. Changed the dirty bandage on her gun graze, thinking of Gosney's belly.

Not enough. Not nearly enough. Not like the pain of not being able to have children. Not like the pain of being a woman, no power, no voice, no one to hear you cry in fucking number 114. In a dirty attic room off Market Street.

She was shaking all over, inside and outside. She'd been ready to die, just like in '37, just like the house on Cordelia Street.

Miranda rubbed her face with a towel, tears coming without the sobs, goddamn salty tears biting into the cut on her left cheek. Took deep breaths, leaning on her right, ankle still misshapen, green and blue and purple.

Grabbed at the sink. Stared at the woman in the mirror.

Fissures you couldn't see. Cracks wide, raw, open, and she felt them gaping, fault lines and crevices, pulling her apart, pulling her in. Falling, falling . . .

She closed her eyes.

Coffee smelled like life again, warming her hands in a white milk-glass mug.

"You owe me a suitcase and some clothes, Meyer. I was fond of the tennis outfit."

"Make me a list, my dear, and you shall

have carte blanche . . . within reason."

Her lips twitched into half a smile. "Within reason. So I gave you the files last night, right? What do you think?"

Hesitant voice. "It should help, Miranda. Any doubt on Duggan's guilt and motivations — any smoke screen we can light —"

She leaned forward on the mattress. "It's not a fucking smoke screen. Those bastards sterilized those women without consent and without just cause."

Sigh. She could hear his fingers tapping on his desk. "I know, my dear. But there's nothing we can do about it. And do you honestly believe Gosney or Parkinson killed Pandora Blake or Annie Learner?"

Miranda raised the Chesterfield to her lips, holding the phone at her side. Bit into the tobacco, inhaled until the end glowed red. Lifted the receiver again. Reluctant.

"No, goddamn it. I don't. Doesn't make sense. Gosney was on the phone with Parkinson, pissing on himself over not making the boss pull strings again. Why go to the trouble? There are easier ways to cover up a murder, especially if you control the medical records at an insane asylum."

"Exactly. They were safe enough, knowing the women had no real recourse. And they don't strike me as the type of men to be involved with that kind of violent, obvious crime."

Her voice was dry. "No indeed, Meyer. Gosney was wringing his hands over the thought of botching my operation."

"But my dear, that's just it. They were going to get rid of you in a way that posed the least amount of jeopardy to themselves and their mission. It isn't personal with these people . . . it's ideological."

"And 'kike' written in blood on a naked woman isn't?" She blew out a stream of smoke, shook her head.

"Yeah, yeah, I know. So it's back to square one again. Back to checking on Henry Kaiser and Pandora's old boyfriend. Maybe he was Jewish, since she identified herself as a Jew on that form they made her fill out."

She stared at the cigarette between her fingers. "Pandora was marked as soon as she listed herself as 'Jewish' and her profession as 'model.' "

"I think you should speak to Mr. Duggan."

She hesitated. "I will, Meyer, but . . . not just yet. I want a few more days."

Silence. She rubbed the Chesterfield stub out in the glass ashtray next to the bed.

He asked it in a cautious way, almost as though he were afraid of the answer.

"What are your immediate plans, Miranda?"

She grinned, skin stretched, gash on her cheek stinging. Imagined the look on her attorney's face.

"I'm going to drop in on Dr. Hugh Parkinson."

She pushed her way through the two center doors at 450 Sutter, glancing up at the ornate gold canopy. Timothy Pflueger's Mayan fever dream, completed the year the stock market crashed. She remembered walking by it a couple of years later, grizzled men with unshaven chins crouched against one of the shiny, patterned columns, empty eyes on the gold, staring. Wishing they could flake some of it off.

Parkinson evidently made money or was born with enough to make it last. Offices in a twenty-six-story Harley Street address, outclassing the old Romanesque Medico-Dental Building over on 490 Post like Hillsborough over Burlingame. The rich didn't migrate much, but they wanted their dentists to move with them.

Miranda limped toward the elevator, ankle held up by bulky wrapping, fried egg, sausage, hotcakes, and coffee from the St. Francis warming her belly. Rain over, skies fog-blind again.

She was wearing a plain black dress, the kind approved for the courtroom, a small flat hat with a veil, and the lowest heels she could find. Small clutch purse, black leather, gold trim. Empty except for her pocketbook, *Chadwick's Street Guide,* a new pack of Chesterfields, and the Ronson Majorette.

Thin elevator operator with slicked-down hair and acne pushed number eight, hugging the wall. Well-dressed businessman in a double-suited serge coat with a navy fedora got in, out again on five. Probably ulcers.

Elevator lurched in time with her stomach. She stepped out on eight, operator sneezing when the door closed.

She walked into the outer office of Dr. Hugh R. Parkinson, D.D.S., suite number 872.

Clean and white. Just what she expected. And open for Memorial Day.

The receptionist was a young woman with mousy brown hair and glasses who kept her desk relentlessly tidy. Even the circled dates on the desk calendar were the same goddamn size.

She peered at Miranda, found nothing to object to on the surface. Long fingernails, clearly her pride and joy, painted a very pale pink.

Twenty-three or -four. Probably still a virgin, hoping the boss would be the One.

"May I help you?"

"I'd like to see Dr. Parkinson."

Confident voice belied her looks. "I'm sorry, Miss, but that is impossible without a prior appointment. Dr. Parkinson's calendar is constantly full."

Miranda smiled, shifted her weight. God-damn ankle, needles all the way up her leg.

"But I do have an appointment."

The young woman looked confused, tapered nails brushing elegantly through the open book. "But — but Miss, there is no one listed for one thirty. We don't schedule on the half hour."

Miranda leaned against the hard rim of the desk edge. Stared down at her.

"It's a personal appointment. Tell him Miranda Corbie is here to see him. And add my regards to Dr. Gosney."

The receptionist's eyes grew bigger behind the thick glasses, and she stood up, modeling last year's dress, Emporium special. Ignored the sliding door that probably led to one of the examination rooms. Walked instead toward the far right, rapped her knuckles above a gold knob, and walked in.

Miranda counted to ten. Braced herself against the desk, wishing she'd taken some aspirin.

The receptionist walked out again, face red.

"Dr. Parkinson will see you now."

Brown paneling, burled wood. Hunting lodge in the city flavor, decorated with sports trophies and blue-and-gold pennants boasting allegiance to the California Bears.

Her first surprise. She'd figured him for a Stanford man.

Her second was when he turned around to face her, cigar between his lips.

Her age. Not a fat, soft, middle-aged lecher getting his kicks from sticking his fingers in women's mouths. Not a big-mouthed braggart with a loud tie and country club connections. Not a distinguished gray-haired businessman, calculating, canny, careful.

Maybe his father. But not Hugh R. Parkinson.

Daddy's little boy. Wouldn't want to endanger Daddy's little boy, would we, Dr. Gosney?

Parkinson was good-looking in that slightly chubby, vacuous way all fraternity boys are, especially after they hit thirty. But the eyes were hard. And very, very cold.

Tried to smile, waved her to a seat. Stubbed out the cigar. Sat back in the brown leather chair, which cost twice as much as the one she'd spent a fee on.

"Now then, Miss Corbie — what can I do for you?"

He bent forward, telegraphing helpfulness, all the goodwill of a fucking Boy Scout.

She lifted the veil. "Mind if I smoke?"

He hesitated. "Smoking is very bad for the teeth."

She shook out a Chesterfield, lit it with the Ronson on the first try. Studied him over the glowing tip, watching him flinch from the curling smoke.

"I'm not here for my teeth."

He sighed, and a muscle inside his jaw moved in and out. First sign.

"Then why exactly are you here, Miss Corbie?"

"I wanted to see you for myself. The puppeteer." She shook her head, said it regretfully. "But I was wrong. I found the puppet instead."

His brow wrinkled, eyes frozen over. "I don't understand."

She inhaled, blowing smoke in the direction of his left ear. "Now that I've met you, I don't either, not entirely. I assume Daddy still has something to do with the county or state or with political campaigns of certain people or still sits on the boards of certain corporations. Or, possibly, hospitals. Yeah. Hospitals make a lot of sense. Is he a doctor? Is that why you chose dentistry?"

Red flush, eyes seemed to get closer together. Second sign.

"My father has nothing to do with any reason you may or may not have come to see me."

She nodded, crossed her legs with effort. "Sure, Junior. He's got nothing to do with a Fascist group of Jew-hating bullies called the Musketeers . . . founded by you. Nothing to do with some heavy strings pulled on the San Francisco Police Department to cover up certain facts about certain murders, encouraging them to railroad a former cop, and do it before anybody else got wise. And nothing at all to do with bombs on Treasure Island, planted around the Federal Building, and your pet surgeon's private eugenics lab at the Napa State Hospital."

She inhaled the Chesterfield, watching him. Glanced down at his hands, fingertips pressed tight across his desk.

"Where's your special decoder ring with the M on it? Didn't you collect enough box tops?"

He jumped up, fists clenched, jerked an arm in the air toward her, then stopped himself. Ran a hand through his slickly oiled hair. Started to pace.

Bingo.

She looked up at him calmly.

"You're an accomplice to attempted murder. Mine. And unless you're willing to go through with it, Parkinson, I swear I'll nail you and Gosney to the wall, however long it takes. You, Gosney . . . and dear old Dad. Because that's who he was talking to when I overheard his phone call."

He glared down at her, contemptuous, features sharper, more well-defined.

"Trash like you wouldn't understand. We're making America a better place. Keeping her out of the Jew war, fighting overseas for a bunch of grocers and garbagemen. Here and in New York . . . all over the country."

She leaned back in the chair. Made an O with her lips and blew a smoke ring. Watched it sail over some framed photographs taken at the St. Francis Yacht Club. Parkinson watched her, unable to look away. Legs and mouth, legs and mouth. He was sweating.

"I thought they were all international bankers, Parkinson. Or are they Reds? Or can't you Hitler-loving assholes make up your little minds?"

He turned white, then red again, rubbing more jelly out of his scalp. Breathing hard, breathing fast.

"Go ahead and call Daddy if you want. And by the way — how is Dr. Gosney today?"

"He's recuperating at home, thanks to you. You almost killed him."

She shrugged. Leaned forward, grinding the cigarette out on the polished mahogany.

"Consider it a warning. I don't like threats, especially from Nazi toadies."

He slammed a fist down on the wood surface, yelling, "We are not Nazis! We're Americans, and — and — you'll see — we're forming a committee, our own party, and our goal — our only goal — is to keep the United States out of this war."

He calmed down, breathing hard and staring at the desk, as if reciting something by memory. "It's a noble enterprise, true to our heritage, to our history. We've been betrayed from both sides, and we're going to make sure American boys don't die in another European war for a pack of Jews."

Her voice was dry, withering. "No. You'll just make sure Jewish girls die in America for a pack of anti-Semites." She stood up, sharp stabs through the ankle, but held her face in place.

"Form whatever committee you want to, Parkinson. Try to take down FDR, hide your fifth column behind the Founding Fathers and the Boston Tea Party and pretty speeches about the U.S. Constitution. But the Musketeers are over — finished. No more bombs. No more recruitment. No more free sterilizations."

His face was canny. "Or abortions?"

Her eyes narrowed. "There are other doctors. You and Gosney are out of business."

"Or you'll what?"

Boyish bravado, eyes on her legs again. She glanced up at the shelf with the golfing trophy from Harding Park. Locked on the weak blue eyes darting over her breasts. She leaned forward, fuck the ankle.

"I'll ruin you. Or I'll kill you. Either way." He shrank under the tone, blinded by the white-hot steel. "The war's already here, Parkinson. And you're the enemy."

He froze, staring at her, while she limped out of the office, banging the door shut behind her.

She couldn't remember the ride to the office. Remembered the receptionist's horrified face, glaring at her, the woman who made Dr. Parkinson scream.

Only patients screamed in a dental office, didn't she know better?

Shaking all the way downstairs. Didn't want to think about whether she was bluffing, didn't want to think about anything except her office and her own chair, and the bottle of Old Taylor in the right drawer.

Hailed a taxi on Sutter.

Gladys not on duty behind the counter, jukebox playing "Glad to Be Unhappy," Lee Wiley sultry and smooth and full of knowing pain.

Look at yourself. If you had a sense of humor, you would laugh to beat the band . . .

No fucking sense of humor. Maybe that was her problem. Maybe she belonged in number 114, men in dirty white smocks coming to feed her Cream of Wheat, watching it dribble down her chin.

Watching her scratch her eyes out, *drip-drop, drip-drop,* red swirls like cotton candy, around and around, wheel of fortune, folks, and where she stops, nobody knows.

Except Miranda. Miranda knew.

It stopped in a coffin, flies and maggots and beetles eating whatever you left behind.

She took a deep breath and closed her eyes, stepping out on the fourth floor.

■ ■ ■ ■

Gummy brown sediment at the bottom of the Castagnola glass, but she poured anyway, tossing the bourbon back until it bit her throat and made her cough. Not the day to call dear old Dad. Not ever the day, but now she had something to say, something to ask him, something to the point.

"Why didn't you tell me she was alive, that she'd left and gone to England? Why didn't you tell me, you sodden piece of shit?"

Oh, Miranda. Must respect our elders, mustn't we, especially our parents. We owe them our lives, after all.

She stared into the glass, swirled the whiskey until tiny drops clung to the edges. If she squinted hard enough, she could see Johnny's face in every one.

Life. Such as it is. Why wasn't she blown up, fallen on the same soil, buried in the same grave, dead, dead, food for the same goddamn worms, ghost floating over a Spanish olive grove . . .

Drained the glass, set it down with a thump.

Too late.

Funny thing about life, mister, it just keeps going and takes you along, like a hitchhiker or somethin'. Yeah. A hitchhiker. And she owed something to her mother, owed something to Johnny. Anything she owed her father she paid off a long, long time ago.

She reached for the phone. Dialed the answering service.

First message: from Lucinda. "About Pandora. Something funny. Call me."

Miranda puffed on the Chesterfield, wrote it down in the Big Chief pad, fresh sheet. Lucinda tried to phone her before Calistoga. Time to pay more attention to Henry Kaiser.

Second message: from Bente. "Got message. Went anyway. Tonypandy bad people."

She was sure "bad people" was a message-service euphemism for something else, an operator's delicate, shell-like ear turned pink by Bente's vehemence.

Third message: "Confidential matter. Please call." Exbrook exchange. Nob Hill and lower elevations. Probably a nervous client. She craned her head to check the calendar on the wall, verified that it was still Thursday, Memorial Day, time for graves and flowers and prayers and tears. No dynamite, Dr. Gosney, not today. She made a note to return the call next week.

Fourth message: "Walter Lodges. Friend at the Hotel Potter. Owe me a ten-spot. Name was Flamm."

She sat back in the large leather chair.

She owed the little man with the rheumy eyes ten dollars and a new pack of Fatimas.

Name of Pandora's boyfriend, he said, rhymed with somebody "gettin' out of town." Taking it on the lam.

Harry Flamm. Lothario, gambler, and the man who was riding Temple Sherith Israel around the track at Tanforan.

Miranda jumped up, ignoring the needles in her ankle, and opened the safe.

Cigarettes with the Black Cat matchbook.

Sat down, opened the flap, read the words again: "Mickey wants to see you."

Stared into space. Reached for the phone, dialed the number. Gruff voice answered.

"Black Cat Café."

She drew in a breath, plunging ahead. "Tell Mickey I want to see him. I know about Harry Flamm and Pandora Blake."

Silence on the other end, except for someone ordering a hamburger, medium rare, hold the onions, and the sound of dishes clanking in the kitchen.

"Who is this?"

"Miranda Corbie."

Silence again. Handset dropped on the receiver.

THIRTY-TWO

Rick wasn't in at the *San Francisco News* office. One of the other reporters, fat cigar clenched in his teeth, mumbled something about Sanders going home to get some rest, pointed tone, your fault, lady, always a goddamn dame in the way of news. . . .

She tried the Hotel Empire, spoke to a politely precise clerk with a Romanian accent. Left a message, Western Union style: "Flamm Pandora's man. Call me. Miranda."

Dug out her *Chadwick's Street Guide,* flipped to the back. Lucinda lived at the La Salle Apartments, 650 Post, fleabag with no phone.

She phoned the central exchange for the Fair, left a message with one of the impersonal clerks that never saw the Magic of the Magic City, one of the thousands of people employed by Golden Gate International Exposition, Inc.: "Set a time, call me, Miranda Corbie."

Miranda hung up, frustrated. Not much hope of reaching Lucinda. She'd have to go in person, try to catch her after the act.

Flipped through the Kardex, found the Oceanic Hotel, dialed direct. Waited for ten rings before somebody answered it, mouth full of mush. No, Gallagher ain't here. Yeah, I'll give her the goddamn message. Hang up.

She bit her lip. Needed to let Bente know about the bombs, about Parkinson, afraid the redhead would put herself in danger. Even if she scared them into shutting down Gosney, Miranda knew the Musketeers would be around in one form or another, swallowed up by the Bund or the Silver Shirts or another hate group.

They'd paint swastikas on buildings, stick posters on buses, break up labor meetings and beat up Jews. She tapped her fingers on the desk. Probably no more bombs. At least in San Francisco.

Didn't check the papers but figured no explosion, no story. Not with the Fair corporation and all those concessions and the Northern California Chambers of Commerce and the whole fucking Golden State, not to mention the West, trying to eke out a solvent year in 1940, '39 floating belly-up. She smiled grimly to herself, thinking of

O'Meara and the firing squad.

Her stomach growled. Goddamn it. Needed to clear her head.

Miranda grabbed her purse, locked up the office. Walked by Pinkertons, Allen's door open a crack. He was leaning forward, offering a lemon drop to a weeping woman in widow's weeds, who probably wasn't really weeping, much less a widow, judging from her red sling-back pumps. She grinned. Allen could take care of himself.

Miranda hurried into the elevator and out into the City, limping on her swollen ankle. She hailed a taxi for Chinatown.

"And the Angels Sing" was still playing on the Fong Fong juke, but no sharp kid from Filipino Charlie's, no gang of girls ogling the bad boys.

Eddie Takahashi was dead and buried, his sister safe.

Something she could be proud of, she could point at when the wheel of fortune stopped turning. Something she could hang on to.

Triumph, of a kind. Justice. Of a kind. Like the Incubator Babies, like Burnett's murder. Like the cases, small and large, she'd made her living. Made her life.

Miranda knew better, always knew better,

than to expect purity in this world. Maybe that was for the fucking angels, the heavenly host, but not here, not now, not in the dirty shacks and dry fields of potato farmers, not in the run-down apartment buildings with families of seven and eight, not even in the Hollywood mansions clinging precariously to the hills, Italian tile swimming pools cool and inviting, just like the call boys and girls stretched out in front of the softly waving water.

You pays your money, you takes your choice. And her choice was to live, but to live with something to clutch in the darkness, something to hold on to that wouldn't leave her, that wouldn't disappoint her, that wouldn't go away, flesh rotting and rotten, white bones blanched by wind and sun. Anonymous dust to anonymous dust, swallowed by the weight of ages.

Dead. Alone. Forgotten.

She shoved aside the remnants of the chop suey sundae, lit a Chesterfield.

Born alone, live alone. Die alone.

She left fifty cents on the counter, waved good-bye to the soda jerk, and walked back into the sunlight of Grant Avenue.

Brick wall on the corner of Commercial and Grant, Far East Bakery, warmed by the sun, fighting the clouds.

Old friend.

She leaned against it, weight on her right foot, braced against the grade. Kept forgetting the goddamn aspirin.

Closed her eyes. Wondered if the boys from Chicago were still gunning for her. Wondered if Parkinson or Parkinson Sr. would believe her threat or whether more phone calls would be made to the state board that licensed her business, to men in dark hats with cheap aftershave, only too happy to get rid of their problem for a fee.

Wondered, for the first time since the beginning, if Duggan was guilty. If he'd killed Pandora in a fit of anger, killed Annie. If she and Meyer had been chasing their own tails, babysitting a murderer, dirty cop set up by Parkinson but guilty nonetheless.

She opened her eyes, spun around. Fingers tugging on her black crepe jacket belonged to Blind Willie. Ned was next to him, grinning up at her from his board.

"Miss Corbie? We seen you 'cross the street. Well, Ned seen you." The blind beggar's voiced piped like a baby chicken, and he smiled big, showing bare, pink gums.

No-Legs murmured: "That offer of a sawbuck still firm?"

She huddled closer to the two men, shielding them from the crowds on Grant. "What've you got?"

Ned reached up, patted Willie on the arm. "You tell it, Willie. You heard it."

The blind man rubbed the wattle of skin on his chin, yellow car driving up Commercial reflected in his dark glasses.

" 'Membered on accoun' a' the name, Miss Corbie. Funny name a' the girl. Never heard no one called it before. Well, I was standin' over by the Ferry Building a few days back — hopin' people comin' from the Fair might be more inclined t' buy a pencil — an' I heard it. Woman, sounded pretty young. She said . . . she said . . . gosh darnit, I get so mixed up sometimes. . . ."

Ned spoke encouragingly. "You know the story, Willie. Miss Corbie ain't in no hurry. Just tell it like you told me."

"That's right, Willie." Miranda hid the eagerness in her voice. "Take your time."

The blind man shook his head. Then his neck craned backward as if he could see the sun, and his face creased in smiles. "I remember now! She said — this here woman — she said two things. Said, 'Pandora wouldn't hold you back.' Tha's why I listened up real quick. 'Membered the name 'Pandora,' No-Legs told me ta listen up for it. Then a man said somethin' I couldn't hear, and then she says, 'She wouldn't lie,' kinda loud, kinda like she was mad or somethin'."

He was smiling wide, tilting his head toward Ned. "I done good, din't I, No-Legs?"

Ned's leathery face cracked a grin, patted the blind man on the arm. "Yeah, Willie. Real good." He looked up at Miranda expectantly.

She opened her pocketbook, handed two fives to the legless man on the plywood board, and pressed the ten into Willie's hand.

"Willie — do you remember what day this was?"

Willie turned his wizened face toward Ned, uncertainty stretching his cheeks into a grimace. "Ned — I don't 'member no days — you know they all seem the same to me."

No-Legs took off his leather cap and scratched behind his ear. "You told me yesterday, I think. Late yesterday. Musta happened that morning or the night before, 'cause we were here in the afternoon."

Willie nodded, voice rising, shrill with excitement. "Nighttime it was — I was thinkin' people might be kinder to an ol' blind beggar after a day on Treasure Island.

Tha's right — Tuesday night, Miss Corbie. Leastwise, I think so."

She squeezed his hand. "Thanks, Willie. And thanks, Ned. Be seein' you."

Ned touched his cap, reached up, and grabbed Willie's hand.

"Glad to help. Be seein' you, Miranda."

He turned the plywood expertly, gloved hands propelling him and the blind man up the crowded sidewalk of Grant.

She lit a cigarette and limped as fast as she could down Commercial to the grassy incline of Portsmouth Square, heading for Kearny and a number 16 White Front to the Ferry Building and Treasure Island.

Lucinda. Had to be Lucinda. She'd catch her before the show, wait around the Gayway if she had to.

Down the side, past some shrubbery, couples on the lawn, old people on the benches. A man in a wide-brimmed fedora got up from the nearest bench, setting aside a newspaper, suddenly not old anymore.

Three steps, and he was even with her. One more, and a gun was poking her in the right side.

She stopped, staring at the Hall of fucking Justice.

"What do you want?"

"Not what I want, sister. What you want. You phoned Mickey."

He was short, doughy, squat. Pug-ugly face, flattened nose, adenoidal growl. He jabbed the pistol a little harder. She gritted her teeth.

"You fucking shove that pistol in me again and I'll scream. That's the Hall of Justice — you figuring I'd drop by, or were you tailing me?"

He shrugged his rounded shoulders, relaxed the gun. "I don't need to tell you nothing. Move. Car's parked 'cross the street."

They walked toward a black Packard, looked like a '36. He stayed on her around to the passenger side, shoved her in, her ankle turning on the slope, needles up her leg and back, sudden intake of breath.

"You goddamn bastard —"

"Save it." He slammed the door, making sure she saw the gun trained on her as he waited for a delivery truck to pass, then slid behind the wheel. Transferred the gun to his left while he started the car, then took the wheel one-handed, pistol back in his right. Let out the emergency brake, rolling to Kearny. Turned right. Not the direction of the Black Cat Café.

"Where are you taking me?"

He stomped on his brake when a taxi hurtled down the intersection, swearing. Glanced over at her, gestured with the pistol.

"Where you wanted to go, sister. Now shut up before I backhand ya. Mickey don't say nothin' 'bout what kinda shape he wants ya in."

He drove on to Geary and headed west, speeding up, slowing down, and she braced herself against the frame of the door, trying to protect her ankle, biting her lip from the pain.

Goddamn it. Bum arm, sprained ankle — and no Baby Browning.

He pulled up next to a nondescript dive with a broken neon sign advertising CHAT NOIR CAFÉ — 2059 Sutter, not too far from Sherith Israel and Harry Flamm's respectable cover. Name rang a bell, but her ankle hurt too fucking much for her to think straight, let alone remember where she'd seen it.

Short and Stubby rubbed out his nickel cigar in the overgrown ashtray, gestured with the pistol.

"Get out. I ain't your goddamn chauffeur."

She opened the door, stood with difficulty,

leaning on it until he came around the front of the car and slammed it shut.

"Inside, sister."

He nodded at the café. She walked in front of him, through a screen door and a wooden one, brittle white paint dropping snowflakes on the copper footing. The restaurant was empty except for an old man slurping chili and onions at a corner table. A burly man in a stained T-shirt presided at the counter, gave Stubby and Miranda the eye.

Stubby said: "Tell the man I brung the Corbie broad."

The counterman nodded, disappeared through a door on the right side of the main room. Small place. Just a few seats, table-cloths unlaundered, thrown sloppily on rickety tables. Flies mating on the silver pickup counter in front of the kitchen, buzzing in slow circles around the cash register. The man in the T-shirt lumbered back through the door, gestured with his head.

"Said to come in."

Stubby flashed his .38, jabbed her in the back to show what a big man he was. She spun around toward her right and threw a backhand as hard as she could at his fleshy face.

Knocked him backward, caught him by

surprise. The man in the T-shirt sniggered.

"I told you to keep your fucking gun off me."

Stubby rubbed his cheek, eyes small and sparking. He cocked the .38. Miranda stared at him, fists clenched.

The side door opened. Another voice drawled: "Well, lookie here. Mitch can't handle the dame. C'mon in, honey, Mickey wants to meet you."

Big man, red suspenders, pungent smell of bay rum and whiskey. Hair slicked back like Muni in *Scarface*. Crooked teeth.

Miranda turned around, conscious of Stubby and his gun behind her, making noises. She limped slowly through the open doorway, brushing by the man in red suspenders.

"Felt good, honey, do it again." He laughed, teeth yellow, throat red.

She ignored him. Walked toward the light.

Behind the door the hallway led to a wire room, about eight men fixing bets on races coming in across the country. They barely acknowledged her presence. The torpedo in red suspenders walked her through to a doorway in the corner. Knocked three times, pushed it open.

Expensive room, expensive desk. Behind

it sat a broad-faced little man, about five or six years younger than Miranda with smashed ears and a scarred nose, chubby with muscle gone to fat. A blonde with her skirt up above her knees was bouncing on his lap. He waved a Havana cigar at them, thick eyebrows lifted in apparent good humor. Scratched a thumbnail on his five o'clock shadow.

He was dressed in a powder blue suit, yellow tie, and display handkerchief. Pricey, tailored, loud. Hat matched the tie, custom job, resting on the desk in front of him.

The blonde looked up, pouted when she saw Miranda.

"Gee, Mickey, ain't I special no more? You cratin' in other broads now?"

He shoved her off, slapping her on the ass. "Business, Doris. Go powder your nose or somethin'." Voice was a growl, with a hint of Coney Island.

The blonde straightened the skirt and sashayed across the room, tossing her head when she passed. Whispered: "Keep your grubby mitts off, sister, or I'll rip your goddamn lungs out."

The bird in suspenders chuckled. The blonde gave him a baleful eye, trying to maintain some dignity. He shut the door behind her. Gestured to Miranda.

"This here's Miranda Corbie, boss. She's the one that called Frankie."

Mickey nodded, grinning. "Nice-lookin' package. I like shamuses what look like movie stars. Where's Harry?"

"Waitin' outside by now. I'll go check." Suspenders left her, softly closing the door. The little man locked his hands behind his head and leaned back in the squeakless chair, grinning at her.

"You know who I am?"

She decided to play it bold. Strode as confidently as she could on a sprained ankle to one of the chairs set crookedly in front of his desk.

"You're Mickey Cohen, Bugsy Siegel's right-hand man. Mind if I smoke?"

He frowned. "I don't smoke and don't drink. I'm as pure as the goddamn driven snow."

She shook out a Chesterfield while he watched. Lit it with the Ronson, inhaled, blew smoke over her left shoulder.

"So is Hitler."

He laughed out loud, slammed his hand on the desk. "I had a feeling I was gonna like you."

The door opened and Suspenders walked in with Harry Flamm. His face was sullen, scared. Mickey waved him to the other seat.

"C'mon in, Harry. Take a pew."

Mickey leaned forward, elbows on the desk, adding to Miranda in a confidential tone, "He ain't the brightest bulb in the room. Say — how you like the suit? Snazzy, huh?"

Harry's face reddened. "I ain't done nothing wrong, boss."

Mickey addressed him with overdone patience. "You know that, an' I know that — and now, Miss Corbie's gonna know that." He looked at her. "So. You called the meeting, honey. Whaddya want? A cut of some action?"

She crossed her legs, drawing their eyes, inhaling the smoke. Looked at Mickey thoughtfully.

"I was wondering why Siegel's lieutenant is in San Francisco, setting up wires under the noses of the Lanza family. Then I remembered something. I remembered seeing a matchbook for this dump in a Cordoba tan Ford." She leaned forward. "Why'd you set somebody after me, Mickey? To protect this bastard?"

She gestured toward Flamm, who started to rise out of his seat until the big man with suspenders shoved him back down hard.

Mickey looked at her with owl eyes, then burst out laughing again, hard enough to wipe his eyes. He said to Suspenders, "Get this — the broad thinks we tried to rub her out!" He laughed again, rough, raucous noise dying in a chortle, gleam behind his small brown eyes. Tongue between his teeth. "You wouldn't be bad to rub out, baby, but not with no gun."

Miranda's breath was quick. She was unsure, in open territory. No-man's-land.

"Why'd you have him follow me, then? Why search my apartment?"

Mickey shook his head, like a priest with a disbeliever. "Lady, lady, lady. You call yourself a shamus. But you ain't no dick." He laughed again, and the men laughed with him, Flamm more relaxed. Mickey coughed, swallowed hard, ordered Suspenders to get him a whiskey. Changed moods, suddenly all business.

"You owe me, lady. Whitey saved your fucking life. You're fishin' around Flamm here 'cause his ex-twist got herself iced. Flamm gets nervous, 'tween the murder and the swastika on the temple — somebody calls it in, he figures maybe it was tied up, maybe he was bein' framed for somethin' he didn't do. You tumble?"

She said it slowly, not taking her eyes off him. "You had me followed, see what I'd turn up. Is that it?"

"Yeah. Figured you could work for us and not even know it. 'Cause we know somethin' you don't know, which is that Lima's got trouble with a wop from Chicago named Benedetti. Now, we get along with everybody out in New York, Jews, wops, micks, Mexicans, whatever. Same way in L.A., no troubles, and up here Lima's a goddamn lamb. Even works with those chink bastards. But these Benedetti sonsofbitches don't wanna play with us 'cause they don't like Benny Siegel, an' they start mouthin' off about Jews, and the whole goddamn deal looks like it's fallin' apart."

She pointed the cigarette at him. "You thought Benedetti might've killed Pandora and the other girl to set you up."

Mickey raised his hands in the air, openpalmed. Exaggerated shrug. "We don't know. The cop could take the rap, no problem. But with you diggin' around, we wanted to make sure if you turned somethin' up on Benedetti, we'd get it. So Whitey's orders were to keep you alive — alive, sister, because Angelo wants you dead."

He leaned back in the chair, hands behind the head again. Smug smile.

"Whitey saved your life. Shot that fuckhead Scorsone out on Treasure Island after he took a potshot at you. Shadowed you but good, sister — when Scorsone pretended to be from the goddamn phone company, when you was being watched. Whitey's your fucking guardian angel."

Last puff on the Chesterfield, crimped the stub out with her fingers. "And now?"

Mickey frowned. "An' now I don't know what to do wit' you. Benedetti's gone back to the hole he crawled out of. We got things set up between Lima an' us pretty cozy, enough for me to get back to some goddamn sunshine. This fucking city's too cold."

She nodded. "And maybe too hot. Clever to launder money between the Black Cat Café and Chat Noir. I heard there was new money in town getting washed. Didn't figure it was from L.A."

He grinned up at Suspenders. "See, Paulie? Smart broad." Back to Miranda. "I'm a man a' culture, Miss Corbie. I like it when my boys speak French." He laughed again, loud and long. Looked at her shrewdly.

"You're a good-lookin' dame, even with that cut on your cheek. And you're smart. You know if you talk, Whitey won't be your guardian angel no more. Besides, you owe me. You owe me personally. An' one of these days I'm gonna collect."

He jerked a thumb at Flamm. "This bozo ain't killed nobody except a racin' form. We checked on him — don't want no heat from nobody, and he's dumb, but not dumb enough for this. He's a runner, picks up chits, uses the temple. Which — by the way — we donate to. You think them funds for the war orphans and such come cheap?"

Shook his head. "No, lady, you're on your own with your case. No Whitey, neither, he's back down in L.A." He looked up at Paulie in the red suspenders, suddenly tired, his face drawn.

"Get her back where she belongs."

"Can I ask Flamm a couple of questions first?"

He thought about it for a few seconds. "OK, sister. But make it quick."

She turned to Flamm, still sullen, Paulie's large hands still on his shoulders. "Harry — did you suggest Pandora go to Calistoga?"

He snorted. "Suggest, hell. I paid for it. We was through ages ago, after she come back from the place. Never the same after that. Nutty broad, she was — talkin' about becoming a Jew, like fucking me somehow made her one."

Mickey and Suspenders laughed, Flamm joining them after a few seconds. Miranda held his eyes.

"Did you know a doctor up there sterilized her? Because she said she was Jewish?"

Mickey's face darkened, his short, thick neck pivoting toward Flamm, chin stuck out. Harry went white. "What's this Nazi shit, Harry? You know this?"

"N-no, Mr. Cohen, no sir. Never heard nothin' about it."

Mickey looked at Miranda, features shoved together, flushed and angry. "This doctor kill the girl?"

"I don't think so. But there's a group — call themselves the Musketeers — a doctor involved was sterilizing Jewish girls. They also tried to bomb Treasure Island."

A vein in Mickey's neck popped in and out. He barked, "Name?"

Miranda shook her head. "I took care of it, Mickey."

He scoffed. "You — a broad? Besides, you ain't even Jewish."

"I told them I'd kill them. And I meant it."

She tried to hide the trembling in her legs, focusing the fear in a cool, unbroken stare at Mickey. A smile slowly spread across his chubby face. He spoke softly.

"See, boys? Investment."

He nodded to the man in suspenders. An

order to leave.

Miranda stood up. Paulie walked behind her to the door.

Mickey's voice was loud behind her.

"You owe me, Miss Miranda Corbie. Don't forget it."

THIRTY-THREE

Mitch was leaning against the counter, propped on a stool, sulking to the man in the T-shirt, face still red. He glared at Miranda, threw some car keys to Paulie.

"You take her home. Only way I wanna see the bitch again is in a casket."

Paulie chuckled. "I'm bettin' on the broad."

Sour smell of day-old dishwater followed them out the door. The big man opened the door of the Packard for her, still smiling.

"Climb in, girlie. Where you wanna get dropped off?"

"I can take a streetcar."

He shook his head, frowning. "Mickey likes his guests treated the right way. You climb in."

She sighed and climbed in, careful of the ankle. He shoved it into gear, grinding the transmission, and pulled out into the Sutter Street traffic. Said conversationally, "Don't worry 'bout Mitch, sister. He ain't so important to Mickey no more."

Fifteen minutes later, he rumbled to a stop in front of the Monadnock.

Paulie leaned over and smiled, held out his hand. "I'm Paulie Fein. Mickey'll call when he needs you."

She hesitated, then shook his hand. Climbed out in front of a flower stand, buckets heaped with carnations and roses, man in a blue serge suit buying one for his lapel. Watched Paulie dart between a Municipal and a White Front, laying on the horn while he flew down Market Street.

So that was the money-laundering racket Fisher told her about. Back and forth, Black Cat and Chat Noir, gambling money, racing wires, Los Angeles extending a warm and sleepy hand north, courtesy of Bugsy Siegel and Mickey Cohen. Big names, big crooks, and the Lanza mob rolled over, glad for company.

She shook her head, walked toward the big double doors. Couldn't tell Fisher. Cohen would be watching for any move of her mouth, and Whitey would come back, not her angel anymore.

Rick was pacing in front of her office door. He looked up.

"Jesus, Miranda, you're pale. What happened? You OK?"

She unlocked the door, hobbled in. Sank into the overstuffed leather chair.

"Yeah. I'm OK. Flamm didn't kill Pandora or Annie."

He raised his eyebrows. "How do you know?"

"Let's just say I have it on solid authority."

Authority from a fucking mobster, Siegel's West Coast lieutenant. She passed a hand over her forehead. Unlocked the right bottom drawer, took out the bottle of Old Taylor. Poured herself a shot in the Castagnola glass, still on the desk, drank half of it down in a shot.

He watched her. Then took off his brown jacket and threw it on one of the chairs in front of her desk. He was wearing the shoulder holster for the Spanish .38.

"Only way I could bring this back without getting stopped by a flatfoot." He unbuckled the holster, slid it off, set it down on the desk in front of her.

"Thanks, Rick." She gestured to the bottle, almost empty. "You want some?"

He shook his head. "Bomb story was squashed. But I figured you'd know that."

She nodded, swirling the whiskey, watching the drops form on the sides of the glass.

"Thanks. For everything. I hope you got something they'll print."

He shrugged. "Sure. A lot of tourists out here for the Fair. Paper likes fluff pieces on where to go for what."

"It's not front page."

"Still pays." He picked up his hat from the chair, put his coat back on. Looked down at her.

"I don't like leaving you like this, Randy."

She winced, staring at the glass. "S'OK, Rick. Gotta get out to the Gayway, soon as I make a few phone calls."

He turned to go. His voice was soft. "Be seein' you, Miranda."

"Be seein' you, Rick."

They thought they owned her.

Something she feared a hell of a lot more than dying.

Battlefield Gayway, not a bad place to die, no place was good, silk sheets or stuffy apartments filled with perfume samples, stage where men could come pay a quarter and get a photograph close-up of your nipples, sell them on the street corner in Los Angeles, tell people it's Lana fucking Turner.

She poured another drink, bourbon sloshing the sides.

Fuck Whitey and his Panama hat, and fuck Mickey Cohen and the twisted, sick bastards at Murder Inc., business of America is business, said Henry Ford, and they made a goddamn killing. Siegel and Costello and Mr. Ice Pick Abbandando, and somehow they never got the chair, never shit their pants with a last meal, last cigar, when the state turned the lights out and the gas came seeping through the cracks.

No, they'd get killed by an upstart, rubbed out by an enemy, but they were too fucking big for the police department or even Thomas Dewey, too big for J. Edgar Hoover and his publicity machine. Because the business of America was fucking business, and that's what they were, what they all were.

Businessmen.

She drained the bourbon, craned her neck to ease the tension in her muscles. Fuck the mob, wherever they came from. She'd handled Martini and Coppa. If Cohen's mob came knocking, she'd handle them. And in the meantime, Mickey might even make sure Gosney wouldn't be practicing much surgery.

Miranda raised the glass in a mock toast to herself. Tried to feel bad, feel guilt, but she wasn't feeling anything at all. Maybe she'd have bad dreams, but fuck . . . she didn't know any other kind.

Phone jarred her awake. Fever dream, half-asleep, whiskey and the late afternoon sun.

Dead girls, cut open, lost children, child and mother. Gosney and Parkinson and a fat little haberdasher in powder blue, chomping a cigar, eyes like dry ice. Flamm and Kaiser and the Gayway, Artists and Models, ice pick through the neck, word written in red. Written in blood.

She blinked. Stretched her hand toward the phone. Fisher.

"Miss Corbie?"

"What's wrong?"

His voice was hesitant. "No leads on the bomb squad. I've, uh . . . I've made reference to your claims, but word from on high is — no dice."

"Figured as much." She yawned. "Excuse me."

Miranda set the phone down. Rubbed her eyes, slapped her cheek to get some feeling back in her face. Picked up the receiver again. "Got some news for you — Angelo Benedetti's gone back to Chicago."

Voice was sharp. "How'd you find that out?"

"Solid authority, Inspector. Solid authority."

He grunted. "Can't say I'm sorry to hear it, but I'd feel better if I knew your sources."

Wry grin. "Not sure if you would."

"What's that?"

"Nothing." She pulled open the drawer, shook the last cigarette out of a pack of Chesterfields. "So why are you calling?"

"I'm sorry about your murder case. No traction here, right now it's 'bomb, bomb, bomb' — narrow squeak, let me tell you, not that the public'll ever know. The, uh — the chief is grateful, and so is Johnson."

Miranda placed the stick between her lips, snapped on the desk lighter. "Johnson's a crooked bastard. I don't know about the new chief. If I live long enough, maybe I will."

He chuckled. "Gonzales is coming back for a couple of weeks, by the way. Told me to say hello."

She felt her pulse quicken, swore under her breath. "Well, he wanted to meet some fifth columnists."

"Yes, yes, he did. I think he'll be taking an interest in the Musketeers." He lowered his voice on the last word. "Not that anyone's mentioned that name down here."

She smiled to herself, puffed the cigarette.

Said: "About the Duggan case. Henry Kaiser's the number one suspect, lion tamer I told you about. But I've got a question. Hugh R. Parkinson, dentist. Is his father still in politics?"

Hesitation, then Fisher cleared his throat. "Not politics, exactly. He's a retired surgeon, was on the former State Board of Lunacy. Does a lot of charitable work these days, made a run for state senate couple of years back. Name's Hugh F. Parkinson." Added in a lower voice, "Owns a number of businesses, including Healthy Holdings, Incorporated — which holds the title to Dr. Aalder's Sanitarium in Calistoga."

"You dug that up."

She could hear him grin. "You were pretty adamant this morning."

"Yeah. It's been a long goddamn day." She stared at the cigarette between her fingers, red ember burning down the white tube of tobacco.

"Inspector — why did you call?"

Low, sad chuckle. "Your instinct's pretty good, Miss Corbie. We, uh . . . we're a little worried about a missing persons case, just phoned in. Another connection to Treasure Island — and Pandora Blake."

Her stomach knotted, hearing the name before it traveled through the wire, seeing his mouth opening, syllable by syllable, smelling the cheap, exotic perfume dabbed behind her ear.

The gaudy jewelry. The phony sarong.

"Lucinda Gerber. Another performer at Artists and Models. Maybe she took a powder, but we found your card in her apartment. . . ."

She phoned Meyer by rote, catching him in the office, updating him about Lucinda, about Flamm. Left out the part about Mickey. Dangerous enough for her, no need to drag in anybody else. She could type it up later, leave a document, last will and testament.

Meyer tried to hide the relief in his voice at Lucinda's disappearance. If it could be connected to the murders, Duggan was as good as released. Goddamn lawyers, all the same, even the good ones.

She hung up the phone. Popped two Pep-O-Mints in her mouth.

Roommate said she hadn't been around for two straight days, and Lucinda wasn't the type to cut and run. Rent was due, so the other girls whined to the police, looking for Lucinda and the lost third of the rent money.

Goddamn it. Lucinda and her sarong, red

nails, languid eyes. Gimmick by Max Factor and whatever product Dorothy Lamour was selling these days.

Miranda leaned out the window, trying to find air to breathe, to get out of the corner, out of the fucking mousetrap. Faces and names, swirling patterns. All of it held together by will, her will, and it was starting to crack, to stumble, to fall and never get up. She passed a shaking hand over her eyes. Wiped the sweat from her forehead. Tried again.

Lucinda had known something, and Blind Willie heard part of it. Something that got her killed, and if Miranda hadn't been running around, blind, stupid, heading to Calistoga, sniffing out bomb threats, and socializing with fucking gangsters, maybe she'd be here. Maybe she'd be alive.

She stared through the window across Market Street, fingers clenched on the scarred white window frame.

Peck Judah Travel Service. Florsheim Shoes. Hyman's Leasing. Names that weren't Washington and Jefferson and Franklin. Immigrants to an immigrant country, polyglot nation, especially San Francisco, gold mines and golden opportunities, visit the West in '49, sister, 1849 or 1939, didn't matter, there was land here and gold and riches to be made.

And with the immigrants came violence. Every wave resisted, beaten back by those already here. Beaten, hated, killed.

Miranda rubbed her neck. C. R. Willett, chiropractor, offices across the street. Maybe he could help her. Crack her spine for inspiration, find the fucking killer.

She limped to her desk and sank in the chair, leg shaking, ankle sharp like knives. No hurry, not now, not to get to Treasure Island, not to meet Lucinda. A chance, maybe, she wasn't dead, but every tick of the clock, less and less and less.

A church bell, St. Patrick's on Fifth. *Dong. Dong.*

Always goddamn church bells.

She poured the rest of the bourbon, drank it in one shot. Waited for the cold to go away. Got up again, limped to the safe. Took out her mother's postcard.

Miranda read the words. Over and over. Grateful to the woman, to Catherine Corbie, memory in a place of darkness. Song, crooning, gentle hands, gentle touch, ripped away, never felt again.

Stolen.

Tears on a thin cotton sheet, tears and pain, and later fear, her father's friends, the hands, the mouths, strange urgency of motion, and she'd run and she'd run and she'd run. Looking for her mother, looking for escape.

Looking for life.

Grateful, oh yes, because she could have never been born, not in the moral world of Dr. Gosney, never grown beyond a momentary bodily impulse, fear and the will to survive. 1906 and God's revenge, and the first and last time her father showed interest in anything beyond Shakespeare and the fucking gin bottle.

She could have been given away, never to remember a mother at all, never to know, to understand. To want. To need.

To love.

Grateful even for the pain.

She sat at the desk, hunched over the card, salt stinging her skin, making it cold. Fingers traced the contours of her face. She shivered.

Miranda Corbie.

Cracked and damaged.

Fissured lines, and she could feel them under her skin.

But she wasn't broken.

Not yet.

She brushed through the paperwork on her desk, reading notes from postcards and matchbooks. Thought of Pandora's card from Nance's, symbol of a time when she could have children and after which she could not. Thought of Lima, Ohio, and words read over and over, held with sweaty hands, edges rough, while Pandora lay in a bed at Aalder's, wishing she'd never been born. Pandora, flesh show model, midwest girl with Hollywood in her eyes. Beloved of an Aquadonis, going places, on his way up.

Pandora, who knew she could never have children.

Miranda closed her eyes. Hearing a whispered song, a blind man's story. A tragedy in five acts, and she could smell the bougainvillea, hear the waves creaming on the Santa Monica shore. Scent of fear, whispered intake of breath, panic, protest, puzzled eyes, aware now, but no comprehension, no understanding, not even enough for horror. The oh-so-easy intimacy of steel through skin, murmured promises, and above all else . . . applause.

She opened her eyes, tears running down her cheeks.

Miranda placed her mother's postcard in front of her on the desk, straightening the edges. Picked up her purse, slid into her coat.

Locked the door behind her.

■ ■ ■ ■

Applause rippled through the spectators, most of them wearing coats while they sat on the hard wooden benches, ogling the women in bathing suits, trying to spot a hardened nipple, a telltale bulge in the men's briefs.

She sat in the front row, clapping dutifully. The Aquacade, Billy Rose's grandiose spectacle of flesh and fantasy, water just an excuse to show off skin.

She spotted Ozzie heading backstage for the dressing rooms. Limped outside, carried by the crowd, seven o'clock show packed, murmurs of appreciation for the swimmers, for Hollywood's Tarzan, for Esther Williams, the swimming star who'd replaced Eleanor Holm.

Miranda smoked a cigarette by the Court of Reflections. Looked into the water, studied her own.

The performers were starting to come out of the stage door along the side of the giant building, where Ozzie led her before. He walked out smiling, towel around his neck, dark hair still tousled.

"You wanted to see me, Miss Corbie? Is there any news?"

She linked her arm through his, no objection. Led him past the reflecting pool, her ankle dragging. Turned left toward the Tower of the Sun, dazzling bright, beginning and end.

Phoenix reborn.

Her voice was gentle. "Yes, Ozzie. I'm — I'm sorry."

He stopped, looked down at her. Puzzled. "What's happened?"

She gazed at the tower, rich and yellow in the setting sun.

Fool's gold. Magic. Magic and lights and fame and fortune, come west, come west, and you might be on the radio, be discovered by Hollywood, find what you're looking for.

What you've wanted all your life.

Applause.

She faced him. "It's about Lucinda."

He grabbed her arm, fingers tightening around her elbow. "Is she OK? What's wrong with her?"

Miranda searched his face, eyes sad and certain.

And said: "Where is she, Ozzie?"

THIRTY-FOUR

He tried to run, but Gillespie stepped out from behind a statue, and another cop was ready with the cuffs. Bewilderment, anger. Tears.

Mad eyes, wet and blue like the water he loved.

The water that was going to make him a star.

They thought she was dead when they found her, unresponsive. Almost too late. He couldn't decide what to do with her, hadn't made up his mind on how to dispose of the body. Another girl from Treasure Island, another Jew, and Duggan would be free, and they'd be looking somewhere else. At someone else.

She was tied up naked, no food or water for two days, gagged. Bruises all over, empty, taken. Used. Cuts on her neck, down her legs, across her breasts, where he'd tested the knife, tried the color against her skin. Not the right shade of red, not quite red enough, so he waited, setting the scene, planning what to do.

Taking his bows at the Aquacade.

Miranda stood by the corner of the Hotel Shawmut, leaning against the soiled brick, watching a Baby Ruth wrapper dance down the street, the gutter still choked with garbage.

They brought Lucinda out on a stretcher. Took her away in an ambulance, another girl for the sanitarium, for the alienists to ask questions. Tell me, Miss Gerber — how did it feel? Lick of the lips, wet the pencil, get their fucking kicks. Sick fucking bastards, sick fucking world.

Miranda would follow up, make sure it wasn't Napa, even if she had to pay for the hospital herself. Come see her, visit her and Phyllis Winters, Martini's cast-a-way, the girl she'd saved for Dante's Sanitarium. They sit in their chairs with a lap rug amid the jasmine blossoms, white-coated doctors shaking their heads, orderlies looking them up and down, saying what a goddamn pity.

But Lucinda would live. And she'd come out the other side.

Cracked, not broken.

Ozzie was crying softly, hands in manacles behind his back. Gillespie and Fisher and a swarm of other cops, reporters waiting for the story. Another murder on Treasure Island? Sells papers, boys, can't have too many rapes and murders, give the public what it wants. . . .

She moved through the blue-coated bulls, parting the crowd, walked up to Ozzie, who in between tears would talk only about Johnny Weissmuller and Hollywood and how he was going to be famous.

Not in the way he imagined.

He seemed to see her for a moment, lucid and canny, eyes still like a hurt little boy's.

Angry. Ignored. Forgotten.

She understood those eyes.

Fisher was at her side, and the moment was broken.

"What I can't figure out is why he wrote 'kike' — was it just to throw us off scent?"

She looked into Ozzie's eyes, his soul, nodding at the pain. Old acquaintance.

"Yes and no, Inspector. Part of him wanted to survive, understood the crime and the risk and tried to minimize it. But the other part wanted recognition. He wasn't trying to fool anyone. He was signing his name."

Once upon a time there was a bright young man who worked for his uncle, the chiropractor. And he was athletic and smart and good-looking, and everybody said he should be a movie star.

Everybody but the popular ones, the blondes and the debutantes. The boys in letter sweaters, whispering behind his back.

Hebe, they'd call him. Kike. Commie, Red, Christ killer . . .

And the boy tried not to listen to the words of derision, the tone of contempt, of anger, of malice. But even out of Oklahoma, he'd hear it when he tried to rent an apartment.

Hebe.

Tried to find a job.

Christian only — *Jew.*

Tried to date a girl.

Kike.

But the boy persisted, believing in his destiny. And he came to California, land of golden dreams, land of Hollywood and movie stars and a chance to be famous on a magic island. And he met a girl who could have made him happy, and did, for a brief time, a few short weeks. His costar, his leading lady. His Ginger Rogers.

She shared some of his dreams, fame and fortune, a contract with Metro-Goldwyn-Mayer. And she wasn't like the others, she liked his name, his heritage, even embracing it as her own.

But he was ambitious. And after she told him she loved him, after they'd wet the sheets in his little bed, damp with the sweat of their bodies — like movie stars, like the love scenes that they always cut out, she said, and laughed — she told him she wanted to quit the show, quit the Island. She wanted to settle down, to be his wife.

Just his wife.

And he saw her then, saw what she really was, the stained apron and the callused hands, fat, frowsy, loud, always yelling. Always wanting.

Ain't got no money for your goddamn magazines, boy, who the hell do you think you are, Clark Gable? Her face a mask, wrinkled, old, her body soft and green.

She'd take it all away from him, the fancy cars and the bungalow, the custom suits. No smell of desert poppies, no neon lights, no golden sand, no celluloid clicking in the camera, click. *Click, click.*

No adulation. No acceptance.

So he killed her. Waiting behind the screen when she came in, key in his pocket. Souvenir of their magic time in his hand, the age before when she wasn't a monster. And he'd stabbed her like he remembered from his uncle's chart, right where she couldn't do

542

anything.

He killed her, slayed the monster.

And to make sure the blondes and baseball players out in Oklahoma would know, he signed her with an autograph, signed his performance, his art. His heroic deed. Signed with the name they'd called him, what everybody whispered when he walked in, the people pretending to be his friend, pretending to like him, pretending to care.

Kike.

He was smart, too, because he signed it twice, this time on a temple where Pandora's old boyfriend worked. Signed it, called the police, boasting. And he thought it was over, but right away, he had to sign once more, this time a friend of hers, another monster, someone else who was going to take it all away. She phoned, and he heard the threat in her voice, smelled the flesh again, green and rotting. So he told her what he told Lucinda. What he told Miranda.

That Pandora loved him, loved him so much she wanted babies. His babies. Their very own.

Well, said the friend, the monster-friend, Pandora can't have babies. This sounds strange, and even suspicious.

And it was strange, strange to him that

Pandora never told him. Maybe she wouldn't have become a monster, maybe he could have saved her, like Clark Gable or Johnny Weissmuller, if only . . . if only he'd known.

So he chatted up the friend and saw her that night. She was a girl who understood the importance of the signature, who recognized what the autograph meant. She was a monster, so he signed her, too.

Kike.

They pieced the story out of Ozzie patiently, promising him he'd play himself if they made a movie out of it. He spoke about it distantly, admiringly, except for the end. The hero, he wondered — would he live happily ever after? The cops looked at one another, heavy-lidded. Wouldn't say anything.

Miranda smoked and answered their questions, over and over.

Lucinda knew Pandora couldn't have children, knew her friend wouldn't have lied to Ozzie, not even to hold him. She took the rent down to the Hotel Potter, guarded Pandora's secret, defended her friend's honor. And after Ozzie said she wanted babies — his babies — Lucinda became confused, just like Annie Learner had. Pan wouldn't say that, wouldn't do that to Ozzie.

Ozzie panicked after Miranda called him with a message for Lucinda. And the girl in the sarong, Pandora's fellow artist's model, confronted and questioned the boy they both loved.

He took her prisoner that night.

Miranda told the story, told it until the guilt became more manageable, told it until she ran out of Chesterfields and Life Savers and her fingernails became chipped and cracked from tracing rivers on the wooden desk.

It was her fault. Miranda's fault. Lucinda almost died because of her.

Meyer flew down, insisted she be given some rest, can't they see the poor girl's been through enough, what with bombs and murderers?

No pity, Meyer, not for me. Save it for Lucinda.

Fisher took her aside, asked her how she'd figured it out. Miranda looked across the crowded room at the Hall of Justice, across the scarred wooden desks, some filled with men who despised her, some not.

She said: "My mother helped me."

The chatter continued, swirling around her, clock ticking in clicks against the pale beige wall.

■ ■ ■ ■

She slept for almost two days straight, stayed in bed for two more. Rick and Bente, Allen and Meyer. All dropping by to see her, offer congratulations.

Didn't feel like she deserved them. If she'd been quicker, smarter, she could have saved Lucinda. Saved her from what she'd gone through. What she was still facing.

Nielsen came over to disapprove. Gave her ankle a proper wrap, checked on the gunshot wound. Graze was healing, no nerve damage. But the gash on her cheek would leave a small scar. Something to remember Calistoga by.

She told Bente everything, Mickey included, made her promise to stay away from Tonypandy. Gave her a ten-dollar bill to pay Walter down at the Hotel Potter, and Bente came back to tell her the place still smelled like cabbage.

Rick played cards with her, but he was too easy to beat in poker, so they switched to gin on the table, bourbon in the glass. He was with her when they listened to Churchill talk about Dunkirk, about the miracle.

We shall fight on the beaches, we shall fight on the landing grounds, we shall fight in the fields and in the streets, we shall fight in the hills; we shall never surrender . . .

She cried. Rick held her close, and she let him.

They didn't have much time.

Meyer phoned on the fifth. Duggan was getting out of Quentin, finally, paperwork finished.

She dressed for the first time, carefully. Studied her face in the mirror, fretted over her cheek. But maybe the Club Modernes weren't her destiny, not for much longer.

She sat with Duggan and Meyer at a little café in Larkspur. He was about fifteen pounds thinner, couldn't meet her eyes.

"So you found out about Annie's operation and you blamed yourself. And visited Pandora that morning to ask her to put in a favorable word." Meyer shook his head. "Poor lad. You should have told us everything from the beginning. I hope Johnson didn't succeed in soliciting information from you. About the IRA."

Duggan's voice was thick, heavy, hesitant, as if he hadn't used it in a long time.

"I kept quiet. 'Bout everything. Didn't want anyone t' know."

His attorney sighed. "Too quiet, Mr. Duggan. A near miss. Pressure was exerted from above, on Johnson and the D.A., and you were very nearly crushed by it. Would have been, I'm afraid, without Miss Corbie's efforts."

The ex-cop raised his eyes to Miranda's for the first time, moist, red, rheumy. She handed him the matchbook and postcards from Annie's apartment. He stared at them as though they were artifacts in a museum.

He muttered: "Thanks."

"Something else, Duggan. Something you should know. Maybe it'll change your life, maybe even give you a life. I don't know — that depends on you."

She dropped a small silver ring in his callused palm. "Annie was planning to keep the baby."

His rounded shoulders caved forward, long arms wrapping around himself. His fist closed around the baby ring, sobs rocking him back and forth.

On June 14, the Germans occupied Paris.

Miranda was in Magnin's, purchasing a new line of cosmetics from Elizabeth Arden, three new dresses and a coat, plus a swimsuit and tennis outfit, courtesy of Meyer, who'd also given her a handsome bonus and a brand-new set of luggage.

The clerk turned up the radio. The last "Marseillaise" was being broadcast as jackboots marched through the City of Light, Arc de Triomphe triumphant no longer.

At the Fair they were showing *All Quiet on the Western Front,* and the San Mateo Junior College was holding its sophomore dance.

Offers of work were pouring in. Attorneys other than Meyer, some crooked, some legitimate. Even an insurance company. And always her bread and butter, the women who were looking for an answer, a verdict, a settlement. Clumsy justice, the only kind she could find.

Miranda looked out the window of her office. Gonzales was coming back in a few days, for a few days. She'd like to see him. And then — she didn't know.

She loved her city, sad city, glad city, loved the smell of incense and fried rice in Chinatown, clink of martini glasses on Nob Hill. Italian crab fishermen on the long wharves, small boats, trawling, bridges golden and gray, and in the middle a magic, Treasure Island, colored lights and elephant trains. Fog and sunshine, gold and green.

San Francisco. Phoenix-city and part of her, raising her up, survivor.

Her home.

Herself.

But there was a postcard in her desk.

And a mother to find.

London was calling.